Regency

LORDS & LADIES
COLLECTION

Two Glittering Regency
Love Affairs

Jewel of the Night
by Helen Dickson
&
A Penniless Prospect
by Joanna Maitland

The *Regency*

LORDS & LADIES
COLLECTION

The *Regency*

LORDS & LADIES
COLLECTION

Helen Dickson &
Joanna Maitland

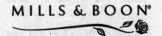

MILLS & BOON®

*MILLS & BOON and MILLS & BOON with the Rose Device
are registered trademarks of the publisher.*

*First published in Great Britain 2006 by
Harlequin Mills & Boon Limited,
Eton House, 18-24 Paradise Road,Richmond, Surrey TW9 1SR*

THE REGENCY LORDS & LADIES COLLECTION
© Harlequin Books S.A. 2006

The publisher acknowledges the copyright holders of the
individual works as follows:

Jewel of the Night © Helen Dickson 2002
A Penniless Prospect © Joanna Maitland 2001

ISBN-13: 978 0 263 85105 2
ISBN-10: 0 263 85105 2

138-0706

*Printed and bound in Spain
by Litografia Rosés S.A., Barcelona*

Jewel of the Night
by
Helen Dickson

Helen Dickson was born and still lives in South Yorkshire with her husband on a busy arable farm, where she combines writing with keeping a chaotic farmhouse. An incurable romantic, she writes for pleasure, owing much of her inspiration to the beauty of the surrounding countryside. She enjoys reading and music. History has always captivated her, and she likes travel and visiting ancient buildings.

Chapter One

1822

Long of limb, six foot three of lean hard muscle, his handsome face with its imperious profile and strong features as fine drawn and almost as tanned as those of the native Indians, Captain Jordan Grant—a cavalry officer tailor-made—stepped out of the boat that had rowed him from the *Eastern Lady*, and climbed the ladder onto the bustling wharf at the East India dock yard at Blackwall. His thick dark hair gleamed beneath the morning sun, and his wide-set silver-grey eyes, beneath winged black brows, were hard and intent.

A man who inspired awe in all those he met, he was completely unreadable and single-minded—and at that particular moment he had an uneasy feeling. He looked back at the ship that had brought him from India, a muscle ticking in his clenched jaw. He searched the faces of those around him, wanting to discover the identity of whoever had invaded his cabin and searched his personal property when he'd been breakfasting with the captain. Nothing was missing, so he assumed they had been unable to find what they were looking for. Instinctively his hand went to his breast pocket, and he was reassured when his fingers closed over a hard object.

His gaze sharpened when he recalled the man with pale features and a drooping moustache he had seen on deck earlier, a man who hadn't been on the ship from India, so he must have come aboard after the vessel docked some time during the night. Something nagged at his memory. His face had been vaguely familiar—seen in very different circumstances. He followed the recollection down the alleyways of his memory. It had to be in India. But where, precisely?

Jordan was still frowning when further along the wharf a carriage pulled up. When the door was flung open and the familiar face of his younger brother Edmund appeared, he immediately put the disturbing incident to the back of his mind, but it was not forgotten. A smile broadened his mouth, revealing a lightening glimpse of very white teeth, and with ground-devouring strides he moved towards him. It was two years since he had last been home on leave, and he was impatient to see his family. The two men shook hands and embraced affectionately, speaking rapidly for several moments.

There was a similarity between them. Like Jordan, Edmund was dark-haired, but he was not as tall, nor was he was so ruggedly virile, and he lacked the aura of authority, of forcefulness and power, that surrounded Jordan. Edmund was friendlier and more approachable, but he did not possess the full measure of the legendary Grant charm that had been bestowed on his older brother.

'Welcome home, Jordan. Good Lord, it's good to see you! You're still in uniform, I see,' he said, passing a quizzical eye over his brother's red jacket. 'Does that mean you will be returning to your regiment?'

'I've worn this uniform for so long that it's become a part of me,' Jordan replied, his voice richly textured and deep. 'But—no, I won't be going back.'

Edmund looked at him steadily. 'Do I detect a note of regret?'

Jordan shook his head as they walked slowly towards the carriage. 'No—although after ten years of military life, it won't be easy adjusting to being a civilian again.'

'I needn't tell you how relieved Mother will be. We'll all be happy to have you back at Landsdowne. Mother has invited Emily and me to spend the summer with you, by the way.'

'It will be good for us all to be together again.' A pensive frown creased Jordan's brow. 'It was rotten news about Father, Edmund. I was stationed in Calcutta when I heard about his ship going down off Madagascar. Tropical storm, I believe. How's Mother taken it?'

'It was a terrible tragedy. Mother was stunned by her grief. As you know, her constitution is delicate and we were all deeply concerned. It might have been easier to bear had there been a body,' he said quietly. 'Still, she's over the worst, thank God, and coping rather well. She's looking forward to seeing you.'

'And Charlotte?' Jordan asked, enquiring about his sister.

'I broke the news to her at the academy. She was devoted to Father and quite devastated. But the tragedy was three months ago, and our sister is young and healthy and strong. She'll be all right now.'

'Is she still at the academy?'

'Yes. She came to Landsdowne for a few days to be with Mother and although Mother suggested that she remain at home, Charlotte was restive. It was her wish to return to her friends. Her education is almost complete. Anyway, she'll be home in three weeks.'

Jordan looked at his brother in astonishment. 'Good Lord! Is she eighteen already?' he asked, as a picture of a golden girl, all ruffles and lace with ribbons in her bouncing hair and a laughing face, danced across his mind.

Edmund laughed. 'She is. Our sister is a woman grown—and a lovely one at that. Mother is going to have her work cut out fending off Charlotte's admirers when she takes her bow. I'm afraid you've been away too long, brother.'

They climbed inside the coach, and Jordan lounged in the corner with his usual careless elegance. Edmund subjected him to close scrutiny. There was an aggressive confidence and strength of purpose in his features, and he had the air of a clever man who succeeds in all he sets out to achieve. From the arrogant lift of his dark head and casual stance, he was a man with many shades to his nature, a man with a sense of his own infallibility.

Whenever Jordan had been home on leave, he'd been much sought after by every hostess and unattached female in town. Dazzling women always surrounded him. They found him irresistible. Edmund had watched with amusement as they had flirted shamelessly with him, using all their feminine wiles to hold his attention. Jordan was not immune, and his name had been linked to some of the most beautiful women in town. But with all his attention pinned on his career, marriage was not on offer. Now he was home for good and still a bachelor, he presented a challenge few would be able to resist. In no time at all half the mamas in London would bring their daughters into his line of vision.

'So, Jordan, you are no longer a military man,' Edmund stated.

'No. I put in my discharge before Father's ship went down. His death has brought my retirement sooner rather than later.'

'I dare say you'll miss India.'

He nodded. 'Very much—but it's good to be home.'

It had been a long voyage—almost five months. When at last the fifteen vessels of the East India fleet—protected by watchful frigates of the Royal Navy—had sailed heavily laden up the Channel and he had seen the English coastline with its crying gulls, it seemed that he had been a lifetime in that swaying, creaking wooden world.

'Still,' he went on, 'involvement with the Company will take me back from time to time. Now, tell me everything that has been going on in my absence—and about Emily. I'm glad the two of you finally tied the knot—and I'm sorry I couldn't be with you.'

Edmund had married Emily Paxton, a young lady of good breeding and enormous wealth, twelve months ago. Being the eldest of two girls, she was her father's heir. Her mother was dead, and when they had married her father had insisted that they live at the family seat in Kent. The old man liked Edmund, and stressed that as his son-in-law and—God willing—father of his future grandchildren, it was important that he learned all about the running of his estate.

Of an indolent nature and without his brother's drive, Edmund had been only too happy to oblige. Jordan was Lord Grant now, and Edmund was content to stand back and let all the responsibilities of running the family's many business concerns—which included being a director in the East India Company—rest on his capable shoulders.

* * *

As Judith walked across the street to Miss Powell's house opposite the academy clutching a letter in her hand, it was not the first time that she had entertained uncharitable feelings towards her Aunt Cynthia. Her shame at her own thoughts in the face of her aunt's generosity swamped her. When her parents had been killed in India four years ago, her aunt, being her only living relative, had sacrificed a great deal to pay for her education. That her aunt held no affection for her—indeed, her manner often bordered on antipathy—had saddened and hurt Judith deeply in those early days.

She felt friendless and totally dependent on her aunt, who saw her as a financial burden and endured her presence at her home in Brighton with resentment. Never had she felt so alone—abandoned, almost—and when her aunt had enrolled her at Miss Powell's academy for young ladies in a quiet part of Chelsea, telling her that she should be grateful, for she was under no obligation to pay for her education, and that if it were not for her she would have been sent to the poorhouse, Judith's misery had been complete.

Miss Powell was seated at a table in her drawing-room reading some correspondence when the maid showed Judith inside. It was a lovely room, homely and full of light, and a fire spluttered cheerfully in the hearth. Miss Powell, the proprietress of the academy, who preferred to live not on the premises but close enough to keep her finger on the pulse, was a tall, stately woman. Her neatly arranged fading dark hair crowned a lined, intelligent face and shrewd blue eyes. Her graceful movements, calm features and soft voice disguised a formidable efficiency and energy. She smiled a warm welcome at her favourite pupil.

The light from the window fell onto Judith's face, il

luminating her fine skin to a soft shade of golden honey,
and lighting her serene hazel eyes with a luminous quality. Her dark brown hair, with highlights of red and gold,
was gathered into a knot at the back of her head, a style
Miss Powell considered far too severe for one so young,
although today the effect was softened by several escaping stray curls brushing her cheeks. She was of medium
height and as slender as a wand. Her gown was dark
green, the bodice tight-fitting, which drew the eye to her
narrow waist and small breasts.

The young woman had a natural poise and unaffected
warmth, but there was always an air of seriousness about
her, a primness, which manifested itself in the square set
of her chin and the firmness of her lips. Some people
thought she was aloof and cold, while others thought she
was quiet and refined. She had a way of looking at a
person, silent and unblinking, like the dark-eyed Indian
women in the land of her birth, with their unfathomable
stares. Having lived among them until she was fourteen,
it was something she had unconsciously acquired.

'What have you there, Judith?' Miss Powell asked, seeing the letter in her hand. 'Is it for me?'

'It's from Aunt Cynthia, Miss Powell,' Judith said,
moving close and handing it to her. 'I think you should
read it.'

Quickly Miss Powell's eyes scanned what was written.
When she had finished, she sighed low and was pensive
for a moment, then, rousing herself, she looked at the
young woman with some concern. 'So, your aunt is to
leave for Europe with friends for an indefinite period, and
suggests that you remain at the academy for the summer
vacation. How do you feel about that, Judith?'

A small shadow passed over Judith's face. 'I am disappointed, of course,' she said slowly. 'I do so love

Brighton and the sea. But Aunt Cynthia is entitled to do as she pleases. Despite existing on a small income, she has placed an excellent education within my reach. I will not repay her generosity by complaining and showing ingratitude. It's no good fretting over something that cannot be changed, so if you would allow me to remain at the academy, Miss Powell, I would be most grateful.'

'Of course you may. Your loyalty to your aunt does you credit, but you've too generous a spirit, my dear. As your father's sister and your only living relative, your aunt had a duty to take care of you when your parents died so tragically—and from what you have told me they were an admirable couple and you are a credit to them.'

Judith felt her heart warm. 'Thank you for that, Miss Powell. No one understands the way you do.'

'You have taken advantage of all the academy has to offer and excelled admirably in all your studies. They would be extremely proud of you. You will make an excellent teacher, Judith, and a valuable addition to the academy—of that I am convinced.'

'At least I will be able to support myself, which is a relief. Apart from visiting Aunt Cynthia in the future, I cannot accept anything now that comes from her.'

Miss Powell had always been extremely sympathetic to the trials and tribulations of Judith's situation. She was eighteen and in three weeks time her education would be complete. Despite the friction that existed between Judith and her Aunt Cynthia, Miss Powell knew how much the young woman had looked forward to going to Brighton for the summer, before returning to the academy in the autumn when she would take up her employment as a teacher. No doubt her aunt thought she had done quite enough, and now Judith was eighteen and old enough to earn a living, she desired to rid herself of her tiresome niece as soon as possible.

The fact was that Judith's parents had died penniless. Her father had held a minor post in the Indian Civil Service, and both he and his wife had been killed. Judith had never recovered from the shock of losing both her mother and father so tragically, and it was something she never spoke of.

Apart from a small allowance her parents' deaths entitled her to from the Company, she had no money of her own and couldn't live off her aunt for ever. She had to find some means of earning a living, and teaching was a respectable occupation for a young woman.

Miss Powell put great emphasis on learning and devoted all her time to crusading for the education of women. She ran her academy efficiently and employed only the best teachers. Judith was her star pupil and well qualified to teach English, French, the arts and the classics, and so she'd had no qualms about offering her employment. She would be paid accordingly, and would occupy a room at the academy. However, when the young woman had accepted her proposal, Miss Powell was saddened, because she knew it wasn't from choice or inclination, but because it was the only thing she could do.

Resigning herself to spending the entire summer in London—although she had to concede that it was a splendid city and had plenty of attractions to keep her occupied—Judith returned to the room at the imposing redbrick establishment in Chelsea that she shared with her friend Charlotte Grant. Not in the least interested in art, Charlotte had gone reluctantly to an exhibition of paintings with one of her tutors and a group of other girls.

Feeling dejected, with a sigh Judith lay on her bed and

stared up at the ceiling, her mind going back over the four years she had been in England, with fragmented images of her life in India intruding. She'd been born there, and had been so happy that she hadn't wanted to leave, but she'd been given no choice.

Oppressed by a terrible feeling of isolation, when she had first come to England she'd felt out of place. With her exotic upbringing and the freedom and vibrant colour of India coursing through her veins, it had been difficult that first year, try as she did, for her to conform to an English young lady's way of life. Eventually she had settled down, but there were times when she still felt like a stranger in a strange land.

She would never forget the day she had come to the academy. She had stood in front of the other girls, stiff and awkward. Self-consciously she had looked down at her boots, twisting her handkerchief in her fingers, feeling the eyes of every girl in the school looking at her. Tortured by shyness and painfully aware of the sorry spectacle she made in her plain grey dress, tears had been very near to the surface.

Brought up in India, she had imagined that she would be at a disadvantage among the other girls, but thankfully she had inherited her parents' gift for learning and had applied herself to her studies with diligence and determination that had surprised herself and brought praise from her tutors.

Charlotte Grant had been her salvation. She had burst into her life like a shining light and, unlike Judith, there was nothing prim about her. When she was not under the watchful eye of Miss Powell, her manners were quite outrageous, her conduct reprehensible. She was wilful, obstinate and made everyone laugh, but she also had a kind heart and a caring nature, for which Judith loved her. All pink and white, with a pair of languishing corn-flower blue eyes that twinkled mischievously and a pro-fusion of golden curls, she charmed all her companions and could not be found wanting in those accomplishments that characterise a young lady. She could play the pianoforte well, dance like a fairy and sing like a lark—attributes unequalled by Judith.

She envied Charlotte her home in Greenwich, her family, and their closeness. The enormous wealth of the Grants brought Charlotte many luxuries. Her elder brother and father showered gifts on her when they returned from India—glorious silks, cashmere shawls, and pretty trinkets.

On the whole life at the academy was pleasant. Judith was reconciled, and the background that made her different from the other girls didn't worry her quite so much any more.

Charlotte returned from her visit to the exhibition in subdued spirits. After removing her cloak she plopped onto the bed, sighing deeply. 'When I leave the academy I swear I will never look at another painting again.'

Judith sat up, her lips curving into a smile at Charlotte's frowning vexation. 'Oh dear! Was the exhibition that bad?'

'Worse,' she grumbled, producing a small novelette from her pocket and beginning to thumb through the pages.

'What is that?' Judith asked, eyeing her friend's reading material suspiciously. 'Is it a romantic novel, by any chance?' Charlotte was certainly not of a literary bent, but she did try.

'Yes, but I didn't buy it,' she was quick to inform Judith. 'One of the other girls has let me borrow it.'

'Then for heaven's sake don't let Miss Powell see you

reading it. You know she considers that kind of literature as frivolous and uninstructive—''it could fill the reader with delusive ideas and even lead to degeneracy,''' Judith said, quoting the proprietress, and yet not unkindly.

'I know.' Charlotte sighed, not in the least concerned. 'But I love reading romances, and if it produces a moral degeneracy and makes me unable to control my passions, then so be it. At least I won't die of boredom from reading the curriculum we are made to absorb day in and day out to improve our minds.' She glanced across at Judith. 'Is something the matter, Judith? You look quite miserable. Has anything happened?'

'I've had a letter from Aunt Cynthia. She's going away for the summer and closing the house. Miss Powell has agreed to let me stay at the academy.'

Charlotte sat bolt upright. 'What? All summer?'

'Yes. Oh, it won't be too bad. London isn't Brighton, I know—but there will be lots to do. There will be one or two other girls staying on, so I won't be here alone.'

'But that's positively ghastly. I can't let you stay here all alone. You must come to Landsdowne and spend the vacation with me,' Charlotte pronounced with her usual enthusiasm. 'Besides, when we leave here neither of us know when we will see each other again. It would be fun to spend the whole summer together—before Mother begins planning my future and finding me an eminently suitable young man to marry.'

'It's generous of you to offer, Charlotte,' Judith smiled, 'but I couldn't possibly.'

'Yes, you can. I shall write to Mother immediately and ask her. I know she would love to have you stay. She likes having people around her—especially since father died. Edmund and Emily—that's Edmund's wife—will be there, and Jordan will be home from India.'

'All the more reason why I must stay here. You will all be together as a family for the first time in two years, Charlotte. I couldn't possibly intrude.'

'Don't be silly, Judith. You wouldn't be intruding. Mother is always urging me to bring you to Landsdowne, and Edmund has expressed his eagerness to meet you. You will like Emily, and Edmund is nice—unlike Jordan, who can be a dreadful ogre at times. Oh, you must come.'

'Very well, Charlotte—but only if your mother agrees. I shall look forward to meeting your brother and his wife, and forget all about your ogre of an older brother,' she teased.

'Good. I'll write to Mother at once.'

The letter from Charlotte's mother arrived the day before the end of term. It was raining hard that evening and Charlotte had just come in from the street. She was standing by the door shaking the wet off her plum-coloured cloak and trying to stifle a sneeze when Judith handed it to her. Tearing it open, she scanned it quickly.

'There you are,' she cried happily. 'I told you Mother would be delighted to have you stay with us. You must go and tell Miss Powell immediately, and then we'll go to our room and pack our trunks.'

Judith was apprehensive about going to Landsdowne and at the same time excited. She knew she would cut a sorry figure staying in such a grand house without the right clothes. Nearly all her dresses were serviceable and hardly the kind young ladies wore to soirées and such, but since she wouldn't be invited to any, it didn't really matter. 'Yes, I'll go right this minute.'

'Wait,' Charlotte said, as she was about to go outside.

'It's raining quite hard. Here.' She handed Judith her cloak. 'Put this on, otherwise you'll be soaked before you cross the street. It's damp, I know, but it will cover you.'

Judith slipped outside into the rain, drawing the large cowled hood over her head. It was almost dark and the street was quiet. She fixed her eyes on the light shining from Miss Powell's windows, knowing she would find her in her drawing-room at this hour. As she was about to step off the pavement she drew back when a coach and matching pair of horses drew near. It halted, and she gasped as the door opened and a black garbed figure with a hat pulled well down over his face emerged.

There was something sinister and threatening about that figure. Becoming alarmed, she turned to go back inside the academy, casting an anguished glance at the closed door, but everything happened with such dreadful speed. The man was on her before she could take a step, his arms going round her. Even as she drew breath to scream, he dealt her a ringing blow on her chin and she went spiralling down into a black hole.

Judith stirred and moaned. As she gradually regained her senses she tried to move, but it was impossible. Her hands were bound tightly behind her back and a blindfold prevented her from seeing. An ache throbbed in her jaw and her head swam as the ache became a pounding pain. She was lying on a hard floor and it was extremely cold.

There wasn't a sound to be heard, but it was an unnatural silence—which was an enemy in itself, while the air was charged with an ugly tension. Menace bristled all around her, and she sensed she was not alone. She strained her ears, her heart pounding with a mixture of rage and fright. Only once before in her life had she experienced the kind of terror that gripped her at that moment. A presence surrounded her like a sickening wall of hatred. She struggled to stay calm, to stop her limbs from trembling. She had no idea what was happening to her, who would want to abduct her—or for what reason.

Finding her voice, she whispered through parched lips into the dark. 'Please—I know someone is there. Why have you done this? What is it you want from me?' There was a rustle as someone moved close and she could hear his breathing.

'So,' a voice hissed quietly, 'our little captive is conscious at last.'

Judith let out her breath on a long sigh of relief. 'Why are you doing this? Why am I a prisoner? At least tell me that.'

'It is not for you to concern yourself with that.'

'My disappearance from the academy will have been noticed. Someone will find me,' she said on a note of desperation, trying to conceal the raging anxiety in her heart.

'No one will find you here—and screaming will do no good. There is no one to hear you. And do not try to struggle,' her captor said, his voice having become flat and deadly. 'If you are to remain here indefinitely, it could save you much pain in time to come.'

The fact that she had been trussed could only mean that her captors were afraid she might escape, and the blindfold was to prevent her from seeing their faces. If there were anyone to hear her screams they would have gagged her. 'But what is it you want from me?'

'From you, nothing. You are merely a pawn, that is all. When your brother has complied with our demands you will be released unharmed.'

Judith puzzled on this. 'My brother?' she asked at last. 'But—I don't have a brother.'

There was silence.

'I said I don't have a brother,' she repeated forcefully, her voice raised.

'I heard you the first time,' the strained voice hissed, as though purposely keeping his voice low so as to disguise it.

Suddenly, realisation of what must have happened hit Judith with the stark clarity of a blinding flash. It was Charlotte they had meant to kidnap, not her. She was wearing Charlotte's cloak and must have been mistaken for her. If she hadn't taken it this would not have happened. Hope stirred in her heart. 'Clearly you have made a mistake. I am not who you think I am—whoever that may be. My name is Judith Wyatt. Don't you see? You have kidnapped the wrong person.'

The terrible silent stillness around her told her that her captor must believe her—that he had irretrievably blundered into an appalling error, for after a long moment of deliberation, he uttered a string of savage curses and moved away. She heard a door open and close and voices raised in anger. Then all was quiet. And so, huddled in her dark retreat, despite her numbness and pain, she waited, vulnerable and afraid, praying that now they knew they had the wrong person they would release her. But then again, in another minute she could be dead, pointlessly murdered by someone she had never seen.

Chapter Two

Jordan was not in the best of moods when he arrived at the academy to escort his sister and Miss Wyatt to Landsdowne.

Being a powerful proprietor of the East India Company and a member of a group representing the banking, commercial and shipping interests of the Company—a position held by his father until his tragic and untimely death—he had yesterday come to town to India House in Leadenhall Street for a shareholders' meeting.

Alighting from his carriage, the sight of three men leaving the building had suddenly caught his attention. His heart gave a sudden jolt of recognition and his face hardened. Quickly he stepped back, not wishing to be seen. One of the men was Lord Jeremy Minton, who had been employed as a district officer in the northern region of India, and whose career in the Company's service spanned fifteen years.

The Company provided useful career opportunities for sons of impoverished landowners, and Minton's family had become almost destitute. Jeremy had been a youth when his father died, and seeking ways to boost the dwin-

dling income derived from his estate, he joined the East
India Company.

Opinionated and susceptible to demonstrations of arrogance that he could not disguise, pride was evident in
all Minton's dealings. He was also a man who couldn't
hold his temper, and as a result had few friends. He had
joined the Company for personal gain, and he had very
soon developed a hunger for gold and jewels that
amounted to a personal sickness. If ever there was a man
whose judgement could be tempted by greed, it was
Minton. It was rumoured that he had grown immensely
rich in the Company's service.

Slightly over average height, he was certainly a fine
figure of a man, with a bull-like strength, the muscular
swell of his shoulders straining against the seams of his
coat. His pale blue eyes were set too close together beneath a heavy brow for his features to be described as
handsome.

Jordan's dislike of the man was intense—the dislike
being mutual—but it was not Minton's looks he disliked
as much as the stench of corruption that surrounded him,
and the suppressed violence within. He was like a dangerous animal trained to behave, while retaining the menacing, wild ways of his birth. But while Jordan kept him
at a distance, he could also keep at bay the memories and
feelings he stirred.

Jordan's eyes shifted to one of Minton's companions.
Suddenly his mouth went dry and clammy sweat sprang
out on the palms of his hands, for he recognised the pallid
features and the thin, drooping moustache of the man he
had seen on board the *Eastern Lady*. At the time he had
been unable to remember where he had seen him before.
Now he knew. The man was Minton's servant, and
Jordan was a hundred per cent certain that under his mas-

ter's instructions, he was the one who had searched his personal property in his cabin.

He gave his attention to the third man—a splendidly dressed turbaned Indian with an effeminate face, flat black eyes and a cruel mouth. His name was Jehan Khan, once a humble retainer of the Rajah of Ranjipur. During his time in India as a soldier of the Crown, Jordan had become closely acquainted with the Rajah, whose small state bordered on Nepal. He had been a man of honour and had earned Jordan's respect and admiration. The same accolade could not be applied to his cousin, Prince Chandu, who had wheedled Jehan Khan into his own service.

What perturbed Jordan was seeing Jehan Khan here in London with Jeremy Minton, whose district had included Prince Chandu's domain. And what deepened his concern was the fact that there was little love lost between them and their distrust of each other ran deep. When Minton made common cause with Khan, Jordan had reason to think something serious and of a sinister nature was afoot. But then, both men were corrupt and ambitious, and corruption and ambition could make strange bedfellows.

Jordan had a multitude of reasons for wanting to avoid contact with either of them. A thunderous frown drew his black eyebrows into a single line as he watched the three men climb into a waiting coach and drive off. Cursing softly, a dull rage ate into him like acid, filling him so completely that for a moment everything went dark around him. He strode into India House, determined to discover the purpose of their visit.

After all those years serving as a soldier in India, wasn't it time for pleasure and peace at his home without

the intrusion of Jeremy Minton and the corrupt machinations of Prince Chandu?

Amidst a great deal of girlish laughter and tears of
departing pupils—happy to be going home but sad to be
leaving their friends—trunks and bonnet-boxes and a
paraphernalia of other articles were being arranged onto
carriages by frustrated coachmen in the street outside the
academy. When Jordan enquired after his sister he was
directed to Miss Powell's house by a sombre-faced
teacher. Looking forward to seeing Charlotte, he was
quite unprepared for the reception he received when he
was shown into the drawing-room.

Charlotte was seated on the lemon and green cushions
of the window seat in an extreme state of distress, with
Miss Powell doing her best to comfort her. On seeing her
brother she rose and flung herself into his arms.

'Oh, Jordan—I'm so happy to see you—relieved, too.
Thank goodness you're here.'

She didn't look at all well and her tearful greeting
alarmed Jordan. 'Charlotte, what is it? Has something
happened to you?'

'No,' she wailed, 'not to me. It's Judith.'

'Judith?'

'Judith Wyatt,' Miss Powell explained. 'As you will
know, Lady Grant has very kindly invited her to spend
the summer at Landsdowne with Charlotte, and has
agreed to assume complete responsibility for her. Unfortunately she has disappeared. We are all so worried as to
what can have happened to her.'

Jordan's stare was probing. He had the distinct feeling
that he was about to be inconvenienced by a girl he had
never met. 'Disappeared? How? How can a pupil go
missing?'

'I wish I knew,' Miss Powell replied. 'Yesterday evening she left the academy to come here to see me but never arrived. A thorough search has been made, but there is no sign of her. It is all very distressing.'

Jordan was incredulous. 'You mean she disappeared crossing the street?'

'Yes, so it would seem. No one has seen her since.'

Jordan frowned impatiently. He had no idea what to expect of Charlotte's friend, but in view of her impoverished state, which left her with no alternative but to earn a living to support herself, he didn't expect much. 'You have informed the constables?'

'Of course. Everything possible is being done to find her, but as yet their enquiries have come to nothing.'

'Is it possible that she could have run away?' he asked shortly.

'Judith had no reason to run away, Captain Grant.'

'Does she have any friends she could have gone to visit—a young man, perhaps?'

Charlotte was clearly shocked at what he implied. 'Jordan, really!' she gasped. 'Of course she hasn't. Judith isn't like that.'

'I apologise, but every possibility has to be considered.'

'You are right, Captain Grant, but Judith's parents are dead,' Miss Powell explained. 'She has no friends outside the academy and her only living relative is an aunt in Brighton.'

'If anything untoward has happened to her I shall blame myself,' Charlotte wailed, crumpling down onto a sofa and giving vent to a fresh outburst of tears. 'I should have gone with her. It was almost dark and Miss Powell has always stressed that we must not leave the academy unaccompanied. I hate to think of her being kidnapped—or worse.'

'Stop it, Charlotte,' said her brother sharply. 'You are jumping to conclusions.'

'I can't help it,' she whispered, sneezing and wiping her nose, for she had contracted the most wretched cold after spending too long in the rain the previous day. 'I can't leave here until I know what has happened to her. I simply can't.'

'I am sure Miss Powell will send word to Landsdowne if she hears anything,' Jordan said, gentling his tone, a sympathetic smile softening his grim features.

'Please, Jordan. Let me stay,' she begged, almost choking on her emotion.

Relenting, Jordan sat beside her and placed a calming arm about her shoulders as she began to cough. 'You look as though you should be in bed, Charlotte. Very well. We will both stay—if that is all right with Miss Powell.'

'Of course. You must remain here. With all the activity going on at the academy, you will be more comfortable. If you will excuse me, I have some parents waiting to see me before they whisk their daughters away for the summer. As you can see, Captain Grant, Charlotte has caught a chill. I'll instruct matron to make up a powder for her and have refreshment sent in to you while you wait.'

An hour after Jordan's arrival, Judith was unceremoniously deposited at the end of the street. Dazed and shaken, and struggling to find some sort of mental equilibrium as she adjusted her eyes to the bright light when she removed the blindfold, she walked unsteadily past a line of carriages towards the academy. Parents and pupils swarmed all over the place. Seeing her, a concerned-looking tutor disengaged herself and came to her. Reassured that she was unharmed, the tutor immediately took her to Miss Powell's house.

When she entered the drawing-room Charlotte threw herself at her friend, enfolding her in the protective warmth of her arms and love. 'Judith! Thank goodness you're all right. I have been so worried. Where on earth have you been?'

Judith swallowed down the lump in her throat, and the tears she'd fought all night finally slid down her pale cheeks. In all the years she had known Charlotte, she'd never seen her so upset, and she felt sick with remorse that her disappearance was the cause of her distress. The heat of the cheek pressed against her own also alarmed her, telling her that her friend was most unwell, which was confirmed when she looked into her fever-bright eyes.

Miss Powell interrupted the reunion, saying in a calm voice, 'I can't tell you how relieved I am to see you back, Judith. Everyone has been most anxious. First of all I must ask if you have been harmed in any way?'

Judith shook her head, brushing the tears from her cheeks. To surrender to the full intensity of Miss Powell's solicitude was a luxury she would have to forgo until she had explained all that had happened.

'No, Miss Powell. I am tired and my head aches, that's all.'

'Nevertheless, you must go to bed and I'll send for Dr Gardner to take a look at you. But first there are a few questions that must be answered.'

Miss Powell placed an arm about Judith's shoulders and turned her round. From across the room a man of uncommon height with his hands clasped behind his back was studying her closely, his lean frame clad in an impeccably tailored black suit, a white shirt and neckcloth at his throat. Dark hair was swept back from his wide brow and curled on his collar. 'This is Captain Grant, Judith.'

Miss Powell left the three of them alone to ask her maid to arrange for Dr Gardner to call.

As Captain Grant crossed the room with long, vigorous strides, Judith stifled an unexpected attack of nervousness. She admitted to herself that Charlotte's brother was a splendid figure of a man, whose movements bespoke a life of action and adventure. His face was darkly handsome, almost saturnine, his nose well-formed above unsmiling lips, and those eyes—silver-grey and almost transparent—which gleamed like bright gems against his skin, bronzed by the Indian sun, seemed capable of piercing her innermost secrets, causing a frisson of unease bordering on fear to course through her.

There was something unbending and self-contained about him, an air of the professional soldier displayed in his dignity and bearing and crisp manner. He moved with the confident ease of his own masculinity, and he had a powerful presence, an undeniable magnetism—a ladies' man, Charlotte would say, the kind of man who filled the pages of those romantic novels she so ardently devoured.

He had done nine years of military service in India— her own beloved country, where she had spent a greater part of her life—and her senses swirled as something as mystical and primeval as India and the ancient rivers that journeyed through that land entered her soul. In that moment all her senses were intensified almost beyond endurance.

She recalled the tales of destiny her Ayah had immersed her in as a child, of how all their lives were dictated by the stars and the heavens, and she wondered if some master plan had been at work and marked her path to cross that of Jordan Grant's. Mentally she shook herself out of her trance. She didn't believe in the influence of fate, nor that she was destined to meet a man who wouldn't give her a second look.

Towering over her and having no knowledge of her thoughts, Jordan saw a young woman of medium height, extremely pale and tense. Her eyes were lowered. She was dressed in a high-necked, unrelieved charcoal grey dress, unbecoming on a girl so young. Her hair was also drawn back severely. He was just deciding that she was the plainest young woman he had ever encountered, when she raised her startling hazel eyes and fixed him with an unfathomable, unblinking gaze.

His breath caught in his throat, for in their depths was the look of another world. He was surprised to find there was nothing actually objectionable about her. Her skin was golden and absolutely without blemish. Her face didn't change as she held out her hand, small, slim, though still slightly swollen from the tight bonds that had secured her wrists during her captivity.

'I'm pleased to meet you, Captain Grant,' she said, with all the confidence she could raise. Regardless of all that had happened to her since she had left the academy, she was determined not to portray herself as some weak-kneed schoolgirl. She sensed that he found her something of an encumbrance and that he was vexed that her disappearance had inconvenienced him. He concealed his impatience well, but it was there, in the tightening of his jaw and the narrowing of his eyes. Captain Grant was an aloof, icy stranger who was inspecting her closely. She was certain that if she were one of his soldiers he would lose no time in telling her that she did not pass muster.

'I am sorry to have caused you so much trouble, but I assure you it was not of my making.'

Jordan was somewhat taken aback by her calm approach, but he would have been surprised to know how exceedingly nervous she was about meeting him. He took her hand lightly in his strong fingers. 'I'm pleased to meet you, too, Miss Wyatt,' he said, with flawless formality and no warmth, which, to Judith, seemed like an unpromising beginning. 'I assure you that you have been no trouble. I am relieved you are returned to the academy unharmed—although,' he said sharply, his gaze shifting to the bruise on her cheek, 'not entirely, it would appear. Who did this?'

'I—do not know.'

His granite features softened. 'Does the bruise cause you pain?'

Judith had recovered both her equanimity and her air of command. 'I'm perfectly all right. It is nothing,' she replied, touched that he should ask. 'I—I was accosted last evening—when I was coming to see Miss Powell— and bundled into a carriage. It was raining and everything happened so fast. I tried to get away, but my assailants were strong. There was nothing I could do.'

Charlotte was outwardly shocked. 'You mean you were kidnapped?' she gasped, staring at her friend in terror, the inadequacy of the question in the face of that monstrous bruise angering her to bitter tears. It was unthinkable that anyone would want to hurt Judith. 'How frightened you must have been.'

'I confess that I was,' Judith admitted, laying a calming hand on Charlotte's arm, 'but please don't distress yourself, Charlotte. I am recovered now.'

'Have you any idea why anyone would want to accost you?' Jordan asked.

'No—or what I mean to say is that they didn't. They had no reason to—although they didn't realise this at the time. Please understand that I lost my senses for a while, and when I recovered I was terribly confused and had no idea what was happening to me. One of my assailants—although I must tell you that I was wearing a blindfold and didn't see his face—told me I was merely a pawn, and that when my brother had complied with their demands I would be released. That was when it occurred to me that they had made a mistake.'

'Mistake?' Jordan frowned, puzzled.

She met his gaze calmly. 'Yes. I don't have a brother, you see. I—I believe it was Charlotte they meant to kidnap.' On hearing a fearful cry, she turned to Charlotte, who was frozen in shock, her eyes staring in consternation.

'Me?' she uttered, a slight tremor detectable in her voice. 'But why would anyone want to kidnap me? For what reason?'

Knowing how fearful Charlotte must be feeling, Judith's heart swelled with pain for her friend. 'Oh, Charlotte,' she whispered, reaching out and taking her hand. 'I'm sorry to have to worry you, but that I cannot tell you.'

'But—am I in danger?'

'I cannot tell you that, either.'

Jordan was giving Judith a strange look, staring at her hard, his eyes boring holes into hers. 'What are you saying? How can you possibly know it was Charlotte they wanted? Did they say as much?'

'No, they didn't. However, I have no doubt in my mind whatsoever that Charlotte was their intended victim. She has two brothers and I was wearing her cloak at the time.'

'And this is significant?' Jordan snapped the question.

'I believe so. I am quite certain that whoever it was that abducted me mistook me for your sister.'

Jordan raised his brows in a scornful gesture. 'Forgive me, Miss Wyatt, but I find that difficult to believe. You and my sister are not remotely alike,' he remarked pointedly.

His reply was startlingly abrupt—almost rude, and Judith flinched. She heard the insult in his smoothly worded statement, and a wave of anger brought a sudden flush to her cheeks. She knew she wasn't as pretty as Charlotte—who was the very picture of perfect sweetness in comparison with what Judith felt to be her plainness, but she didn't care to be reminded of it. Her eyes did not flinch from the piercing silver gaze and she faced him with a flicker of hauteur she could not quite conceal. Pushed to retaliate by his arrogant calm, and the recollection of her own ill-use at her assailants' hands, when she spoke her voice was cold and threaded with sarcasm.

'You are absolutely right, Captain Grant, and it is an affliction I have learned to live with.'

'I apologise if my clumsy words offended you. It was not intended. I am sure you have many admirable qualities.'

'If I have then I doubt very much that they are of the kind you would admire, Captain Grant,' she replied tartly. 'However, I don't know what it was the men who abducted me want from you—or your brother, but it has occurred to me that they could decide to pursue whatever it is and that Charlotte's life might be in danger. Being extremely fond of her, this concerns me greatly, as it should you.'

'No,' Charlotte cried, choking on her emotion. 'Surely not.'

Judith turned and saw naked fear in her friend's eyes. 'I'm sorry, Charlotte, but it could happen.'

Affronted and furious that this chit of a girl had the temerity to remind him of his duty, Jordan's voice turned positively glacial and his eyes gleamed like shards of ice. 'Be assured, Miss Wyatt, if, as you say, my sister was their intended victim—and I have to say that I am inclined to believe you—then every precaution to safeguard her well-being will be taken by me.'

'For heaven's sake, Jordan,' Charlotte intervened, distressed by the thought that some unknown assailant might be planning to abduct her and carry her off to heaven knows where. 'Do you have to be so unkind? Why, anyone would think Judith asked to be kidnapped. You must realise that if she hadn't borrowed my cloak none of this would have happened—although I shudder when I think that if they had been successful and abducted me, then I would still be their captive waiting for you or Edmund to concede to their demands. Goodness! What can it be they want? Have you any idea, Jordan?'

Guilt tore at him as he abruptly replied, 'None.'

There was an edge to his voice which made Judith glance at him sharply. She looked at the tight line of his mouth and the disturbing light in his eyes, and the truth hit her then. Captain Grant did know, and knowing this cast a haunting and uneasy cloud over her. She could not have put into words the feeling of discomfort, but it was as though some spirit had groped its way into her heart.

'Then when we arrive home we must ask Edmund,' Charlotte quipped. Taking Judith's hand she drew her down onto the sofa beside her. 'Please forgive my brother, Judith. He's not usually such a crosspatch—although I do recall that he has an evil temper when vexed.'

'I have a rather formidable temper myself when

roused,' Judith admitted, meeting Captain Grant's gaze. It was true, although no one had tested it for some time.

Mild interest stirred in Jordan's eyes and warmed with a mixture of amusement and admiration. For one brief moment he glimpsed the proud, spirited young woman hidden behind that calm façade.

'Really?' he drawled. 'I am surprised, Miss Wyatt. To me, you have the appearance of placidity and patience personified.'

'Appearances can be deceiving, Captain Grant.'

'It would appear so,' he said, inclining his head slightly, the rigidity leaving his jaw and a smile lurking at his mouth.

After her gruelling night, all Judith's defences were down, her spirits low. As a result her deep sigh and the weary smile she gave him was unintentionally personal. 'Please forgive me. I feel quite worn out and truly do not want to argue with you.'

'I am glad to hear it. And I don't argue—I'm diplomatic,' he stated. 'How quickly you become angry and defensive, Miss Wyatt, which is something I shall have to guard against since you are to be our guest at Landsdowne.'

'I am only angry when I feel the need to be defensive, Captain Grant,' Judith countered.

A smile moved across his lean brown face. 'Truce?'

Judith told herself that her presence at Landsdowne would be of no real consequence at all to Captain Grant, but she smiled anyway, her first genuine smile of their meeting, her soft lips curving with winsome humour that made her eyes glow. 'Truce,' she agreed.

'Now—tell me what you remember of your ordeal.'

'It was all very confusing at the time. I was knocked

senseless out in the street, and when I came round I had no idea where I was.'

'Miss Wyatt, I am extremely sorry that you have been drawn into a matter which is none of your concern. However, I don't think I need to stress how important it is that you remember something so these men can be apprehended. Nevertheless, if they do intend pursuing this matter with either me or my brother, then they will have to show their hand sooner or later. Do you remember anything? The smallest detail could be crucial. Did you see your assailant? Did you get an impression of his build?'

'I didn't see anything. My eyes were covered the whole time. The blindfold remained in place until I was released at the end of the street.'

'Do you remember anything about the location of the place they took you to?'

'No, nothing—except that it was extremely cold.'

'How long did the journey take from where you were being held to the academy?'

'About fifteen minutes.' She sighed, suddenly tired of his questions, which bordered on interrogation. 'I'm sorry I cannot be of more help. What I do know is that there was more than one person involved. I heard them arguing when they realised their mistake. Before that, one of them told me I would not be released until my brother had conceded to their demands. That was when I realised there had been a mistake. I don't have a brother, you see.'

Jordan nodded, becoming detached and cool once more. 'Yes, I do see,' he said, moving towards the door, intending to leave. 'I also see that you will not be travelling to Landsdowne with Charlotte and me this morning.'

Her heart leapt with disappointment. 'Oh—but after a change of clothes and—'

'Please don't interrupt,' he said with an insistence that brooked no argument, his face having set itself into the implacable mould which would have been instantly recognised by the men in his regiment. 'Clearly you need to rest after your ordeal, and Miss Powell is quite right to ask the doctor to examine you. Charlotte is feverish and I want to get her home as quickly as possible. My brother and his wife will be coming to town tomorrow, in which case I shall instruct them to collect you at three o'clock. Now, before we leave I must have a word with Miss Powell.' He glanced at his sister. 'Be ready in a few minutes, Charlotte. Goodbye, Miss Wyatt. It's a pleasure to have met you.'

His curt dismissal of her annoyed Judith, but she was too well schooled to show it. She rose, making a conscious effort to keep all emotion from her voice. 'Goodbye, Captain Grant,' she said with quiet dignity. 'And thank you.'

He gave her one last look as though he wanted to say something further, but then he changed his mind and left.

Chapter Three

The following afternoon, feeling rested and pronounced well enough to leave the academy by Dr Gardner—despite having slept fitfully and dreaming she was still tied up in that cold room—Judith was ready when Edmund Grant and his wife arrived to take her to Landsdowne. But her ordeal at the hands of her assailants was still at the forefront of her mind, and she wondered what was behind it and how deeply Captain Grant was involved. It was all very mysterious.

In spite of the fact that she had prepared herself for what she must expect at the Grant family home at Greenwich, she viewed the proposed visit with some trepidation. Her trunk, which had seen much service over the years, seemed even more battered as it was placed on the rack at the back of the splendid coach.

With her husband, Emily got out of the coach and greeted her warmly, referring with a great deal of concern and sympathy to her abduction. Emily was petite, fair-haired and extremely pretty. There was an air of kindness about her and Judith liked her immediately. Edmund Grant was natural in his behaviour and charming. His looks were pleasant and friendly, and he put on his most engaging smile when he saw her.

'It's good to meet you at last, Miss Wyatt—or may I call you Judith?'

'Yes—I would like that. Thank you for collecting me, Mr Grant.'

'Edmund,' he corrected firmly. 'I have been urging Charlotte for a long time to bring you to Landsdowne. Unfortunately my poor sister was quite unwell when she arrived home yesterday.'

'I know. She did have a sore throat and a headache. She was out in the rain the day before and got quite wet, I'm afraid.'

'Mother took charge of her at once and in no time at all she was tucked up in bed with a hot water bottle. But please don't worry, Charlotte has such miraculous powers of recuperation that I'm sure she'll be on her feet in no time at all. Now,' he said as he handed her into the coach, 'come and meet Emily's sister, Alicia. She's been staying with friends in town and is coming to Landsdowne with us for an indefinite period.'

It was only then that Judith became aware that there was another occupant inside the coach. At the sincerity and warmth of Edmund's and Emily's greeting, Judith knew she would enjoy her visit to Landsdowne. This opinion lasted only a moment. One look at the beautiful young woman Edmund introduced her to—whose nose was long and straight and perfect for looking down, and with a mouth resembling Cupid's bow—made Judith's heart sink. It only took her a moment to realise that Alicia, who was twenty years old, was unlike Emily in every aspect.

As Judith settled herself opposite this aloof young woman, Alicia gave her a faint inclination of her elegantly coifed auburn head and a frosty smile, before settling her austere gaze on her in a cool and exacting way. Impersonally her eyes raked her with a single withering glance, noting her plain attire with a look of distaste. Judith knew she had decided there and then that she was as poor as a church mouse and had no social credentials to recommend her. Immediately a wall of antipathy seemed to spring up between them, and Alicia seemed bent on putting her at a disadvantage from the start.

'So you are Charlotte's friend,' she commented wryly and with a practised smile when Edmund had introduced them, giving Judith a flash of sharp white teeth from between her parted lips.

There were hidden connotations behind the smile and Judith was not quite sure how to read them, but whether meant as insult or compliment, the two of them were both to be guests in the Grant household and it would not do to get off on a bad footing. There was nothing like a smile to confuse a foe or charm a friend and Judith's lips curved graciously. 'Yes, I am,' she replied pleasantly, self-consciously tucking a stray curl beneath her bonnet. She might resemble a pauper, but she had no wish to look as dishevelled as one into the bargain. 'We have been friends ever since I began attending the academy four years ago.'

'And have you finished your education at the academy, too?'

'Yes—although I am to return in the autumn to take up a teaching post there.'

Alicia gave her an arch look. 'You are to be a teacher? Goodness! How awful for you. I cannot imagine anything worse than having to teach hordes of children how to read and write.'

If Alicia hoped to see a flicker of emotion pass across

the girl's face she was disappointed, for Judith continued to smile. 'Your conjecture is quite wrong, I assure you. I'm looking forward to it.'

With a slight nod and a look of boredom, Alicia turned to look out of the window at the passing scenery. She made no further attempt at conversation, clearly considering Judith of no consequence.

There was a strange air of unreality about the journey as the coach travelled through London and across the river to Greenwich. She chatted amiably with Emily and Edmund and, having decided to ignore Alicia, Judith found that the couple had succeeded in putting her at ease.

Almost at their journey's end, they travelled down a lane which brought them to a set of tall iron gates. A wide avenue of stately limes led to the most beautiful house Judith had ever seen. Built in warm red brick, its lines were pure and simple, with tall windows of shimmering glass. As the coach passed through the gates, which swung open on well-oiled hinges, she gazed at the exquisitely landscaped gardens, which consisted of acres of rolling green lawns and clipped box hedges, of sculpted pools reflecting flowering shrubs and trees with variegated leaves.

After climbing out of the coach she entered the house in dazed disbelief. Standing in the spacious marble hallway with a graceful, curving staircase sweeping upwards in the centre and forming a gallery, it surpassed anything she had ever seen.

'Mother is resting just now, Judith. You probably know she hasn't been too well of late. I dare say she'll be down later,' Edmund informed her, explaining his mother's absence. 'Jordan is in town and hopes to be home for dinner. Emily will show you to your room.'

'I'd be happy to,' Emily said obligingly. 'Come this way, Judith.'

Judith's room was pale blue and cream, charming and restful, with a splendid view of Greenwich and the Thames in the distance. Immediately concerned about Charlotte, she asked Emily if she might see her. Emily could see no reason why not and took her to Charlotte's room, which was just next door.

Propped against her pillows, her eyes red, cheeks flushed and sneezing into a handkerchief, poor Charlotte really did look quite poorly, but she was delighted to see her friend.

'I'm so glad you're here, Judith,' she said, patting the bed for her to sit down when Emily had left, 'but how I wish I didn't have this wretched cold.'

'You'll soon be feeling better, Charlotte.'

'I do hope so. If I have to stay in bed another day I'll go mad.' Rearranging her pillows with Judith's help to enable her to sit up, she settled back. 'Tell me about your journey and what you think of Edmund and Emily.'

'They are everything you said of them. They were both charming and very kind.'

'And Alicia? What do you think of her?'

In Judith's uneasy mind the memory of those cool green eyes resting on her was far too vivid. 'I—have to say that her manners are not equal to those of her sister's,' she replied cautiously, without implying that she had found offence in Alicia's behaviour towards her, 'but she is extremely attractive,' she conceded.

Charlotte glanced at her sharply. 'Alicia can be quite stuck up sometimes. I do hope she wasn't rude to you, Judith.'

Judith smiled, having already decided to avoid Alicia's company as often as possible. 'I think Alicia sees me as something of a ''blue-stocking''—one of that frightful band of women who openly parade their intelligence. I always find it strange that those who are prejudiced against educating women to the same level as men are those that one might expect to appreciate them. I suppose Alicia finds somebody as plain as I am, who has been taught to a degree that enables me to teach others, thoroughly unfeminine and therefore unattractive.'

'That's because she doesn't have an imaginative brain. Alicia puts great emphasis on fashion, status, social advancement and being seen in all the right places. She is a dullard and has no literary leanings, you see, that's why she resents it in others.'

'Then perhaps she is to be pitied and better understood and I have been too harsh on her, Charlotte.'

'No, you weren't. It's very rare that you see fault in anybody, Judith, but I'm afraid that where Alicia is concerned you are too generous by far—which, in my opinion, is more than she deserves. Every time she opens her mouth I expect to hear her rattle,' Charlotte said unkindly. 'She is a natural flirt, proud, vain and conceited, and thinks far too highly of herself, if you ask me.'

'I suppose with her looks and being the daughter of a very rich man, she has everything in her favour and is entitled to think highly of herself.'

'That may be, and I would be ready to forgive her, if she had not been rude to you. You are a guest at Landsdowne as much as she is, and I won't have her upsetting you.'

'She won't,' Judith smiled. 'I won't let her—but you didn't tell me she was to be here.'

'I didn't know myself until I arrived home and mother

told me—although my dear brother is her true reason for coming to Landsdowne, not, as she would have it, to be with Emily. When Jordan came home two years ago, Alicia had visions of being his wife, but however much she hoped he would ask her, he went back to India without saying a word. Yet when he returned and she saw him in town recently, I suspect her aspirations have been revived. She's quite besotted by him—and I know Emily would be delighted if anything were to come of it. Although I'm not so sure about Mother.'

'And your brother? How does he respond?'

'He's not immune to the overtures she's making towards him,' Charlotte told her, stifling a yawn. 'When it comes to wheedling her way around people Alicia is a genius—and when it comes to affairs of the heart, in my opinion all men are weak and foolish. From what I have seen when the two of them are together, Jordan is no exception.'

Judith disagreed with this. There was nothing weak or foolish about Jordan Grant. 'Then I wish her success.'

'Perhaps she was rude to you because she sees you as some kind of threat for my brother's affections.'

'Me?' Judith responded incredulously. 'Don't be ridiculous, Charlotte. As plain and ordinary as I am, what man would give me a second look? Especially when the competition is someone as beautiful as Alicia.'

'Plenty would, if you'd encourage them more. If only you would accept some of my dresses and do something with your hair—which is lovely when you brush it out— you would confound them all.'

Judith was saved having to reply, for at that moment Charlotte was overcome by a fit of sneezing. Her refusal to accept any of her friend's dresses was an old argument, one she preferred not to enter into just then. She sat with

Charlotte a while, but as her eyelids began to droop it was clear she was not up to any more conversation. 'Do you think anyone will mind if I take a walk in the gardens before it gets dark, Charlotte? They look so lovely.'

'No, of course not. I just wish I could come with you,' she grumbled miserably, closing her eyes and settling down to sleep.

Realising she had strayed further that she had intended, Judith was about to turn back when she saw Captain Grant walking with long strides towards her. She was totally unprepared for the way her heartbeat suddenly started to quicken and the warmth that flooded her whole being. He had returned to Landsdowne from his business meetings in town, and when he had enquired of the butler if Miss Wyatt had arrived, he had been told that she had gone into the gardens. Immediately he had come to look for her. He was frowning and his jaw was tightly clenched.

Frozen into stillness, Judith waited for him to reach her. With his tall, lithe figure, she thought how handsome he was, how confident and assured of himself, and she wondered what it would be like to be close to such a man. But Judith knew, and her heart lurched with pain, that she was a million miles away from being his equal, that she was not of his world and never would be. The realisation shook her out of her trance, and she was shocked that she should venture to think this way.

'Miss Wyatt! I wish you wouldn't walk too far away from the house alone,' he said curtly.

Judith bristled at his tone. His coolness damped the warmth she had felt on seeing him walk towards her, and when she looked into his eyes, unable to find any gentleness or kindness, and seeing that they were as cold and unwelcoming as glaciers, she withdrew inside herself. 'I—I am sorry. I didn't think anyone would mind if I took a stroll before it gets dark.'

'Usually it would be perfectly in order for you to do so, but in the light of what happened to you the other day, as a precaution I would prefer it if you didn't,' he said. His tanned features were set in lines of implacable authority, and he spoke in a voice of strained patience, reminding Judith of the brutality of her abduction and the terror of her incarceration.

She gasped with alarm. 'Captain Grant! Are you saying I might be abducted again? You seem to forget I was released—that it was not me those men wanted to kidnap but Charlotte.'

'I do not forget, and I can see you are still upset by what happened.'

'Of course I'm upset,' she said heatedly. 'I'm not used to being set upon in the street by a total stranger, viciously attacked and bundled into a carriage, where whoever it was bound my hands and tied something over my eyes and carted me off to heaven knows where. Are you going to tell me what it was all about? You know who was responsible, don't you?' she challenged.

There was a hard gleam in his eyes when he looked at her, giving no inkling of his thoughts. He nodded slightly. 'All I can say is that I have my suspicions and no proof. However, if the people who abducted you are still intent on kidnap—for whatever reason—then now that you are our guest they may realise they were too hasty in releasing you and abduct you again. The truth of it is I don't know what they intend, but I am sufficiently worried not to take any chances until there is an outcome to my enquiries. I tell you this for your own safety. Come—I'll walk with you back to the house.'

Jordan's quality of detachment as they walked side by side was peculiar to himself. It wasn't until the house was within their sights that his mood softened. Slowing his pace, he looked at the young woman properly for the first time, his silver-grey gaze considering her closely. When he had first seen her he had looked at her with a critical eye, but on closer inspection he found her features uncommonly intelligent. She was a strange young woman, and with her looks and plain attire did not belong to the fashionable world. But with her fine, slender form and handspan waist, which reminded him of the frail white moonflowers that grew in abundance in India, she was deserving of a second look.

She moved with a natural grace and poise that evaded most of the European women he knew, in fact her movements were more reminiscent of Indian women. There was an aura of prim innocence about her that he found appealing, but behind her calm façade he sensed an adventurous spirit tinged with obstinacy.

She really was the opposite of Charlotte in every way. Charlotte could be described as adorably pretty, whereas Judith Wyatt's face was arresting. Her hair was a rich dark brown, attractively highlighted with shades of red and gold. Her face was heart-shaped, with a small determined chin and soft, pink mouth. Her hazel eyes, outlined with thick sooty lashes, were large and slanted slightly.

They were lowered as she walked beside him, so he was unable to read their expression—which was just as well, for Judith was irresistibly drawn to her companion from that moment, and the realisation of it shone deep in their depths. Her profile was pure and serene, and Jordan was suddenly curious to know her better.

'I trust you are suffering no ill-effects from your ordeal?'

'No—none.'

'Tell me about yourself,' he said without preamble, watching her steadily and fixing her with a lazy smile.

Turning her head she looked up and met his gaze, her incredible eyes candid and expressive. 'There's nothing to tell. Usually I never talk about myself.'

'Never? Might I ask why not?'

'Because there are so many other things to discuss that are far more interesting.'

Raising his brows he looked at her expectantly. 'Come now,' he prompted softly. 'You are eighteen years old, Miss Wyatt. There must be something.'

Clearly he had no knowledge that she had been born and raised in India. If he did she was certain he would have asked her about it. But she was glad he didn't know, since there were some memories that ran deep and were too painful to recall. 'There isn't. I'm quite ordinary, really. My parents are dead, and when I'm not at the academy I live with my aunt in Brighton.'

'I understand that your aunt is abroad just now.'

'Yes—which is why Charlotte kindly invited me to Landsdowne. I did thank her for her consideration for me. I would not have you or Lady Grant believe me ungrateful. I confess it sounded more agreeable than spending the summer at the academy.'

'I suspect you will miss not going to Brighton. Is that correct?'

'Yes, I will. I love the sea.'

'And your aunt? Do you love your aunt, Miss Wyatt?'

Judith opened and closed her mouth without uttering a word before turning her eyes away from his penetrating gaze, wishing he hadn't asked such a personal question. Her face was a mirror of such confusion that Jordan took pity on her. 'I apologise. It was rude of me to ask that. You don't have to answer.'

'No—it—it doesn't matter,' she said, looking at him once more. 'I—I respect her—and I will always be grateful to her.'

He frowned, eyeing her quizzically. 'But you are not close. Why?'

Perhaps it was the low timbre of his voice or the intensity of his gaze, for as Judith looked at him, the truth seemed to be squeezed from her. 'Because she dislikes me. I am also burdensome and an expense she can ill afford,' she answered, wondering what a man with all his privileges would make of that.

Jordan nodded, digesting her words. 'Why do you want to teach?' he asked pointedly.

His question took her wholly by surprise and she felt herself flushing. She was in a situation for which she was ill-trained, but she answered with admirable calm. 'Why does anyone want to do anything? I want to teach because I can—and because I need to. I find it necessary to support myself. Besides, I like being independent and self-sufficient. I prefer it that way.' When he gave her an enquiring look she said, 'I have my pride and my reasons, Captain Grant.'

'You have just given me three answers to my question, Miss Wyatt, but you have not given me the most important one. You have not said that you enjoy teaching.'

'Oh, but I do,' she said on a rush. 'And teaching is a respectable profession for a woman.'

'And being respectable is important to you?'

'Of course. Miss Powell already allows me to teach French to the children in the lower school, and I shall be happy to take up my position in full at the academy in the autumn.'

'Does being a governess not appeal to you instead?'

'Not really. I enjoy teaching more than one person.'

'And no doubt you are well-drilled in all subjects necessary to make a good teacher.'

'I hope so, Captain Grant.'

Having come to a small gate in a beech hedge, he paused in opening it, looking down at her upturned face. 'And what are your pleasures?' he inquired softly, waiting for her reaction and her reply with enigmatic eyes, knowing perfectly well that her idea of pleasures would not conform to his own—which were the kind she would not approve of and certainly not admire. He was ten years her senior, wiser and centuries older than she in experience. There was an innocent vulnerability in the purity of her features, and when she replied and he noted the enthusiasm that crept into her voice and the glow that lit her wide hazel eyes, he suddenly felt ancient and worn out beside her youthful idealism.

'I have lots. I take pleasure from listening to music, reading and painting and visiting various exhibitions when I can. I also enjoy discussions on current affairs—but I do have opinions of my own which do not always agree with those of my associates and that often leads to arguments,' she told him, her light laughter bursting from her like sunshine. 'I like walking and sight-seeing in town—and I do so look forward to going to my first opera or a play.'

Jordan's reaction was sharp, his voice holding a trace of irony. 'Whatever happened to such things as needlework and housewifery and etiquette? I was under the impression that the curriculum was heavily weighted in favour of those accomplishments as might make an appealing wife.'

'And so it is, but unfortunately—and much to my tutors' dismay, I am not much good at any of those things,' she confessed without embarrassment.

'I expect you play the pianoforte and sing, too, Miss Wyatt?'

'Unfortunately I do not excel at playing any instrument—no matter how hard I practise,' she answered, undaunted by his tone and with laughter still shimmering in her eyes. 'I don't play the piano half as well as Charlotte—who puts me to shame, and my voice is less than tuneful so I always avoid inflicting it on sensitive ears.'

A faint smile tugged at the corner of Jordan's mouth. 'And will you go on teaching at the academy until you are of an age to retire?'

'Maybe.'

'That is certainly proof of your attachment to the place,' he remarked. 'And marriage? Does that not enter into your scheme of things? Doesn't every young woman want to marry and have children?'

'Marry? Why is it that men seem to think the goal in every woman's life is to marry and have children?'

'So, you plan to remain a teacher all your life?'

Judith flushed. 'Well—no—I mean—I do not know at this time,' she replied with some confusion. 'If it happens then maybe I will consider it.'

Jordan simply smiled crookedly and opened the gate, standing back to let her pass through.

They walked on in thoughtful silence for a few moments. Having studied Captain Grant's profile from beneath lowered lashes, Judith recognised authority when she saw it, and everything about this man bespoke power, control and command. The hard set of his face did not suggest much tolerance or forgiveness, and she felt quite small and vulnerable when she was in his presence.

'What about you, Captain Grant?' she asked coura-
geously, capturing his gaze with her mesmeric eyes. 'I
imagine you must be missing India. Are you enjoying
being a civilian again?'

'My mother is happy to have me back in one piece—
and my brother is relieved to have someone take over
my family's many business affairs. Since Father died he's
had his work cut out keeping the wheels turning and travelling between here and his home in Kent.'

'I was sorry to hear about your father. I met him several times when he came to collect Charlotte from the
academy. I liked him. Poor Charlotte was inconsolable
for a time. But—that is not the question I asked,' she
said quietly.

His face took on a masklike look, deliberately expressionless, like his voice, and his eyes narrowed on her
face. 'True—and please feel free to ask any question you
like. I am tied to India by affection, not by blood, and
for now, Miss Wyatt, I must give my heart and soul to
the task of the moment.'

'I suppose you must find life here very different.'

'I do, but no doubt I'll adjust given time.'

'And can you turn your back on your military life in
India with no regrets?'

'No. That is not possible. No one can have no regrets.
Whatever military duty I carried out, I did so with a clear
mind and never sought to justify myself—even though I
am convinced of the fallibility of all human judgement.
Most of the officers of my acquaintance and subordinates
accepted the ideal of working hard and playing hard. I
believe it was playing hard that kept everyone sane.'

'You sound hard, too, Captain Grant,' Judith stated, in
a tone that was not meant to give offence.

He looked directly ahead, his face set in harsh lines.

'I was in India for nine years, Miss Wyatt, and it would be hard for you with your English upbringing to understand the nature of the people there.'

Judith stiffened and was about to inform him that she knew all too well the nature of those people he spoke of, but he gave her no time.

'India is a country where a man has to rely on his own wit and his own power of command to survive. It is a country accustomed to stern measures and respectful of power—be it Indian or British—and it is careless of human life. The things a soldier does and sees tend to harden him.'

'But not beyond recall.'

'No,' he said, smiling, his gaze warm and gentle as he captured her own once more and looked deep into her eyes. 'I hope not.'

Judith returned his smile, and in that second she saw something in his gaze that spoke of his interest, and she knew that for the first time he was aware of her.

They had reached the house and before either of them could say anything else Alicia hastened to claim him. Her appearance had a sobering effect on Judith. Alicia's cold green eyes met the hazel ones of the young woman by Jordan's side. For the merest instant a current of tension passed between them, and then, with a little smile, Judith turned away, breaking the contact.

Alicia looked extremely elegant in a lime-green shot silk dress, making Judith feel positively shabby beside her. 'You look very nice this evening, Alicia,' she said generously. 'Please excuse me. I will go and change for dinner.' She knew as she said this that she had nothing better than what she was wearing to change in to.

Not waiting for either of them to reply, she slipped into the house, but not before she had seen Alicia bestow on Captain Grant her most dazzling smile. Charlotte was right: it was plain that Emily's younger sister was very taken by him. The fact that he had first sought out Judith on his return to Landsdowne—who was not even a member of the family—was quite clearly indefensible to Alicia.

When she had changed into a lavender muslin dress she looked at her solitary figure in the long mirror, finding no comfort in what she saw. The dress, with its high neckline and long sleeves, was far from flattering. How she wished she'd something pretty to wear and someone to arrange her hair in a grand style like Alicia's.

Feeling oddly alone, and wishing Charlotte was not indisposed, she went to the open window and looked out. The sound of Alicia's tinkling laughter drifting up to her from below and echoing around the walls of her room with merciless mockery made her feel worse. Looking down into the garden, she saw that the auburn-haired beauty was still in conversation with Captain Grant, who was perusing her in the ageless way in which a man looks at a beautiful woman.

Judith watched Alicia laugh and lean towards him, placing her hand in a familiar gesture on his arm, and what she said was soft and muted. Her companion said something in reply and laughed with her, gazing down into her upturned face, and whatever it was he said to her, she lapped it up like a kitten with its face in the cream.

It amazed Judith that Alicia could remain so calm when she was so close to him, when she herself—just an observer—was as much a-tremble as a blade of grass in strong wind. Charlotte was right, Alicia was very taken by him, she could see that. She was not sure of Captain Grant, but there wouldn't be a man alive who didn't find

Alicia attractive, and Captain Grant was certainly speaking to her and looking at her in a way that bespoke interest.

Quickly she pulled back from the window, feeling ill at ease and very much the intruder, yet at the same time a warmth began to course through her body. Suddenly the thought of being as near to him as Alicia was, of having him lean close and speak tender endearments, made her heart knock frantically and a strange excitement pulsate through her veins, and she felt a yearning that was completely alien to her. Catching sight of her reflection in the mirror once more she sighed, wishing she weren't so plain and uninteresting. Compared to Alicia she was as naïve and unsophisticated as a babe in arms.

As Jordan prepared himself for dinner with the aid of his valet, he was quiet and detached—lost in his secret self. He tried to concentrate on the meeting he'd had at India House earlier that day, and the information he'd been given regarding Jehan Khan's reasons for coming to London, but in his relaxed state he was more inclined to dwell on the quirk of fate that had caused Miss Judith Wyatt to be a guest in his home.

As he'd begun to escort her back to the house he'd tried to ignore her, to pretend she wasn't there, and after their few minutes of conversation he had been sorely tempted to do so once more. She had made him reflect on his life in India, on all the things he was missing, and on what his life in the future would lack.

There had been many pleasurable diversions for him in India, but none of them had been of a serious nature. This had been mainly down to him. Because of his military duties, which were often fraught with danger and took him away for many months at a time, he had purposely steered clear of becoming closely involved with any woman.

Until he began his military career he'd been surrounded by family and servants, whose presence and the things they did for him reminded him of his social superiority. He couldn't remember a woman ever talking to him with such unaffected candour as Miss Wyatt had done. He had never met anyone like her—but then, he hadn't been anywhere to meet anyone like her.

Young ladies of Miss Wyatt's station in life had never entered his sphere, and if she had he would have overlooked her because she wasn't spectacularly beautiful like all the other women who floated around in his social world—women of unbridled self-indulgence, whose lives revolved around the latest fashions and expensive jewels, women who had a raging ambition to marry a high-ranking officer or a nabob—women like Alicia Paxton.

It had been brought to his attention by one of the gentlemen at his club in town that Alicia had been more than generous with her favours with one of her father's employees last summer. Alicia was one of those women so basically beautiful that even artificiality heightened her, with all the confidence of a young lady born of a well-to-do family. She had a way of smiling teasingly into his eyes, and from witnessing her body language her interest seemed genuine enough.

Her sole priority was marriage. Unfortunately Jordan found her shallow, somewhat lacking in intelligence, with her head stuffed with nonsense. Nor had she any perception of what love between a man and woman could mean. She might have hopes in his direction, but he had no intention of becoming romantically involved with her.

Her slightly slanting green eyes gave her a feline look, and he'd wager she could produce claws if necessary! But whatever shine she possessed had become somewhat tarnished by the presence of Judith Wyatt.

Chapter Four

Judith was the last to come down to dinner. The butler showed her into the drawing-room where everyone was gathered, all partaking of a glass of wine. It was the first time she had been inside this luxurious room, and the sumptuous decoration, the paintings, the furniture and silk upholstery, the porcelain and the Aubusson carpet, were far removed from her little room at the academy and her Aunt Cynthia's modest house in Brighton.

Unable to stave off looking at Captain Grant, her eyes immediately sought him out. She was surprised to find he was watching her entrance like a large, predatory hawk, his wineglass arrested halfway to his lips.

He had changed his clothes and looked extremely handsome and dignified in a rather splendid ivory silk embroidered waistcoat beneath his black suit, which stretched without a crease over the breadth of his shoulders. His shiny black hair had been brushed in merciless neatness, but an errant lock threatened to dip over his forehead at any moment. There was a restlessness about him which reminded her of a caged animal, and she sensed he would feel more at ease outdoors than confined to the house.

He was standing with Edmund by a huge, heavily carved mahogany sideboard, pouring wine. Alicia, her face aglow and clinging to his side like a limpet, was more haughtily, breathtakingly beautiful in the candles' glow than Judith had realised earlier.

Judith went directly to Lady Grant. She was always struck by the elderly lady's dignity. Like her friendly, charming manner, it was so much a part of her and demanded immediate respect. She was seated on a sofa beside the fire, discussing a variety of topics with Emily, who sat opposite.

Lady Grant was slight in stature, softly spoken and her movements graceful. Her brown hair was sprinkled with grey, her skin smooth, and the appealing beauty of her youth lingered on into middle age. Having met her on those occasions when she had come to the academy to collect Charlotte, Judith thought her a lovely lady, and was saddened that her husband's death seemed to have affected her health. They had been very close. Today she looked pale and drawn and had been lying on the sofa in her room for most of the day, but she had come down to dinner to welcome Alicia and Judith to Landsdowne.

'Judith! I'm so happy you're here,' Lady Grant said, her face wreathed in a smile. Taking her hand, she drew the young woman down beside her. 'When Charlotte wrote and asked if you could come I was delighted. You are so sensible and level-headed and such a great influence on my daughter. I do so hope you enjoy your stay with us.'

'I know I will. I just hope Charlotte is soon better enough to get out of bed. I'm so sorry you're not feeling well, Lady Grant. If there's anything I can do to help, please don't hesitate to ask.'

'Thank you, Judith. That's extremely kind of you.' She

glanced to where Jordan stood. 'Be so kind as to bring Judith a glass of wine, will you, Jordan? I'm sure she could do with one.'

It was quite unnecessary for her to remind her son of his duties, since he was already halfway across the room with a glass in his hand. Alicia, evidently resentful of Jordan's brief desertion, scowled her displeasure, her black brows drawn together like wings.

Lady Grant looked at Judith once more, her eyes filled with concern. 'But how are you feeling, my dear? Jordan told me all about your abduction. I'm so relieved you were unharmed. I was very concerned about you. It was a dreadful business—truly dreadful. Whatever it was those men wanted, we must all be very careful until Jordan's enquiries can throw some light on the matter.'

Handing Judith the glass of wine, Jordan bowed his head with a studied degree of politeness. 'Is your room to your satisfaction, Miss Wyatt?'

'It's charming, thank you. I'm sure I shall be comfortable,' she replied, trying to ignore the warmth tingling up her arm as her fingers accidentally touched his when she took the glass.

'I thought you might like to have the one next to Charlotte,' Lady Grant said. 'It also offers a splendid view of the park and the river.'

'That was very thoughtful of you. When I go down to Brighton my room overlooks the sea. I hear it every morning when I wake.'

'Which you will miss, I'm sure,' Lady Grant sympathised. 'Do you swim, Judith?'

'Yes—when I can.'

'Don't you find the sea cold?'

'At first. But you soon get used to it.'

'What else do you do when you are in Brighton—when you're not swimming?' Jordan asked.

Shifting her gaze from Lady Grant's, she gave him a hesitant smile. 'I love the beach—collecting shells and things. I suppose it's the child in me,' she laughed. 'I also walk a great deal, and Aunt Cynthia has friends calling all the time. I often accompany her on her visits to them.'

'Well, we can't promise you any swimming but there are some lovely walks in Greenwich,' Lady Grant said, 'providing you don't wander off unaccompanied, that is. If it rains—knowing how much you enjoy reading, there are plenty of books in the library. I'm sure you'll find something to your taste.'

'Do you ride, Miss Wyatt?' Jordan asked.

'Not since I was fourteen.'

'Then it's time you were back in the saddle. We have some excellent horses. I'll select one that is suitable.'

Her face brightened, her expressive features glowing with such genuine delight that Jordan was completely captivated. 'Thank you. I would like that,' she replied, although having heard nothing but praise from Charlotte for Captain Grant's horsemanship, she prayed she wouldn't make a fool of herself if she rode in his company.

At that moment the butler entered with great dignity to tell them that dinner was ready.

The Grants lived in a style of elegance Judith was not accustomed to and she felt completely out of her depth, despite Lady Grant's efforts to put her at ease. She hardly noticed what she ate or drank, but the food was delicious. The conversation was interesting and animated, although Alicia, who was seated across from her, tended to raise matters completely alien to her. Judith felt it was intentional, to make her feel excluded. Alicia also had a subtle way of disparaging her through compliments, telling everyone how clever Judith was, that her intellectual powers were no different from those of the opposite sex—a blue-stocking personified, in fact. Judith was irritated by it and tried to laugh it off, but she knew Alicia was placing great stress on what some considered to be unfeminine traits in order to emphasise her own femininity.

'Judith was telling me on the journey down that she is to return to the academy to teach in the autumn,' Alicia said over dessert.

'That is what I intend,' Judith responded calmly.

'Do forgive me,' she smiled, 'but I can't help thinking how very odd that seems.'

At first Judith believed Alicia jested in light repartee, but the malevolent gleam in her eyes destroyed all such thought. She felt her cheeks go hot. 'Odd?' she queried.

'Yes. I find it quite extraordinary. Apart from my governess, I've never met a female teacher before. It's hardly a profession one would embrace from choice,' Alicia remarked with a tight smile.

'It was not forced on me. I enjoy learning for its own sake. It is necessary that I provide for myself,' Judith explained unashamedly, in a controlled voice, determined not to let this rude woman score a hit. 'So it is indeed fortunate that I do enjoy teaching.' Out of the corner of her eye, from where he sat at the end of the table, she could see there was a mixed expression on Captain Grant's face. It was one of disbelief and amusement. She shot him a look and he arched his brows and grinned lazily in the face of it, before settling down to watch and listen in speculative silence.

Alicia saw the exchange and seethed to think that Judith shared some secret with Jordan. 'What is the use of science and commerce and such like to a woman who will spend all her time making her husband happy and raising children?' she went on clumsily.

Judith listened patiently to Alicia's antiquated ideas. Much as she would like to give her the setdown she richly deserved, four years of strict adherence to rules and good manners, and not wishing to give offence to her hosts, could not be disregarded. Clearly Alicia hadn't excelled at her studies, and resented those who did.

'Father doesn't hold with boarding schools for girls,' Alicia went on. 'A governess taught Emily and me everything it is necessary for young women to know at home—is that not so, Emily?'

Emily responded with amused indulgence, but she was determined to have a quiet word with Alicia later, to remind her of her manners. 'So we were, Alicia, but I do envy both Charlotte and Judith the freedom of being taught at a boarding-school with other girls. Miss Powell is respected and very much admired by those both inside and outside her profession. I hear she is to found a charity school for both boys and girls in Chelsea. Edmund has already offered to subscribe to the school—you too, I believe, Jordan.'

Jordan's reply was a barely discerned nod and a sardonic lift to his brow, and Edmund heartily aired his opinion in support of education for women.

Miffed that she didn't have the support of either Edmund or her sister, and beginning to feel her cheeks grow hot with the sting of defeat, Alicia raised her chin haughtily. 'Nevertheless, one cannot escape the fact that the stain of being a ''blue-stocking'' is enough to scare away certain gentlemen, and as a result the accused woman may remain a spinster until the day she dies.'

Judith suppressed a smile, pitying Alicia her ignorance. 'Oh, my,' she said in a moment of sheer mischief. 'Now that is a daunting prospect for any woman. You make securing a husband sound like a holy crusade for all women, Alicia. Still, I have no intention of breaking one of my cardinal rules.'

'What rule is that?' Alicia enquired reluctantly.

'Never to accept a proposal of marriage from a man unless he is of the same intellectual calibre as myself. We must be equal in all things. I refuse to dance attendance like a witless fool on any man who will expect me to submit to his authority, and not to say anything other than yes and no, and insist on my calling him my lord and master, a man who will list me among his possessions, like his dogs and his horses. I consider ideas such as these unacceptable and more than a little insulting.'

'You are rather harsh on the male sex, Miss Wyatt,' Captain Grant remarked coolly.

She turned her head and met his gaze directly. 'It was not my intention to give offence.'

'None taken,' he smiled, 'but you have just damaged my ego beyond recall. How about yours, Edmund? Still intact?'

'After that? Hardly,' Edmund laughed in mock horror.

'I think what you were trying to say,' Jordan went on, returning his sparkling, penetrating gaze to Judith, 'is that you have no intention of being owned by any man.'

'Yes, that's exactly what I meant,' she replied, her eyes holding his. 'Although I must make it quite plain that I believe it is a wife's duty to be an asset to her husband in every way, and that there must be respect and consideration on both sides.'

'It sounds quite mad to me,' Alicia quipped.

'Sane, I think,' Judith countered.

'Oh, I don't doubt your sanity, Judith. It is simply that with ideas such as these, a woman is in danger of becoming eccentric and developing undesirable characteristics.'

Judith arched her brows at Alicia. 'If you mean she is capable of taking care of herself, then I admire her for it. In my opinion men are superior to women in one thing only.'

'And what is that, pray?'

'Brute strength.'

Judith's reply brought laughter from all present, which increased Alicia's irritation further. 'Really? Then I wish you success in your hunting,' she remarked frostily. 'Among the gentlemen of my acquaintance, most of them are opposed to the idea of having an intellectual wife.'

'In which case I shall have to remain a spinster and bear it as best I can,' Judith said, sighing with mock resignation and folding her hands quietly in her lap. 'Although some women might consider it a privilege to enjoy such independence without the shackles of matrimony.' Was she mistaken or did she see a smile of frank admiration gleam in Captain Grant's eye? As if to confirm it he cocked an eyebrow and raised his glass in a subtle salute, before drinking his wine.

After dinner, while Judith exchanged pleasantries with Emily and Lady Grant over coffee, Alicia was noticeably silent as she watched Edmund and Jordan across the room. When she'd finished her coffee Judith rose.

'Please excuse me. I'm very tired and would like to retire,' she said in a quiet voice.

'Of course, my dear,' Lady Grant said. 'I shall be going up myself presently. Is there anything you need?'

'No, thank you. I'll look in on Charlotte before I go to bed. Goodnight.'

With a thoughtful frown Lady Grant watched her go. She had carefully noted the warmth of Jordan's smile and the absorbed way he had watched their young guest as she had valiantly responded to Alicia's barbed questions during the meal, and was both pleased and encouraged by it.

Jordan was in quiet conversation with his brother. He had not so much as glanced in Judith's direction since they'd left the table and she'd assumed he'd forgotten her presence, but when she moved towards the door he lifted his head and looked straight at her. When she was about to climb the stairs she was surprised when he came out of the drawing-room to say goodnight, closing the door behind him. Clasping her hands together, she waited for him to speak to her.

'Congratulations,' he said, striding towards her. 'You did well.' Admiration had swelled in Jordan at how valiantly this young woman had faced up to Alicia's barbs at the dinner table. He was beginning to see that she was a mass of contrasts, most of them vastly appealing.

'Did I?'

'When you imparted your pearls of wisdom earlier I confess to being a little alarmed at the content—but I admired the sense of what you said. There does seem to be a great disparity between the sexes, which I have not given much consideration to before tonight. However, there's nothing that pleases a woman more than victory over another.'

'Oh? Please explain to me what you mean.'

'That when one woman strikes at the heart of another, she usually hits the target.'

Her mouth twitched. 'You mean it's fatal?'

His silver eyes danced as though he had found her altercation with Alicia vastly entertaining. 'Nearly always—but in your case it was an exception. Alicia was too outspoken about your profession. You were too tolerant.'

'One thing I was taught at an early age, Captain Grant, was how to employ tact when it is most needed. As a guest in this house I would not be so rude or so ill-mannered as to argue with her. Besides, it was nothing really. I refuse to let Alicia upset me.' Inexplicably, the laughter was rekindled in her eyes and Jordan saw her bite back a smile. 'I'll do better next time.'

One dark brow arched and his eyes danced with devilish humour. 'How? Would you like to ask her outside onto the lawn, so you have the requisite twenty paces?' he asked, gently teasing.

Judith's lips answered the laughter in his eyes in a smile that revealed shining teeth. 'If I do, will you be my second, Captain Grant?'

Jordan shook his head with mock gravity. 'I'm afraid that would not be appropriate. You are both guests in my home, so it is only right that I remain neutral. Besides, I think you are more than capable of taking care of yourself.'

His expression became serious as he continued to hold her gaze. The depth of this young woman's composure amazed him, as did the delicate softness he saw in the expressionless young face that was looking up at his. He had seen enough of her to realise she had many pleasing attributes, and he was surprised to find that she stirred his baser instincts. 'You should laugh more often,' he murmured. 'It suits you. Tell me. Are you always so outspoken?'

'It's an attitude I seem to be growing into. No doubt

you must have found some of my remarks quite outrageous and think that I'm dreadfully ill-bred.'

'Nothing is further from my thoughts. I thought you were quite magnificent,' he said softly. 'You, my dear Miss Wyatt, are a refreshing alternative to all the other ladies of my acquaintance. Something tells me there's more about you than being a blue-stocking. Did you mind Alicia accusing you of that?'

There was laughter in her voice when she answered. 'I could be called worse, I suppose, but—perhaps you share Alicia's opinion and cannot imagine what could be worse than for a young woman to be accused of blue-stockingism.'

'I hope,' he said softly, 'that I'm not so antiquated in my ideas as to think that. I'm not prejudiced against brains in the opposite sex—indeed, it should be considered a premium amongst both sexes. You are a remarkable lady, Miss Wyatt. All my life I've harboured the delusion that all young ladies yearn to snare a husband— and the wealthier the better. You have just taught me something new. I'm beginning to think there is no substitute for a clear-sighted, intelligent woman.'

Judith warmed to the compliment. 'Then I am pleased my outspokenness has achieved something. I'm not like other young ladies, Captain Grant.'

'I sensed that the moment I met you.'

His remark was by no means insulting, in fact the warmth in his voice indicated quite the opposite. Aware of the searching intensity of his gaze, embarrassed colour stained Judith's smooth cheeks. Perplexed, she lowered her eyes and moved away, convinced that he could see the pink flush which heated her body. Making a conscious effort to keep her voice from shaking, she said with calm dignity, 'Thank you. I must go. Goodnight, Captain Grant.'

'Goodnight—and—Judith?'

She lifted her head. 'Yes?'

'I may call you that?'

'Yes. I would like that.'

'My name is Jordan. I'm not a soldier any more.'

It was the first time in five days that Judith had left the confines of the house and grounds when she attended the morning service at the parish church of St Alfege, which was situated on Greenwich High Road beyond the woods. She was glad that Charlotte was sufficiently recovered to accompany her. Lady Grant preferred to ride in the carriage with Alicia—whose manner towards Judith was more amiable since that first day, which gave her reason to think that Emily must have had a quiet word with her.

Charlotte and Judith declined the use of the carriage, for they both sought the exercise provided by walking. Besides, the sun was shining and the air was fresh. Judith's abduction and the dangers that still threatened were uppermost in all their minds, but with Edmund and Emily accompanying them they felt quite safe. With pressing matters of business to attend to in town, Jordan had left Landsdowne the day following Judith's arrival and was due back some time that day.

When the service was over and they were walking back to the house, Emily and Edmund paused to speak to some people they knew. That was when Judith discovered she had left her prayer-book in the church. Her parents had given it to her on her tenth birthday and it was one of the most precious things she possessed. She couldn't bear to think of losing it. Telling Charlotte she wouldn't be long, she hurried back to retrieve it, finding it on the pew she had occupied.

Leaving the church she hurried to catch up with the others, slightly concerned when she found they had gone on ahead without waiting for her. Entering the woods, she followed the path that snaked between the trees, welcoming the chill that fell on this twilight world after the heat of the sun. As she walked she sensed that she was being watched. She paused and turned to look to her left, seeing a man standing among the cover of the trees staring at her strangely. But what she found stranger still was that the man was Indian. His turbaned figure was dressed in a glistening silk mulberry tunic, his heavily ornamented belt shining with jewels. A feeling of unreality crept over Judith and she shuddered, feeling extremely vulnerable and afraid. It seemed that someone had stepped onto her grave.

Through a veil of confusion and fear, what she now saw was a scene from her past. She glimpsed the dark, shadowy images creeping with stealth out of the locked doors of her mind, and she was sure they were catching up with her. All her deepest, darkest fears lay among the ghosts this Indian resurrected. Since coming to England her nightmares had lain dormant, but now those ghosts were beginning to raise their ugly, dangerous heads once more.

Overcoming her initial shock, she automatically found herself speaking in Hindustani, a language she was fluent in, even though she had not spoken it for four years. 'Who are you? What do you want?'

The man remained silent, but there was puzzlement in his eyes, which narrowed when he heard her speak his own tongue.

Judith forced herself to back away. With her heart

thumping she turned and walked quickly towards the others, who had paused to wait for her, and when she glanced back the man had gone. Gradually her pulse steadied, but she wore an air of acute fear as she recounted what had happened. Deeply concerned, Edmund told them to go to the house. He went back and searched the woods, but there was no sign of the man Judith had seen.

When Jordan arrived home Edmund lost no time in informing him of the incident. Jordan listened, and when his brother had finished speaking, for a split second there was total silence. But then Jordan's face hardened.

'In spite of all my warnings Judith was alone in the woods, you say?'

Edmund nodded. 'Emily and I had paused to speak to an acquaintance and had no idea she had run back to the church to retrieve her prayer-book. We began to walk on and it wasn't until we were halfway through the wood that we realised she wasn't with us. When she appeared her eyes were full of fear. She was clearly quite upset.'

'Where is she now?'

'In her room, I think.'

'Ask her to come to the study, will you, Edmund? I'll speak to her privately.'

Chapter Five

Ever since Judith had arrived back at the house she had puzzled over her encounter with the Indian. Who was he? Undoubtedly he was somehow linked to Jordan and had something to do with her abduction, but what did he want?

When she was summoned to Jordan's study she found him alone. He was sitting at his desk in his shirtsleeves, looking through a pile of correspondence. Uncertainly she moved across the carpet. His dark head was bent over his work and she felt a pang of longing and a need so strong she felt weakened by it. How she wished he might find her as pleasing to look at as she found him.

'You asked to see me,' she said quietly.

He raised his head and looked at her, throwing down his pen. 'Yes,' he answered sharply. Shoving back his chair, he stood up and walked round the desk. Perching his hip on the edge, he crossed his arms over his chest. His face was set hard, the lines around his mouth tight, and his silver eyes bored into hers. When he spoke his voice was like steel.

'Tell me, Judith. Do you make a habit of being disobedient—of doing the opposite to what you are told to do? What did you think you were doing?'

Judith started, her eyes snapping wide open at this surprise attack, her heart contracting at his tone, merciless and cutting. 'Why—I—I cannot think what you mean.'

'No? I thought I told you not to wander off on your own. No sooner do I return home than Edmund is telling me that you did precisely that. You, more than anyone, must be aware of the dangers. It was the height of folly. I advise you to heed my warnings in future.'

The unexpected rebuke stunned Judith into momentary inaction, but she regained her senses quickly and drew herself up with cool hauteur. 'If I wanted advice,' she retorted indignantly, her eyes sparking with ire, 'I would ask for it. I should tell you that I have a streak to my nature that fiercely rebels against being ordered what to do by anyone.'

'I have a formidable temper myself,' he informed her with icy calm, his eyes locking on hers with a deadly glitter.

'So I've been told. If you must know why I was alone, it was because I discovered I had left my prayer-book in the church. It happens to be extremely precious to me and I returned to retrieve it.'

Jordan's black brows snapped together and his eyes narrowed, but his voice was carefully controlled when he spoke. 'It doesn't matter why you disobeyed me—it makes no difference. From this day forward, while the threat of further abduction remains, while you remain in this house you will do as I say,' he continued, immune to the wrathful expression on her face.

Hot colour of indignation exploded on Judith's cheeks and his look warned her not to cross him, but this merciless analysis of her behaviour and the unfairness and harshness of his attack was too much. If he thought for one moment he could dictate where she went and what she should do then he didn't know her. She should have withered beneath his icy blast, but she was too angry to be intimidated by him. Undaunted, she lifted her chin with a small but obstinate toss of her head. It was a gesture of defiance.

'By what right do you appoint yourself my guardian?'

His eyes seized hers in an unrelenting gaze. 'I don't. While your aunt remains abroad Miss Powell has placed you under my mother's care and my own.'

'Then I sincerely hope it is a habit you do not feel obliged to continue.'

'Until such time as your aunt returns or you go back to the academy, you will abide by my rules and accept the hospitality of this house. Is that clear?'

These words were delivered in a cold, lethal voice, and Judith grew pale. She bristled inwardly. Her pride had been pricked, and she was hardly in the mood to forgive Jordan his high-handed manner, but his words were an order and, automatically, she managed to dominate her anger and obey. 'Yes—I understand.'

Jordan had caught the flare of anger his words brought to her face, but he also saw something that resembled pain and hurt in the depths of her lovely eyes. The complexity in them stunned him. Their warm colour was brightly exposed to the sunlight slanting in through the window. She really was quite lovely and he couldn't believe he had once thought her plain. Feeling his anger begin to fade, he relinquished his perch on the desk and walked slowly to the hearth to escape the fresh tender smell of innocent youth that stood before him.

'I apologise if I spoke harshly to you just now, Judith,' he said, still with his back to her, 'and you have every right to be angry. It was insensitive of me. I was alarmed when Edmund told me what occurred earlier. I am concerned for your well-being while you are here. You could so easily have been hurt. Clearly the incident has upset you.'

Perhaps it was the low timbre of his voice or the steadiness of his gaze when he swung round and came to her, but as Judith stared at his grave features she began to relax, finding herself believing him. 'A little,' she confessed. 'But coming upon the man in the wood like that reminded me of something else I would like to forget.'

He raised his brows. 'A secret?'

'No—not really. It—it's something I prefer not to talk about, that's all.'

Jordan was curious to know what it could be, but it was her own private affair so he asked no further questions. Shoving his hands into his pockets, his eyes held by the pale, graceful figure, he moved closer. He contemplated her for a moment and Judith stood, riveted by that sparkling gaze, like a sparrow mesmerised by a bird of prey.

'The man you saw,' Jordan asked at length. 'Tell me what he was like.'

'I am sure Edmund told you he was an Indian. Apart from that I cannot tell you anything else.'

'He didn't speak to you?'

'No.'

'What did he look like? Describe him to me.'

Judith quickly gave Jordan a description of the Indian, omitting nothing, not even the rather splendid huge black pearl she had seen fastened in the centre of his turban. 'Who is this man?' she asked when she had finished. 'You know him, don't you?'

Jordan nodded. 'His name is Jehan Khan.'

'And was he responsible for abducting me?'

'I suspect he might have been involved in some way.'

'The man who spoke to me when I was blindfolded was English. I'm certain of that. Who is Jehan Khan?'

'Apart from being the envoy to an Indian prince called Chandu, by all accounts he is enjoying himself and has become extremely popular. He's cutting quite a dash about town and is frequently seen in society with his entourage of servants and seemingly unlimited funds. What he is doing here in Greenwich, however, is a mystery.'

'Did you know him in India?'

'Yes, we met several times.'

'And Prince Chandu? Were you acquainted with him, also?'

He nodded.

'Why is Jehan Khan in London?'

'To negotiate with the directors of the Company for the return of his master's land, which was annexed by the British when the Prince's cousin—the Rajah of Ranjipur—died leaving no direct male heir.'

'And will he succeed?'

'No. The Company has no intention of doing anything that is against Company policy. Besides, being guilty of crimes against Company property and maladministration of his own domain and his people, Chandu has not adhered himself to the British.'

'So, Ranjipur has become just another bastion of British India,' Judith commented, not without bitterness, for she did not approve of the way the British gained control of disputed territory. But her opinions on this very sensitive and highly controversial issue she diplomatically kept to herself. 'Where is he staying—this Jehan Khan?'

'At the home of Lord Jeremy Minton in Highgate—which, I confess, confuses me. An open dislike and distrust existed between them in India. Khan deeply resented the closeness between Chandu and Minton, which is why I'm surprised they're here together, and that Khan is partaking of Minton's hospitality.'

'What kind of man is Lord Minton?'

'Ambitious. Like others before him, Minton saw India as a place for quick riches. He lived like a king in his district way up country—close to the border with Nepal. It was so remote he had no reason to fear interference from Delhi, so he was able to do very much as he liked—while portraying himself as a gentleman of business carrying out his work for the Company rather than himself.

'He is unscrupulous and avaricious, and has acquired a private fortune while in the Company's service. There is a restriction on receiving gifts and private trading by Company workers, and with a huge question mark over him he has been recalled to London, where he is to be investigated by the select committee. It is highly probable that he will have to face charges of native intrigue and the abuse of his office—which is no bad thing, for there are many more like Minton who need weeding out—pompous men with an inflated sense of their own importance, their brains addled by the sun, liquor and opium.

'The Jeremy Mintons who have grown fat on vice have to be curbed, or everything and everyone connected with it will become so mired in corruption that the rot it will generate will spread and destroy everything admirable about the Company. Whatever the outcome, with his name tainted by dishonesty and dissolution, his career with the East India Company is over.'

Judith was quite bewildered. 'But—what has all this got to do with you?'

'As to that I'm not certain.'

Judith eyed him quizzically. 'You have an idea, don't you?'

His expression became grim and his voice stern. 'You are very persistent, Judith, but that need not concern you.'

'I beg to differ. I have every right to know who abused me that night. I cannot forget it.'

'You have need to remember,' he said, glancing at her sharply, 'and to fear both Jehan Khan and Jeremy Minton. If I discover that either of these men were behind your abduction, then I promise you they shall pay.'

There was a quiet warning in what he said. 'If you're thinking of me, then please don't waste your time. One thing I have learnt is to rely on myself.'

'I know, but I do worry about you,' he said softly, his eyes fixed on her face. 'For all your courage, you are a fragile thing, Judith Wyatt. You put me in mind of a moonflower—a slender, beautiful white flower that grows in India. They are so transparent you can hear them pop when they open.'

She smiled, remembering them, too, but she made no comment. Tilting her head to one side, she looked at him with speculative hazel eyes. 'Do you suppose whoever abducted me intended abducting Charlotte and holding her until you paid them ransom money?' she asked, her agile mind having already reached this conclusion.

A hint of humour stole into his face as he met her gaze. 'There's maybe a bit more to it than that.'

'Is there? Well, I could be right. After all, it's no secret that you are immensely rich,' she reminded him with art-less candour.

'Do you always speak your mind?' Jordan asked, astonished by her unguarded question.

'Always. I think it's best, don't you?'

He nodded. 'At least one knows where one stands—
although your question is difficult to answer just now.
It's possible that you are right and those men were intent
on procuring money from me. Greed is a powerful mo-
tivation for risk. However, I strongly believe it was for
something else.'

'If not for money, then could it be of a different nature
entirely?' Suddenly her eyes opened wide as a fascinating
yet outrageous thought occurred to her. 'Are you involved in some kind of conspiracy. Is that it?'

He raised an eyebrow at this, and when he looked at
her, amusement struggled with amazement on his face.
For a moment he didn't say a word. His eyes gleamed
as he shook his head slightly, but he had a peculiar trick
of hiding all his thoughts behind an inscrutable mask. 'I
can assure you that I am involved in no such thing.' Suddenly his expression relaxed and his eyes brightened as
a smile moved across his lean brown face. 'And now I
think it's time we did something else.'

'What have you in mind?'

'Edmund, Alicia and myself are to take a ride in the
park before dinner. Perhaps you would care to join us.
As you know, Charlotte has a fear of horses and doesn't
like to ride, so she won't be accompanying us.' The way
her face lit up with a radiance like the sun coming out
from behind a cloud Jordan found utterly endearing. Captivated by the depths of the hazel eyes looking into his
and by the freshness of the lips slightly parted to reveal
small, perfect teeth, he felt an unfamiliar ache in his heart
and his mind became momentarily preoccupied with how
adorable she looked, and another, less welcoming but undeniable awareness—desire.

His growing attraction to Judith Wyatt astounded him.
It was insane! His tastes ran towards sophisticated, ex-

perienced women and he had diversions a-plenty—with Alicia hovering persistently by his side and the pick of every beautiful female in London society eager to trade themselves for an alliance with the Grants of Greenwich. The notion that a young woman fresh out of the school-room could arouse him was almost comical.

'Unless you wish to offend me, you won't refuse,' he said gently.

Judith lowered her eyes beneath the heat of his gaze in case they should give her away. Even as the blood raced through her veins and her heart was doing strange, unfamiliar things, there was a voice reminding her firmly of pride, self-discipline—and the foolishness of unrequited love. She could not believe the effect this man always had on her—but Jordan Grant, titled, wealthy, and devastatingly handsome, would never be interested in a penniless, plain young woman, whose only ambition in life was to teach.

'Come, what do you say?' he persisted. 'You're not thinking of an excuse, I hope?'

She smiled shyly. His gaze never wavered from hers, and she wondered if anything escaped those alert grey eyes. 'I wouldn't dare.'

'Good. Now that's settled I'll see you at the stables in fifteen minutes.'

Fifteen minutes later Judith watched a groom leading a white mare into the stable yard, her coat gleaming silver in the afternoon sun, her floating mane and tail brushed to perfection. Edmund was already mounted, and so was Alicia, who looked stunning in a blue velvet riding habit with gold frogging, and a matching hat, cocked at an impudent angle atop her hair.

But Judith only had eyes for the white mare and the

man who came to take the reins from the groom. The horse stretched out its nose and shook its mane vigorously when Judith moved confidently towards her. The animal's soft brown eyes were alive and intelligent, and removing her glove Judith rubbed her velvety nose affectionately.

'She likes you,' Jordan said, pleased that Judith wasn't nervous about approaching the horse.

'The feeling is mutual. She's beautiful. What's her name?'

'Tilly.'

'And does she have any peculiarities that I should know about before I risk life and limb?'

'None that I know of. She's as docile as a lamb.'

'I only hope I haven't forgotten how to ride.'

'Four years is a long time, but don't worry. Once you're in the saddle it will come back.' He grinned when he saw her wrinkle her nose at the side-saddle. 'What is it? Do you have an aversion to the saddle?'

'I've only ever ridden astride. Seated on that, it is more than likely that I shall become unseated at the first hurdle and make a complete fool of myself—providing I don't break my neck. And if I do,' she said, smiling up at him, 'no doubt you'll blame my poor horsemanship and not the saddle.'

He grinned down at her. 'I'd offer to change it but should you be seen you will be ostracised from society for ever.'

She gave him a wry smile, probing the depths of those clear grey eyes. 'Since I cannot claim membership to that ancient and exclusive set, that does not concern me. Society can be vindictive, and I am glad I don't have to worry about social acceptability. Now,' she said, turning her attention to the instrument of torture she was expected to sit upon, 'about this saddle.'

'If you're afraid to ride side-saddle—if it's more than you can handle, simply say so,' Jordan generously suggested, a lazy, challenging, almost taunting smile tugging at his firm lips.

Judith glanced at him and laughed brightly. 'I'm not afraid, so don't you dare try putting me off,'

Jordan felt total admiration for her competitive spirit, and before Judith knew what he was about he'd placed his hands on her waist and lifted her effortlessly into the offending saddle, watching as she hooked one knee around the pommel and placed her small foot in the stirrup, letting his hand linger for a moment on her thigh.

'Does that feel comfortable?' he asked, his forehead suddenly furrowed in concern.

'Yes,' she replied, taking the reins with one hand and stroking the mare's neck with the other. 'We'll soon get used to each other—won't we, Tilly,' she murmured into the horse's ear.

'You don't feel faint?'

'Not a bit,' she smiled, controlling her mount easily when she moved restlessly and danced a couple of steps to one side.

Jordan swung himself up onto his own horse, a huge nut-brown stallion, and together they rode towards Edmund and Alicia. Alicia, coolly poised and elegant, her nose tipped disdainfully high and her green eyes hostile when they settled on Judith, had to struggle to hide her annoyance at the attention Jordan was showering on her. She walked her horse beside Judith's out of the stable yard as the two men went on ahead.

Although Alicia considered Judith far too slender to be described as womanly—presenting no competition to her own roundly proportioned form—she had to concede that dressed in the right clothes and with her hair arranged in a more fashionable style instead of that ridiculous bun at the back of her neck, with her wit and brightness, she could attract a covey of young men to her side. Alicia considered it high time she knew her place at Landsdowne.

'I've just been telling Jordan that I've never ridden side-saddle before,' Judith said in an attempt to relieve the tension between them, her nostrils invaded by a heavy scent of French perfume that wafted across to her from the other woman.

'You mean you have always ridden astride?' Alicia said, favouring her with a cool, level stare.

'Yes—always.'

Alicia's eyebrows raised as she stared across at her, her red lips twisting scornfully. 'Really! Another peculiarity of yours,' she quipped with silken malice. 'How very unladylike.'

Judith adopted a tolerant smile. 'Considering I was a child at the time, Alicia, your accusation is somewhat misplaced.'

They rode on in silence for a few moments until Alicia calmly said, 'I don't know what you have in mind where Jordan is concerned, Judith, but whatever it is, forget it.'

Judith stared at her with a coolness that astounded Alicia. 'Would you mind telling me what you mean, Alicia?'

Alicia returned her stare, her green eyes shining ruthlessly. 'That no matter how much you throw yourself at him, you'll never succeed in getting him to look at you the way he looks at me.'

'Do not suppose that I would encourage him to do so,' Judith laughed, delighting, as she always did, in the ridiculous. 'Dear me, Alicia. What on earth's got into you?'

'Righteous anger, if you must know,' Alicia flared, astonished and infuriated by Judith's calm, cool manner, 'which means that I have just cause. So don't deceive yourself into believing Jordan's interested every time he speaks to you. He's being polite to a guest in his house, and nothing more. Why,' she scoffed, wanting to humiliate and shatter this woman's most sensitive feelings and wipe the simpering smile from her lips, 'he'd laugh you right out of bed.'

'I doubt it, since such a thing is unlikely to happen,' Judith responded, meeting her gaze squarely, refusing to be intimidated by such cutting remarks. But Alicia was right. Any healthy, virile man would desire Alicia, with her voluptuous curves, her beauty and her sensuality. She was also ruthless, and any man she desired she would want to possess body and soul. Judith began to feel sorry for Jordan, and she also felt a small frisson of distaste when she thought of her own plainness. 'You're being quite absurd, Alicia. You let your imaginings run away with you to the point where you are in danger of becoming hysterical.'

'I don't think so. I've seen the way you look at him, how much you want him. But I'll get him in the end. I've been patient. I've waited for two years for him to come home, and now he has I won't see them wasted. I won't stand by and watch a mere schoolgirl jeopardise my plans.'

The anger and bitterness seeping out of Alicia was so palpable that Judith could almost feel it. 'You may be assured that I have no intention of doing any such thing.'

'Then we understand each other. You will stay away from him?' Alicia queried.

'I'm sorry to be a fly in the ointment, Alicia, but that's going to be difficult, since we inhabit the same house,' Judith answered flatly. 'But I'm sure if you want him so much then nothing will stand in your way.' She looked at Alicia and calmly pointed out, 'But the matter between the two of you is not absolutely settled, is it? First, you have to make him want to marry you.'

'And I will,' Alicia continued emphatically. 'I will do everything within my power to bring about a relationship that will be completely advantageous to myself.'

Judith gazed somewhat pityingly at her. 'If that's what makes you happy then I see nothing wrong with it. But don't overestimate your ability to manipulate him, Alicia. I would not equate Jordan Grant with the other gentlemen of society. I have known him just a short time, but I already know he is nothing like them.'

'How can you—a pupil at Miss Powell's academy, a person who is quite destitute—possibly know anything about gentlemen of breeding? Such things are way beyond your sphere,' Alicia said scathingly, her eyes travelling with abhorrence over Judith's plain garb. 'Why, you'll be lucky if a man ever looks at you.'

'How coarse you are, Alicia. If you're through with your insults,' Judith murmured, flinching inwardly at Alicia's words, half convinced that what she said was true, 'I'll ride on.'

Perceiving that her thrust had hit its mark, Alicia watched her go, her eyes shining with triumph.

Having nothing but contempt for Alicia's paltry attack, seeing nothing in it but ignorance and malice, refusing to be hurt by the cruel barbs, Judith shoved them to the back of her mind and rode on to join Jordan and Edmund.

They walked their horses towards the park, where they gave them their head and galloped over the grass. Judith breathed in deep, delighting in the feel of the horse moving beneath her and riding better than she'd imagined. She might not have a fashionable habit to wear and she might not sit her horse as elegantly as Alicia, but she didn't let it spoil her enjoyment or take away the pleasure of being on a horse again. How she wished Charlotte was there to share it with her, but Jordan was right. His sister had an aversion to horses and you couldn't get her near one.

She sneaked a glance across at Jordan admiringly. There was an aggressive virility about him and an uncompromising authority and arrogance that had been imbued into him during his years as a soldier. Alicia was right. Jordan Grant was beyond her sphere of things and she didn't know how to deal with him.

He made her uneasy and made her heart do strange things, but in a moment of dreaming of what might have been had she been born with a silver spoon in her mouth, she allowed herself a moment to dwell on how handsome he looked astride his powerful horse, with his shining dark hair ruffling in the light breeze, and his swarthy features enhanced by the gleaming whiteness of his neckcloth. He was resplendent in an impeccably tailored dark green riding-coat that stretched across his broad shoulders without a crease, and snug-fitting buckskin breeches disappearing into highly polished tan riding-boots.

They rode among the tall elms and chestnuts and up the hill to the Observatory, where a splendid view of the Queen's House and the busy river was to be had. Riding back they slowed their horses to a leisurely walk, Jordan and Edmund pausing now and then to acknowledge others they knew who were either strolling or riding in the park. Alicia, who was doing her utmost to engage Jordan in bubbling conversation, never left his side for a moment.

Happily chatting to Edmund, Judith failed to notice that Jordan was studying her. His sharp eyes told him that despite being out of the saddle for the past four years she could certainly ride, and her handling of Tilly was impressive. She adopted a no-nonsense attitude and dealt firmly with the skittish mare, commanding her movements superbly. His gaze rested with admiration on the confident poise of her head, her straight back and perfectly relaxed shoulders and arms.

His curiosity about her increased. She must have had an excellent teacher. Where had she learned to ride like that? He suddenly realised that apart from what she had told him, he knew absolutely nothing about her. It was a situation he was determined to rectify at the earliest opportunity.

Chapter Six

A gold-embossed invitation was delivered to Landsdowne inviting Lady Grant, her family and house guests to a ball to be given by Lord and Lady Penrose in town. The Penroses were close friends of the Grants, Lord Penrose being a director of the East India Company. The ball was in honour of their youngest daughter's betrothal.

Immediately Lady Grant started discussing the arrangements and Charlotte excitedly began deciding what dress and jewellery she would wear, speculating on the gentlemen who would be present. But she was not insensitive to the feelings of Judith on the matter, who had quietly and firmly proclaimed she would not be going.

'I can't possibly go, Charlotte,' she said when they were alone cutting flowers for the house in the rose garden.

'Of course you can,' Charlotte said, snipping a splendid red bloom and placing it neatly in her basket. 'You have been invited—and if you're worrying because you have nothing appropriate to wear, that's easily remedied. I have plenty of gowns you can choose from—although no matter which one you choose it will have to be altered to fit. You are much more slender than I am. Mother's maid can arrange your hair.'

'I like my hair the way it is,' Judith told her stubbornly.

'We are to travel up to town two days before,' Charlotte went on, ignoring Judith's comment about her hair. 'Edmund has promised to escort us to Vauxhall Gardens, and we are to go shopping with Emily. I dare say you would prefer a more cultural repertoire of exhibitions and museums, but you get enough of that at the academy. You are on holiday and should enjoy yourself.

'Jordan continues to rent the house in Piccadilly our father used whenever business commitments kept him in town. It's large enough to accommodate the whole family when the need arises. The Penroses live in a magnificent house in Mayfair, Judith, and there's not a society girl in London who wouldn't kill for an invitation to their ball. You really can't allow yourself to miss such an opportunity.'

'No, Charlotte.' Judith was adamant. 'I'm just a dowerless girl from Miss Powell's academy. I'm not a society girl.'

'You're going to be—even if it's just for the one night.' Charlotte glanced down the garden and her face broke into a joyous smile when she saw Jordan striding towards them, having just returned from spending three days in town on business. 'Hello, Jordan! Come and help me persuade Judith to go to the Penroses' ball. I've tried my best but she refuses to consider it.'

'I am not going, Charlotte,' Judith said, happiness soaring through her on Jordan's arrival. Suddenly the garden, which had been up till then just another garden, became an enchanted place. The banks of roses became more splendid, the scent of flowers sweeter, the air warmer. It was absurd, she thought, for she seemed to be in danger of falling in love with this handsome captain.

Jordan looked at her for a long moment with those incredible silver eyes of his, one of his sleek black brows elevated, and then he smiled.

'We'll see about that,' he told her.

Judith's abduction and the mysterious threat of further danger hung uneasily over the household. No further light had been thrown on the incident, but Jordan reassured them all that it was still being thoroughly investigated. Apart from everyone being careful not to wander off unaccompanied, everything carried on as normal.

After dinner on the same day that Jordan arrived home, Emily became engaged in a game of piquet with Lady Grant, while Alicia observed with an expression of extreme boredom. With profound annoyance she kept glancing across the room to where Jordan and Edmund were in deep conversation.

Emily always looked faintly anxious when they were all gathered together, as though worried that the obvious antipathy her sister felt for Judith would break into open warfare. Whenever the two of them looked at each other it was with something less than pleasure. There was always a curious sense of constraint between them, and yet they felt obliged, because they were both guests at Landsdowne, to converse in the most formal and stilted manner. Emily was thankful that Judith was a sensible, level-headed young woman who knew better than to provoke Alicia, and was always careful to avoid sitting next to her.

Charlotte was entertaining them on the pianoforte, and Judith sat apart from the others, engrossed in a book.

Unable to stand being ignored any longer, Alicia got up and sauntered over to Jordan and Edmund.

'Why are you neglecting us?' she complained, pouting sulkily. 'It must be a full fifteen minutes since either of you spoke to us—and you just back from town, Jordan. I have not set eyes on you for three days. I object to being excluded from your conversation and cannot imagine what you are discussing that is so interesting.'

'It may be of interest to us, Alicia,' Edmund said lightly, 'but I doubt you would find a discussion on industrial investments and the continuing famine in Ireland of any interest whatsoever.'

She wrinkled her nose with distaste. 'You're right, I wouldn't, and I don't see why you have to discuss such matters now.'

'I apologise, Alicia,' Jordan said, smiling in an attempt to dispel her sullen look. 'It's simply that now I've left the army and taken over my father's affairs, I must familiarise myself with everything and fit myself to the role—which is the reason why I am frequently absent from Landsdowne for several days at a time.'

'Are you missing India and your regiment, Jordan?' Emily enquired politely, pausing in her game of cards to look across at him.

He seemed to contemplate her question before answering, and when he spoke his face had taken on a grave look. 'I shall always regard England as my home, but I became truly fond of India. I do miss it, yes.'

'I cannot for the life of me see why you should, and nor can I understand what the British are doing there,' Alicia said in some indignation, for she had resented the time Jordan had spent in India with his regiment, and her resentment was increasing daily now he was home, for he seemed in no hurry to press his suit as she had hoped. 'India is so far away.'

The mention of India interrupted Judith in her reading and she raised her head. A cold, tight feeling began to form in the pit of her stomach as she desperately tried to think of a way to avert a topic she feared would strike straight at her heart. Her palms were perspiring where they rested on the book in her lap.

'There are trading posts there, Alicia, and trade is necessary and important not only to the prosperity of Britain and India, but also to the entire world. It's called progress,' Jordan explained, patient as a teacher with a slow pupil. 'The British army is there to sustain order and to protect them and the people who are employed to run them from rebels, whose aim it is to disrupt the peaceful order of things—not without a heavy cost in human life, I might add.'

'Nevertheless the natives must feel oppressed beneath the might of the British.'

'They have suffered oppression for centuries at the hands of their own overlords,' Jordan commented dryly. 'It is our aim to bring peace to India.'

'Still—it seems to me that the Indians have exchanged one master for another and their oppression is no less,' Alicia continued with all the clumsy ignorance of a person unfamiliar with their subject, stubbornly refusing to let the matter drop. 'From what I hear and read in the newspapers of the British in India, they consider the natives to be culturally inferior and themselves a superior race.'

'From my own experience,' Jordan went on, 'much of their prejudice is rooted in fear and ignorance, and unfortunately some of the Company servants are not renowned for the sophistication of their manners.'

'I suppose that if the Indians do feel oppressed, they don't have to put up with it.'

'And in your opinion, Alicia, what should they do?' Edmund asked quietly.

'Why, there are millions of them to a handful of Company workers and the army. If they feel they are suffering hardship and injustice under British rule, then why don't they do something about it?'

'That's a very unpatriotic thing to say, Alicia!' Emily rebuked, scowling darkly at her, quietly wishing her sister would cease her mindless chatter and sit down. 'Besides, from what we read in the newspapers they do revolt— all the time, and the massacres and atrocities they carry out on British communities are quite dreadful. Is that not so, Jordan?'

'I regret that is so. But I must point out that there is often savagery on both sides.'

Alicia shrugged. 'I fail to understand why Company workers want to take their wives and children there any- way—to live among uncivilised heathens who worship heathen gods, killing each other and burning widows— where one is likely to be attacked and carried off by a tiger.'

Judith saw Jordan suppress an amused, tolerant smile, while she existed in a state of jarring tension as she sat perfectly still and listened to Alicia air her misinformed views.

'How they can take on a mode of life that strikes me as being the very epitome of stupidity never fails to sur- prise me. I cannot think of anything worse than exposing oneself to the fevers that are prevalent there, of adopting a nomadic existence, sleeping under canvas and travelling about in that intense heat, forgetful of the conventions that dictate our own lives.'

'And I, Alicia, cannot envisage you suffering such discomforts, either,' Emily said sharply. 'But you really should go to India and see for yourself, before you condemn what the British are trying to do there.'

'No, thank you. I have a fair skin,' her sister quipped, touching her cheek to indicate this well-known fact. 'The hot sun would not treat it kindly.'

'Nonetheless, I think you have said quite enough on the subject and it would be nice if you remembered your manners,' Emily rebuked.

In her vulnerable state Alicia's careless remarks had hit Judith like daggers, gouging holes into her emotional barricade. She put down her book and in a trice was on her feet, her eyes blazing at Alicia, unable to conceal her feelings.

'Nobody in their right mind would endorse your ignorant view, Alicia. You have no idea what you are talking about. Like most people outside India you are abysmally misinformed of the nature of the people and the country. However, being unacquainted with the East I suppose you can be excused what you have just said. But has it not occurred to you that husbands and wives should be together wherever that happens to be, that they may have no wish to be separated, often for years at a time? Many people who go to India find it enchanting and actually enjoy the nomadic existence, and rejoice in the absence of a social system that stifles freedom of any kind in the modern world.'

Alicia, somewhat shocked by Judith's outburst, looked at her directly. 'Nevertheless, one cannot help but wonder what would happen in a society where everyone could do very much as they please, where there were no rules to be broken. No doubt everyone would become tired of it and die of boredom. And in India where there is a lack of rules to dictate how people should live, one cannot escape the fact that there are tribesmen who can be described as nothing less than murdering savages.'

'Yes,' Judith replied angrily, feeling her legs begin to tremble. 'I know that, too.'

'Why, Judith,' Alicia mocked, 'anyone would think you speak from experience.'

The eyes of everyone in the room snapped wide open, and they looked at each other with an identical look of consternation.

As he was about to drink his brandy, Jordan's hand paused with the glass halfway to his mouth. Judith had caught all his attention. Her face was a mirror of anguish, and he watched it lose what little colour it had.

Judith swallowed, the faces around becoming blurred, but she was wretchedly aware that she had become the focal point of five pairs of eyes. Quietly and with a trembling voice she answered Alicia's question. 'I do. Please—excuse me.'

Her words scored through Jordan's brain as he stared at the closed door through which she had hurriedly disappeared. She had been close to tears, he had seen that.

'Good gracious!' Alicia exclaimed, seemingly amused by Judith's angry reaction to what she had said. 'Who on earth would have thought it?'

An uneasy silence had fallen on the room and Lady Grant was looking decidedly uncomfortable. Charlotte rose from the piano stool and strode towards Alicia, incensed.

'Alicia! How could you! That was the most insensitive, cruel thing you could have said to Judith. You have no idea what you've said, have you?'

Jordan slowly put down his glass, all his attention riveted on his sister. His jaw tightened and he stood up. 'Charlotte! What are you talking about?'

Charlotte's head swivelled round to her brother. 'Judith was born in India. She lived there until she was almost fourteen years old—until her parents were murdered and she had no alternative but to come to England.'

Jordan stared at Charlotte, her revelations pounding in his brain like hammer blows. 'What? In God's name, why didn't she say anything?'

'Because she saw her parents killed and everyone else at the cantonment in India where she lived—yes, Alicia,' she flared, directing her gaze at that haughty young woman once more, 'women and little children, too. She was the only one to survive the massacre. She suffered terribly and still has nightmares about it—and she never talks about it to anyone—never. It's much too painful for her to remember.'

Frowning with disbelief at what he was hearing, Jordan looked at his mother. 'Did you know?'

Lady Grant shook her head slowly. 'Only that Judith was born in India and that she came to England when her parents died.'

'Then why the hell didn't anyone think to tell me?'

Charlotte moved towards the door. 'I'll go to her.'

'No,' Jordan said in a voice that brooked no argument. 'I'll go.'

Alicia quickly stepped in front of him. 'Jordan, you can't. Listen to me…'

When he looked at her, his brows lowering and his features as hard as granite, she shrank from the blast of his freezing gaze. 'My compliments, Alicia. This time your tongue has achieved its aim. Now get out of my way.'

The tone of his icy command almost sent her scuttling

for cover. Automatically she stood aside and watched him stride out of the room, her face devoid of emotion, but hate was beating a bitter note in her heart. She recalled the ride they had taken in the park several days earlier and the way Jordan had pandered to Judith, concerning himself with her comfort and well-being, and how his gaze had strayed to her repeatedly during the ride.

Inwardly she seethed. The hatred and scorn she felt for that dark-haired witch was all over her contemptuous face. Judith Wyatt had inveigled her way into the household and everyone's affections in a way Alicia could not forgive. She lowered her eyes to hide the feral gleam in their depths, her thoughts upon revenge.

Jordan knocked on Judith's door. When she didn't answer he entered anyway. The room was in semi-darkness. Judith was standing in front of the window, gazing out at the night, and with her back towards him she was just a dark, slim figure silhouetted against the light. He walked towards her and still she didn't turn, but he knew she was aware of his presence.

'Judith. Why didn't you tell me about India and your parents?' he asked quietly.

'Because it would have led to questions,' she answered, her voice barely above a whisper. 'I didn't want to talk about it.'

'Have you ever? To anyone?'

'No—not really. To speak of what happened would be like reliving the experience—when all I want to do is forget.'

'And have you?'

She shook her head. 'No.'

'Then it might help if you were to talk about it.'

She turned and gazed up at him. His face was all angles and planes and shadows, and a heavy lock of dark hair fell over his forehead. In the subdued light he looked mysterious. His expression was firm, his eyes glittering and faintly troubled. 'To you?'

'Why not?' he murmured, looking down into her huge, clear hazel eyes, which were always steady and direct, giving her a waiflike innocence. 'Because I know India, because I know its customs that seem strange to people not acquainted with that country, because I've seen what happens to people when cantonments fall into rebel hands, I'm willing to listen.'

'It isn't your problem.'

'Then I'll make it my problem.'

She looked deep into his eyes. He really did seem disposed to listen.

'Share it with me, Judith,' he persisted gently. 'Hasn't anyone ever told you that a trouble shared is a trouble halved, that two can bear a cross more easily than one?'

She smiled. A softness entered her eyes and a haziness that suggested tears. 'Yes. My mother—once.'

Jordan was relieved to see her smile and her shoulders relax a little. It was a start. 'What was she like, your mother?'

'Gentle, warm, loving. She adored my father and me, and they both loved India passionately.'

'Was your father connected to the army?'

'No. He was an Assistant Collector and a linguist. Having been educated at Cambridge he was extremely clever—if a little eccentric. He wasn't ambitious or any of the things that drove others who went out to India with the East India Company—which was probably why I was forced to accept my aunt's charity when I came to live in England. My father's love of India was such that he would have given it anything—love, loyalty—and he ended up giving his life and my mother's. But he was where he wanted to be, and he wanted to be left alone to live and work in peace.'

'Where was he stationed?'

'For a time he was in Madras—which was where I was born and spent most of my childhood, but then the Company posted him to Calcutta. We'd been there five years when he was moved again, and we went to live between Bombay and the Maratha states in central India. Have you been there?'

Jordan nodded. 'Having passed through the Carnatic I am familiar with the area. But much of my soldiering was done among the hills of the North West Frontier, and the Nepal border.'

Her eyes lit with interest. 'Did you see the Himalayas?'

Jordan nodded. 'A great deal of my time was spent among the foothills on horseback with my regiment. We slept under the stars, with nothing to hear but the night birds and the hum of the cicadas, and the purring of panthers in the trees—all sounds that became as familiar to me as the traffic and the cries of the cities. I remember how invigorating it was to feel the first flush of dawn, and to feast my eyes on the glens where there were seas of columbines and forget-me-nots. I don't deny that one had to be tough to survive as a soldier in those northern territories, but it had its compensations.'

'I would like to have gone there. The Hindus are very superstitious about the hills. They believe the Gods live there. Did you know that?'

'Yes. And who is to say that they don't?'

'No one, I suppose. Mother wanted to stay in Calcutta, but father was happy to go anywhere the Company sent him if it meant seeing more of India. We lived at one of the military stations, which scattered the Company raj and its boundaries. It was quite small compared to some. Unfortunately there was lawlessness and constant disturbances from the feared Pindaris, who roamed at will.'

Jordan knew all about the Pindaris. They were mercenaries of the old Maratha armies who had split up into small groups and penetrated Company territory back in '16, even going so far as to threaten Bombay. Plundering and massacring was their livelihood. To deal with this menace Lord Hastings—the Governor-General of Bengal—had assembled the largest British force seen in India, and it had turned out to be the most difficult campaign they had ever conducted in that country, lasting two years. The incessant marching and broiling heat had made it a wearisome business, but the Pindaris were eventually destroyed.

Judith had paused in her telling, and although Jordan appeared calm, he waited in a state of tension for her to go on. She wasn't looking at him, she was looking out of the window into the dark, back over four years to the time when she had been afraid, as if the images of the past were marching with each shifting shadow. With an effort he restrained the urge to move closer, to take her in his arms and soothe her as he would a frightened child.

'What happened then?' he asked gently, loathing himself for adding to her torment by forcing it from her.

Judith looked at him long and hard before turning away. She wrapped an arm around her waist as if to contain the horrors, pressing her free hand to her forehead in an attempt to relieve her over-burdened mind. Jordan's scrutiny unnerved her, and no matter how she tried to push the memories from her, they returned, lapping inside her head like an ascending sea. Still she hesitated, but in the end she turned to face him once more, and a flicker of sanity lit the chaos of her thoughts.

'You are right. Maybe I will feel better if I tell you.' She held his eyes a moment, and then her gaze slid away. 'Almost every day we heard of fresh outbreaks of lawlessness, but they were always far away and, being protected by the military, we never thought we would be involved. But one day most of the soldiers marched out to settle a dispute on the border, and the next day we awoke to find all the servants had run away. Something was about to happen. We could feel it.' She paused and looked up at Jordan. 'One can smell it in the very air in India—you must know that.'

Jordan nodded. Watching her, he clenched his hands into fists, having to struggle to stop himself from dragging her into his arms. Her voice tore through him, but he couldn't make it easier for her. He had to let her go on.

She bit her lip, her face strained, her body tense. Wringing her hands in front of her, she turned away and hugged herself again. He saw a shudder pass through her. As she shook her head tears formed in her eyes and spilled over her lashes, running unheeded down her cheeks, and he could only guess at her wretchedness.

'It was towards midday—when the sun was at its hottest—when the Pindaris came, armed with talwars and guns. I had gone to the river that ran outside the station to walk in the cool water—although I remember the river being as calm as a lily pond that day and like a warm bath. I was thirteen years old and had disobeyed my parents by wandering off—which I realised afterwards saved my life.

'When I was about to return to our bungalow all the birds on the river rose in a cloud. That was when I heard gunfire and people screaming. I was too frightened to run so I hid in a thicket of thorn and elephant grass beside the river and waited, lying down with my hands over my ears to shut out the sounds. I stayed there all night—but I can't remember when the screaming stopped.'

She wiped her face with her hands, her eyes registering horror as she realised that the door in her mind, kept closed and locked at such great cost for so long, was wide open, and she was about to let all the horrors spill forth. Very slowly she took hold of her emotions, controlling herself with will.

'Eventually I felt brave enough to leave my hiding place. When I entered the cantonment, what struck me most was how quiet everything was. I could not believe what the Pindaris had done. Everyone—forty families and the remaining soldiers—had been killed—although I think butchered would be a more appropriate word to describe what I saw. Bodies had been left where they had been struck down, others thrown into the well or burned in their bungalows. I—I found my parents on our verandah. My mother's head had been shattered by a talwar— and—and my father…' She swallowed, shaking her head, the memory too shocking to tell.

Her toneless monologue was a story of pain and a tremendous sorrow so great that if she told it with emphasis she would surely break. Jordan listened, feeling a pity begin to melt his heart as she went on with her tale of horror.

'An orgy of burning and looting had taken place and there was dried blood everywhere. It was quite extraordinary really because at the time I felt nothing. I was numb inside. It was as if I stood outside myself. I remember looking at the shattered flagpole and wondering what the Pindaris had done with the British flag. But what

I remember most when I look back is the smell, the flies and the carrion.

'The smell was not the familiar smell of charcoal and burning cow-dung, but of scorched wood and earth and baking flesh. The scene, with its bloated bodies of people and animals, was like a vultures' table, and they were already devouring the spoils. It was horrible. I'll never forget it.'

'And then?' Jordan gently prompted when she fell silent.

'I went back to the river. Not knowing where the Pindaris were, I was too frightened to move on. Besides, the nearest station was nearly twenty miles away and I knew I would never make it on foot—all the donkeys had been slaughtered, you see. We had some bullocks and two elephants at the station, but the Pindaris had taken them. So I waited until the soldiers returned.'

'How long was that?'

'Three days. After that—when my parents had been buried—along with all the other bodies, I was taken to Bombay and sent to England.'

'And the rest I know.'

She nodded. 'Yes. I left India when the monsoon had begun and the whole country was under a deluge of rain, but I will never forget how beautiful it was—and how sweet its fragrance. I have since discovered it is a fragrance unique to India—of spices and garlic, musk and sandalwood, heat and dust.' Her eyes had gone a softer colour, remote with memory. 'My parents loved it so much—me too, and despite what happened and the bitter memories, I shall always feel like a person divided. I am tied to India by affection and will for ever consider it to be my home. It runs through my life like the blood in my veins.'

Jordan placed his hands on her upper arms and scrutinised every detail on her pale face upturned to his. 'Thank you for telling me, Judith. Unburdening yourself to someone who can fully understand the complexities of your situation was necessary. Perhaps it will bring you peace and help rid your mind of its ghosts.'

'I hope you're right. I often wake in the night dreaming about what happened, but when morning comes and the dark hours have receded, all the demons are back in their box.'

'When a person has experienced the worst that can happen to them, they can never be so afraid again. I believe that, and so must you.'

Judith tilted her head to one side, her look curious. 'Did something awful happen to you, too?'

'Yes. So I do understand what you've been through.'

She smiled softly, a playful glint in her eye and an adorable little dimple appearing in her cheek. 'Would you like to tell me about it, Captain?'

Her puckish humour brought a warm gleam to his eyes and he returned her smile, confounded by the spirit of this young woman. 'It's a long story. I think we'll save that for another day.'

His voice was so soft it made Judith's blood run warm. The pull of his gaze was too strong for her to resist and her whole being melted with its impact. It was as though his clear silver eyes, shining with the brilliance of diamonds, were looking into the very depths of her heart and soul. She felt the touch of his empathy like healing fingers soothing her pain like balm. She had seen in his eyes the reflection of her torment and she knew he understood. She had told her story without knowing how he would react, and in opening up to him he now shared

the secret of her past with her. She had included him in
something very personal, and that was what counted.

'Thank you for listening. After four years of silence,
being able to speak of what happened has given me reassurance—and the best thing of all is the knowledge that
I have told it to someone with whom I can talk freely of
India, to someone who has been as closely linked to it
as I. You were right when you said it might help to talk
about it. It has brought me an enormous feeling of relief.
But what must you think of me?' she laughed a little
nervously. 'I must be so different from most of the
women you are acquainted with.'

'You are indeed—which is one of the reasons why I
find you so attractive.' Reaching out he gently touched
the fine line of her jaw, and he smiled at her with something half-rueful in his expression. 'You know, when I
told you that you remind me of the moonflowers that
grow in India, I meant it—particularly when I look into
your eyes. Their petals are so white and pure, free from
moral taint or defilement, and so translucent that the light
shines right through. You will have seen them.'

She flushed, flattered and deeply touched that he
should liken her to such a beautiful thing. 'Yes. They
fascinated me. I used to watch them. The popping noise
they made when they opened was always magic to hear.
I pressed some in a book, and now they resemble crumpled silk handkerchiefs. But they're still lovely and remind me of home.'

At that moment they were interrupted by a knock on
the door. Without being told to do so, Charlotte came in
full of concern. She paused and looked at them both with
some consternation—the fact that Jordan still had his
hand on Judith's cheek not escaping her notice.

'Oh! I'm sorry to interrupt, but I had to come and see

if you were all right, Judith. You seemed so distraught when you ran from the room. I know how much Alicia must have upset you.'

'I'm fine now, Charlotte, really,' Judith said, smiling in an attempt to rid Charlotte of her concern. 'Jordan has been very kind and understanding and I feel much better.'

Looking up at her brother, Charlotte saw in his expression admiration and something else when he looked at Judith, something that was more than polite regard and brought a slow smile of understanding to her lips.

'If you'll excuse me, ladies, I will bid you goodnight,' he said, crossing to the door. 'Unfortunately I have some pressing meetings in town tomorrow so I have to make an early start.' Before going out he turned and looked back at Judith. 'You'll be all right?'

'Yes—thank you.'

When they were alone Charlotte gave Judith a sideways smile. 'So, my brother has been both kind and understanding, has he?'

Judith found herself blushing. 'Yes. He was very nice.'

'And what where the two of you talking about when I interrupted?'

'Nothing in particular.'

'And?'

'And nothing, Charlotte,' Judith said with a nervous laugh.

'Come now, even you don't walk around in blinkers. Half the female population in London has imagined themselves in love with Jordan at one time or another.'

'Have they indeed? Then I applaud their judgement.'

Charlotte's eyes widened. 'You do?'

'But of course. It would be ungenerous of me to do anything else after his kindness to me just now.'

'So you *have* noticed after all that my dear brother is probably the most handsome, virile man around?'

'I am human and I have noticed. He's also a gentleman and I am a nobody and therefore quite beyond the pale. His friendship is welcome, but anything else would be out of the question.'

'We'll see,' Charlotte said, flouncing to the door where she paused and turned round, mischief written all over her pretty face. 'But I must warn you that if the two of you carry on like this then you are in danger of making Alicia insanely jealous.'

Rolling her eyes in helpless dismay, Judith went and shoved her out of the room.

Chapter Seven

When she was alone she sat on the cushioned window seat, and with her knees drawn up to her chin she gazed up at the full moon and the myriad of stars that hung in the clear sky. The distant horizon to the west was awash with a deep pink flush, heralding another fine day.

She sighed, resting her cheek against the cool glass, thinking about what had just transpired and the man who had sought her out to comfort her. Her rampaging emotions and imaginings where Jordan was concerned were of a personal nature and were beginning to disturb her greatly.

Ever since their first meeting she had tried to ignore them, but they invaded her mind constantly, beckoning like mischievous imps playing a teasing game, flitting to and fro when she was least expecting it. Over the past few days he had established himself firmly in her thoughts, and she was becoming painfully aware of him as a man, of his blatant sensuality, and of the excitement that coursed through her with his every glance and each spoken word.

She didn't regret telling him about what had happened to her in India. It was something she had never shared

with anyone else—not even Charlotte knew the details—
and it formed a bond between them. But she could not
quell the warmth that suffused her body whenever she
thought of him and she trembled slightly, feeling the
blood pumping strong through her veins when she remembered the unique power of his silver eyes whenever
they settled on her, as if reading her innermost thoughts
and marking her down as his victim.

With no knowledge of men of the world like Jordan
Grant, she was afraid and yet strangely excited by the
melting she felt within her when dwelling too long on
his image, and she knew she would very soon be out of
her depth if she did not take care.

Journeying to town the following morning, as Jordan
lounged against the padded upholstery of the carriage,
for the first time since returning to England his concentration wandered away from matters of business. Ever
since he had left Judith's room the previous night she
had filled all his thoughts.

He thought long and hard about what she had told him,
and he was caught somewhere between torment and tenderness. He remembered her agonised face when she had
told him what the Pindaris had done—they were the kind
of images that were familiar to him also, images that had
once turned his own life into a living hell. But he was a
man and he had chosen the life of a soldier. He had also
known that the Asian continent was careless of human
life, so he had expected to witness such barbarities,
whereas Judith had been a thirteen-year-old girl who
should have been spared such trauma.

Ravaged and raw and alienated from the country she
had come to look on as her own, she had come to
England. How confused, alone and threatened she must

have felt; but she was resilient and had survived better than most young girls would have done.

Whenever he was with her he was physically stirred by her closeness. In fact his growing attraction to her was disquieting. When he had sought her out in her room and seen the soft look in her eyes, shining with recent tears, he had thought how vulnerable she looked, with a sweet, wild essence that would always belong to her, reminiscent of the fragile Indian moonflowers.

He felt a consuming, unquenchable need to know her better, but for the present he had an important meeting with the directors at India House and he immediately immersed his thoughts in that. But then a face with a pert, round chin, a lovely expressive mouth, and thickly fringed hazel eyes crept unbidden into his mind, teasing him, beckoning him. A slow smile curved his lips, and when the carriage was about to turn into Leadenhall Street, with a gleam in his eyes he immediately instructed the driver to head for Bond Street instead.

When a large box elaborately tied with a broad silk ribbon arrived at Landsdowne during the afternoon, Judith was absolutely amazed when Lady Grant laughingly handed it to her, and she was stunned when, having taken it to her room accompanied by Charlotte, she opened it and discovered among the tissue paper an exquisite white silk, star-spangled dress and matching slippers.

There was also a shawl, which had rapidly become a fashionable and practical accessory to any outfit, and it was not made of serge or cotton or wool—which would have been the case had it been manufactured in England. The shawl that Judith feasted her eyes on was one of the best—a luxurious cashmere, which had been imported from India.

'Oh, Charlotte!' she gasped, gently fingering the material of the dress and guessing at once who had sent it. 'It's exquisite. But—there must be some mistake. It can't possibly be for me.'

'Yes, it is. Here, see for yourself,' Charlotte enthused, handing her a card that had been attached to the box. 'Now you have no excuse for not going to the Penroses' ball.'

Glancing down at the card in her hand Judith's flesh warmed. It simply read—Yes, you shall go to the ball. J. 'It's from Jordan. But—I can't possibly accept such a gift.'

'Why ever not?'

'It's much too grand—and far too expensive. I'll be afraid to wear it for fear of spoiling it.'

'That's a ridiculous objection.'

'Not only that, there is Alicia to consider. She will be hurt when she finds out.'

'Livid, you mean. Alicia will turn green when she finds out—and I hope I'm there to see it. You may be sure you'll outshine even her in this dress,' she said, lifting it out of the box and gasping when the tiny spangles caught the light and gleamed, sending tiny dancing shapes around the walls. 'But it's an unusual dress. I can't remember seeing one quite like it. It's most unlike Jordan to choose anything so—so extraordinary.'

Judith didn't think so and smiled secretly to herself. She knew that as soon as Jordan saw it he would have been reminded of the moonflowers, the beautiful white Indian blooms he had told her she reminded him of. On seeing the dress he would have known instantly that she would like it.

* * *

Charlotte, who had looked forward to the ball like a child anticipating Christmas, could hardly be contained on the journey to town two days later. Jordan hadn't returned to Landsdowne so Judith had as yet been unable to thank him for the dress. She accompanied Lady Grant and Charlotte in the carriage. Emily and Edmund had travelled on ahead with Alicia, whose reaction, when Charlotte had lost no time in telling her of Jordan's gift to Judith, had been to smile thinly and say 'How nice.' But her eyes when they had rested on her rival had been quelling.

The house Jordan rented when in town was in Piccadilly. It was huge and very grand and stood back at the end of a short, tree-shaded drive. Jordan was absent when they arrived. When they had eaten, Charlotte took Judith's hand and dragged her up the stairs to show her the rest of the house.

Between meetings at India House and the daily demands of his other business commitments, Jordan's life was full. When Charlotte learned he was to visit the East India docks at Blackwall immediately after breakfast on the morning following their arrival in town—on a day when the East India fleet was outward-bound, because it was one of the greatest sights to be seen passing down the River Thames, she begged him to allow herself and Judith to accompany him.

Jordan, who had just strode into the breakfast room, his sister and Judith being the only occupants, refused outright. 'No, Charlotte,' he said, helping himself to some coffee on the sideboard. 'It's out of the question. The very idea is preposterous. The dockyard is no place for you—what with the noise, smell and the workmen—whose language is unguarded and not fit for the ears of gently reared young ladies.'

'Oh, please, Jordan,' she begged, her eyes enormous with longing. 'We promise not to be a nuisance. We shall remain in the carriage at all times. No one will even know we're there.'

'Have you forgotten that Edmund is to take you to visit the gardens at Vauxhall today?' he reminded her brusquely.

'No, but we can go another day. Besides, Alicia has a headache and is to remain in bed, so we could save that until another day. I know Judith would like to see the fleet prepare to sail, wouldn't you, Judith?' she said, looking to her friend for support.

Jordan's gaze shifted to Judith, where she sat folding her napkin. Her face was animated and brilliant with hope, her eyes fixed on his with ardent expectancy as she waited with bated breath. Of course she would like to witness the great ships setting sail for the east, he thought. It was only natural. They were a link to her past. But he was reluctant to take either of them to the docks this morning, which would be teeming with all kinds of humanity. He shook his head, a denial working its way to his lips, but as he continued to look at Judith he could feel himself wavering, and in no time at all his resolve slipped away.

'Would you like to go, Judith?'

'Oh, yes please. I'd love to.'

'Then you shall,' he conceded. 'Edmund will accompany us. Run along and get ready, the two of you. But I want your word that you will remain in the carriage at all times.'

'You have it,' Charlotte cried gleefully, disappearing upstairs in a swirl of taffeta and lace with Judith in tow to prepare for the outing.

* * *

It was a spectacular sight that met them at Blackwall. The dockyard had been built to Company specification in '06, with a masthouse enabling an Indiaman to be fully rigged in a matter of days rather than weeks. The number of heavily armed Company-owned vessels at anchor in the deep water, the workshops and warehouses—all within half a mile of India House—storing all kinds of exotic commodities from the East that stirred the imagination, and all employing thousands of people, gave an individual a very respectful idea of the Company's worth.

Hundreds of people had turned out to see the fleet set sail. The bustling wharves were a seething mass of noisy humanity—sailors, workmen and onlookers. Some were rough and unkempt, and ladies held onto their skirts to avoid contact. Company shareholders stood in groups, their faces wearing identical expressions of pride as they conversed with each other. Crew and passengers were swarming all over the scrubbed decks as the heavily laden vessels shifted restlessly with the rising tide, the charcoal grey water lapping at the great hulls, lying low in the water.

The ships carried additional surgeons, sailmakers, smiths, tailors, barbers, caulkers and joiners, making sure they were run efficiently and maintained like a small town. The holds were packed with all manner of goods—food and drink, tar and oil, powder and ammunition for the guns in case of attack from pirates, and a hundred other things—not counting the precious cargo.

Sandwiched between Emily and Charlotte in the carriage on the edge of the crowd, Judith feasted her eyes on the vessels, watching the tall masts and webs of rigging swaying with the motion of the water. Remembering her own journey from India on one of these vessels, she breathed in the familiar, comforting smells of hemp and pitch, which welcomed her like old friends. Those great ships represented home, and the elusive faces of her mother and father passed wraithlike through her memory. The memories of her last days in India were all too fresh, and the breeze blowing off the river suddenly seemed very cold.

Jordan glanced across at her. He could see the dark memories crossing her face as she looked at the scene, and that her hands were clenched tightly in her lap, as if by dint of will she could hang on to the remembrances associated with India.

'Are you all right?' he questioned anxiously.

Slowly she brought her gaze round to his. She looked at him intently as he silently reached out to the part of her she had laid bare to him not so long ago, when he had touched and lightened a dark corner of her mind. She smiled, feeling a faint, unexpected drift of happiness. 'Yes, I'm fine. Truly. My mind was assailed by memories, that is all.'

He nodded, understanding. 'Then if you ladies will excuse Edmund and me, we will leave you for a few minutes.'

When the two brothers had climbed down to mingle with other Company shareholders, Charlotte moved across to make more room, her eyes sparkling with excitement out of a rosy, flushed face.

'I wish we could get out and mingle with the crowd. It would be so exciting to get a closer look. I think the whole of London must have turned out to watch the fleet get under way.'

Judith's eyes followed Jordan and Edmund as they made their way to a group of gentlemen who were gathered on the quayside, influential, too, by the richness of their dress and the attitude of those around them. After a few moments she watched a man approach and speak to Jordan. He lowered his head to listen to the man, who was pointing towards a warehouse some distance away. After excusing himself to Edmund and his acquaintances, Jordan accompanied the man in the direction of the warehouse.

Judith could see nothing unusual in this and was about to look away, but a man, following closely in their wake and who looked like a beggar, caught her eye. He was wearing a heavy coat, too heavy for the hot day. The sleeves were far too long and concealed his hands, and the wide-brimmed hat hid his face. The crowd was thick, the man inconspicuous to Jordan. His gait had a measured, almost sinister steadiness that set alarm bells ringing in Judith's head. Her gaze slid to his hand by his side, and she froze, for she caught a glimpse of steel— evidence of malign intent. A cold hand gripped her heart and she gasped, sensing that Jordan was in grave danger. She must warn him.

'Emily—go and fetch Edmund and tell him to go to the warehouses over there,' she said breathlessly, pointing towards them. 'Jordan is in danger—I'm certain of it. Please hurry.'

Both Charlotte's and Emily's eyes snapped wide open with astonishment, and they watched in some consternation as, in a flash, Judith was out of the carriage and pushing her way through the throng, her heart beating so hard she thought it would burst. Without attempting to call her back, sensing the urgency of the situation, immediately Emily went in search of her husband.

Entering the dim interior of the warehouse, the man accompanying Jordan melted into the shadows. Jordan couldn't have said what it was that alerted him to danger—it might have been the sound of a footfall or a passing shadow, but there was a sense of evil on the air, and he felt a prickle of warning on the hairs at the back of his neck. Hard and motionless as a rock, every muscle in his body became tense, but pulsing with raging energy, ready to explode into action. Quickly and concisely, his mind worked in an icy calm, severed from the emotions that could cloud his judgement. These were the responses that had carried him through a thousand similar situations that had kept him alive so far. He always travelled fully armed, and slipping a small pistol from his pocket, he whipped his head round just in time to see a man closing in on him, his hand half raised to expose a sliver of metal.

The beggar's hand reached towards him. Down the knife came and like a cat Jordan leapt aside. The blade cut harmlessly through the air, finding no soft flesh to flay, only the fabric of his jacket sleeve. Reluctant to fire his weapon, Jordan crossed the intervening distance and there were frenzied movements between the two of them, as they became locked in a devilish embrace. Jordan managed to grab at his assailant's hand and wrest the knife away from him, sending it clattering to the floor.

Clutching a coil of rope, the man who had brought him to the warehouse leapt out from the shadows between the packing cases, at the same moment that Judith entered. When he saw her pressed against the door, momentarily rendered speechless by amazement, he panicked and dropped the rope. Regaining his senses quickly, he drew a knife and advanced towards the still struggling pair.

Judith's eyes opened wide to see the man lunge forward with his arm raised ready to strike. His eyes glittered hard in the dim light, and his teeth showed in a ragged snarl. Her gaze became riveted on Jordan, who had his back to this new danger. Anguish and desperation can be a powerful opiate against fear. It wasn't a conscious decision that propelled Judith forward, but suddenly she was running towards him wildly. A cry broke from her lips, a high, deadly shrill.

'Jordan! Watch your back.'

Heeding her cry, Jordan spun round just as this new threat was upon him, and he was unable to prevent the man from sinking his knife into his accomplice's back, before running out of the door and becoming lost in the crowd.

Feeling the man go limp, Jordan stepped back and looked at him, his chest heaving breathlessly. His assailant gagged and suddenly clawed at his back, from which the hilt of a knife protruded. He fell to his knees before slumping forward onto his face, his body jerking violently with convulsions before becoming still.

Immediately Jordan glanced round at Judith. She was frozen, staring at the corpse, her eyes wide with horror, her arms wrapped round herself. He strode swiftly towards her.

'You saved my life,' he said quietly. 'Thank you for that.' His tone held a moderate note—of gratitude, pride, and perhaps awe, that made Judith lift her face to him. Jordan drew a deep breath. With her face as white as death, her eyes wide and staring, something in his chest tightened. Placing his hands on her upper arms he drew her close. 'Judith, are you all right?'

She nodded, gulping hard. The relief of knowing that Jordan was safe and unhurt made her legs go weak. 'Yes. I—I thought—I was afraid you would be killed.'

Whatever it was that Jordan saw in her face at that moment made him utter hoarsely, 'Dear Lord!' and pull her against his chest.

Judith gave up all pretence of courage and clung to

him, burying her face in his solid warmth. Having just been subjected to several dreadful moments of fear, the realisation that he was actually holding her nearly broke her fragile grip on her control. 'I was so scared,' she whispered. 'I thought—I feared—I was terrified they were going to kill you.'

Remembering the devastating moment when he had heard her cry out, and realising the danger she had put herself in, made Jordan take hold of her arms and gently push her away. Holding her face between his hands he looked intently into the wavering depths of her eyes. 'Don't you ever,' he breathed harshly, 'disobey me again. What you did was both reckless and foolhardy. I made you promise to remain in the carriage and not do anything foolish. Are you crazy? The light in here is so bad I might have mistaken you for an assailant and blown your brains out.'

'I didn't think,' she whispered. Content that he was safe, she felt the terror of the last few minutes and the fears of the future fall away. Pulling herself together she said lamely, 'I—I'm sorry. I—I saw the man following you. When I saw the knife in his hand I knew he was some miscreant intending harm. It was clear to me that you were in danger—but I was too far away to warn you—so I followed you in here. How could I do otherwise?'

'What the hell's going on?' a voice shouted from the doorway. It was Edmund. After sending Emily back to the carriage to sit with Charlotte, he had come to see what all the fuss was about. Glancing at the dead man on the floor, Jordan's dishevelled appearance and Judith's trembling form, he took in the situation at once. 'Good Lord! Are you all right?'

Jordan nodded. 'Our unappealing friend here,' he said,

turning the corpse over with the toe of his boot, 'has just tried to kill me—or kidnap me, I'm not sure which,' he growled, his eyes going to the coil of rope on the floor. 'His accomplice lured me in here on the pretext that someone concerned with the Company wished to have a word with me.'

'Do you recognise him?'

Jordan looked down at the upturned features, at the glazed eyes and the matted brown hair revealed by the discarded hat. Satisfied that the man was dead, he shook his head. 'Never seen him before—or his accomplice.'

'How did you manage to stab him in the back?'

'I didn't.'

'The man who lured him here killed him,' Judith said, stepping forward.

'Jordan, why would anyone want to kidnap you—or kill you for that matter?' Edmund inquired.

'I believe it was kidnap they had in mind—but as for the reason, you would have to ask our assailant,' he replied grimly. 'I think they hoped to take me by surprise. When it became clear I had the upper hand, no doubt his accomplice waiting in the shadows considered it best to remove him altogether. Captured alive, there is no knowing what he might have disclosed under interrogation.'

'I think we should get out of here,' Edmund said, looking uneasily into the dark corners of the warehouse, which smelt strongly of spices and tea. 'I'll get someone to take him away.'

When Edmund had gone Jordan turned his head towards Judith. His expression was grave and serious as his relentless gaze locked with hers. 'I apologise, Judith. I should not have spoken to you so harshly just now. You must understand that I did so out of concern.'

There was no mistaking that he spoke in earnest, and

Judith felt a sudden warmth in her heart at his kindness. The numbness was melting from her limbs and she moved towards him, conscious of the dead man lying at a grotesque angle a short distance away. 'That's all right. You had every right to be angry with me.' Dropping her eyes she saw the damage that his assailant's knife had done to his jacket. 'Your—your sleeve is torn,' she whispered.

Jordan drew back and barely glanced at the tear. His teeth flashed in a sudden, unexpected smile. 'I've been through worse. It would take more than an assassin's blade to finish me.' Her eyes must have clouded suddenly, for his smile vanished. 'I'm grateful for your concern, Judith. Truly. I can only consider that with what my assailants had planned for me, your arrival might have saved my life.'

'Someone must have a very deep grievance against you.'

'It looks like that.'

'And you meant it when you said you don't recognise either of your assailants?'

'Never seen either of them before in my life. But then, when someone is out to do you harm, they don't have to commit the act themselves.'

'Are you saying the man was a hired assassin?'

'It's possible.'

'Isn't that a bit extreme? What would anyone gain from having you killed—or kidnapped?'

'Revenge—and something else, perhaps.'

Judith was deeply concerned by what had happened. Since her encounter with Jehan Khan at Landsdowne they had not spoken of it. At the time it had seemed important, in so far as it represented a threat from that direction, and now she could feel the threat tightening.

'You told me not so very long ago that I should fear Jehan Khan and Lord Minton. Have you reason to fear them?'

'I don't fear either man—but I have reason to be wary of them.' He put a gentle hand beneath her arm, looking down at her face in the dark shadows that surrounded them. 'Come, Judith—let's get out of here. It's all over now. One of the villains who set this pretty trap for me is dead and I am lucky to escape. I will have Emily take you back home. Edmund and I will stay and clear this mess up with the authorities.'

When they reached the carriage and Jordan instructed Emily to return to the house, Charlotte looked at him with enormous disappointment and murmured something about unfairness under her breath, but when she caught a searing glance in return, she had the good sense to shut up.

Jordan was consumed by a cold, violent rage as he strode off in search of his brother. If Judith's abduction and this attempt on his life were anything to go by, as it turned out, he was completely wrong in one judgement he'd made when he'd returned to England. The effect of his close friendship with the Rajah of Ranjipur was not nearly so insignificant as he'd imagined, though just then he had no way of foreseeing the extent of its profound, violent consequences in his life. It all implied something he hadn't wanted to think about, but found he could no longer avoid.

The powers of Prince Chandu were far-reaching, although here in England the man was virtually untouchable. His ability and his vast wealth, and those he could hire with it, put him above the law and beyond reach—or so he thought. Not unless Jordan himself was willing to settle with Prince Chandu on a personal basis. Jordan reminded himself who he was, and the family he represented, and he didn't want to be accused of conducting his affairs the way Prince Chandu conducted his. But if he wanted to preserve the lives of those closest to him, and his own, he had to be realistic.

Chapter Eight

Judith was deeply troubled by what had occurred earlier. The incident had taken the shine off her preparations for the ball, but Charlotte, not one to let her concern for Jordan dampen what was to be an exciting event, soon put her into the spirit of things.

'When I have finished with you you won't recognise yourself,' she told Judith, almost bursting with enthusiasm as she took Jordan's gift off its hanger.

And every word she said was true. When she stood Judith in front of the long mirror to inspect her handiwork, Judith could not believe what she saw. The gown was of a fine white silk and spangled with tiny stars that caught the light. The skirt was full and flowing, and on Charlotte's advice she had declined the wearing of a hoop. The bodice was modestly cut and silver Brussels lace hung from the elbow length sleeves so that the material draped softly over her forearms. Lady Grant's maid had curled her thick wealth of hair into a mass of ringlets that fell in gentle tiers from the crown of her head to the nape of her neck.

Judith stared at the elegant figure in the gorgeous gown and white satin slippers, more than a little bewildered by her reflection. But then her lips parted in pleasure and a delicious sensation welled up inside her.

'Oh, Charlotte. Is that really me?'

'Every inch.'

'It—it's rather like an ugly duckling turning into a swan.'

'No, it isn't. You were never an ugly duckling, Judith. You just didn't make the best of yourself. You really should take advantage of your attractive looks upon occasion. You look spectacular. You'll eclipse every other woman at the ball—even Alicia in her lemon and gold.'

However, it wasn't Alicia Charlotte was concerned about but her eldest brother, and she dearly longed to see if Judith, in her exquisite gown, would have a noticeable effect on him.

When it was time to leave for the ball Judith tried to compose herself as she left her room, trying to stem her nervousness about what would be her first and last experience of a society ball—and about meeting Jordan and praying that she wouldn't make a fool of herself. She descended the stairs with Charlotte. Apart from the butler hovering in the hall everyone was in the drawing-room, but suddenly Jordan emerged to see where the carriages had got to.

His eyes became riveted on the young woman accompanying his sister. Completely transfixed, he was rendered speechless for the first time in his life. Judith's appearance could not be faulted. The material of her dress was so thin that it did not disguise the wearer's slenderness and grace. It complimented her lustrous hair—a vibrant, glorious colour. The large hazel eyes, pert nose and perfect, soft pink mouth were gentle against the honeyed skin. She was lovely, more than Jordan had imagined.

They paused when he moved to the bottom of the stairs. He was impeccably groomed. Judith took note of this proud and darkly handsome man, magnificent in a claret-coloured coat and white trousers, ivory silk waistcoat and pristine cravat. Slowly they continued their descent, and when they reached the final step, Jordan reached out and took Judith's hand. She felt his fingers, strong and firm, wrap themselves around her own. There was a twinkle in his silver eyes, and a slow appreciative smile worked its way across his face as his gaze leisurely roamed over her body. The unspoken compliment made her blood run warm.

'Now what do you think of our prim little school teacher, Jordan?' Charlotte asked, laughter bubbling on her lips.

Prim? Jordan thought. There was nothing prim about Judith that he could see at that moment. 'You look entrancing, Judith,' he murmured. 'I'm happy to see you have agreed to go to the ball after all.'

'The dress persuaded me—as you knew it would. Thank you, Jordan. I should have thanked you earlier— but somehow we became distracted by other matters. No one has ever given me anything so beautiful.'

'It was my pleasure.'

Unable to tear her eyes away from Jordan, Judith was blind to Charlotte's satisfied smile, and to her look of smug triumph when Alicia—accompanied by everyone else in the party—emerged from the drawing-room. On seeing Judith looking so stunning, compliments tripped over each other from everyone's lips, which she accepted gracefully, but when she looked at Alicia her happiness dimmed. Alicia's face hardened and her eyes burned with a jealous malevolence as her gaze passed insolently over her dress, before she turned away. At that moment a footman announced that the carriages were waiting and they left.

The streets outside Penrose House in Mayfair were congested with private equipages carrying the distinguished and sophisticated members of society. Dignified footmen arrayed in crimson livery were kept busy opening carriage doors to allow the guests to spill out. Judith existed in a state of breathless unreality and was overcome by an almost childish excitement as she drank everything in. She stepped into the hall, which was so big it reminded her of a cathedral. The whole house was a blaze of light and a sea of shimmering hooped gowns, sparkling jewels, dancing plumes, and alive with a cacophony of vivacious chatter. The scene was like a brilliant, joyous pageant, elaborate and bizarre, magnificent and strangely unreal.

The scent of flowers spilling out of baskets and vases hung like an intoxicant on the warm air. Penrose House was extremely grand. Two marble staircases swept up from either side of the hall, coming together at the first landing to form a gallery, and one huge crystal chandelier hung in the centre.

'Lord and Lady Penrose certainly have a taste for the erotic,' Judith commented in a conspiratorial whisper to Jordan as they slowly inched their way towards their hosts, indicating with her eyes the nude statues in every niche and balancing on every pedestal around the hall and up the stairs.

Jordan's eyes twinkled down at her and a seductive smile formed itself on his lips. 'Are they acceptable in your opinion?' he murmured, for her ears alone.

'Oh, yes. They're beautiful objects. They look so elegant.'

'I agree. Lady Penrose chose them herself. You will

note that Aphrodite and Adonis make up the main—their purpose being to stimulate the pleasures of the imagination.'

Feeling her cheeks burning at what he implied, she looked away.

Jordan chuckled softly, absolutely enchanted by her innocence. 'I think you misinterpret my meaning, Judith, and if so I apologise for confusing you.'

She favoured him with an irrepressible sideways smile, her eyes telling him she did not believe him. 'Did I? You are certain of that, are you?'

'Of course. The pleasures I speak of I associate with taste. They are not the same as the gratification of appetite.'

'And what is your definition of taste? Do you believe it is a matter of feeling—or scientific knowledge?'

'The issue is not straightforward and few can say what it really is, but I think taste is a matter of feeling—and sense—and must be distinguished from lust.'

'Now I am truly confused,' she laughed. 'Please explain to me what you mean.'

'When a person views a work of art, I believe they should do so directly and unencumbered, and not be distorted by lower forms of sensuality and desire.'

'Then I can see that must pose a problem for a great many gentlemen.' At that moment they were passing a particularly alluring statue of Aphrodite. 'Beautiful, is she not? Aphrodite, the Greek equivalent of the Roman deity of Venus, representing all the qualities of love and beauty,' Judith quoted from her studies. 'I fail to understand how a man can look at her objectively and not desire her?'

A slow, roguish grin dawned across Jordan's features.

'I agree. In fact, I would say that is virtually impossible,' he replied quietly.

Judith looked at him, her eyes full of mischievous laughter, and she was unable to stifle the smile that tempted her lips at the complete absence of contrition on his handsome face. 'I was right, wasn't I? I did not misinterpret your meaning in the first place.'

His eyes twinkled wickedly. 'You did not,' he confessed unashamedly.

'You are quite impossible,' she said, laughing under his amused gaze.

'I know. Infuriating, isn't it,' he chuckled, placing his hand under her elbow and guiding her in the direction of their hosts.

Jordan found this delightful young woman truly amazing. At one and the same time she managed to be an innocent young girl and a beautiful, alluring woman, full of beguiling contrasts. To discuss a subject with such jaunty impudence—a subject most young ladies of his acquaintance would find either boring or beyond them, he found utterly exhilarating.

When Lord and Lady Penrose and the betrothed couple had received them, they passed on into the ballroom, filled with men and women already dancing to the strains of an orchestra. There was a host of people waiting to meet Jordan. He was accosted at every step. It seemed as if he knew nearly everyone present.

The ball began in grand style. Calmly watching Judith as the evening progressed, Jordan noted how the reflection of hundreds of candles and the Venetian mirrors became accomplices in illuminating her gentle beauty. Despite her inexperience at social gatherings and polite repartee, she seemed to find her feet admirably. She became a laughing, beautiful young woman, in possession

of a natural wit and intelligence that soon had a crowd
of admiring young swains eagerly vying for her attention
and the chance to add their names to her dance card. It
was soon full, and she had one after another of them
sweeping her off her feet into the dance.

As she dipped and swayed to the music, her slender
form floating with a fluidity and grace over the floor in
a swirl of white skirts, the tips of her satin slippers visible
as her feet darted to and fro, the more Jordan watched
her the more irritated he became at all the attention she
was receiving. He could not bear to see other men vying
for her attention, coveting her, to watch the appreciation
in their eyes as they devoured her upturned face, smiling
and flushed from dancing. He guessed their thoughts
were not so very different from his own, and he despised
them for it.

For the first time in his life Jordan experienced an
acute feeling of irrepressible jealousy, which twisted his
heart and caught him completely off guard. It was a feeling he found decidedly unpleasant.

The lively music and fast steps, the thrill of being
swept around the dance floor in the arms of handsome
young men, filled Judith with an unaccustomed gaiety.
She could not escape if she'd wanted to from the zealous
swains who gave her no respite. She felt wonderfully
alive, and even Alicia's cold glowers could not penetrate
the aura of excitement that surrounded her.

There was a respite in the dancing when everyone descended on a room next to the ballroom, where a most
extravagant supper had been set out. Fortunately for
Judith, unlike most of the ladies present, her slender body
was not encased in a whalebone corset, so she wasn't

prevented from savouring most of the mouth-watering dishes.

Later, when one of her partners returned her to Lady Grant, finding the room had become warm and stuffy and feeling the need for some air, she slipped out of some tall French doors onto a small balcony situated a few feet above the level of the ground. Lanterns hanging in the trees lighted the darkness.

Suddenly she was startled when a black-garbed gentleman appeared through the doors and stepped in front of her and bowed. When he spoke his voice was a gravelly baritone.

'So here you are, Miss Wyatt—and all alone, which is most unwise. Why, any disreputable scoundrel could whisk you away without anyone knowing. I'd be failing in my duty if I didn't take you indoors.'

'Oh! And your name, sir?' she asked as she allowed him to lead her back inside, thinking it an odd thing for him to say.

'Lord Jeremy Minton—and this is our dance, I believe.'

The name hit Judith like a cold blast. Lord Minton! This was the man Jordan had told her about, whom he disliked intensely. And now here he was, expecting her to dance with him! There must be some mistake. How could it have happened? How could his name have appeared on her dance card without her knowing?

Gracious rejection was already on her lips. 'Oh—but you must be mistaken. I—I don't recall—'

'Check your card, Miss Wyatt. You will see there is no mistake. It is mine by right.'

Quickly she scanned the names on her card and her heart plummeted when she saw his name was indeed entered for the next waltz.

His smile was one of smug satisfaction. 'There you are, you see. At the time there were so many gentlemen flocking around you that you appeared to be in a state of some confusion. I will forgive your oversight.'

Feeling a small frisson of alarm, Judith glanced around hoping to see Jordan. She recognised his tall figure across the room immediately, but he was in conversation with a group of gentlemen and had his back to her.

The musicians had already started playing when Lord Minton took her hand and led her out on the dance floor. She tried to disengage it, but arching one dark eyebrow he looked at her imperiously, appearing not to notice. As they danced Judith was conscious of the hard bulk of his muscles beneath his coat, and the strength and power of the shoulder that flexed beneath her hand.

She had already noted that despite the hard line of his thin lips, and the cruelty she saw in his weathered face, he was quite good-looking, but it was marred by too heavy a brow and penetrating, pale blue eyes set too close together. He was surprisingly nimble on his feet and his limbs moved with impressive tensile power, despite having a large build, and she had the momentary notion that she was dancing with some well-regulated machine. Suddenly she felt the contact with him quite revolting.

'You look divine, Miss Wyatt,' he murmured, watching her face closely. 'Are you enjoying the ball?'

'Yes—very much.' Judith had collected her thoughts sufficiently to respond with grace, but her reply was stilted, and she was praying the dance would be of short duration. Her brows drew together in a puzzled frown when a thought occurred to her. 'Tell me, Lord Minton, how did you know where to look for me?'

He smiled, but the smile did not reach his cold eyes. The scented nearness of her body, coupled with his

delight at his success in getting her alone so that he could
speak to her, combined to lift him to a pitch of heady
excitement, and an old ache revived itself in his loins.
He looked down at her, at her straight shoulders rising
above her firm breasts, observing how the dress highlighted her collarbones perfectly—so fine, so breakable.

But where she was concerned his lust must be held in
check for the time being. The target of his interest was
Jordan Grant, and it was necessary for his own survival
to get even for past differences and obtain something that
did not rightfully belong to him. He would give ten years
of his life to see Grant lying dead, and he was convinced
that with a little persuasion—tender or otherwise, it mattered little to him, Judith Wyatt could be coerced into
aiding him to achieve that goal.

'I was watching you,' he said at length. 'I saw you
slip through the French doors onto the balcony. I didn't
expect to find a lady disappear outside alone. I made up
my mind that you either had an assignation or you must
have a taste for the air.'

'And as you have discovered, sir, it was the latter—
especially when a room is stuffy and warm.'

His eyes locked on hers and he said meaningfully, 'After living in India for most of your life, you will have
become accustomed to the heat.'

Judith stared at him, her eyes widening in amazement.
'You are extremely well informed, sir? To the best of my
knowledge I've never seen you before in my life.' Suddenly, something about his deep voice stirred the ashes
of an unpleasant memory and her brow creased in a puzzled, questioning frown. 'That is so, isn't it? We have
never met before?'

A small smirk appeared on his lips. 'If we had, I should

be mortally offended that you could forget it. However, I do know a great deal about you, Miss Wyatt.'

Judith listened in stunned disbelief as he went on to recite her life's history, wondering how he could possibly know so much about her, but before she could question him, suddenly something caught her eye. Someone had appeared in the ballroom and was causing quite a stir among the throng. It was the turbaned figure of a man exotically dressed in a long tunic of saffron-coloured silk sashed with turquoise. Accompanied by two white robed servants, he came forward into the pool of light that embraced the dancers and stopped, his face expressionless when his eyes settled on Lord Minton and his partner.

It was Jehan Khan.

Quick as a flash Judith remembered that unnerving moment when she had met him on her way back from church, and that when she had spoken to him in Hindustani she had seen his eyes register surprise. She also recalled Jordan telling her that the Indian was residing with Lord Minton. Had Jehan Khan told Lord Minton of their encounter, and had the latter, on learning that she was familiar with the language, made enquiries about her? She stared up at him, two bright sparks of anger showing in her eyes.

'I am concerned why a gentleman I do not know should show so much interest in me. It is none of your business.'

'I was exceedingly curious to learn more about a young woman who speaks Hindustani like a native. How could that be? I asked myself, unless she has spent some considerable time in India.'

'What do you want from me, Lord Minton?'

His hooded eyes levelled on hers. 'I want you to remember at all times that you have reason to fear me, Miss

Wyatt. I find you are in a position to help me acquire something I want. We have things to discuss, you and I.'

When the waltz was halfway through and Jordan standing beside Alicia, had calmly observed the arrival of Jehan Khan, his eyes did a broad sweep of the dancers in a search for Judith. He saw her image in a maze of bodies. Never had he seen her look so provocatively lovely, and he had a sudden urge to beat a path to her feet and send all her persistent suitors packing. His eyes shifted to her partner and the shock of recognition blanched his features. His emotions shattered from all rational control and fury seared through him like a knife.

Unbidden, a small mountain retreat in the foothills of the Himalayas seeped into his mind. Against a backdrop of these majestic mountains he remembered the smell of pine trees, and that the glens were full of snowdrops and lilies. But he also remembered the dust and the heat of one particular day, the flames—reaching, dancing, leaping and devouring—and more, much, much more. It was a sight that would haunt him for the rest of his life.

Hearing Jordan utter a low, savage curse, Alicia looked at him. His eyes were glacial, his jaw taut, and his mouth drawn into a ruthless, forbidding line. Curious as to what could have brought about this change in him, she followed his line of vision, her eyes lighting on the man dancing with Judith. 'Why, Jordan, you seem determined to harass that poor gentleman. Who is he?'

'Lord Jeremy Minton, and I have a thousand reasons for disliking him.'

The dark frown that accompanied his statement surprised Alicia. This black side of Jordan's mood was new to her. She realised that the gentleman who held all his attention had unleashed in him all the concealed forces of his passionate nature, all the more terrible because he was a man who was normally in control and able to master them.

'Excuse me,' he ground out. 'There are one or two things I have to say to that blackguard.'

Having expected him to claim the next dance, Alicia's mouth opened to vent her displeasure, but he was already moving across the room towards the couple on the edge of the dance-floor with the stealth of a panther. She glared at his retreating back but then shifted her gaze to his quarry, interest beginning to stir in their depths.

Without warning, a hand reached out and snatched Judith out of Lord Minton's arms, startling the couples closest to them.

Jordan's features were tight as his narrowed eyes swept over his implacable enemy like whiplash. He looked at him from his superior height with such a cold and barely contained rage that for a moment Judith thought he was going to murder Lord Minton right there and then. The look that passed between them crackled with hidden fire.

'If you have a shred of sense, or if you have learned anything from the past, Minton, you would know better than to approach anyone remotely connected to me or my family,' he said in an explosive underbreath.

'I beg your pardon?' the other said, without emotion.

Jordan's fists clenched in a visible effort not to drive them into Lord Minton's face. 'You heard me the first time,' he ground out between his teeth, in that same deadly voice. 'Let me give you a piece of advice, Minton. Get out of here before I give way to my inclinations.'

'Which are?'

'To throw you out myself. It would not be good for your dignity, your friend watching you over there,' he said, gesturing towards Jehan Khan with a brief nod without removing his eyes from the target of his hatred, 'or your health. So get out.'

Lord Minton's muscles tightened visibly, and a hot flush had risen from his white stock. His eyes were glittering with unspeakable rage, and for a moment something savage and raw stirred in their depths. It was clear that he was tempted to throw himself at Jordan, before the fury was replaced with icy contempt and he had the sense to step back. He bowed stiffly to the young woman. 'It has been a privilege to meet you, Miss Wyatt. I trust you will enjoy what is left of the ball.' To Jordan he said, 'We will meet again, you and I, Captain. Soon.'

Jordan took a step forward. He was standing quite still, showing no more expression than a stone. Whatever lived behind those silver eyes was hidden. 'Beyond the requirements of formality you will never speak to me, to Miss Wyatt, or to any member of my family again, Minton— not until you are on your knees begging for your life at the barrel end of my pistol or the point of my sword. Then I will give you leave to address me as you please— for they will be the last words you utter.'

Too anaesthetised by shock, Judith listened. She was trembling in every limb. Lord Minton turned and made straight for Jehan Khan, and after speaking quietly to each other, together the two of them quit the room. Fortunately the unprecedented altercation had passed unnoticed by anyone. Only Alicia, who had moved closer to hear what transpired, was aware that anything was wrong, and she turned and looked at the retreating figure of Lord Minton and his companion with a curious interest, not at all fooled by their apparently harmonious departure from the room.

Chapter Nine

In a moment Jordan turned to Judith. Still trembling from her encounter with Lord Minton, she saw that to her utter disbelief he was still livid, and that this time his anger was directed at her. Never had she seen such savage, scorching fury as that emanating from Jordan at that moment.

He bent his head and said in an ominously calm tone that belied the leaping fury in his eyes, 'Come with me.'

His hand moved as rapidly as a striking snake and clamped on her forearm. He steered her towards the French doors which she had disappeared through earlier, but before he stepped outside he took two glasses of champagne from the tray of a passing footman and handed one to her. It was a gesture designed to add to the charade of two people wishing to partake of some intimate conversation in private. When they were alone Jordan drank the sparkling wine in one draught and placed his glass on the stone balustrade. Judith put hers down untouched.

His look cut through her. The anger and rage were gone from him. What there was instead was ice.

'You little fool. After I'd spelled out the vicious nature

of Minton's character, I thought you'd have more sense than to add his name to your dance card. Damn it, Judith!' he snapped, raking his fingers through his hair and beginning to pace the narrow balcony with angry, frustrated strides. 'Are you so simple that you didn't know what you were doing?'

Stung by the unfairness of his attack, Judith's fists clenched by her sides and her cheeks flamed as she glared at him. 'How dare you say that to me? The least you could do is consider my position in all this.'

'That is precisely what I am doing.'

'I honestly don't know how it happened and I deeply regret the unfortunate incident. I didn't want to dance with Lord Minton and I know I should have made my excuses the minute he approached me, but I had no idea who he was until it was too late. Besides, he's not an easy man to say no to.'

'I do know that.'

'Then you should try and understand how difficult it was for me instead of berating me so unjustly. Through no fault of my own I have been dragged into something I know nothing about and cannot even begin to comprehend. I don't mind admitting,' she whispered, with a shiver of revulsion when she recalled the cruelty Lord Minton's snake-like eyes had revealed, and how she had recoiled against his arm which had been like an iron thong about her waist, 'that I'm scared.'

Jordan stared down at the tempestuous young woman in the gorgeous white dress, her face both delicate and alive with her emotions. The fury within him died, and as he looked down into her glorious eyes, his stomach clenched.

'I'm sorry, Judith. Above all things I want to shield you from hurt, not be the source of your anguish. It was not my intention for you to become involved in any of this.' He perched his hip on the balustrade and folded his arms across his chest, his look one of extreme gravity. 'As yet I do not fully comprehend it myself. Since returning to England I've had no contact with either Minton or Jehan Khan—in fact I've only seen Minton once and that was from a distance. I have my suspicions about what is behind all this—that it concerns something that occurred in India some time ago.'

'Then please tell me so that I can at least understand some of it.'

'I told you that I spent much of my time on the North West Frontier, but before that—back in '15 and for more than a year afterwards, I was engaged in the Gurkha War in Nepal. You will have heard of it.'

She nodded. 'Yes, and the treaty which followed, bringing the Company large tracts of land in the foothills. It was shortly afterwards when our own troubles with the Pindaris began.'

'It was at this time that I first met the Rajah of Ranjipur. The Rajah and I became friends and I did him a service for which he was deeply grateful at the time. He was a man for whom I held the utmost admiration and respect, a man who was fair and just in all his dealings with his fellow Hindus and the British. Jehan Khan—who was one of his retainers—was weaned away from his service by the Rajah's cousin, Prince Chandu, and elevated to the high position of adviser to the Prince himself. Chandu is the Devil's own. He is cruel, utterly ruthless and selfish, and he turns others into murderers to suit his own ends. I have already told you that the Rajah died without a direct male heir from his body shortly before I left India, and that the Company annexed his estate, which is the usual practice in such cases.

'Prince Chandu, who found British rule intolerable and was constant in his wish to rid India of these foreigners, accusing them of plundering, injuring and disgracing the people, considered it his right to inherit his cousin's estate and was vicious against the Company. But all the time Chandu had only one motive and that was to serve himself. He rules his land as despotically as his forebears have done, and his people live in fear of him. If he wants something he believes it is his right to take it.'

'But where do you fit into all this? You are no longer connected to the army so why are you being pursued?'

Jordan stood up, his face tense and wrapped in secrecy. His tall figure dominated Judith, and his eyes fixed compellingly on her lovely features. 'I cannot divulge that until certain facts have been made clear.'

'I thought you would say something like that. Why won't you tell me?' she persisted.

His face became grim. 'Because you are safer not knowing,' he said, which was true. If she was abducted again and she knew too much, she would soon tell her assailants what they wanted to know. She would be unable to resist their methods for long.

'What I will tell you is that I became involved in a long-standing quarrel between the Rajah and Chandu. It was of a highly sensitive nature, involving the Rajah's beloved daughter. It was a long time ago and I thought the matter ended—but maybe it isn't—at least, not where Prince Chandu is concerned.' Suddenly Jordan's forehead creased with concern. 'Tell me, Judith, did Minton threaten you in any way?'

'Yes, I believe he did,' she answered, trying to piece together the fragments of the puzzle of all Jordan had told her—and what he'd left out. Resting her hands on the balustrade, she gazed out from their small circle of light to the garden beyond, hearing the silvery notes of a fountain somewhere amongst the trees. The warm, honeysuckle and rose perfumed air lapped around them, whispering that it was a night made for lovers, but dark storm clouds were already gathering in the distant heavens.

'Lord Minton told me that I have reason to be afraid of him, and that we had things to discuss, but I was not fated to learn how far his words would have carried him because that was when you interrupted—and thank God you did.'

'What else did he say to you?'

'He—he knows all about me—everything. He knows how old I am, that my father worked as a clerk for the East India Company, and that I was born and raised in India and came to England when my parents were killed. He knows that when I am not at the academy I live with my aunt in Brighton. He also knows that at present she is abroad and that I am residing at Landsdowne as your mother's guest. How did he find out?'

'It wouldn't be too difficult. What puzzles me is why he should want to.'

'He also told me that he became curious to learn more about me when I spoke to Jehan Khan in his native tongue when I encountered him that day.' She smiled softly. 'I don't suppose it's every day you meet people in London who can converse fluently in Hindustani.'

Jordan looked at her in amazement, his admiration increasing the more he got to know her. 'You speak Hindustani?'

She nodded. 'And Urdu and a smattering of other languages, of which there are many in India—as you know yourself. There's nothing unusual in that, so you needn't look so surprised. When I was growing up I spent most of my time with the natives.' She paused and looked up at him, saying on a more serious note, 'I—I think it was Lord Minton who abducted me.'

'Why do you think that? Has he said anything that might imply that he did?'

'No. It was his voice. I'm sure it was the same. At one point in our conversation there was a sudden change in his tone that caused shards of fear to prick my spine. It brought back the nightmare of my abduction, and I didn't know who or what the person who had spoken to me had been. Lord Minton, though,' she said, her expression becoming thoughtful, 'his voice… But that was impossible, I declared to myself, and too fanciful by far. Absurd, even—but could it be the same?' She looked at Jordan. 'I don't think the similarities are coincidence.'

Jordan nodded, his expression grave. 'I believe you are right. I've thought that all along, but until I have proof we'll just have to be patient—and on our guard in case he tries something like that again.' Suddenly the musicians began playing another waltz and he smiled down at her. Taking her hands he drew her towards him. He was standing very close and she had to look up to him. His gaze dipped lingeringly to her soft lips.

The focal point of his gaze did not escape Judith and she felt herself melting.

'I think this is our dance,' he murmured.

Automatically Judith pulled her hands away and consulted her card. 'No. I have already promised it to a gentleman by the name of Sir Babbington Smythe.'

Jordan's grin was tigerish. 'Blast Babbington Smythe! I'm claiming it for myself.'

'But—I can't let him down. It wouldn't be proper.'

'Yes, it would,' he said, and taking her hand he propelled her through the French doors, where he drew her into his embrace and swept her into the waltz.

Like the man himself, Jordan's movements were relaxed and bold as he gently swirled her in graceful circles, with none of the mincing steps her other partners had demonstrated. Meeting his engulfing silver gaze with warmth, Judith relaxed against his arm, feeling that he was holding her closer than was seemly. But she told herself she didn't care as a glow of warmth and happiness surged through her. The gentle, spicy cologne he wore, mixed with his own manly smell, touched her senses and filled her head.

Catching the admiring looks of other women both on and off the dance floor, she smiled to herself. Jordan was by far the most handsome man present, and no doubt many of them yearned to be in her position, to bask in the aura of his powerful masculinity, and have his bold eyes capturing and imprisoning theirs—which was exactly what they were doing to hers at that moment.

A glow warmed her, and she realised she was falling victim to the curious power of attraction he possessed over all other human beings she knew, an attraction which was already beginning to blaze into something more profound. It was mad, impetuous, abandoned and sensual—impossible to deny or halt.

Where Jordan was concerned her mind was a battleground of conflicting emotions. She couldn't ignore the treacherous leap her heart always gave at the sight of one of his enthralling, intimate smiles, and the softness in his eyes when he looked at her, the smiling tenderness she heard in his voice, were both utterly shattering to her self-control. There was nowhere she could hide from the truth, for the truth was that she wanted him, and she could well imagine the pleasure that he could give a woman. With a mixture of quiet acceptance and nervous anticipation, she realised that what she felt for Jordan was actually out of her hands.

Judith could have no comprehension of what was going through Jordan's mind as he looked down at her glowing face, of where his imaginings were leading him. He was thinking what a glorious sight her shimmering mass of dark hair would be, brushed out of its ringlets, draped over his pillow and spilling over his bare flesh, and how pleasurable her supple young body would feel writhing in ecstasy beneath his own. The meanderings of his mind amazed him, but the path along which they travelled was not displeasing.

Judith Wyatt had somehow found her way into his blood. He was drawn to the sincerity in her eyes, her smile warmed his heart, and feeling her slender form pressed against his in the most innocently provocative way sent desire raging through his veins. Her charms were subtle, her personality unlike other women he knew. There was a sensuality about her, a natural sophistication and inspiring liveliness that drew him to her. He wanted to hold her against him away from prying eyes, to mould her body to his, and he wanted all the Babbington Smythes here tonight to know that she belonged to him.

'Oh dear!' Judith said, when her eyes lighted on a thin, uninteresting-looking gentleman with red lips and a po-face, who was glaring at them from the edge of the dance floor. 'I've just caught a glimpse of Sir Babbington Smythe, and he looks fit to commit murder.'

'Then I shall permit him to call me out,' Jordan teased, grinning, 'after the dance and not before.'

'You would fight over me?' she asked, laughing delightedly, finding the idea of two grown men fighting a duel over her extremely flattering.

'But of course. I would take on a whole regiment of men if necessary. You, my beautiful little moonflower, are captivating.'

His term of endearment warmed her heart. 'That's why you bought me this particular dress, isn't it? Because it reminded you of our conversation about the moonflowers. I am right, aren't I?' she asked, enjoying the feel of his hand on the small of her waist. It seemed to pulsate with life, sending shock waves through her entire body.

He nodded, his eyes locked on hers.

'And you would really fight over me?'

'You are a very rare specimen indeed, and worth fighting for,' Jordan murmured, his eyes openly and unabashedly displaying his approval as his gaze ranged over her face upturned to his.

'And you, Captain Grant,' she replied, giving him a coy smile, 'say the nicest things.'

'Only to those I like,' he told her, his eyes glinting with amusement. 'But where Sir Babbington Smythe is concerned he has every right to be angry. You have humiliated him by overlooking his name on your dance card, and I have compounded it by taking his place. So, you see, it would be most impolite of me to end his life when he has done nothing wrong and must be wretchedly bemoaning his loss. My sympathy is with the poor man entirely.'

'Then it is obvious to me, that he is better off humiliated and alive, than dead and proud,' she said, laughing softly, enjoying herself enormously and falling in with his mood.

'My sentiments exactly,' Jordan said, spinning her round until she was almost breathless. 'Are you enjoying yourself, Judith?'

'Absolutely—and I know I have you to thank for that.

Unfortunately, I don't think Alicia is enjoying herself very much,' she remarked, having caught Alicia's eye where she was standing next to Charlotte. Alicia was glaring at her with an expression that could have crushed rock, and for one brief moment Judith sensed her overpowering jealousy and rage. She had the impression that Alicia would not let Jordan out of her sight for a moment, in which case she must have seen them disappear onto the balcony. She suddenly felt her spirits sag, deriving no pleasure at flaunting the close relationship that was developing between Jordan and herself before the other woman's gaze. 'She's standing with Charlotte and looks extremely put out about something.'

'You really shouldn't worry about Alicia. Perhaps her dancing partner has let her down,' Jordan said lightly, knowing this was the case, because he was to have partnered her in this waltz. 'Do you think we should introduce her Sir Babbington Smythe?' he suggested teasingly. 'Maybe they can inject some humour into each other.'

'Jordan—that is a cruel thing to say,' Judith rebuked, but she was unable to stop herself from smiling back at him. She found something irresistibly comic about Sir Babbington Smythe and Alicia dancing together. But then on a more serious note she said, 'I'm afraid Alicia doesn't like me. You must have noticed.'

'Alicia can be extremely trying and vexing at times.' He paused, frowning thoughtfully, and then he said, 'I shouldn't have said that. She has many attributes to her credit. Alicia is beautiful and vivacious. She is also fun to be with and popular with everyone—and I am not unaware that she has aspirations where I am concerned. I am not insensitive to her overtures,' he said, having recognised the bold gleam in Alicia's eyes on more than one occasion issuing an invitation. He also knew she was no innocent, and that she'd had at least one affair in the past. There was a sultry promise which emanated from her like a sexual aura, but it failed to fire his own need.

'Then—why do you not respond?' Judith asked impulsively, realising too late that it was the height of bad manners to ask a gentleman such a personal, intimate question, but it had tripped off her tongue before she could stop it.

He grinned. 'Because I have a well-developed instinct for self-preservation.' After a brief pause he continued, his arms tightening and his lips nearly brushing her hair. 'When I marry,' he said, his smile fading, his voice softening and his eyes shining down at her with a caressing, purposeful light, 'I want my wife to have more than women like Alicia can give me. I want her to be the most special woman of all.'

The slow curve of his firm lips and the sparkle in his translucent eyes that followed his statement, combined to a disarming degree to sap the strength from Judith's limbs. She didn't know what it was, but there was an inflection in his voice and a warmth that seemed to suggest that he was talking about her, as if he had already made up his mind that she was the one he wanted. She lowered her eyes and stared at his shirt front, much too conscious of the magnetism of the man and the uneven beat of her heart. She flushed with confusion—and regret, for her common sense raged, and she knew she could not allow that to happen.

But she refused to have her happiness ruined—not when there was another hour or more of the ball left to enjoy.

Jordan's feelings for this unassuming woman were indeed serious. Although Alicia was undoubtedly beautiful,

her features were not as fine and delicate as those of the
young woman in his arms. Nor was her skin as fair. But
then, it would be difficult in his eyes for any woman to
surpass those features of the maid he had decided to make
his own. His eyes feasted on the creaminess of her neck
and shoulders, and the gentle swell of her breasts. A
strong yearning to hold her tighter, a yearning that cau-
terised his mind with his physical need, seized him.

Now he was home his plan was to take a wife, which
was something he had put on hold in order to pursue his
military career. He had stayed a bachelor long enough—
but to look outside his own circle, to marry a girl of the
lower class... An amused smile touched the corners of
his mouth at the thoughts that were filling his mind, and
of the shock that would explode upon society if he did
marry a girl of Judith Wyatt's pedigree. He smiled inwardly. It would be worth marrying her for the reaction—
not that he cared a damn what anybody thought.

Taking a respite from the dancing, standing beside
Charlotte, who was chattering away in fierce animation,
Alicia let what she said pass over her with no interest.
Her eyes were fastened on Jordan whirling Judith in the
waltz—their second waltz, and the last, for to dance more
than two dances with any one lady would be quite improper and commented upon, and not even Jordan would
flout convention so brazenly. But then, she thought angrily, the mood he was in tonight, he just might.

'They dance beautifully together, don't they, Alicia?'
Charlotte said, following Alicia's scowling look and purposely rubbing salt in the wound with her casual comment.

Alicia ignored her remark, continuing to glare at
Jordan. His look was one of complete absorption as he

gazed down at the woman in his arms, which made Alicia both furious and frightened. He had never looked at her that way, and she was unprepared for this insult, this humiliation. Suddenly she wanted to hit out at them both for his rejection of her—casting her aside for a nobody. No one treated her like that. Nobody! Not even Jordan Grant, no matter how rich and powerful he was.

Rage almost consumed her. Her beautiful face was convulsed with it, and she was filled with a loathing that brought out everything cruel and fierce in her. Her whole being was filled with a fierce hatred for the woman Jordan was smiling at with so much lovesick passion it made her feel sick. So much the worse for you, Judith Wyatt, she thought as her jealous heart hungered for revenge. I'll get even with you some day, she vowed. I swear it.

Turning sharply, she left the ballroom to go in search of her sister, who had gone to sit in an anteroom with Lady Grant. She was finding the excitement, the oppressive heat from the candles and the large contingent of people, all too much. Alicia came to an abrupt halt when she saw Lord Minton in conversation with Lord Penrose. Suddenly a malicious smile curved her lips and she looked at him with keen interest. He was handsome enough, she thought, but there was a coarseness about him.

Deciding that it might be to her advantage to make it her business to get to know this gentleman who had roused Jordan to such fury, slowly she began moving towards him, watching him closely when he paused in his conversation with their host when he became aware of her approach. His eyes narrowed, and something that went beyond interest ignited in their depths. His lips curved in appreciation of her beauty, but Alicia was not deceived, for when she drew close and looked into those cruel, pale blue eyes, she recognised that which was in herself. She knew in that instant that they could never be friends, and she realised that Lord Minton would make a dangerous enemy.

Two hours later, after Jordan had released Judith from his arms and allowed her to dance with someone other than himself, the party assembled on the steps of Penrose House to return home just as the first flash of lightning streaked across the sky, and thunder rumbled over London.

Having just returned from the room which had been set aside for the ladies to retire to, Judith had been both surprised and puzzled to see Alicia conversing with Lord Minton with the ease and confidence of long acquaintance. And yet she could swear that neither had known of the other's existence until tonight. It was plain that Lord Minton had not been intimidated by Jordan's threat on the dance floor, although he had been prudent enough to keep his distance and not provoke another unpleasant incident.

From Judith's point of view she could not think of a more disagreeable man than Lord Minton for Alicia to attach herself to, but it was no business of hers who Alicia chose to associate with. Neither Alicia nor Lord Minton had seen her pass by on her way to join the others to await their carriage, but the cold calculation she had seen in Lord Minton's eyes when they had looked into those equally calculating eyes of his companion had made her shiver, and she was interested to know what they had discussed with such intensity.

Bringing her thoughts back to the present, she was disappointed when Jordan excused himself and climbed into his own carriage, which he had arranged to have brought to Penrose House when the ball ended. He explained that he had an engagement to keep and would return home later.

Secretly he intended visiting a certain establishment close to the river, where he knew some of Jehan Khan's servants could be found when they were not dancing attendance upon their master. It was his intention to glean as much information as he could from them regarding the purpose of Khan's visit to London, and also to confirm his suspicions that Minton and Khan had been behind the attack on his own person at the warehouse at Blackwall that day. But as his carriage left Mayfair, he was unaware of the closed, black equipage following in his wake.

Chapter Ten

Jordan alighted from his carriage a short distance from the tavern. The thunder was passing over but the wind had risen, and he raised the collar of his redingote to shield his neck from the slanting rain. Knowing a multitude of dangers lurked in the dark alleyways, he told the driver not to wait, that he would find his own way back.

Approaching the tavern, he stepped aside to let a trio of inebriated sailors pass by, their arms slung around the shoulders of a couple of whores. Momentarily distracted, he failed to see the coach that halted in the shadows a short distance away, or the two men in white robes who climbed out and darted across the street, crouching low among coils of rope close to the tavern to avoid being seen.

Jordan entered the tavern and pushed aside a beaded curtain. He was a stranger to the place, but he knew of its popularity. The Crescent Moon was no ordinary tavern, nor was its presiding tavern-keeper any ordinary tavern-keeper. His name was Ali Shah. His short body was cushioned in fat, his voice as sweet as a maiden's, and his eyes and hair as black as a raven's wing. He had left Bombay and sailed to London on one of the Company's vessels twenty years ago, never to return.

The air inside the main room was thick with the smell of spiced food, burning sandalwood, tobacco smoke and human sweat—and the all-pervading smell of opium. The ceiling was low and heavily beamed, the walls hung with a strange mixture of English artefacts and traditional Indian mosaics and murals. Pipe-smoking, somnolent figures lounged at scratched tables, while others sat cross-legged on heaps of velvet, golden-tasselled cushions—in fact Jordan could have been in a Joyhouse anywhere in India.

Ali Shah's rich Indian background and his long association with the British made his tavern and his manner of entertainment rather different from the usual. Night after night business was brisk. Every kind of traveller flocked to his tavern—mainly sailors and employees of the East India Company who, during their travels in the East, had developed a fondness for the Joyhouses and the dancing-girls.

From as far afield as Goa, Kashmir and Calcutta, these dusky-skinned girls—whom Ali proclaimed were the choicest jewels of India—with large dark eyes heavily rimmed with kohl, their hair sleek and oiled, their bodies clad in glittering, diaphanous fabrics from the East, swayed among the customers, performing their slow, rhythmic, ritualistic dances to the sound of the sitar. They were also expected to pleasure Ali's customers in the age-old way, and when their bodies lost their beauty and they were no longer desirable, they would disappear like others before them into London's seething metropolis.

The travellers who found their way to the Crescent Moon had also developed an unbelievable passion—for many an addiction—for opium, the strong narcotic dulling their senses into languor and forgetfulness.

When Jordan was seated at a table with a clear view of the beaded curtain, with a nod from Ali one of the dancing-girls attached herself to him. She leaned close, and even before he looked at her, the cloud of her perfume—which smelled heavily of seduction and musk, enveloped him. Her black hair was parted down the middle and hung in a heavy plait to her waist. He met her kohl-rimmed, velvety eyes and smiled. Her soft, fully-fleshed mouth, darkened with red salve, parted in response, exposing small, perfect white teeth. She was young and decidedly lovely.

Eager to oblige the handsome customer, she poured him some wine when he declined a pipe. He gave the impression that he was there to relax and watch the dancing, but inside he was tense and alert as he watched for Khan's servants to appear. He saw Ali disappear through the beaded curtain and return a few minutes later, but thought nothing of it.

Looking around he saw no familiar faces. His eyes were drawn back to the beaded curtain when it parted to admit three more customers. Ali beamed a welcome and told them how delighted he was to offer them the hospitality of his establishment. After glancing around the tavern one of the newcomers grinned broadly when his eyes lighted on Jordan. Immediately he detached himself from his companions and weaved his way through the somnolent bodies and the haze to Jordan's table.

'Jordan! Good Lord! Good to see you, but I never expected to see you here of all places.'

Jordan rose and put out a hand, his lips smiling a welcome, genuinely glad to see him. The man's name was Thomas Parry, and he was one of the Company's repre-

sentatives in the Spice Islands. He was home on leave
for the first time in eight years. The two had become
acquainted in Calcutta and had travelled from India on
the same vessel, getting to know one another well.

'After all I've heard about this place I thought I'd take
a look close at hand,' Jordan replied sociably. 'Didn't
expect you to be here either, Tom.'

Tom shook his hand and slipped easily into a chair
across from him, already well-oiled. Tom liked Jordan
Grant. He was a fine figure of a military man who didn't
parade himself like some of the British in India. He got
on well and was highly respected by the native troops. It
was said that during the Anglo-Nepalese war back in
'14–'16, when more territory had been won in Nepal for
the Company, Captain Grant and his regiment of bearded
Sikhs had put the fear of God into the Gurkhas—who
were known to be a formidable fighting people—and later
into the rebels on the North West Frontier.

'Are you here alone?' Tom asked, summoning Ali to
bring him a drink.

Jordan nodded, retaining the lounging indolence of his
long body as he picked up his glass and took a sip of the
dark red wine.

'Then you must stick with my companions and me.
The streets hereabouts are riddled with corruption and
vice—some of the roughest damned streets in London. A
man's life isn't worth that after dark,' he said snapping
his fingers into the air. 'Many a cut-throat will do you in
for a nickel-plated brandy flask or a silk handkerchief.'

'And what of you, Tom? Are you here for a pipe—or
the female company?'

'Nothing wrong with both, is there?' Tom chuckled,
his rugged, good-humoured face splitting into a grin as
he eyed appreciatively the girl who had served Jordan

and was hovering within his reach. Leaning over, Tom stretched out his arm and traced his finger along her naked abdomen. She responded with a sultry smile and teasingly danced out of his reach, inviting him to follow.

'You don't change, Tom.'

'They do say something like that,' he replied, lounging back in his chair and continuing to watch the dancing-girl from beneath lowered lids. 'They also say the flesh is weak—and I'm not ashamed to confess mine is weaker than most.'

'A fact I have observed for myself.'

'Ah, Jordan. I've seen enough pallid redheads and fair-haired maidens with their giggles, their simpering and dissembling to last me a lifetime. My mother's been parading them before me for the last few weeks—in the hope that I'll marry one of them and settle down in England. May God preserve me from such a fate.'

'From that, Tom, I take it you are no admirer of European beauty.'

'Damned right I'm not. The indolence of the English women—and their preoccupation with matters of fashion, etiquette and rank—is enough to drive a man into an early grave. Give me the dusky, exotic wenches of the East any day. It's true what they say—the East gets into your blood,' he said on a sigh of nostalgia. 'Even at home a man has to go looking for it. What the hell does a man do in London for six months?'

'Are you telling me that's a problem for you, Tom? I thought you were looking forward to your vacation.'

'I was, but it's beginning to lose its charm damned fast.'

'Then I suppose when one is obliged by society to live by society's rules, the promise of unconventional amusement offered by our host in this exotic establishment tends to give rise to the most irregular stimulation. Is that not so, Tom?'

'Absolutely. And you must agree with me, Jordan, otherwise you wouldn't be here.'

Jordan's expression remained bland, giving no indication that his reason for visiting the Crescent Moon was entirely different from that of his friend's.

Tom's lips curved into an ironic smile. 'My imaginative solution to the problem created by society would definitely not appeal to my dear mother. But unfortunately this is not the East, where my friends are aware of my pattern of living, and it would be expected of me to visit an establishment such as this in the early hours.'

Jordan laughed. 'I've always admired your standards of morality, Tom, which are wonderfully uncomplicated.'

Tom's eyes narrowed as he dragged them away from the swaying hips and coolly surveyed his friend. 'Your own, too, Jordan—at least they were,' he said meaningfully and with unusual gravity.

Jordan's smiling face had set itself into an implacable mask. It was the face that had won him many a battle or a game of chance. It was cool, self-controlled, and without a flicker of emotion, and like his face his manner gave no indication of the way he felt. 'I'd like to think they still are,' Jordan admitted. 'I'm the last man to judge another man's morals.'

'True. Those who live in glass houses should never throw stones.' Drinking deep of his wine, Tom turned his attention back to the girl. 'Dear Lord, what a beauty. Feast your eyes on that, Jordan. Look at those eyes—and that mouth. A man would give a year of his life to place his lips on that.'

'I doubt the All Mighty would ask that of you, Tom. I think you will find that a few shillings will suffice,'

Jordan drawled with mild cynicism, amused by the look of complete absorption on the other man's face as his eyes did a slow, salacious sweep of the girl. To Tom she was simply an object, her body having the requisite firm-fleshed litheness and provocative movements of a dancing-girl, her languid grace awakening all his carnal needs.

It wasn't too long ago that Jordan would have thought like that, when he thought each day might be his last. Then, he had refused to think of the women he made love to as people—it was so much easier to regard all women that way. It worked. Life is never made easier by complicating it.

Tom introduced him to his companions, who joined them at their table. Jordan began to relax, despite beginning to feel hot and having to loosen his neckcloth. In jovial spirits one of them insisted on toasting India, the Company and friendship, and as one toast followed the other, all the time one of the servants was there to re-plenish their glasses. This was not the case with Jordan, who was determined to remain alert and kept one eye fixed on the beaded curtain, scrutinising everyone who entered. He had no intention of becoming inebriated and sipped the deep-coloured liquid slowly. His glass re-mained almost full, and was topped up only once by a grinning Ali himself.

Lounging back in his chair, the voices of his compan-ions becoming somewhat distant and the haze beginning to thicken around him, he looked at the girl who had served him and was dancing among the customers in more detail. Swaying to the music, she was a living, breathing embodiment of all those voluptuous women of India, as sleek, beautiful and predatory as a cat.

Small and well-rounded and possessing an abundance

of sensuality, she was dressed in a silver choli and diaphanous, voluminous trousers, caught in round her hips by plaits of beads and at her ankles, above tiny tinkling bells, bangles and her gold sandalled feet. Becoming mesmerised by the bright jewel in her navel, which darted before him like a one-eyed firefly, Jordan tried tearing his eyes from her, but time and time again they were drawn back like metal filings to a magnet—in fact, he couldn't keep his eyes off her.

He shook his head. What the hell was the matter with him? The haze was thickening around him and voices came to him from down a long reverberating tunnel. And still the dancing-girl writhed before him, teasing and tantalising, and each time he reached for her she laughed and nimbly evaded his questing hands. Suddenly there was something strange in his sensations and indescribably new. He seemed to lose all identity and suffered pangs of dissolution. He wanted the dancing-girl—he must have her. He was unable to focus on anything else. She had become an obsession.

He was conscious of distorted sensual images running in his fancy, and an unknown freedom of the spirit and soul that delighted him like a heady wine. He hastened to partake of the pleasures flitting and dancing in front of his eyes, feeling soft hands touching his face like the fluttering wings of an exotic butterfly. He stretched out his hands to capture it, but it deftly slipped away.

As he travelled on these excursions of the mind, he was plunged into a kind of wonder at his depravity. This situation was peculiarly apart from the ordinary run of his mind. Normally he would stand aghast before the acts he was imagining committing with the dancing-girl, but his conscience slumbered.

Taking his glass, when he looked into the deep red

liquid something stirred. He must have stared at it for a full thirty seconds before sanity struggled to the fore as sudden and startling as a crash of cymbals.

The wine! The heat, the giddiness—it was drugged. It had to be. He shook his head to try and clear it, and looking up, through the haze he saw that Ali was watching him closely, his dark eyes hooded and hiding all expression. Tom's face swam before him and he heard his voice coming from somewhere far away.

'Jordan? Are you ill? What in God's name is wrong with you?'

'Get me home, Tom,' he managed to gasp, his words slurred. 'I don't care how you do it—but get me home. The—the wine—drugged.'

Tom was incredulous. 'But, how?'

'Not now, Tom—not enough time. Just get me out of here.'

Immediately Tom and his companions helped him to his feet. He reeled and lurched but they managed to get him out of the tavern, unaware of the two silent figures lurking in the shadows, disappointed that their plan to abduct Grant-sahib had failed.

It was probably a combination of the excitement of the ball, the rain whipped by the wind lashing at the window-panes, or thoughts of Jordan, that prevented Judith from sleeping. Tired of tossing and turning in the warm darkness, she climbed out of bed and padded over to the window. Pulling back the drapes, she looked out on the dark watery world. When the rain fell with so much ferocity it reminded her of the rainy season in India. She loved the fury of the storm. It never failed to touch a chord inside her.

Hearing the rumble of wheels and seeing the soft orange glow of a light suddenly appear beneath an archway of trees at the end of the short drive, she peered out, straining her eyes to try to make out what it was. On seeing the bulk of a coach and that the light was its lantern, she realised it must be Jordan returning from his club or wherever it was that gentlemen went to until the early hours. She watched two blurred and indistinct figures alight, noticing that the taller of the two was being held up by the other.

'Oh, my goodness—it looks like Jordan! He must be drunk,' she gasped in alarm, unable to think of any other explanation why he would return home in this condition. Immediately she reached for her robe, thrusting her arms into the sleeves at the same time as her feet found their way into her slippers.

But then she paused. What was she was doing? Ladies didn't go wandering about the house in their night attire, and she couldn't possibly go down at this hour and bring Jordan in off the street. Besides, it might shame and humiliate him to find he was being helped inside his own house by one of his female guests. But then, she knew he wouldn't want any of the servants to see him in this condition, or his family, and with Lady Grant having retired to bed feeling most unwell, to see her son tumbling about in a state of inebriation would only distress her and make her feel worse.

She did consider waking Jordan's valet or Edmund, but Edmund and Emily's room was on another floor at the back of the house, and his valet's room was somewhere in the attics. By the time either of them appeared Jordan could have woken the whole house.

In a state of acute indecision she glanced outside. Seeing him stumble and sink to his knees, the decision was made for her. Leaving her room, she sped noiselessly along the dark landing and down the stairs to the hall, hoping everyone had gone to sleep hours ago and wouldn't hear a thing. Opening the heavy door she stepped into the drive, glad to find there was a respite in the rain if not the wind. It took hold of her hair, whipping it about her face, and tugged at the hem of her robe. Finding its way underneath, it cheekily touched and caressed her bare legs.

She ran down the drive and confronted the two men, able to make out that the smaller and more sober of the two was staring at her in amazement.

'Captain Grant, I believe,' the man said, his eyes taking in her dishabille in one sweeping glance that seemed to penetrate through her night robe.

'I know who he is,' she said shortly, having to raise her voice above the noise of the wind. She was embarrassed that this stranger should see her in her night attire, and infuriated with Jordan for putting her in this position in the first place.

'I'm Tom Parry, friend of Captain Grant. On finding him in this unfortunate condition in an establishment I wouldn't dream of offending your delicate ears by mentioning, I thought I'd better do the sensible thing and bring him home.'

Suddenly Jordan started forward, unintelligible words tumbling from his lips. The light of the lantern showed his face drawn and ashen. He looked like a man so drunk he was about to pitch forward. Tom caught him and slung his arm about his shoulders to keep him upright.

'Oh, this is quite shocking,' Judith said in a furious whisper. 'I would have thought Jordan to be man enough to hold his liquor.'

'He can. Jordan has the capacity to consume colossal quantities of alcohol without losing an ounce of dignity.'

'Then what's wrong with him? Is he ill?'

'No. He's been drugged.'

Judith stared at Tom aghast, her fear for Jordan over-riding all else. 'Drugged? But—but—how? And why would anyone want to?'

Tom shrugged, unable to come up with an answer. But he was curious, especially since the Crescent Moon was frequented by people from the subcontinent, and one of them might hold a grudge against Jordan. But he gave away nothing of his mystification to the young woman, who was clearly so concerned about Jordan's condition that she had thrown decorum to the four winds and come rushing out in her night attire to assist.

'The only explanation I can come up with is that some-one put it in his drink. Why, I don't know. What I do know is that it took effect so quickly he was unable to tell me anything. Take it from me, Miss—?'

'Wyatt,' she replied in an aching whisper, swallowing past the awful lump that had risen in her throat. 'I'm a friend of his sister and I'm staying with the family for a few weeks.'

Tom nodded, digesting this. 'Well—in my experience it'll be useless trying to talk to him while he's in this state. He wants putting to bed to sleep it off—but he'll have one hell of a head in the morning, if you'll pardon me saying so.'

'I'll pardon anyone anything if I can get him inside and to his room without waking anyone,' Judith replied, looking at Jordan's handsome face with his hair tumbling in disarray over his brow. At that moment she had no wish to dwell on how he came to be drugged, or the sinister implications of it. Time for that later, when she had got him safely to his room.

'Would you like me to take him inside?' Tom offered.

Judith shook her head. 'Goodness, no—but thank you, anyway. His mother, Lady Grant, is unwell and would be most upset to see Jordan in this condition. I'll try and manage him. At least he's upright and seems able to walk—if a little unsteadily.'

Tom took in her slight figure, unconvinced that she'd succeed in getting him up the stairs, but he could see by the firm set of her chin that she was determined to manage. He took Jordan as far as the door, and after draping the drugged man's arm around the slender shoulders of the girl and saying goodnight, he closed the door noiselessly behind him.

On her own with Jordan, Judith knew it was going to be no easy task getting him to his room. 'Now just you help me as much as you can. And don't you dare go to sleep just yet,' she whispered, knowing as she said it that he didn't hear her.

Staggering precariously beneath his greater weight, which seemed to get heavier with every step she took and almost sent her crashing to the floor, with superhuman strength she managed to cross the hall to the stairs, where she paused, leaning against the newel post to get her breath.

Jordan stirred and looked down at the woman in white. Her image was indistinct. Through his confused, drug-clouded mind his thoughts strained for clarity, but continued to meander through fantasy. Everything struck him as odd and his brain refused to register certain things. He had a peculiar sensation of standing in the middle of a slowly turning sphere, and he could find no explanation for the girl to be there. But memory and a swaying, tantalising vision of a dancing-girl floated through the caverns of his mind like a butterfly and penetrated his torpor.

For the sake of his health he had not been the kind of

man to visit the whorehouses in the East—to slake his lusts with any female who could be bought for a few rupees. But since he had admitted this girl to his home he assumed he must have invited her, which seemed a perfectly reasonable explanation for her being there, so he accepted the situation and could see no earthly reason why they shouldn't proceed to his bedroom—which was what he must have intended in the first place.

He grinned down at the white apparition in the dim, swirling light. Her hair was a cloud of darkness, her eyes large, dark-lashed and lustrous, and he welcomed the idea of some intimate, female companionship—even though he could not place a definite image to identify the one only inches away. When he thought she was about to move away, he suddenly reached out and caught her to him like a small bird captured in a storm, placing her back against the hard balustrade with his full weight pressed against hers so that she couldn't move.

'Oh, no—my lovely dancing-girl,' he murmured, his voice slightly slurred. 'Truly you are as beautiful as a star. But—to my torment—you flit and twirl in my sight and then dance away to tease me. But enough, I say. I will not be turned away until this craving hunger still gnawing at the pit of my belly has been relieved.'

In a shivering trance, Judith stared up at him. Clearly Jordan was still not himself. His eyes had a fixed, unnatural brightness and were without expression. She knew then that although he saw her, he didn't know who she was—that she was no more to him than a pretty dancing-girl he had met somewhere earlier.

Before she could react, his mouth had swooped down and locked onto hers with a desperate urgency, parting her lips in a deep languorous kiss that took her breath. To struggle was useless, for his enveloping embrace entrapped her, and it was impossible to protest when his mouth slanted fiercely over hers.

At the back of her mind she told herself that this was only a performance, and to keep Jordan quiet she had no alternative but to participate in the performance and behave like the dancing-girl he believed she was. She could see no harm in the subterfuge if it meant getting him to his room without waking the whole house. And so she yielded to his kiss, tentatively returning it and relaxing against him. But she could smell his skin, his hair—and his presence, like a magnet, was drawing her to him and doing strange things.

Suddenly she felt a throbbing heat creeping into her body, and everything began to change. She felt as if the whole world had gone mad. His lips became more insistent, his tongue sliding and probing, his hips hard and demanding against hers.

Sensing her capitulation, Jordan's ardour increased and he kissed her with a hunger he saw no reason to control. The lips beneath his were soft, the body he clasped supple and yielding, her perfume intoxicating and unmistakably real.

Dazed by the confusing messages her body was sending to her brain, and afraid that if she didn't stop him he would make love to her there and then on the stairs, with a shaky breath and a frantic throbbing of her heart that would not be calmed, Judith placed her hands against his shoulders and exerting pressure pushed him back, but it was weak at best. Raising his head Jordan gazed down at her, his anger at being interrupted apparent. Passion had turned his face hard and intense, and Judith felt a stirring of panic when his eyes, translucent in the ghostly dark and holding a fierce glitter, moved restlessly over her inadequately clad body.

'Shush,' she breathed near his ear, placing her hand over his mouth when she thought he would say something, thinking nothing of resorting to mindless bribery in an effort to get him upstairs. 'Not here. Someone might see. We must go to your room. Help me get you upstairs, Jordan. Please. Do you understand?'

She thought he must, because he turned his head and looked up at the flight of stairs. Hauling his arm once more about her shoulders, her free hand gripping the balustrade for support, she began to stagger up the stairs, tripping over the hem of her robe halfway up, banging her shin and almost falling in the process. Physically she was quite strong, which was a good thing considering she was supporting a man twice her weight.

On reaching the top she uttered a sigh of relief. Without respite she proceeded with her burden along the landing, all the time aware of his closeness and his virile masculinity. Whether it was the promise of what they would do when they reached his room, or because somewhere in his subconscious he was concerned about disturbing his mother, Jordan seemed to sense he must accomplish his goal quickly and with the minimum of noise, and ceased to be the dead weight he'd been. Judith uttered a silent prayer of thankfulness when they passed Lady Grant's door without making a sound.

Chapter Eleven

When they entered Jordan's room and the door was
firmly closed on the world outside, Judith exhaled a profound sigh of relief. Jordan seemed to sense where he
was and immediately struggled out of his redingote and
threw it on the floor. He shook his head in an attempt to
bring some semblance of normality to his thoughts, but
nothing was as it should be. He saw the shape of the bed
and his mind and body reached out to it for sleep. But
there was still a compulsion inside him that told him to
hold on to the vision of the woman hovering in his sights,
not to let her go until he'd satisfied his burgeoning need.

The storm had passed over and the moon had risen,
casting its silvery light over the furnishings. Jordan sat
on the bed and began pulling off his shoes and unbut-
toning his waistcoat and shirt with amazing speed, and
casting them aside.

Judith watched him in trembling disquiet, mesmerised
by the uncovering of his magnificent male body, aghast
at the way her gaze caressed his shoulders and the ta-
pering, furred chest. It was lean and broad in all the right
places, strong, proud and savage. Suddenly his nakedness
embarrassed her, and when he began fumbling at the but-

tons on his trousers, the merest thought of what he was
about to uncover brought hot colour racing to her cheeks,
even in the privacy and semi-darkness of the room. That
was the moment she knew it was time to make her escape
before it was too late.

With her heart thumping in rapid beats, she began edg-
ing towards the door, but his eyes were fastened on her,
his lips smiling about his white teeth, and when she
reached out for the handle, as quick as a striking python
he was on his feet, blocking her escape. Nimbly she
bolted past him and scampered across the room, her only
thought to avoid him, but impatiently he flung himself
after the pale, darting shape of her and caught hold of
her arm, pulling her back against the hard rack of his
chest.

'Oh,' she gasped, unsuccessfully trying to wrench her
arm from his grasp.

'Ah,' he said exultantly, turning her round in his arms
and lowering his face to her hair, breathing deeply of it,
his fingers tangled in the luxuriant tresses. 'I have your
full attention now, my sweet. No more flitting about, no
more teasing. This is what it's all about—a man and a
woman—with nothing between us.'

'No,' she cried, fighting him wildly, twisting and
writhing in an attempt to gain her freedom, but his iron-
thewed arms held her fast.

'Be still,' he murmured, cupping her face in his lean
hands and brushing her lips with his own. 'Why do you
fight me? Is it because I haven't paid you? Is that it?'

'Yes,' she gasped, latching onto this in the hope he
would realise his mistake and release her.

But that was not what Jordan intended. Mindlessly
driven by a strong compulsion to have this tantalising
creature, holding onto her wrist, he fumbled in his jacket

pocket and produced a small key. With great difficulty he opened a drawer in a large armoire and removed a box. Snapping it open with one hand, he removed something and slipped it over Judith's head. Feeling a hard, cold object come to rest in the little valley between her breasts, she realised it was a pendant of some kind.

'There, that should be payment enough.' Immediately his mouth came down hard on hers once more, sending jolt after jolt of wild sensations pulsating through Judith and silencing any objections. They were standing close to the bed and Jordan pushed her back onto it. Placing his arms on either side of her like two strong pillars, he lowered his weight until he lay upon her. His dark hair tumbled over his brow, and his eyes gleamed down into hers.

Judith knew that physical resistance was useless against his unswerving passion. Feeling his hard, thrusting body pressed against hers, and knowing her own vulnerability, she seriously doubted that she could hold him off—and she was no longer sure that she had the will to resist, nor that she wanted to.

Drained of strength and beset with nerves—almost with a kind of terror, at the speed with which events were taking over—Judith felt his lips upon hers once more, moving hungrily, twisting and demanding, warming her to the very core of her being. His tongue passed between her lips to probe and taste the honeyed sweetness within with a ferocity that drew a moan from her throat, breaking her resolve and lacerating her will, causing every one of her senses to erupt in a ball of flame, arousing her to heights she couldn't yet imagine.

She knew she could not withstand his persuasive, unrelenting assault for long—and she also knew that what he was doing to her could be a prelude to other pleasures.

And why shouldn't she experience them? She confessed to herself that she wanted him so much. Why shouldn't she continue to play the dancing-girl for an hour or so? Slowly, encouraged by his mouth and his caress, the thought took root and began to grow and to blossom into something wonderful. When his lips left hers and travelled to the warm, pulsating hollow at the base of her neck, her chaste body came alive beneath his questing hands. Desire swept through her, warm and hungry, gathering force until it became a storm of passion.

The thought of what she was about to do flashed through her mind, but she rejected it quickly. And yet beneath the waves of pleasure she was aware of a faint sense of shame. This was not how she had wanted to experience her first night of passion. There had been no vows said between her and Jordan, and because she was a nobody and quite penniless there never would be. Despite the tender words he had spoken to her at the ball, she wasn't going to fool herself into believing he was going to make any undying declarations of love. She was unhappily aware that he had made love to countless other women, and that he simply needed her now because he thought she was a dancing-girl—clearly a dancing-girl he wanted desperately to possess, and in his drug-induced mind he believed she was that person.

She had always sensibly believed in the teachings of her mother and her tutors at the academy, that it was a sin for a woman to give herself to a man in carnal lust outside wedlock, and that she must learn to exercise the strictest discipline over the demands of the flesh. Indeed, her ideals had always dictated that for her there would be no frenzied coupling with a lover, that would engage body and mind but not the heart. Her self-respect demanded more. Not only must she love, but she must be

loved equally in return. She had always regarded her virginity as something infinitely precious, wanting to keep
it for her husband for their wedding night, and if there
were to be no husband then she had intended taking it
with her to her grave.

But she hadn't realised that love when it came would
be so powerful and all-consuming. She loved Jordan with
all her heart, and if she could just have this one night of
happiness to remember, to savour and memorise in the
years ahead, then surely God would forgive her this one
weakness. She realised that tomorrow the pain of what
she had done might be intolerable, but regardless of this
and what came after, tonight she wanted to belong to him
completely.

When his fingers began fumbling with the fastenings
on her robe and he tried to tear away the encumbering
garment, gently she pushed him away.

'Wait,' she whispered. 'Don't be in such a hurry.'

Kneeling up on the bed, she slipped the offending robe
off her shoulders and whipped her nightgown over her
head in one single, glorious stroke. An almost wicked
smile tempted Jordan's lips as his silver gaze followed
each of her movements. Judith felt his eyes on her—on
her breasts, on her legs, and she rejoiced in the sensation
as if it were a caress. How she would like to light the
candles, to have as much light as possible shine on her
body, her face, when he made love to her, so he would
know she was the girl he called his moonflower and remember. But she couldn't do that. Best to let him go on
believing she was the dancing-girl.

Her senses reeling and lifted by a love that was
stronger than modesty or reason, proud and unashamed,
believing she was in control, she leaned over and kissed
his mouth, slipping her arms about his neck and letting

her hands caress the hard, smooth, rippling muscles of his back, but Jordan took control away from her. Bending his head, he flicked the tip of his tongue over the hard, rosy peaks of her firm breasts, letting it wander with tantalising slowness over her flat stomach, before tipping her back onto the bed to explore in detail the more intimate secrets of her body. He did so possessively, with the sureness and expertise of a knowledgeable lover, deliberately and slowly rousing her to dizzying heights.

There was a moment when Judith thought she heard a sound—a low, creaking sound of a door being pushed open or of someone treading on a loose floorboard. She listened for a moment, but when Jordan raised himself above her and caught her mouth in another drugging kiss, she could not deny the hot, sweeping excitement that gripped her, the throbbing need that was building and growing with such intensity she thought she would die of it. Reality no longer mattered as her mind ceased to function and her body became soft and pliant, taking on a will of its own.

Unable to resist any longer the erotic demands, the heat, the pressure of him, when he moved between her trembling thighs, no longer able to retreat from the course she had set herself, she opened them willingly and allowed the boldness of his rigid manhood to enter and fill her aching void. In that one irretrievable moment, when the pain of her shattered maidenhead had subsided and been replaced by something new, something infinitely wonderful, when she began to move as he moved and answered his demanding, thrusting hips, that steadily increased in power and force, in joy and a beauty that became unbearable, driving her to a terrifying precipice, Judith knew what it meant to become as one with another human being.

Jordan took her in a wild, ravenous passion, curving his hands around her hips and forcing her into a tempo to match his own. Wild spasms drove his fullness higher and deeper within her, their bodies moulded together, as he slaked himself with her like a man offered water after a prolonged thirst. Her arms and body welcomed him, and she arched to meet him, with her head thrown back and her hair a stream of tangled silk. With his name on her lips she allowed herself to be possessed, clasping him and caressing him, abandoning her body with all her heart and soul and a hurricane of love.

It was near dawn when Jordan rolled away from her and fell into a deep sleep. As sanity slowly began to return, summoning the remains of her energy, Judith left her lover's lair and quickly donned her nightgown and robe, her skin still throbbing and tender from his caresses.

There was something almost childlike about his naked, masculine frame outspread across the turbulent bed, his tousled head almost buried amongst the pillows. The bed was huge, but when he was lying down it looked too small to hold him. He was truly magnificent and she felt a great, aching love for him. Bending over, she softly placed a kiss on his brow.

'I love you,' she breathed, letting her eyes linger on his profile for one blissful moment, before she slipped silently from the room and down the landing to her own.

Like Judith, Alicia had been unable to sleep. In the small hours she heard a sound and went to investigate. Seeing no one, she realised Jordan must have come home and had gone to his room. She paused outside his door when she heard a voice. It was the voice of a woman. Unable to stifle her curiosity, softly she opened the door. Apart from the moonlight the room was in darkness.

Straining her eyes she saw the naked bodies of a man and woman entwined on the bed making love. The woman's sighs and groans of pleasure reverberated in her ears. It was Judith, she knew it. As she watched the shameless pair she was consumed with a primitive desire to kill—to be avenged.

The slut! The bitch!

Silently she stepped back. Closing the door, she returned to her room, her only conscious thought being that one day she would be avenged. She had no idea how long it would take, where or how. That didn't matter. All that mattered was that one day she would take her revenge on Judith Wyatt and make her wish she'd never accepted Lady Grant's offer to spend the summer at Landsdowne.

When the dawn was beginning to lighten the sky and the house was stirring to life, Judith perched on the window seat with her knees drawn up to her chin and hugged her secret to her. Was it possible to feel such happiness, such elation shimmering inside? Daydreaming, she went over in her mind the splendour of Jordan's lovemaking, unable to believe it had happened, but it had—her body, still pulsating from his caresses, gave evidence to that. When she'd returned to her room and looked at her face in the mirror, she had wondered if she would see a difference. There was a sparkle in her eyes and a gentle flush on her cheeks, and her expression was one of perfect tranquillity, but otherwise she looked the same.

The fact that her future could not be shaped and shared with the man who had wakened her body to divine, sweet torment, that her happiness wasn't destined to last, didn't seem to matter just then. It wasn't until the door opened and someone entered her room that she was forced to face the enormity of what she had done.

Turning her head she expected to see one of the maids or Charlotte—although she would be most surprised to see her friend up and about at this hour, in fact, she would be surprised if Charlotte surfaced before midday following her exertions at the ball. She saw Alicia with her back pressed against the closed door, a sneer on her lips and a cruel gleam in her green eyes. Never had she looked so vicious. Judith felt the colour drain from her cheeks, but she managed to control the shaft of dislike that twisted through her at the sight of her. In no mood for a confrontation, she stood up, sensing that the other woman's presence boded nothing but ill.

'What do you want, Alicia? What are you doing in my room at this hour?'

Alicia stood with her hands on her hips, eyes slightly narrowed, surveying her rival's pale face and taking in her unbound hair, which tumbled about her shoulders in a luxuriant mass. 'I've come to salute you. You're a cunning one and no mistake. You certainly know how to worm your way into a man's arms—and his bed.'

Judith stared at her in blank astonishment, taken off guard by her accusation. In alarm she made a great effort to steady herself. 'How—how did you…?' Suddenly she remembered the sound she had heard when Jordan had been making love to her. All the years of schooling her features into a polite mask were forgotten. The disgust she was feeling showed clearly on her face. 'So—that was you—the sound I heard. Snooping, were you, Alicia?'

'You slut,' she hissed, moving forward, her pretty face disfigured by anger and spite. 'You miserable little tramp. I could strangle you with my bare hands. I know your sort. I knew what you were the moment I set eyes on you—a scheming, jumped-up nobody who came to believe you could suddenly better yourself. You couldn't keep away from him, could you? What a proper little snake in the grass you've turned out to be.'

'It wasn't like that.'

Alicia smiled a thin smile. 'Wasn't it? I know what I saw. I saw you. It appeared to me that you were submitting with the greatest enthusiasm.'

Judith lifted her chin. Alicia believed she had her exactly where she wanted her. She expected her to cringe and cower. Judith looked at her coldly, showing not the least sign of shame for what she had done as she attempted to explain a little of what happened. Not that she felt she should—especially not to Alicia, but it would not go amiss for her to know the condition Jordan was in when he'd arrived home.

'I was still awake when Jordan came home. When I looked out of my window I saw he was with an acquaintance, who was holding him up. Seeing him lurching and staggering, the general impression I got was of an inebriate rolling home from the tavern, so I went downstairs to help him inside. I was afraid he would wake the whole house, you see.'

'How considerate. And he wasn't drunk?'

'No. Through no fault of his own he had been drugged. When his acquaintance left, my only thought was to save him from embarrassment, and to get him to his room without waking Lady Grant. As you know, she wasn't feeling at all well after the ball, and I had no wish to add to her distress by letting her see Jordan in that condition. I swear that what happened was not what I intended to happen. I only wanted to get him to his room without disturbing anyone.'

'You succeeded admirably,' Alicia sneered.

'I know how you feel about Jordan, Alicia, but no matter what you think I did not do it to spite you.'

'I don't believe you.'

'You are entitled to believe what you like. I never thought—never dreamt—Jordan would lay a finger on me in that way. But—he is strong—and very persuasive.'

'Are you saying he forced himself on you?'

'He didn't rape me, if that's what you mean.'

Alicia arched her brows. 'Rape! That's such an unpleasant word to hear from you, Judith. Gently bred ladies would know not to use it,' she jeered.

'Normally I am the very model of respectability and it is not a remark I would make to just anyone,' Judith replied, in no way defensive. 'But I am sure you don't need me to explain its full meaning.'

Refusing to play the part of a broken victim, Judith considered the word and what it meant. Jordan had not taken her by force—he didn't have to. Her only reservation lay in the fact that his thoughts had not been of love, but of a primeval fulfilment—the desires of the flesh. To him their coupling had meant nothing more than the mating act. When he awoke he wouldn't remember any of it, and it was for this reason that he must never know she had shared his bed for that brief time, even though her whole being hungered to repeat their turbulent consummation.

'What I am saying is that I couldn't get away from him—and I confess,' she said softly, 'that after a while—I had no desire to. But if it makes you feel any better, Alicia, being under the influence of a narcotic, he didn't know who I was. When he wakes he won't even remember what happened—and if he does, I promise you he won't remember who shared his bed.'

Alicia's eyes narrowed, and for one exquisite moment she began to fondle her dreams of revenge. What was to prevent her using the situation to her advantage? Only Judith would know, and she would have to live with it for the rest of her life.

'I don't think we have anything further to say. I think you'd better leave, Alicia.'

'With pleasure. And I think you'd better start packing. After this I imagine the whole family will be outraged by your unacceptable conduct. I can't see Lady Grant wanting you to remain in her house. It's hardly the way to repay her hospitality.'

'If you have one iota of consideration for Lady Grant, Alicia, you will not tell her,' Judith snapped. 'There is no need.'

Alicia looked at her, her eyes steady. 'What are you saying?'

'That I have no intention of confronting Jordan with any of this. Regardless of what you may think of me, I am not a fool. Socially I am beneath him, and the last thing I want is for him to feel that he is obliged to marry me—that I have tricked him into it. There would be a terrible scandal.'

'Jordan is a natural survivor. He'll live it down.'

Judith shook her head. 'I don't want him to know— he must never know.'

She sounded as if she meant it, and Alicia was certainly not going to argue about it.

'I told you,' Judith continued, 'he won't remember any of it so what's the point? It would serve no purpose. I will bear the burden of what happened between us. Do you understand what I'm saying, Alicia?'

In answer, Alicia's mouth settled in a thin line and she

looked at her scornfully. 'Oh, yes. I understand more than you realise.'

'What do you mean?'

'That I am quite prepared to follow your example. Don't worry,' she said, and with a haughty toss of her head she turned and strode back to the door. 'Your oh-so-sordid little secret is safe with me.'

When Alicia had marched from the room in a swirl of white lace, Judith finally allowed her defences to crumble. Engulfed in a well of misery and loneliness, she sank onto the bed, her shoulders slumped, her euphoria of the moments before Alicia had come in shreds. There raged within her the full realisation of what she had done, and there was no way she could deny the dreadful truth. Last night she had been completely irrational, and it was equally obvious that she'd let emotion drive her to do something that was incredibly impulsive. In one desperate moment to share Jordan's love, she had sacrificed her virtue, her morals and her principles, and it left her with a mass of shame.

As brief as it had been, it was over. She would return to the academy and pick up her life and pretend last night had never happened. But she would never forget.

A sob rose in her throat, and for the first time in four years she felt despair fill her soul completely. She felt emotionally drained and afraid. With tears streaming down her cheeks she covered her face with her hands and wept out her misery, which seemed to have no end. She was branded by Jordan, and she would ache with love for him every waking hour. But she would have to leave Landsdowne. Her actions had left her with no choice. The decision was hers to make, and she had made it the moment she had let him make love to her. Besides, she had no way of knowing how he felt about her, except that he had implied he enjoyed being with her, and their Indian backgrounds gave them much in common.

Unconsciously her hand rose to fondle the necklace he had placed round her neck as payment for her services. He had believed her to be a whore, and never had a whore made love to her client as willingly as she had.

She raised the pendant and looked at it closely for the first time. She knew very little about jewels or their worth, but even her inexpert eye could see it was a magnificent design. It was of a rare beauty. There was a huge central diamond, roughly cut with a yellow glow in its depths, and smaller diamonds and rubies were set around it. The gold mounting and chain alone would be of great value.

It was certain that Jordan would miss it and search for it, but would he remember giving it to his companion of the night? She didn't think so. Still, she couldn't return it to him otherwise he would demand she tell him how it came to be in her possession. It looked extremely valuable, and she decided it would be safer kept around her neck than concealed in a drawer, until she could make up her mind what to do with it.

Her eyes alight with concentration, her mind coldly calculating, formulating and deciding, Alicia left Judith's room and went directly to Jordan's. She pushed the door open quietly. Naked and lying on his stomach, he was stretched out across the bed, his head buried in the pillows, fast asleep.

Feasting her eyes on the absolute perfection of his masculine body, she felt something warm kindle in the pit of her stomach. She had no doubt whatsoever that being made love to by Jordan would be a far different matter from the adolescent fumblings and pawings of

Philip Mason. Philip was her father's steward, whom she had taken as her lover for just one short week last summer when boredom had set in, as it often did when she was forced to spend any length of time in the country. The affair had meant nothing to her and they had been very discreet, for if her father ever found out about it he would take a shotgun to his steward.

Closing the door, she padded across the carpet, her eyes taking note of the rust-coloured stains on the sheets. Her smile was one of pure malice. Judith didn't know it but she had done her a favour. The evidence that intercourse had taken place would explain away the fact that she was no longer a virgin, which was something she had always known she would find difficult to explain to her husband on their wedding night. When Jordan awoke and found her lying beside him, he would believe the entire responsibility for her first intimate encounter with a man was solely and exclusively his.

Stripping off her robe, she lay down beside his inert body, nestling close, feeling immensely smug and pleased with herself. Getting Jordan to the brink of matrimony had been a lengthy process, but she was certain it would be well worth the wait.

Chapter Twelve

Wandering in and out through the depths of sleep, something formless and as black as the hounds from hell was sitting on Jordan's head and preventing him from moving. It was mid-morning when it lifted and he floated out of a flickering, golden haze comprised of bright sunlight and fragments of memories. Completely disoriented, he lay without moving, watching the play of light on the floor, pain stabbing through the sockets of his eyes and embedded in his brain. He tried to lift his head, but there was a regiment of soldiers at full charge at work inside his skull.

Closing his eyes, he tried to remember the events of the night before that had made him lose all contact with reality. He recalled what happened at the ball, going to the Crescent Moon and his meeting with Tom Parry and his companions, but he couldn't remember anything after that. There had been an exceedingly pretty dancing-girl, but her face was a blur to him now. He tried to remember more of the details, but the tableau etched inside his brain was a blurred, ominous vignette.

He forced himself to concentrate on a certain face—Judith's face, when she had been in his arms, gazing up at him as they danced. He focused on that one special thing, tracing every detail of her delicate features, feeling the throbbing on the perimeter of his mind begin to lessen—to become bearable. It was a technique he'd used frequently in the past, a technique that had been as successful then as it was now.

But there was something else, something far more important that he had to resurrect. He lay there trying to bring to mind the memory, which was competing with the regiment when it began pounding once more. Opening his eyes he saw the clothes he had worn for the ball strewn on the carpet, but something was amiss. One of the garments was white and gossamer thin. He stared at it for what seemed like an eternity, slowly becoming aware of a warm body pressed to his back. More sharply than he intended, he raised his head. It began swirling dizzily and he put a hand on the top, since there was every possibility it might explode.

Rolling onto his side, he leaned on one elbow and stared at the naked woman lying beside him. A cloud of auburn hair was spread out on the pillow, and the face was indisputably one he recognised. Reality struck him with enough force to set off a further explosion of pain in his head.

'Good God! Alicia!'

Her eyes fluttered open and she smiled up at him, stretching languorously like a cat in the sun, unashamed by her nakedness. 'Good morning, my love,' she crooned, trailing a finger over the crisp mat of hair on his chest and over his brown, muscular shoulder. She yawned behind one slender white hand and snuggled into him, placing her lips in the warm hollow of his throat. 'Mm. You were wonderful last night, Jordan. I'm already looking forward to a repeat performance.'

Jordan was incredulous. He couldn't figure it out. He couldn't accept that he'd spent the night with Alicia and was unable to remember their animal coupling in the dark—empty of tenderness or joy—and nor did it do anything for his masculine vanity.

'Alicia,' he repeated sharply, once he'd recovered from the initial shock. 'Kindly explain what happened.'

She bent her head back and looked up at his thunderous countenance, pouting her soft lips, making a pretence of being hurt. 'Really, Jordan! If I had any hope that you might be pleased to see I am still here, your tone of voice would have taught me otherwise.'

'That is beside the point. I wake up and find you in my bed—without being aware how you got here—and you are surprised when I ask you to explain?'

'Do you not remember? Cast your mind back.'

Jordan tried, but all he could conjure up were misshapen images of an enchanting creature—part angel, part spirit—who had writhed beneath him and made his blood stir hotly. The image did not fit the woman lying beside him. He froze at the mere thought of having made love to Alicia, and the abjection and passion of the attachment.

Pushing her away, he swung his long legs over the edge of the bed and pulled on his trousers, feeling less at a disadvantage with his clothes on. 'I would be grateful if you would refresh my memory of the entire night. I don't mind admitting that it is extremely hazy and I really cannot recall a damned thing,' he gritted furiously. 'Did you come to my room of your own accord?'

'Why,' she cried, his words bringing her to her knees on the bed. 'I would never enter a gentleman's bedroom uninvited. How can you think that, Jordan?'

'Then what the hell are you doing here?'

'I—I heard you come home—very late—but I didn't know it was you at the time. I left my room to investigate—and you were in the hall—shockingly in your cups, I might add. In fact, I had to help you up the stairs to your room.' She smiled softly. 'That was when you became extremely amorous and one thing led to another and—well—I'm still here.'

'Don't look like that, Alicia,' Jordan snapped when he saw her simpering smile and the enticement in her look, his tone carrying anger and frustration. 'I have no intention of ravishing you again—if that's what did happen. It's precipitated an infernal mess, and I'm not about to repeat it.'

Jordan gave her a hard look, his mouth tightening as he stared down at her, at the pink mouth and long-lashed green eyes. He found it strange that he got no pleasure in perusing her naked form, that she no longer had the power to attract him—the only emotion she was capable of rousing in him now being revulsion. She might look soft and fragile, but he was beginning to suspect she was as strong as steel inside. He felt disgusted with himself— and with Alicia, for allowing it to happen.

Running an impatient hand through his dark hair, he turned away, rubbing his brow, when a moment of flame and vision rushed over him, and for one single second he was of clear sight. He saw Ali Shah, and the knowledge that he had been drugged by some act of evil at the Crescent Moon crashed through his mind like the report of a cannon.

'Jordan—I hope you remember our conversation—our agreement.'

With an awful sense of foreboding and dread in his heart, Jordan growled, 'I don't. Remind me.'

'Why—you said we would be married.'

'Then I am more of a fool than I thought.'

'But—you must. You cannot refuse—you will not. If I've learned one thing about you since we became acquainted, it is the fact that you are a gentleman, and gentlemen do not renege on their word.'

'Thank you for your trust, Alicia. I shall try and take heart from it,' he replied with dry sarcasm, which Alicia prudently ignored.

'You have compromised me and now my reputation is completely ruined. How do you think it will look—cohabiting in your bedroom while your mother is sleeping almost next door?'

'Leave my mother out of this.'

'You can't possibly expect me to weather the scandal alone.'

His dagger gaze pinned her to the bed. 'Why? Is there to be one?' He took a deep breath, trying to stay calm.

'I sincerely hope not. You made love to me, Jordan. You—you were the first.' She lowered her eyes at that blatant falsehood, lest he should see it.

Jordan's patience snapped. 'Blast it, Alicia, stop badgering me. Have you nothing to say about your sordid affair with your father's steward—Philip Mason, I believe his name was?' he reminded her brutally, speaking sarcastically, with a kind of cold contempt in his voice. 'Bearing that in mind, it seems to me incredible that you accuse me of robbing you of your virginity.'

Alicia paled. How could he possibly know about Philip? 'I—I don't deny that Philip and I were close— for just a short time—but we were never lovers,' she lied. 'I would never stoop so low as to let one of my father's employees do what you did to me.'

'Don't feign innocence with me, Alicia. You know as well as I do that it's true.'

'Then what of this? You can see by the evidence that I speak the truth,' she said, her eyes burning with green fire as she indicated the small bloodstains on the white sheets. A silence fell between them, and with a surge of triumph Alicia realised she had hit her target. She saw Jordan blanch, and when he lifted his gaze from those tell-tale marks, his eyes were watching her with an expression that was at last attentive.

Jordan had been convinced that Alicia had disposed of her virginity long before he returned from India, and he had a peculiar, humiliating feeling that somehow she had cunningly forced his hand. But he could not call her a liar when the evidence of their mating was emblazoned on the sheets.

Alicia watched him closely. His profile was harsh and forbidding. She knew he was thinking madly of some means of escape from marrying her, and she also knew that behind that taut façade boiled a terrible, violent rage. But she had no intention of letting him off the hook.

'Oh, Jordan,' she sighed. 'Why—last night you were so enthusiastic about being a bridegroom.'

'I don't remember,' he growled, gritting his teeth in frustration. 'Now—I think you should leave. Get dressed and return to your room before my valet or one of the servants comes in.' He turned away as she slipped her clothes on, but he didn't miss the flare of temper in her eyes, or the fright that he might not comply. 'You must forgive me, Alicia, but I have much to think about,' he said curtly. 'We'll discuss this later.'

Alicia shrank beneath the icy gaze he levelled at her, but she persevered nonetheless. 'You mean you want to wait for the ceremony to take place?'

The thought of being joined in holy wedlock to Alicia was one that froze Jordan to the marrow. 'I have no wish for the ceremony to take place at all—ever—but it seems I am left with no alternative.'

Jordan watched her go, shaking his head to clear his senses as a multitude of emotions marched to war within him—confusion, anger—and a bitter regret that his actions, through no fault of his own, had brought about this intolerable situation. He was unable to deny what he had done—and then again, because he couldn't remember, he was unable to admit it. But the proof on the sheets was damning.

Dear Lord! he exclaimed silently, bowing his head and massaging his temples, which were beginning to ache. Why couldn't he recall what had happened? There was a vague memory of making love, and a smiling face, and a great wave of feeling surged through him as he began to remember dimly that the woman writhing beneath him—so soft and warm and smelling of roses, had not been of the common kind. He tried to focus on her face, but it shifted like a thing in a mist, and his reason wavered. But it did not fail him utterly, for again his memory was beginning to stir among deep layers of cloud, and he was following his companion of the night down a sensuous path in his mind.

He had an inability to distinguish between Alicia and the passionate woman he had made love to. However, if she answered his passion with such zeal and unforgettable pleasure if he made her his wife, then perhaps marriage to her would have its compensations, he thought bitterly.

His feelings were nebulous, chaotic, and much as he would like to avoid doing so, he knew he must give some thought to the problem that faced him. Already he could feel the noose of matrimony tightening around his neck—a noose he would gladly have placed there himself if he

were marrying the woman of his choice: Judith. He recalled how happy she had looked at the ball in the dress
he had bought her, and the memory pierced his heart.

He clenched his fists, fury sweeping through him like
a whirlwind that he was being pushed into a marriage he
had no stomach for. He was caught in a trap, knowing
full well that Alicia would make it known what they had
done—out of spite, if nothing else—should he turn his
back on her. The scandal that would ensue would destroy
his mother, and he would not allow that to happen. Besides, if, as Alicia claimed, she had shared his bed, then
it was not beyond the bounds of possibility that a child
could result from the union.

Already resigning himself to his fate, he turned when
his valet entered and ordered the man to bring coffee and
prepare a bath. Even though his heart was still full of
rage, it was steadier and more resolute.

On edge about her first meeting with Jordan, with careful grooming, Judith dallied over her toilet as long as
possible. She would have preferred to stay in her room
until the following day, but her absence would be commented upon and someone was bound to come looking
for her. When she was ready she went in search of
Charlotte.

But she need not have worried about encountering
Jordan. When they entered the drawing-room they found
Lady Grant, who was feeling much better, seated on the
chaise-longue reading. Raising her head, she smiled and
informed them that Jordan was out and Alicia was still
sleeping off the effects of the ball. She also told them
that they would be leaving for Landsdowne within the
next hour or so. Jordan would not be accompanying

them. He was to remain in town with Alicia, Edmund and Emily.

When they drove away from town, it seemed that Judith's heart would break, but she was stubbornly determined to get through that day and the next. She refused to cry. She would go on. She would survive. Time would help, but she did not believe then that it would heal.

On their arrival at Landsdowne, Judith was surprised to find a letter waiting for her from her Aunt Cynthia. Her aunt had written to inform her that she had come back from the Continent early due to ill-health, and Judith could travel down to Brighton if she so wished. Judith was surprised that her aunt had taken the trouble to write, but she was glad she had—even though she suspected Aunt Cynthia had an ulterior motive: that she wanted someone to look after her. Just when she felt as if there was no way to save herself from drowning, she had been thrown a lifeline, and she was determined to grasp it.

She would hate leaving Landsdowne, but it would solve her immediate problem. In the light of what had transpired between herself and Jordan, she didn't dare stay, not close to him, in the same house. She had considered returning to the academy, but she knew Lady Grant and Charlotte would think this strange following her enthusiasm to spend the summer away from it.

Understanding Judith's concern for her aunt, Lady Grant accepted her decision to go to Brighton, but Charlotte was less than happy. Her face fell as Judith explained that she was leaving.

'You can't go to Brighton, Judith.'

'I think I must, Charlotte. If Aunt Cynthia is unwell then I have a duty to go and see her. When I return to the academy there's no telling when I'll be able to go down. Besides, there are some things I want to bring back with me—clothes and a few books I'm going to need.'

'But you haven't had a chance to get to know Jordan properly,' she argued.

'I think I know him as well as I am ever likely to,' Judith replied softly. 'He did ask me to dance at the ball—twice, in fact. And he bought me that lovely dress. I have much to be grateful for.'

Judith sounded faintly regretful, which was not lost on Charlotte. She gave a sigh of exasperation. 'Oh—he really can be extremely vexing at times. Why on earth he had to remain in town escorting Alicia here and there baffles me. Anyone can see he doesn't care about her in any romantic sense. Can't you stay at Landsdowne for another week or two?' she pleaded. 'That will still leave you with enough time to visit your aunt before you have to go back to the academy.'

'No, Charlotte. I'm sorry, but I would like to leave within the next few days.' Seeing Charlotte's look of despondency, she smiled reassuringly. 'Don't worry. When I return to London I'll come and visit you at the earliest opportunity. I promise.'

'Oh, very well. If you insist then I suppose you must go. But life will be extremely dull without you.'

'You won't feel so deprived when the others return from town.'

'No—I suppose you're right.' Suddenly Charlotte smiled and took Judith's hand affectionately, then frowned, concern showing in her eyes. 'There I go again—thinking of myself as usual. You are right to go to Brighton, Judith. Truly you have not looked yourself since the ball. You are quite pale. Perhaps some sea air will not come amiss.'

'I'm fine, Charlotte—really, so you must banish all fear for my health. Don't fuss.'

Charlotte was not convinced and she gave her an inquiring look. 'Did something happen on the night of the ball you haven't told me?'

Uneasy under the unwavering gaze, smiling broadly in an attempt to allay Charlotte's concern, Judith said, 'Something did happen. I had a wonderful evening. I enjoyed it so much and met so many nice people. Everyone was very kind.'

'That wasn't what I meant. It's just that you seem—well—different, somehow. You would tell me, wouldn't you, if something was wrong?'

'Of course I would,' Judith replied, wishing she could unburden herself and certain she would find a willing listener in Charlotte. But it was a knowledge she could not share with anyone. Why, the whole of London would ridicule her if they knew what she had done—and that she had thought she could make a man of Jordan Grant's standing love her.

After four days, Jordan and the rest of his party arrived at Landsdowne. During the time Jordan had spent in town he'd returned to the Crescent Moon—not only to question Ali Shah, but also to try to recall something of what had happened to him that night—all to no avail. The tavern-keeper was nowhere to be found. He had even gone to the home of Tom Parry, but his mother, a flamboyant lady who adored her only son, had informed him that Tom was out of town for a few days visiting friends.

It was mid-afternoon and Judith was reading in the library. She waited fifteen minutes before putting her book down and going to join the family in the drawing-room, where everyone seemed to be in good spirits.

Unobserved, she stood in the doorway, a small, isolated figure clutching a hand over her pounding heart as her eyes were drawn to the man she had not laid eyes on since she had left his bedroom.

He stood in front of the hearth facing the room, with one arm casually draped across the mantelpiece, his gleaming booted foot resting on the hearth, his long legs encased in superbly tailored fawn trousers. The lean, hard planes of his cheeks looked harsh and forbidding, his jaw set and rigid. Her pulses quickened and her cheeks grew warm, for she could still see the sprawl of long, powerful limbs, and the tumble of dark hair against the white sheets.

The growing ache in Judith's heart attested to the degree of her love. Seeing Jordan in the luxurious splendour of the drawing-room, so very much at home and every inch a gentleman of wealth and quality, never had he looked as handsome—or as unattainable, to Judith as he did just then. And to make matters worse a positively glowing Alicia, dressed in a gown of shimmering gold silk, was clinging to his side. In an attempt to calm her nervousness, she let out a slow, steadying breath and went in, bringing Jordan's eyes to focus on her. His face was a pleasantly smiling mask that hid all thoughts.

Edmund immediately got up from where he was sitting beside a smiling Emily and went to the sideboard, where he poured some wine into a crystal glass. Judith accepted it with a little smile. Assuming it to be champagne, her mind began to register that something was happening she knew nothing about. Cold fingers of apprehension traced her spine.

'It's a little early in the day to be drinking champagne, isn't it, Edmund?'

'It's for a toast,' he explained, putting on his most

engaging smile. Arching a brow at his brother he touched the rim of his glass to hers.

When his mother had returned to Landsdowne after the ball—on Jordan's instructions taking Charlotte and Judith with her, Edmund had been concerned and puzzled by his brother's condition and his behaviour. Having no knowledge of what had happened to Jordan when he'd left them to keep an engagement after the ball, when he'd seen him the following morning, his face so deeply etched with lines of strain and fatigue, it had struck genuine alarm in Edmund. In fact, his brother had looked like hell.

Like everyone else, over the weeks since his supremely self-confident, invulnerable older brother had arrived from India, Edmund had quietly watched a closeness develop between him and the hazel-eyed girl from Miss Powell's academy, so he had been both surprised and puzzled when he had dispassionately told him that he was to marry Alicia. Considering it wise not to involve himself in Jordan's personal life, he had not queried his reasons, but he sensed that this young woman, who was looking at him with wide-eyed apprehension, was about to be battered by the announcement.

'What's the occasion?' Judith asked, looking directly at Jordan. An expression she couldn't recognise flickered across his face, and his silver eyes seemed extremely bright beneath his dark brows, but there was no smile, no word of affection. Perhaps he felt nothing for her after all, she thought bleakly. He looked at her coolly and inclined his head slightly.

'Judith! I trust you are well?'

Thrown off her balance by his cold, almost ceremonious tone, with a painful effort to dominate her disappointment she managed to say, 'Perfectly. I hope you all had an enjoyable few days in town.'

'Oh, absolutely,' Alicia enthused. 'Why, we've hardly had time to pause for breath, have we Jordan?—what with a visit to the opera—and last night there was a lavish party at Sir Matthew Joseph's house in Grosvenor Square.'

As Alicia continued to prattle on, Judith looked at Jordan again. All of a sudden she wanted to cry. She couldn't understand it. Could this cold, polite stranger be the same man who had danced and spoken so light-heartedly to her at the ball, who had made love to her with such tender passion in the dark, secret hours of the night?

'Jordan and Alicia have some good news to impart,' Emily said.

'Oh?'

'Jordan and I are to be married,' Alicia burst out, unable to contain herself any longer.

Judith stared. The pronouncement was beyond her worst imaginings. Alicia's green eyes gleamed tauntingly, glorying in her victory. Her lovely features were transfigured with joy at flinging the announcement in the face of her hated rival, but to the others listening it seemed no more than the exuberance one would expect from a bride to be.

When Judith caught Alicia's stare and saw her green eyes gleaming with triumph and malice, she thought she was going to be sick. So, this was Jordan's destiny! Glancing up at him she saw that his dark, hard-featured face showed little pleasure. That wretched woman had done her utmost to snare him, and she had succeeded— and Judith had an awful suspicion that this situation had come about because of the night she herself had spent in his bed.

Shock drained away what colour she had as she realised how complete her humiliation was, and that her own position was irredeemable. Suddenly she didn't want to be there, and in a state of suspended anguish she secretly began counting the minutes until she could politely excuse herself from this family gathering and end her ordeal. Displaying a calm she didn't feel and managing to bring a smile to her lips, she said, 'Congratulations. When is the happy event to be?' She knew it was a mundane, inadequate thing to say, but she had to say something and there was nothing else she wanted to say.

'Of course it isn't official yet—and when it's formally announced, I know all the ladies in London will envy me. Jordan has to speak to father—but that is only a formality, of course. The wedding will take place as soon as it can be arranged. Jordan doesn't want to wait,' Alicia said, linking her arm possessively through the prospective bridegroom's and looking up at him adoringly. 'That is so, isn't it, Jordan? So, Judith, what do you say to that?'

The tone, haughty and lightly contemptuous, made Judith's hackles rise. A slight surge of anger momentarily diverted her thoughts from her own shock, grief and bitter hurt, which helped her to regain her self-command. 'What can I say?—except that I hope you will both be very happy.'

Excusing herself, she went across the room and sat beside Charlotte, who was not looking at all pleased about the situation. Setting her untouched glass of champagne carefully on the small table beside her, Judith refused to let anyone see how Jordan's presence or the unexpected announcement affected her. She looked down at her lap, for she could feel Jordan's scorching gaze on her, and she could only control her feelings as long as she didn't look into his eyes.

'It's hardly a love match,' Charlotte whispered to Judith when the others began conversing among themselves. 'Jordan looks more like a man going to his execution than his wedding. He doesn't want this engagement, I can tell. I'd like to know what Alicia's done to coax him into it. And no matter how brave a face mother is putting on, she looks quite despondent. In fact, she looks as if she's about to dissolve into tears at any minute. Alicia is not right for Jordan and mother knows it. So does Edmund,' she said, looking to where he sat on the sofa beside his wife. 'He doesn't look overjoyed, either.'

Judith smiled, agreeing with Charlotte, but she wouldn't dream of saying so. 'Love matches are rare in the society-conscious world of the *haute ton*, Charlotte. Why—who knows? They might deal well together,' she replied quietly. 'They may not be much alike, but many couples start married life together with less in common than Alicia and your brother.'

'Less? They have absolutely nothing in common at all, Judith, as well you know,' Charlotte whispered fiercely. 'But I love Jordan so much that I'm not going to make any unwelcome comments. I just hope he knows what he's doing and comes to his senses before it's too late.'

Me too! thought Judith sadly.

'And what are you young ladies whispering about?' Edmund asked, looking around to where they sat, and getting up to help himself to another glass of champagne.

Judith glanced towards him and smiled, managing a look of innocent confusion. 'Why—Charlotte was just wondering if she is to be a bridal attendant—is that not so, Charlotte?' she said, observing Charlotte's indignant features with a look of glowing amusement.

Charlotte glared at her. 'I suppose it has crossed my mind,' she replied stiffly.

'Of course you will be my attendant,' Alicia told her in a rush. 'It would be such a blessing to me.'

'And you, Judith! I'm sure Alicia would simply love to have you, too,' Charlotte quipped mischievously, determined to get her own back on her friend.

Judith was amused that Charlotte's suggestion seemed to throw that ambitious creature across the room into a frenzy. She relieved the situation at once by saying imperturbably, 'Then I would have to decline, naturally.'

'Naturally,' Alicia agreed icily.

Judith was relieved that she wouldn't have to become involved in the complications and details of Jordan's wedding. 'I'm sure Alicia will have bridesmaids enough without me. Besides, that is simply not possible anyway, and you know it, Charlotte.'

'Oh? And why is that, pray?' her friend asked.

'I won't be here.'

Jordan's head jerked in her direction, all his attention riveted on her. 'You won't?'

'Sadly, Judith is to leave us,' Lady Grant explained.

Surprise flickered over Jordan's handsome face. Judith watched his tall figure disengage itself from Alicia's side and stride towards her. He stopped, looking down at her face, tipped back to meet his gaze. The sun slanting through the windows shone on her lavender dress and gleamed in the attractive arrangement of glossy curls about her head. Her eyes were wide and clear and watching him calmly, darker and more lustrous than he remembered, her skin more golden, softer. He didn't know whether to set the changes down to fault of memory or the days that had passed without seeing her.

Something stirred in his mind, something frail and elusive, but it was trapped beyond his recall. She seemed tense, he thought, as if keeping her emotions under control only by the greatest effort. To him, at that moment, her character was both strong and desperately vulnerable. She seemed young, a girl, almost, and yet it was a woman who was looking at him, with a woman's eyes—as if she concealed a secret. A chill settled deep in his bones, and he didn't know the reason for it. He thought he knew her, knew all he needed to know about her, so what could have happened to bring about this transformation?

He had an unbelievable longing to take her hand and pull her to her feet, to feel her body pressed close to his— and he had the absurd idea that he knew exactly how it would feel if he were to do so, but when he spoke, all that he said, in level tones, was, 'Leave? What foolishness is this?'

'It's not foolishness,' she answered quietly, wishing she knew what he was thinking. 'I've received a letter from my aunt informing me that she has returned from the Continent. Unfortunately she is not well. I'm leaving for Brighton in the morning.'

'I see. You feel that you must?'

'I—have obligations. It is my duty. If I don't go now, I may not have another opportunity for weeks—or even months—when I begin teaching at the academy.' She waited, searching his harsh, sardonic features, indulging in a brief, tormentingly sweet fantasy that he would beg her to stay, but he looked supremely unconcerned.

'That's settled then.' He turned on his heel and strode towards the door. 'Excuse me. There is something I have to do.'

Alicia made a move to follow him. 'But—Jordan—'

'Not now, Alicia,' he said with a look of sorely strained patience. Turning his back on her he walked out.

When the door had closed behind him, Judith had never felt so unhappy in her whole life. When everyone began discussing wedding arrangements, after listening to the conversation until she could bear it no longer, she stood up. 'If you will excuse me, I have to get my things together.'

'Of course, my dear,' said Lady Grant. 'Edmund will take you into town first thing tomorrow for the stage-coach. But you must not leave without first coming to my room to say goodbye.'

'I won't. But I—can quite easily go into town by myself. I don't want to be any trouble.'

'We can't allow that, Judith,' Edmund said. 'It's no trouble at all.'

'Thank you. I do appreciate all your kindness.'

'Nonsense!' Lady Grant said, smiling fondly. 'It's been like having another member of the family in the house. We're going to miss you.'

Chapter Thirteen

Judith was carefully folding her clothes and placing them in her trunk when the door opened. Thinking it was Charlotte, she carried on, and it wasn't until the person spoke that she jerked her head towards the door.

'I do hope you're not running away, Judith,' Alicia said calmly, her eyes aglow with smug satisfaction.

Judith looked at her, her face cool and exquisitely set. Yet inside her the anger that she managed to keep under ruthless control swirled around her in waves of heat. 'I never run away from anything, Alicia—and didn't your governess teach you that you should always knock on doors before entering anyone's room? What do you want?'

'Oh dear! I can see that the news of my betrothal to Jordan is not to your liking.'

'It doesn't matter to me,' Judith said flatly, directing her attention to placing personal items in her trunk. 'It really is none of my affair. I don't know how you did it, Alicia, but you succeeded admirably. Congratulations.'

'That's very noble of you, considering the circumstances. Would you care to hear how I did it?'

'I'm not interested.'

'I'll tell you anyway. You were right when you told me that Jordan would have no recollection of making love to you that night. When he awoke and found me in his bed—with the evidence of our coupling and the loss of my virtue all over the sheets—he was left with no alternative but to do the honourable thing.'

There was a silence, a silence occupied by Judith examining this dreadful disclosure. The harsh reality of what Alicia had done when she'd left her room struck her with horror, and the look she cast her was one of profound disgust.

'Now I realise what you meant when you told me you were prepared to follow my example. What you have done goes beyond the bounds of immorality. It makes me feel sick to think that you could blithely climb into the bed I had so recently vacated and pretend you had been there all night—and you had the audacity to call me a tramp!' Judith seethed scathingly. Oh, what she would give to topple Alicia off her smug pedestal and tell everyone the truth. 'You do realise that I could expose what you have done, don't you, Alicia?'

'And I you,' Alicia countered calmly, her eyes narrowing and glittering viciously as she prepared to deliver her trump card. 'What I have come to say to you is this. I shall enjoy being married to Jordan—and I shall also enjoy the prestige of being Lady Grant. I cannot allow the truth of that night to be known—not after I put my reputation on the line.

'I am not prepared to let anyone take my new life from me, so if you attempt to do any such thing, I will create so much unpleasant publicity that not one of the parents who send their darling daughters to be taught at Miss Powell's academy will allow you anywhere near them. Not only will the scandal destroy you, but also the much admired and highly esteemed Miss Powell. Do you understand what I am saying?'

Alicia let Judith's silence be her answer. With a toss of her head she turned to leave. 'I think you'll adhere to reason. In time—if you can spare it from the classroom, that is,' she mocked, 'perhaps you will find someone else—who belongs to your own station in life—to love.'

'Love!' Judith exclaimed with maddening calm, while quietly fuming beneath Alicia's blatant threat. 'What do you know about love? You have never loved anything beyond yourself. Yet *I* dare say that I have loved Jordan. I may not be a lady but I am a gentleman's daughter, and I have been Jordan's equal in love. However, perhaps I should remind you of what I told you when you came to my room after the ball—just in case it has slipped your mind. I don't want Jordan to know what happened between us—he must never know. So your threats are pointless, Alicia.'

When the door had closed on Alicia, leaving the ruin she had brought about, Judith sat down calmly on the bed to contemplate her situation. Her hand rose unconsciously to the pendant she still wore hidden beneath her dress. Removing it, she held it in her hands and gazed down at its exquisite beauty, running her finger across the bright diamond. She still hadn't decided what to do about it, but now she did consider giving it to Alicia.

The most painful, agonising part of it all was that she didn't have a choice. She had never dared to reach above herself, had never aspired to be a lady—but she had dreamed of being Jordan's wife. Sadly, she accepted that Alicia belonged to this life, more than she did, and if she did give the necklace to her she would be rid of it without raising Jordan's curiosity as to how it came to be in her possession. He would believe without any shadow of doubt that he had made love to Alicia that night—unless his memory of it returned. This was something she refused to contemplate, for the results to everyone concerned could prove disastrous.

However, on reflection she decided to keep it for the time being, for should she find herself with child, she would tell Jordan. She would want nothing from him for herself, and would not want him to feel under any obligation. But she truly believed that every child had a right to know its father, and every father his child. The necklace would be proof that she had been the woman in his bed that night, and that the child was his.

Briefly she did consider the dire consequences this would bring to Alicia if this should happen—that Jordan might refuse to marry her, but she couldn't help that. If there were a child, to avoid any embarrassment for all concerned, she would go away until after it was born. Unfortunately the child would not be spared the stain of illegitimacy.

Should there be no child, then she would have the necklace delivered in secret to Alicia with a note explaining how she had come to have it, and that she must return it to Jordan on the pretence that he had given it to her that night.

She fastened the pendant back round her neck and shoved it inside her dress. Then she placed the last of the items on the bed into the trunk, tightening the straps securely. What was left she would pack into a small valise in the morning. Feeling the need to stretch her legs, she went down the servants' stairs to avoid meeting anyone and out into the yard at the back of the house. With the threat of being accosted still hanging over everyone at Landsdowne—which was highly probable since Jordan's

ordeal at the hands of someone unknown, she had no
intention of wandering away from the house.

She strolled into the stable yard, relieved that there was
no one about. With her noble head hung over the stable
door, Tilly whickered on seeing her, blinking her big dark
eyes. A fat ginger cat, with huge whiskers, was perched
on top of the stable door keeping her company, but it
jumped down when Tilly stretched out her nose and
shook her mane vigorously on Judith's approach.

Judith did not, however, look to her right, and so she
didn't see the open half-door to the tack room, or the tan-
coloured jacket slung over it, or the solitary man who
stood motionless in the shadows, watching every move
she made, from her easy gait—which suddenly seemed
to him both graceful and seductive—to the bounce of her
luxuriant arrangement of dark curls.

Smiling broadly, Judith rubbed Tilly's velvet nose affectionately, wishing she'd brought a little treat to feed
to her. 'Poor thing,' she whispered. 'I'm sure you'd much
rather be galloping through the park or in the field
munching grass, than cooped up in your stable on such
a fine day as this.'

Suddenly a deep voice that seemed to leap out of the
tack room next to her said, 'That could be arranged, if
you'd care to accompany me on my ride.'

Judith turned in astonishment as Jordan's tall figure
materialised from the shadows. He was watching her
calmly, his hands thrust into his pockets, his dark hair
gleaming beneath the sun's rays and falling over his
brow. But she sensed he was keeping himself on a short
rein, that he was wound as tight as a spring, and she
feared the release. She panicked on seeing him, her eyes
taking in his immaculate white shirt—casually open at
the collar, his fawn riding breeches, and his gleaming

brown boots. With a sublime effort she managed to bring her rioting nerves under control.

'Oh! I—I'm sorry. I didn't mean to intrude. I didn't realise anyone else was around.'

'There isn't. I thought I would take a ride before dinner. Shall we saddle Tilly and ride together?'

'No—we'd better not,' she murmured hesitantly.

'Don't tell me. Alicia would object,' he said with cynical amusement. 'Still, I'm glad you've come. I would like to have a word with you in private before you leave in the morning. Have you a minute?'

His features were hard and impassive, but Judith sensed danger. 'Of course,' she said, and then she added, 'I only came out for a moment. I—I have things to do,' as if it were some kind of protection.

'I won't keep you long. There's no need to ask what everyone else is doing,' he said, his eyes boring down into hers with cynicism, his jaw set and hard. 'No doubt they're all making plans for my wedding.'

'It's quite normal when two people are to be married.'

'And have you nothing to contribute to the conversation?'

'No. It—it's got nothing to do with me.'

He nodded. 'Since I can't persuade you to accompany me on my ride, perhaps you would allow me a few minutes of your time. Come in here.' Striding back into the tack room, he traced a path towards the opposite wall where saddles and bridles were hung. Feeling strangely reluctant to enter the quiet warmth of the building, Judith paused on the threshold, inhaling the smell of saddle soap, warm horse leather and hay. Seeing her hovering in the doorway, Jordan threw her an impatient look and strode back to her, taking her arm and drawing her inside.

'You can come in. You stand there looking at me like

the deer that senses the hunter. Do not fear me. I don't bite.'

She flushed. 'I don't fear you.'

Through every fibre of her body she could still feel the touch of his hand on her arm when he released it. Watching Jordan, she wondered what was on his mind, what he was thinking. As she waited for him to speak, her eyes searching his granite features, she saw no sign of the passionate, sensual side to his nature. The expression on his face caused her an involuntary shiver.

'Do you remember the conversation we had on the night of the ball?' he asked suddenly. 'When we were dancing?'

'Yes—of course I do. It made a deep impression on me. Why do you ask?'

'Because I want you to forget it,' he said firmly, thrusting his hands deep into his pockets once more to keep them from clenching as he tried to bring under control a new onslaught of feelings that the mere sight of her had on him. It had the devastating impact of a rock crashing into his chest, and he strained to endure her closeness.

'May I ask why?'

'I said things I have since had cause to regret. I hope you understand what I'm saying.'

She stiffened, insulted, and her eyes flashed irately. 'Perfectly. When I asked why you did not respond to Alicia's overtures, you told me it was because you have a well-developed instinct for self-preservation,' Judith reminded him bluntly, so unbearably, agonisingly hurt that she wanted to test his discomfort to the limit. 'It would seem that your instinct for self-preservation has deserted you all of a sudden. I remember there were other things you said, but I will not embarrass either of us by repeating them.'

'Things are different now.'

'I know. You are to marry Alicia—and it is clear to me that you are not happy about it. Whatever happened between the two of you does not concern me. But was it necessary to go to such lengths?'

'Yes.'

'You don't love her. I can tell.'

'No.'

'Ever since I came here, Alicia has left me in no doubt that she would marry you. Whatever happened between the two of you after the ball, Jordan, she has certainly succeeded in accomplishing her goal.'

'When I returned home later that night, I was not myself,' he informed her irritably. 'I have no excuses to make and no recollection of what happened.'

'You were drunk?' she queried, wondering if he would tell her the truth. He didn't.

His firm lips twisted with cynicism. 'Something like that. I had no alternative but to offer marriage to the woman who…' he stopped, the words he had been about to say left unsaid.

Judith provided them for him. 'Who shared your bed. I know. Alicia lost no time in telling me,' she explained quietly when his eyes widened with questioning astonishment. 'You should be more careful, Jordan. You know the saying—he who plays with fire! You don't need me to tell you the rest.'

'Thank you for that piece of edifying information,' he ground out. 'I shall strive to remember it.'

'I can see the delicate situation you suddenly found yourself in must have been a difficult moral dilemma for you. However, your morals are entirely your own affair— and I am the last person in the whole world you have to explain anything to.'

Jordan looked down at the tempestuous young woman in the lavender gown, her face alive with her snapping hazel eyes, and he suddenly saw her as she had looked at the ball when they had danced—when he had decided to make her his wife. He was furious with himself and fate for having placed him in this untenable situation. His stomach clenched at the thought that he was going to have to let her walk out of his life.

When he next spoke his gaze settled on her with such iron control that she was deeply shaken. 'Alicia is to bear my name. She knows I am not in love with her—but she does expect consideration and respect, and I have every intention of giving the outward appearance of a happy and contented—if not a loving—marriage.'

'I'm sure you will.' Judith moved to stand before him, looking up into his eyes, rebellion drawing her out of her natural reserve. Her voice, so normal an instant before, was suddenly vibrant, filled with a restrained fury. 'You made a mistake, and you must carry it with you for as long as it takes, Jordan. A soldier you might have been—an adventurer, even, bold and brave enough to take any risk required of you. But I think I know you well enough to know you will never deal dishonestly with yourself or the woman you marry. So why have you brought me in here? If you wish to unburden yourself, why not to Edmund or someone else? Why me?'

'Because of all the people I know,' he said, mentally cursing himself for having felt the need to explain himself to her, 'I thought you would be the one to understand.'

'Well, I don't,' she flared, tears of humiliation burning the backs of her eyes and a lump of emotion clogging her throat. She wanted to run from the tack room without giving her feelings away, but knowing that was impossible, she turned and strolled over to the window in an effort to maintain her self-control. She was deeply in love with Jordan, but her love was unrequited. How she longed to share her confidence, but she must keep it to herself. How much easier it would be if it wasn't true, and she cursed herself for falling under his spell.

Tentatively Jordan made a move towards her, but unable to tell if she would want him near, he halted himself. He could almost feel the alert tension of all her muscles. Her very stillness was like a positive force. 'Didn't you hear any of what I was saying to you that night?' he asked quietly.

She turned as the threat of tears passed, and the lump of emotion in her throat began to dissolve. Without removing her eyes from that proud face, she gave a light, brittle laugh. 'I would like to tell you that my memory of that entire evening is extremely hazy,' she said, 'but I can't—and if I did, I am sure you would strongly doubt the truth of it. You see I do remember, and for a little while—with the beauty of the night—the champagne and the music, I allowed myself to dream. But that's all it was—a dream. Nothing more.' As she turned to go he strode after her.

'Judith—wait.' Taking her arm, he slowly turned her round to face him. 'I would have said more—as I could now, but I no longer have the right.'

'The right? No, Jordan, you don't. It's best not to say anything else.'

With the warm pink glow of the sun lighting up her lovely eyes, Jordan succumbed to the impulse which had been tormenting him from the moment he had seen her walk into the stable yard. With his hand still holding her arm he drew her closer. The warm scent of her body assailed him. He glanced down at her face, so near his that he could see the tiny hairs curling around her ears and the soft down on her cheeks. There was the most innocent expression on her face, and her bright eyes beneath the gentle sweep of her black lashes would not meet his. She tried to pull away from him for fear of what might happen next, and he could feel her fragrant breath on his cheek.

'Dear Lord,' he whispered, pulling her closer still, surprised when she came willingly and leaned against him, yielding her mouth to his with a low sobbing moan. His arms closed round her, crushing her to him as he kissed her possessively. The miracle struck like a spark from their embrace. His mouth gentled, parting her lips in a long searching kiss.

The achingly poignant discovery that it was as wonderful as she remembered was almost more than Judith could withstand. She felt all the old demons, dormant since the night of the ball, awakening inside her, clamouring hungrily for release. Allowing herself to be carried away, instinctively her hands crept up his chest and over his shoulders and round his neck, moulding her body to his. They kissed in mindless rapture while the dwindling afternoon sunlight slanted through the small windows.

As she responded with more ardour than he had expected, the effect on Jordan was devastating. Desire like scalding fire raced through his veins, and as quickly as he had caught her to him, so he cast her away. Half conscious, she opened her eyes and looked at him. Her face was so tragic that he was moved by it, but then his eyes hardened to icy flints and he spoke with chill precision.

'I want you to forget about me. Pretend that night never happened. Go to Brighton and see your aunt, and then return to London and take up your teaching post. That's what I want you to do.'

They looked at each other in a struggle that racked them both, and Judith clung to the sudden coldness between them as a shield. Drawing herself up proudly, she raised her chin. He would never know how much she was hurting, nor would he ever again catch the faintest glimpse of the happy girl she had been at the ball—his moonflower that had shrivelled up and died, like those once-living blooms she had pressed in her book. Fighting back her tears, she said with as much dignity as she could muster, 'You're right. That is exactly what I shall do. Now, you must excuse me. I have things to see to.'

Looking for diversion to keep his mind off Judith's departure for Brighton, Jordan went back to town. That same night saw him at White's in St James's Street, the most exclusive gentleman's club in England, to which he belonged, but no matter how hard he tried to relax, or how many brandies he drank, he had difficulty concentrating on conversation with friends and acquaintances and the game of cards.

His thoughts constantly drifted back to Judith and their kiss. He recalled the feel of her, the sweet scent of rosewater on her skin. He found himself lost in that memory, and it stirred others, but afterwards he was left with a lingering feeling of failure. He had fallen in love with her, and not known it.

Around midnight, when he was on the point of getting up from the card table and leaving, he was surprised when Tom Parry took the vacant chair across from him.

'Good to see you, Jordan,' he said airily, stacking a pile of chips in preparation for the next game of heavy play. 'Mind if I join you?'

'Normally I'd stay and take your money, but I'm leaving,' Jordan replied, giving him a sardonic look.

Tom looked across at him sagely. 'Why? Cleaned everyone out? Or have you lost your touch and allowed your partners to thrash you instead?' he quipped lightly, though he doubted it. To his cost, Tom had discovered Jordan's skill at cards in Calcutta, and he was just one of a large band of unhappy gentlemen to have lost considerable amounts of money to him.

'Neither,' Jordan replied coolly.

'Glad to find you in a better condition than the last time we met,' Tom remarked in a grinning undertone.

Jordan winced slightly at this, but nodded in wry agreement. 'Now you're here, Tom, I would appreciate a moment of your time.'

Tom nodded. 'I thought you might. Mother told me you'd called at the house, by the way, and I believe I know why. I knew when you came round after your visit to the Crescent Moon that you'd come seeking answers.'

'I am. After eight years fighting rebels and dodging shot and steel in India, it does nothing for either my vanity or my self-esteem to find myself taken in by a mere tavern-keeper in London's docklands,' he remarked dryly. 'Come, let's find somewhere less conspicuous to talk.'

Tom put down his cards and Jordan picked up the chips that represented his winnings. They retired to another table where they could converse in private, ordering a couple of brandies from a footman.

'I don't mind admitting that I'm experiencing difficulty remembering what happened that night, Tom. The full possession of my memory has not been restored. I was hoping you could throw some light on it.'

Tom shook his head. 'Can't tell you much. All I know

is you were drugged.' He looked at his friend closely, exhibiting signs of cautious interest. 'Someone must have slipped it into your drink. Who would want to render you unconscious—and for what reason? Has it anything to do with your time in India?'

Jordan nodded, his face set in grim lines. 'I'm afraid it has.'

'Does it have anything to do with that Indian whose name is on everyone's lips—in particular the ladies? Jehan Khan, I believe his name is. Apparently he arrived in London shortly before we did—with Jeremy Minton of all people. I know he's staying at Minton's home— and I know there is no love lost between you and that particular gentleman.'

'You're damned right there isn't,' Jordan growled.

'Want to talk about it?'

Jordan shook his head in frowning concentration. 'No, Tom. Thanks anyway. How did I get home?'

'Under my escort.'

'And when we got there? How did I get into the house?'

'Just when I thought I would have to knock the whole house up, an angel of mercy came to my assistance— said she was staying with your family.'

'I see.' So, Jordan thought, gazing thoughtfully into his glass and gently swirling the amber liquid, Alicia must have seen him come home and the state he was in. But then another thought struck him and he frowned. The room she had occupied did not overlook the street, so it would have been impossible for her to see anything. 'What did she look like—this angel of mercy?'

Tom shrugged, lounging back in his chair. 'It was dark and difficult to get a good impression.' His expression became thoughtful as he recalled the young woman who had come running out of the house in her night attire, terrified that everyone inside was about to be shaken from their beds by a drunken master returning home from one of the dubious establishments gentlemen frequented until the early hours. 'She was small with dark hair—pretty face—in fact, come to think of it, she was quite lovely. Her first impression on seeing you was that you were in your cups and damned irate she was, too. But when I told her you'd been drugged—through no fault of your own, I did stress—she was full of tender concern.'

Jordan arched a quizzical brow at his friend. Tender was definitely not a word he would apply to Alicia. 'Tender?'

'Extremely—in fact I was quite touched, I can tell you. Insisted on taking you inside herself—although how she managed it is beyond me. You're about the weight of a small tiger, and unfortunately she didn't have any servants to hang you upside down from a pole and carry you to the slaughterhouse,' he chuckled. 'Oh, and she told me her name was Miss Wyatt,' he added as an afterthought.

A mixture of incredulity and amazement worked their way across Jordan's face. He stiffened and slowly came erect in his seat. 'Are you sure, Tom?'

'Absolutely.'

Jordan stood up. 'Thanks. I owe you for this. You've just cleared up one matter that's been giving me one hell of a headache.'

When he was in the carriage returning to his house, resting his head against the quilted upholstery, he closed his eyes and again tried to think himself away and back to that night—to commune with the invisible woman who was the very source of his vision, for it was along these lines that his mind always worked, and the habits of years as a soldier had become crystallised and were hard to break.

A vision rushed over him, and in a blinding flash he saw the woman he had held in his arms at Landsdowne yesterday as the woman who saturated and tormented his every waking moment, the woman he had struggled so hard to resurrect. He grappled with his memory, but all he saw was—what? Something hard and jewel-bright around her neck—something familiar. That ''something'' had also been pressed hard to his bare chest when they had made love.

As quickly as the vision had flashed upon him it was gone. He experienced a sudden sinking of the heart, accompanied by a deep sense of foreboding.

When the carriage drew up outside his house, he leapt out and went in, bypassing the startled butler without any acknowledgement. Taking the stairs two at a time, he went to his room. His eyes immediately went to a large armoire in which he kept several of his personal possessions. He kept one drawer permanently locked, and in this his valet had placed certain items that always travelled with him. He recalled thinking it strange when his valet had handed him the key the morning after the ball, telling him he had found it on top of the armoire. Thinking nothing about it at the time, he had thrust it into his pocket and not given it another thought.

Now he strode towards the armoire with the certain conviction in his heart that he would find the long leather case—in which he kept the sacred heirloom that was part of the state regalia of Ranjipur—devoid of its treasure. Taking the small key from his pocket and unlocking the drawer, he took out the case and snapped it open. He stared down at the bed of purple velvet, seeing the imprint where the necklace had lain, and the image of having placed it around a woman's neck was suddenly clear.

Once again he remembered embracing the young woman yesterday at Landsdowne in the tack room, the smell of her gentle perfume—of roses, and there flashed into his fogged mind, like a shaft of sunlight bursting through thick cloud and drenching the land with its heat, the realisation that Alicia hadn't been the one to share his bed that night, but Judith.

Judith!

His heart pounding with disbelief, he experienced a wrenching pain of unbearable guilt, and a profound feeling of self-loathing. Dear, sweet Lord! It had to be! Had she given herself willingly, or—heaven help him—had he forced himself on her? How could he have done that to her, when all he wanted was to love her, to be her husband and her friend, to share her hopes and dreams, her laughter and tears? In a drugged stupor he had robbed that beautiful, laughing, unforgettable girl of her most precious possession—her innocence.

And the awful shame of it was that he didn't even remember the joy of her.

But then he remembered their encounter the previous day, and he realised she must have forgiven him, otherwise she would not have walked into his embrace and kissed him with such tender passion. The sudden, startling vision of Judith's slender limbs, locked in wild abandon with his own, their two bodies twisting in ecstasy in his bed, was so shocking in its specificity that it left him trembling.

However, one thing did worry him about all this, and that was the fact that she must still have the necklace. If so, and should Minton or Jehan Khan get wind of it, then she was in grave danger. He frowned. One mystery was explained, at least, only to deepen another. He was puzzled as to why she had kept it. For what reason? Why hadn't she left it in his room when she'd left? Deciding that Alicia might be able to answer some of his questions, he immediately left for Landsdowne.

Chapter Fourteen

Alicia was both angry and worried when Jordan took himself off to London. She told herself that she was mistress of the situation, but underneath she felt fear. Jordan's lack of enthusiasm to be with her made her uneasy, and her unease deepened when he returned just twenty-four hours later and insisted on speaking to her alone in the drawing-room.

He was cool and calm—and he wasn't smiling. Something was different about him. What could have happened? His eyes were like steel flints, and the lines on either side of his mouth looked as if they'd been cut with a chisel.

Poised and beautiful, Alicia sat gracefully on the sofa with her hands folded in front of her. Jordan looked at her hard. Until Judith had appeared in his life he had enjoyed her company on occasion, but she lacked Judith's goodness, her humour and fresh and lively wit, and she didn't look at him with two adorable hazel eyes, and smile that wonderful warm smile.

'I must say that I'm glad your stay in town was of short duration, Jordan. I take it that your business was concluded satisfactorily?'

With his hands clasped behind his back, Jordan looked down at her, finding it virtually impossible to restrain his anger. 'Business was not my reason for being in town. The necklace, Alicia,' he said without preamble, watching her closely. 'Where is it?'

For a moment she floundered and then she said, 'Necklace? What necklace?'

'The one I gave you when you were in my room on the night you allege I seduced you.' His voice was low and even, and he was watching her like a fox watches a hen in a coop. 'Come, Alicia—don't tell me you've lost it. When a woman is given a gift of such rare beauty, it is not something she is likely to mislay. Allow me to refresh your memory. It's a rare diamond—priceless, in fact. It is of great value to me for sentimental reasons— but unfortunately there are others who are desperate and ruthless enough to kill for it.'

Alicia stared at him, her face as white as the petals of the huge daisies which filled the porcelain vase on the dresser. Her stomach churned as she gazed up at Jordan's relentless features. He looked so tall, so intimidating, and she wished he'd sit down. Unable to lie her way out of a predicament she had not foreseen, she said, 'I have never seen a necklace such as the one you describe. You must be mistaken, Jordan, and only think you gave it to me. After all, you said yourself that your memory of that night is extremely hazy.'

Jordan watched her face as several emotions struggled for supremacy in her. He could read her like a book. He knew what she was thinking and he stood there, fixing her with a penetrating, relentless silver gaze, all feeling ruthlessly extracted from his face. He had no intention of making it easy for her. He smiled, an absolutely chilling smile.

'I congratulate you, Alicia,' he said sarcastically, slowly pacing the carpet. 'That was quite a convincing performance you put on the morning after the ball.'

Her dark brows arched. 'I wasn't aware that I was putting on any kind of act,' she replied, trying to remain composed, yet at the same time assailed by a creeping fear that everything was going drastically wrong. Quietly alert and suspicious, she tilted her head and looked up at him. 'Are—are you beginning to recall things about that night?' she asked hesitantly.

'Unfortunately for you, yes. For reasons of my own, I will not bore you with the details of how I came to be in the state I arrived home in. I'd been drugged, and I was brought home by a friend who left me in the drive—not with you, as you would have me believe, but with Judith.'

Alicia's reaction to his words brought her to her feet. 'No!' she exclaimed heatedly, her own anger beginning to rise, but deep down she knew that when challenged she would be unable to come up with evidence to endorse the truth. 'That is a lie. I told you nothing but the truth.'

'Truth? You wouldn't know how to tell the truth if it leapt up and hit you in the face. Somehow Judith managed to get me to my room without waking anyone. It was Judith who occupied my bed that night, wasn't it, Alicia?' he demanded. 'Judith and no one else. It was Judith I made love to and gave the necklace to. Not, as you would have me believe, you.'

Alicia cringed at his tone. 'Really, Jordan! It is quite preposterous. You must stop this. I have no idea what you're talking about.'

'Don't insult my intelligence with your simpering denials,' he said harshly, looking down into her green eyes with a hard, murderous gleam, his lips curled over his teeth. 'I've known some dirty fighters in my time, but never have I known a woman who would stoop as low as you. Everything that happened to me that night was hazy, I admit it, but one thing I do remember is how much pleasure the woman who shared my bed gave me. That woman was certainly not you. So whatever you contrived, Alicia, you have no one but Judith to thank for its success—at the time, of course. Why did you do it?'

'Because I loved you, and I couldn't bear to think I might lose you,' she said, trying to put the softness back into her voice, and school her features into a tender look, but it didn't work on Jordan.

'If that is what you think, then you deceive yourself,' he told her scathingly. 'Not once have I given you reason to believe you are anything more than an acquaintance, but I always knew you were available—too ready to grasp everything I could give you. You bitch! And to think I almost made you my wife.'

With an indignant gasp, Alicia's eyes opened wide. 'Almost? What do you mean?'

'It's quite simple. There will be no marriage negotiations.'

'And what am I to do?'

'You should have thought of that before you stripped yourself naked and climbed into my bed like a London whore.'

'And you behaved like the vile, unprincipled lecher you are, Jordan Grant,' Alicia flared accusingly.

'Did it not occur to you that my memory might not be irretrievably lost—that when it returned it would shatter all your carefully constructed plans?'

'Judith told me you wouldn't be able to remember.'

'Did she, indeed? Then she was mistaken. Just how did you come to be in my bed, Alicia? Did you see Judith leave my room and challenge her? Is that what happened?'

'Yes—if you must know,' she admitted hotly. 'She also made it quite plain that she wanted nothing more to do with you—and that she wanted no one to find out what had occurred between the two of you.'

'And did you tell her what you intended?'

'No. Why should I?'

'And so you took advantage of her—and my own weakness. You tricked us both. You deceived me into believing I had made love to you.' His eyes raked her with an insulting glance. 'I never realised you could be so deceitful or conniving,' he said with biting contempt. 'Oh, I know how soft and persuasive you can be, how caressing your tone and beguiling your smile, but that does not overrule the hatred and treachery concealed in your heart—the hard, calculating core of you. Until now I would not have accused you of this, but at last I am beginning to understand you.'

Alicia's hands were clenched by her sides and her face so contorted with rage that it was almost ugly. She knew all was lost, that there was no longer any reason to keep up the pretence. 'Believe what you like. But if, as you say, you gave Judith a necklace that night, ask yourself why, Jordan. Could it possibly be because it was in payment for her services—the kind you give to a whore?'

Jordan's anger was pitiless and so powerful his eyes glittered, and he had to clench his hands by his sides to prevent them reaching out and throttling her. 'Be quiet, Alicia. Whatever happened between Judith and me was not some meaningless encounter with a woman of the streets.'

'Ha! So—the truth hurts,' she cried, plunking her hands in the small of her waist and leaning forward slightly, her bosom heaving with anger. 'Your "Oh-so-pious little school-ma'am" certainly showed her true colours that night, did she not? Little wonder she wanted no one to know about her sordid coupling with you, or why she left for Brighton in such a hurry—with such a valuable bauble dangling round her neck,' she sneered. 'No doubt she's already hocked it and will live off the proceeds for the rest of her life. It will be interesting to see how precious her teaching career is to her then—but no matter what she tries to aspire to, she will always remain what she is. A plain little nobody.'

The bluntness of her statement jarred every one of Jordan's nerves. He moved close, looming over her, and never had Alicia seen such an expression in any man's eyes. 'And you have a warped definition of how a well-bred young woman should behave. Judith could give *you* lessons in the art of being a lady. Dear Lord, how you must hate her.'

'Yes, I do hate her. I hated her the first time I laid eyes on her—with her hoity-toity manner and boasting a superiority of mind that was positively sickening. What do you think will happen when it gets out what sort of woman she really is? It will do her no good—the academy and Miss Powell even less.'

No human emotion could be traced on Jordan's face. In a silky, menacing voice, he said, 'If it is your intention to disclose any of this, or cause Judith any unnecessary suffering, then I advise you to reconsider. I shall have a word with Edmund to take you home. You will say nothing to my mother about why you are leaving. I do not want her upset. Of course, you may tell Emily what you like. I know she is sensible enough to be discreet—pity the same cannot be said of her sister.

'There will be no scandal. If you so much as breathe

one word that will bring disgrace to either Judith or Miss
Powell, I swear I will personally wring your neck.' These
words were spoken in a cold, lethal voice, leaving Alicia
in no doubt that he meant it. 'Is that clear enough?'

She drew herself up with nervous hauteur. 'You can't
threaten me.'

'No?' he inquired. 'I meant every word. One thing you
should know about me, Alicia, is that I'm a very determined man, and if any harm comes to Judith by your
hand, I'll destroy you. Believe me when I tell you that
you don't want me for an enemy.'

He turned from her and walked to the door. Opening
it he looked back. 'Remember that being a woman you
have much to lose. You must also remember you will
have your father to answer to. He is an upright, moral
man, and when he learns how you set out to entrap me
into wedlock—and the sordid methods you used to do
it—and not forgetting your little affair with his steward,
I might add—a man he trusts implicitly, by all accounts—he'll not be lenient.'

Alicia watched him go. Embittered and with anger
burning a hole in her chest, she paced the length of the
room as she considered her predicament. She hated
Judith, and she would never forgive her for the humiliation she had brought upon her. And what added to the
injustice of it all was that after behaving like a slut, Judith
Wyatt wasn't suffering for her wrongdoing.

Catching her reflection in the large gilt mirror on the
wall above an ornately carved bureau, she stared at it
hard. The slut would pay for her treachery—and Jordan
for his rejection of her, Alicia. But how? There had to
be a way. It was no good fighting Jordan, she wasn't
strong enough, so she would have to outwit him. She
recalled the necklace he had mentioned. He had told her

it was priceless, of sentimental value to himself—and that others who wanted to possess it were ruthless enough to kill for it. The cogs of her mind began turning faster. Who had he been speaking of? Lord Minton? This was highly probable, if his irate encounter with this gentleman at the ball, and her own conversation with Lord Minton about his association with Jordan in India, was anything to go by—along with the bitter enmity that clearly existed between the two of them.

She smiled at her reflection, a satisfied smile and one of pure malice. Behind her, the fire gave the room a golden glow that suddenly seemed brighter. With purposeful strides she went to her room and immediately sat down to write a letter to Lord Minton.

Jordan had the impression that his mother shared his relief at Alicia's sudden departure for Kent, and that she was to be spared having Emily's sister as a daughter-in-law. She certainly looked happier and more relaxed than she had in days.

When Edmund and Emily whisked Alicia back to Kent, offering no explanation other than that she was missing her father, Lady Grant did not question this or try to persuade her to stay. Her own marriage had been a happy one, and so too was Edmund's. She could only hope that Jordan's would be equally so, and she felt that Alicia was not the right woman for him—although she would never dream of saying so.

She had been perplexed by the seeming contradictions in Jordan's life since his return from India. Something was troubling him deeply. She sensed it was of a serious nature and, not one to involve herself in either of her sons' private affairs, she hoped that it would soon sort itself out.

His moodiness and unhappiness over Judith's absence made her wonder, too, as did Judith's behaviour before she had left with undue haste for Brighton. Judith had come to her room to bid her farewell on the morning following the announcement of Jordan's betrothal to Alicia, and as the young woman had looked at her, Lady Grant had seen something in the depths of her eyes that could only be seen and understood by someone who had felt it themselves. Judith was in love with Jordan, of that she was certain.

Now there was a match she would approve of. Judith might have nothing to recommend her to society, and she might not have the kind of pedigree to rival Charlotte's, but she was warm and kind and extremely clever. She was the kind of woman who would make Jordan happy and be a credit to him, of that she was certain. And so, when he told her he was leaving for Brighton to ask Judith to marry him—his eyes glowing in a way she hadn't seen in a long time, she embraced him warmly and sent him on his way with her blessing.

Cynthia Wyatt lived in a solid, respectable house of three stories in the heart of Brighton, close to the Steine—a broad stretch of grassland that spread northwards from the promenade, on which the fishermen dried their nets. Up on the Downs, several windmills overlooked the town, where wholesale development of crescents, squares and terraces was taking place around a labyrinth of medieval streets called the Lanes.

Despite the discord that existed between Judith and her aunt, she loved to come to Brighton, so situated that a stagecoach leaving London in the early morning reached the resort by noon, returning to the capital during the afternoon. The town had grown rapidly from small beginnings as a poor fishing village. The arrival of the Prince Regent to live with his mistress in '83, and the restorative values of drinking and bathing in seawater, had set the seal on Brighton's development, making it the most thriving seaside resort in the country. Life there was chic, dashing and extremely enjoyable, its reputation as a centre of frivolity and fashion well established.

The Prince Regent had acquired a small house, which he had enlarged. Over the years bits were added onto it in all directions. People at this time were fascinated by China and India, and it was at this house, which became the Royal Pavilion, that the eastern fantasy was born. It was transformed into the most exotic and outrageous of all European palaces. Most people loved or hated it. Judith loved it, the onion-shaped domes and minarets that made up the skyline of the Pavilion reminding her so much of her beloved India.

Having been to her room to tidy her appearance after the journey, Judith joined her aunt in the drawing-room that overlooked the Steine. Cynthia Wyatt was forty years of age, with neat brown hair and plain though not unattractive features. Once slender, her bosom and waist had thickened and she now had a matronly look. Her air was not conciliating, and Judith always felt a sense of unease when in her presence. Seated on a gold and green sofa pouring afternoon tea, the older woman's face, paler than usual due to her recent illness, was one of deep concentration.

'How are you feeling now, Aunt Cynthia? Better, I trust,' Judith inquired with some concern, seating herself opposite.

Cynthia nodded. 'I am tolerably well. It was just a gastric ailment—nasty while it lasted, that caused me to cut my visit to France short.' She looked across at her niece, lifted one brow and frowned. 'You've dressed your hair differently, Judith,' she stated, in such a way that Judith wasn't sure if she approved of the softer style she had adopted or not.

Self-consciously she brushed a loose curl from her face. 'Yes. Charlotte persuaded me—she said it made me look less like a school-ma'am. Do—you like it?' she asked hesitantly.

'It suits you. It's certainly more fashionable and makes you look less severe.'

Judith almost dropped the teacup she was holding into her lap. Compliments from Aunt Cynthia were a rarity indeed. Taking a sip of the fragrant beverage, she studied her aunt over the rim. There was something different about her. Her expression was as cool as it always was when they were together, but there was an excitement behind it. She seemed to be suppressing some inner emotion. Judith didn't have to wait to find out.

'I'm glad you managed to get down to Brighton—although I hope I did not concern you unduly when I mentioned in my letter that I was unwell. It was considerate of you to cut your stay with the Grants short, and I hope you're not too disappointed. Still, I'm glad you came, for there is something I have to tell you that will affect you.'

Judith placed her cup on the small round table between them. 'Oh?'

'Mr Wakeman has made me an offer of marriage, and I've accepted. You are aware that we have known each other some considerable time, so it shouldn't come as any surprise.'

This was true, but Judith was surprised enough to look at her aunt with unaffected astonishment. Her thoughts were in such disorder that she couldn't say anything at all immediately. Aunt Cynthia had always dreamed of marrying a title and mingling with the real aristocracy, of wearing sumptuous gowns and dancing in marble ball-rooms, but it wasn't to be. After all her years as a spin-ster—hoping for something better—she realised that mar-riage to Mr Benedict Wakeman, a lawyer who had a legal practice in Chichester, fifty, small and balding, who doted on her with excessive admiration, was the best she was ever likely to get. Quietly studying the look in her aunt's eyes, Judith could see they were filled with bitterness and something very like despair, and she found herself feeling sorry for her.

'This is not the first time Mr Wakeman has asked you to marry him, Aunt Cynthia,' Judith returned after a short silence, 'and you have always rejected his proposal.'

'Be that as it may, Judith, but I am not getting any younger, so this time I have taken his offer seriously. Benedict is a quiet man and will suit me admirably.'

'Then I hope you will both be very happy.'

'Of course it will mean selling this house.'

Judith's throat tightened and she had a strange, trem-ulous feeling inside. The pain of losing Jordan was so deep she didn't know how she would endure it, and to be told she was to be denied her visits to Brighton, too, was almost too much.

'Of course, now you are about to embark on your teaching career,' her aunt continued, 'you will be spend-ing more of your time in London, but you must feel free to visit us in Chichester any time you wish.' Suddenly a thick gold chain exposed between the side of her niece's collar and her throat caught her attention. 'What is that you're wearing around your neck, Judith?' she asked. 'It looks far too heavy for comfort—or to have concealed beneath your dress.'

Judith hastily put a hand to her throat, feeling a loop

of the chain holding the diamond. 'Oh—it—it's nothing, really,' she said nervously, trying to shove it back inside her dress.

'No, don't hide it,' her aunt said, leaning forward. 'Let me see.'

'It's nothing, Aunt.'

'I insist on you showing it to me.'

Reluctantly Judith complied. Moving closer, her aunt peered at it with wide-eyed astonishment, clearly impressed.

'Goodness! Where on earth did you get it?'

'It—it was given to me.'

'By whom?' she demanded.

Judith stiffened. 'If it is all the same to you, Aunt—I choose *not* to answer your question.'

Cynthia bristled, quite incensed. 'Really, Judith! Your insolence is not to be borne. You are being most unreasonable. Until you are of age I am your guardian—the nearest relation you have in the world. You cannot deny the claims of duty and gratitude. I am entitled to know what concerns you.'

'You are not entitled to know what I do not choose to tell you,' Judith answered resentfully, for to reveal how the pendant came to be in her possession was impossible. 'On this matter I have reason for silence and will not be explicit.'

Cynthia eyed her niece suspiciously as a dreadful thought occurred to her. 'It isn't stolen? You must give me assurance of that.'

'Of course it isn't stolen,' Judith gasped, offended that her aunt should ask such a question of her.

Cynthia reached out and took the pendant in her hand to give it a closer inspection. 'I'm no expert on these matters, but I have seen enough jewels around the throats of others to recognise quality when I see it. It could be valuable.' There was a very determined expression on her face and a sudden gleam in her eyes, and she smiled a thin, greedy smile. 'You must sell it.'

Judith gasped, appalled by the suggestion. 'No—I cannot. I wouldn't dream of doing such a thing. Besides, I have every intention of returning it.'

'You are talking in riddles, Judith,' Cynthia said, getting up, her taffeta skirts rustling crisply. 'Either it is yours or it isn't. I'll arrange for someone to examine it who will tell us its worth.'

Judith gave her aunt a sharp, resentful look, knowing she saw the necklace as the means of stepping into a different world, but said no more on the subject. That avaricious gleam in her eyes was even more apparent. She looked hard, very hard indeed, and Judith knew she would not give up the point. No doubt she would endeavour to coax and threaten until she got her own way.

Mid-morning the following day found Judith walking on the beach, her feet bare and her hair flowing behind her in the breeze blowing off the sea. She was trying to recover her spirits, and to dwell without interruption on the subject that was closest to her heart. Not even the warm sun on her face and the smell of the sea could relieve the deep sadness that engulfed her. Everything seemed so empty and meaningless without Jordan— hopeless, even.

Carrying her shoes, she strolled past the fishing-boats drawn up onto the shingle, and the bathing-machines, where the dippers were already hard at work submerging the bathers in the water. Eventually she came to a rocky stretch that was quite deserted. With her skirt and petticoat bunched in front of her, wistfully she clambered over the rocks, gazing down into the rock pools to see how many sea creatures the tide had left behind. Taking pity on a small kittiwake that appeared to have injured its wing, she put down her shoes and picked it up, cradling it gently in her hands to assess the damage. One of its pale grey, black-tipped wings hung limp, but otherwise it was quite robust. Stroking its head with her finger, she turned, intending to make her way back, speaking softly to calm the bird's fear, and wondering what to do with it.

In the distance she saw a man with his tan jacket hooked over his shoulder walking towards her. He was too far away for her to see his face clearly, but there was something familiar about his gait. He was very tall, with the same dark hair and taut grace, the same air of cool self-possession as Jordan. She looked into the sun's glare, blinking hard, telling herself that she was losing her mind, that it was her imagination playing tricks on her. But she sensed it was him. It was as if some tangible, powerful force told her so. She even recognised the elusive, tangy smell of his cologne, borne to her on the warm breeze.

On trembling limbs, still holding the injured bird in her hands, she stood stock still and waited, her heart pounding as she looked with loving eyes at his tall form, afraid to blink lest he disappeared, afraid to move, gazing at that sternly handsome face that haunted her dreams and tormented every hour of every day.

The closer he came the harder her heart hammered in nervous anticipation, with a mixture of hope and dread as she recalled their parting. What was he doing in Brighton? Why had he come? she thought wildly. Had he finally regained his memory of the night she had spent in his bed and come to claim the necklace?

Or, merciful God, hope upon hope, had he come for her? Had he come to tell her how much she meant to him, that he couldn't live without her and he could not marry Alicia?

When he stopped and a pair of penetrating grey eyes looked straight into hers, she was too afraid to speak, to move, as she gazed at the unbearably handsome face that towered above her, his broad shoulders blocking out her view of anything but him. His white shirt, tucked into doe-coloured breeches, was open at the throat to reveal the strong muscles of his neck, and she fixed her gaze on a small pulse she saw beating just below the surface. An expression she couldn't recognise flickered on his face, and his eyes seemed bright beneath the shading of his hair. Then he smiled, the smile she knew so well.

'Hello, Jordan,' she heard herself say. 'How are you?' She knew it was a stupid, inadequate thing to say, but she had to say something, and with her heart beating so fast she could almost hear it, she couldn't think of anything else.

Chapter Fifteen

All the way down to Brighton Jordan had been rehearsing in his mind what he would say to Judith, and now he was with her he couldn't remember a thing. When she lifted her eyes to his and he saw the quiet yielding in their clear depths, it nearly sent him to his knees. He wanted to lose himself in her eyes, to pull her into his arms and unburden his heart. Taking a neutral course, he looked at the bird.

'What happened?' he asked, reaching out and gently brushing its white plumage with the backs of his lean fingers, because he didn't know what the hell to say to her.

Judith met his gaze and swallowed nervously, smiling with shy uncertainty. 'I—I found it among the rocks. I think it's injured its wing, poor thing.'

The sound of her voice was so soft and sweet, Jordan almost dragged her to him. Instead he threw his jacket onto a rock and took the bird from her. Placing it on the smooth sand, they watched as it limped away. When Jordan looked at Judith again his face was inscrutable.

'You're surprised to see me?'

'Yes. I—I never expected to see you here in Brighton.

H-How did you know where to find me?' she asked softly.

'I called on your aunt and she told me you had gone for a walk on the beach. It wasn't too difficult to locate you.'

'Why are you here?' she asked, unable to bear another moment of this awful suspense. With her new understanding of her own feelings, how she wished she understood his.

Jordan's brows drew together, and he continued to study her. 'What brought me here today has nothing whatsoever to do with the restorative values of this seaside resort.'

'No—I don't suppose it has,' she whispered. Acutely aware of her dishevelled appearance, she ran an ineffectual hand through her hair, which hung down her back in a shining, tangled cascade, thinking what a sight she must look. But at the admiration she saw in his eyes, and the inexplicable, lazy smile that swept over his face as he surveyed her—from her head to her small and slender bare feet, she had the staggering impression that he actually liked what he saw, that the girl walking on the beach was far more appealing to him than the prim schoolteacher. She had thought never to see him again, and now he was here she wanted to weep with joy.

'H-how are you?' she asked, echoing the first words she had spoken, giving him no indication of how she felt.

'All things considered, I am remarkably well,' he assured her dryly, fixing her with a level stare, 'for a man who has made love to a woman and been unable to recall her identity. It did nothing for my male ego, my self-esteem or my pride—and a man is most sensitive about his pride. Only the remembrance that the woman I made love to on the night of the ball was passionate, warm and responsive acted as a balm of sorts. She had an ardour that matched my own—a woman I could not equate to Alicia.'

The words hit Judith with a jolt, and hot, embarrassed colour flooded her cheeks. She looked up at him in help-less appeal. 'Oh!' she whispered, the silky smoothness of her voice beset with confusion. 'You—you know? How did you find out?'

'I worked it out for myself after Tom Parry—the man who took me home that night told me that no sooner did we arrive at the house than you emerged and took charge. I must thank you for getting me to my room without waking the entire household. Although how you managed it is quite beyond me. Alicia confirmed what Tom had told me.'

'I see. How she must hate me.'

'In that you are correct,' he answered with wry amuse-ment. 'But at this moment I don't know who she hates most. You or me.'

'Do—do you know everything?' she asked hesitantly.

'Almost everything. What I don't know, I am sure you will fill me in on,' he said, a softness entering his eyes. Idly he brushed a tumbled curl from her cheek, becoming preoccupied with the way the wind caught her hair, lifting the tresses so that they streamed out like banners. He admired the way it sparkled in the sunlight like rich, dark brown honey. Here in this open, relaxed setting, with the sky as blue as sapphire, and the sea as calm as a mill pond, he could see she was a very beautiful young woman. Her face was flushed with the sun and exertion, and her eyes on closer inspection were not so much hazel as amber and cinnamon.

'You have lovely hair,' he murmured. 'You should al-ways wear it so.'

Judith laughed and smoothed it back with a careless gesture. 'I don't think Miss Powell would approve if I were to appear in class with it in such abandon,' she replied, seeking safety in light humour, but she was vibrantly aware of the compelling magnetism emanating from Jordan's powerful body standing so close to her own.

Once again Jordan's gaze captured hers, probing with a blazing intensity. 'When I awoke the morning after the ball—still under the influence of the narcotic a certain tavern-keeper had applied to my drink—for which he has yet to be brought to account, I was in a somewhat nebulous state. Finding Alicia in my bed confused me even more. My memory of everything that had occurred was unclear, with disjointed, faceless shadows flitting about in my mind.'

'You don't have to explain, Jordan.'

'Yes I do. I owe you that, at least. When Alicia told me she had been with me all night—that we had made love, I doubted it but I could not disprove it. And you let me go on believing it—which was quite wrong of you, Judith,' he admonished, 'but we will go into that later. I was soundly caught in a trap. Every time I thought of marrying Alicia, I was tormented with images of you. You see, my desire for you was unquenchable. It nearly drove me insane. Ever since that night you have put me through a living hell.'

His voice sounded harsh, as if forged from his chest. Reaching out, he threaded his fingers through her hair and framed her face with his hands, gazing down at her lovely golden features, knowing perfectly well that he deserved her hatred and contempt for what he had done to her.

'My behaviour to you that night was unforgivable—

but I sincerely hope you can find it in your heart to do so, and allow me to put things right. Circumstances, I'm afraid, played a heavy hand upon my actions. When I realised that you were the one who had shared my bed—having touched you, and not being able to remember—I became most anxious to touch you again.'

'You did much more than touch,' she whispered shyly.

'I know—and I intend doing so again,' he told her fiercely. 'I intend taking you to bed and making love to you as thoroughly and leisurely as I can. I accept that the loss of your virtue was largely my fault, and I find the responsibility a heavy burden to bear. If I could turn back the clock and put everything right, I would, believe me, but it's too late for that. For a whole week I have been dying inside because of what I did to you.'

Judith gave him a tearful smile, feeling herself melting at the tenderness she saw in his expression. An aching lump began to swell in her throat. 'It's been a difficult week for me too.'

Unable to look at her a moment longer and not hold her, Jordan pulled her against him with stunning force, his mouth opening over hers in a kiss that demanded she return it with equal passion. With unbelievable joy Judith slid her hands up his chest and around his neck. Beneath the thin fabric of his shirt, his chest was solid and warm. She arched herself against his rigid thighs, and Jordan shuddered with pleasure, his hands caressing her back, and then pulling her hips tighter to him. He groaned aloud with rampaging desire, and with the pleasure of having her in his arms and feeling the sweet softness of her mouth.

Tearing his lips from hers, he placed scorching kisses on her cheek, her temples. 'Say you forgive me,' he murmured. 'Say it, Judith.'

All the forgiveness that filled her heart was in her eyes for Jordan to see, a forgiveness so intense he was humbled by it. And when she opened her mouth to tell him so he silenced her words with his lips, his kiss becoming hungry, searching, primitive and potent, sending her spinning off into another world of exquisite bliss. Slowly she began to resurface as the pressure of his lips lessened, but she didn't surface from the state of mindless pleasure until he broke contact with her mouth and raised his head.

Breathing deeply, Jordan looked down at her glowing eyes and soft mouth and had an impulse to bend his head and kiss them again, but a loud burst of laughter from a jolly party of people coming onto the beach snapped them both back to the present. Irritated by the lack of privacy available to them, he shot the group an irate, disapproving scowl.

'Let's find somewhere quiet where we can talk.'

Taking Judith's hand he led her towards a dry piece of sand close by. Lulled by his kiss and the lazy slap of the water on the shore, finding a place in the shade she sank down, tucking her feet beneath her skirts. A welcome breeze rippled off the water, and she turned her head better to feel its coolness on her cheeks. Jordan sat with his back against a rock and drew one leg up at the knee, resting his arm across it. A heavy, dark fall of hair had tumbled over his brow. With a casual gesture he brushed it back, before taking her hand once more and placing it to his lips. He looked into the wavering depths of her large, clear eyes, as if seeking the answer to some burning question.

'I want you to be perfectly honest with me, Judith. It is important to me that you tell me the truth, because ever since I discovered it was you I made love to that night, I've been in hell. Do you have any idea how much

I hate myself—how I feel every time I think of what I did to you?'

'Please, don't,' she whispered.

She wanted to tell him that it was the most wonderful thing that had ever happened to her, that she had felt completely, incredibly, unconditionally, his, and that if it were never to happen again, she would be content to live on the memory for the rest of her life. Her pride and her passion were waging a terrible war inside her. Jordan had given her no indication that he was looking for a permanent partner, a helpmate, and as things stood she could only assume that he wanted what women could give him, as a means to slake his physical lust. She wouldn't humiliate herself by letting him know how much she craved his kisses, his touch.

'I've said that you are forgiven,' she went on, 'even though you did think I was an Eastern dancing-girl and paid me generously for my services,' she said with a whimsical smile.

Jordan grimaced. 'I'm not proud of that, either.'

'Why did you go to the Crescent Moon that night?' she asked curiously.

'I knew that was where Khan's servants could be found when not attending their master. I hoped to find out more about Khan's visit to London, and to confirm my suspicion that he—and Minton—were behind what happened to me at Blackwall. Unfortunately,' Jordan remarked dryly, 'they must have seen me first—hence what followed.' Still holding Judith's hand, after a moment's silence he looked at her once more, his expression one of deep concern. 'For my peace of mind, what I must know is did I force you into my bed? Could you have got away from me?'

She gulped, nodding slowly. 'Yes,' she confessed, her voice a whisper. 'If I'd tried.'

'Then why didn't you?' Jordan questioned, his gaze searching hers.

'I—I don't know.' She sighed deeply. 'I've made such a mess of everything, haven't I? It was a mistake—I can see that now.'

'A mistake that cannot be put aside. So,' he murmured, his eyes gleaming seductively from beneath lowered lids, 'I can only assume that you stayed purely for your own enjoyment.'

'It looks like that,' she replied, her smile sheepish. 'My behaviour was quite shameless.'

'Absolutely,' he agreed. 'And outrageous.'

'Now you're mocking me,' she reproached lightly.

He grinned. 'No I'm not. You're much too adorable to mock.'

'And if I were to tell you that I acted purely on impulse?'

His lips twisted with cynicism. 'I can't imagine you doing anything on impulse. You're far too sensible for that—and I always thought you too prim and proper to let any man touch you as I did out of wedlock.'

'So did I, so what I did goes to prove I'm not always sensible. I can be extremely foolish.'

'The only foolish thing you've done was to climb into my bed. Do you regret your foolishness?'

Judith shook her head, and with a raw ache in her voice she said, 'No.'

Jordan saw tears shimmering in her lovely eyes, and watched one trace its way down her cheek. 'Thank God for that,' he said hoarsely. 'That was my second greatest fear.'

'And what was the first?'

'That I inadvertently hurt you,' he said, with something like despair in his voice.

He was looking at her hard, and she could almost feel the pain inside him, sharp as crystal pieces of ice. 'It's all right. You didn't hurt me. What I did was wrong. I knew the rules, and I broke every one of them when I climbed into your bed,' she admitted quietly.

'For God's sake, Judith,' he said, his voice edged with remorse. 'Will you stop exonerating me. I know what I am capable of when my ardour's aroused.'

She gave him a wayward smile. 'Since you put it like that, you certainly can't be complimented on your subtlety. But—you were most persuasive,' she murmured, tilting her head sideways and laughing lightly.

Jordan grinned. 'You have the advantage over me, but I have no doubt of my abilities.'

'I believe you. I'm sure you've proven yourself to countless ladies in the past.'

'True, but it is the one who has made the deepest impression that has eluded me. My only regret is that almost everything about that night is still obscure, and I despise my weakness.' His face suddenly grew sombre as he considered his next words. 'There is something else we need to discuss. I think you already know what I am going to ask.'

His voice was calm, much too calm, carefully modulated, and that worried Judith. She felt a weak, tremulous feeling inside. 'I think you want me to explain how it came about that Alicia found her way into your bed.' When he nodded she drew a long breath. 'You must believe me when I tell you that when I left I had no idea Alicia would step into it and pretend she had been there all night.' She went on to tell him the whole story, simply, without trying to hide the anger she had felt towards Alicia for her conniving interference and treachery.

Jordan listened without interrupting. Only when she had finished did he speak. 'And the necklace?' When she glanced at him sharply he smiled thinly. 'That is one thing I do remember about that night.'

'You—you thought I was a woman of ill repute and—'

'Gave you the necklace in receipt of your favours,' he finished, a brittle quality having entered his voice. 'Why did you keep it? Why didn't you take it off before your left my room?'

'I—I didn't intend to keep it,' she answered in a small voice, hoping he didn't think that. 'And just in case you are wondering, I have it safe around my neck. You must understand that when I left you I was not in full possession of my thoughts. To be quite honest, I forgot all about it until I returned to my room. After that it was too late. When you arrived at Landsdowne and announced your betrothal to Alicia—when I discovered the lengths she had gone to to secure you, I—I did consider giving it to her—'

'Why? To sanction her deceit?' Jordan said. His voice was mocking, his stare accusing and never wavering from her face.

Judith nodded. 'Something like that,' she admitted wretchedly.

Jordan was disappointed with her reply. 'One thing I have always admired in you is your determination always to speak your mind, your honesty and your courage, but this time the truth digs deep, Judith.'

She flinched, drawing away from him a little. The tenderness of a moment before was no longer evident. Jordan sat regarding her, his face an impenetrable mask. She realised suddenly that there was so much she didn't know about him, that he'd been a soldier in some of the most remote and savage areas of India for years—the ability to hide his thoughts was as much a part of him as his handsome features and dove-grey eyes. The tremulous feeling increased.

'Why are you looking at me like that?'

'Suppose you tell me why you didn't give Alicia the necklace?' he countered.

'You—might not like the answer.'

'Try me,' he clipped, refusing to spare her until he knew the whole of it.

She drew a long, fortifying breath, raising her eyes to his impassive face, speaking awkwardly. 'I—I thought—' Dropping her eyes, she faltered, unable to proceed beneath his penetrating gaze.

'I suppose it was when you thought that you might be carrying my child,' he said quickly, taking pity on her confusion and coming to her rescue.

She nodded, swallowing hard. 'Yes. I—I didn't know if a child might result from what we did together,' she whispered, realising as she spoke that she would be adding more pain and guilt to his memory of that night.

'And has it?' he asked impatiently, his eyes as hard as ice floes.

She flushed. 'I don't know. It—it's too soon to say.'

He nodded, continuing to look at her, his face expressionless. 'And what did you intend doing about it— should you find yourself *enceinte*? Would you have had the child adopted?'

Bristling at his crisp tone she looked at him sharply, deeply offended by his question. 'No. I would never do that,' she answered fiercely. 'Whatever my circumstances, I would never part with my own child. It's just that—I hoped it wouldn't happen.'

'Why? Does the thought of bearing my child bring you such misery?'

'Of course not,' she answered, repaying his sarcasm with characteristic honesty. 'I would be proud to bear your child, Jordan, and I would not fail it—but I would prefer not to do so out of wedlock. I have no wish for any child of mine to bear the stigma of illegitimacy.'

His eyes were hard and probing. 'And if there should be a child, did you intend informing the father?'

'I confess that my mind shied away from any confrontation with you, but I have examined very carefully what I would do, and was forced to conclude that I would tell you. I firmly believe that every man has a right to know his child, and every child its father. That was why I kept the necklace,' she explained, conscious of the diamond caressing her bare skin between her breasts. 'It would prove beyond doubt that I was the woman in your bed that night, and that the child was yours.'

'And did you not consider the dire consequences of telling me I had fathered a child when I was married to Alicia?'

'I would have found out before you married her. I would have told you, and after that the rest would be up to you. But one thing you must understand, Jordan, is that if I should find myself in such a delicate condition, I had thought of going away until after the birth. I wouldn't want anything from you. The last thing I wanted was for you to feel under any obligation to me.'

Jordan sighed, feeling the tension of the last few moments go out of him. Reaching out, he gently caught her shoulders and drew her close beside him so that she leaned against the rock. Holding her in his arms he turned her to face him. Desire was there in his silver gaze, and something more, something so profound it held Judith spellbound. 'You little fool. I am going to marry you,' he said finally. 'I will make you my wife—child or no child.' For a moment Jordan thought that she was not going to answer him, and when she did it was in a whisper.

'Your—your wife? I—I did not think… When—when I left Landsdowne I never expected to see you again. Please don't feel you have an obligation towards me.'

'I don't.'

Judith stared at him, knowing he was doing the honourable thing because he had taken her virtue and because there was every possibility that she might be carrying his child. Not for one moment did she delude herself into believing he loved her, but how she wished he would say it, even if he didn't mean it. She had no doubt that she was deeply and irresistibly in love with him, and she would nurse her secret until, God willing, in time he would come to feel the same about her.

When he spoke his voice was low and his eyes gleamed, so gentle, so full of tenderness. 'Any man would be proud to have you as his wife, Judith.'

'But—you're a gentleman,' she said. 'I'm a nobody—a schoolteacher. Men of your class don't marry women like me. Your friends—society—would reject you. You'd be ostracised. It wouldn't be right, Jordan. I'm not of your world—whereas Alicia is.'

'I think I should be the judge of that. And, anyway, do you seriously believe that would matter to me? If so you do not know me.'

Judith unclasped the necklace and pulled it out of her dress, handing it to him. 'This is yours. Keep it safe, Jordan. It's beautiful—and extremely valuable, too, I imagine. If my aunt could have her way she would sell it and live off the proceeds for the rest of her life.'

Jordan looked down at the exquisite gem for a moment before bringing his gaze back to hers. The wind ruffled his hair, and giving her a rueful smile he got to his feet. 'If she were to do so, she would be able to live like a queen, and no mistake.' Taking Judith's hand, he hoisted her to her feet, picking up his jacket. Taking a handkerchief from an inside pocket, he wrapped the necklace in it and put it back, casually hooking it over his shoulder. 'When we are married I will shower you in jewels, my love,' he said, placing his free arm about her waist as they slowly made their way back along the now empty beach. 'Unfortunately, this particular jewel is not mine to give.'

'Who does it belong to?'

'The Ranee of Ranjipur—the Rajah's widow. When he died of injuries he received in a riding accident, his wife was in Calcutta visiting her family. Knowing the state of Ranjipur would be annexed and all his treasures confiscated, before he died the Rajah placed the necklace in my care—to give to his wife. When he entrusted it to me I had no idea of the trouble it would bring. The jewel— which at one time would have been worn in a turban and belongs to the state regalia, has been prized by various owners in his family for hundreds of years, and he was reluctant to surrender it to the British.'

'He must have trusted you a great deal to place it in your care.'

'He did. Over the years we became close friends. It was an affection that survived until his death. After that a revolt ensued—led by Prince Chandu, who wanted to proclaim himself ruler and make the state of Ranjipur independent. Afraid for her own life and that of her only surviving daughter, his wife—along with her daughter and a large contingent of servants—left for Bombay, where they boarded a ship for the Red Sea. From there they travelled overland to Alexandria, where I have learned the Ranee has decided to spend a little time. I expect her to arrive in England very soon, when I shall be able to relieve myself of the necklace.'

'And what happened to Ranjipur? I recall you telling me that it was annexed by the British.'

'It was. Ranjipur is of strategic importance to the British, and what Prince Chandu intended was not acceptable to them. They stormed the Rajah's palace. Many people on both sides died in the fighting. Prince Chandu escaped back to his own lands and there he remains.'

'So, apart from the necklace, all the Rajah's wealth became the property of the British?'

'Some of it—gold and jewels beyond anything you and I could imagine. Prince Chandu creamed off most of it before they could get to it.'

'Goodness! I can't believe I've been carrying such a precious object around my neck all this time. Is this the reason behind my abduction and the assaults on you, do you think?'

'Yes. I'm certain Prince Chandu has promised Jehan Kahn and Minton a bounty if they can retrieve it.'

'Why do you hate Lord Minton so much, Jordan?' she asked, glancing up at him. 'It was evident to me when the two of you came face to face on the night of the ball.'

Pulling away from her, Jordan became perfectly still, his stare hot and unblinking on the distant horizon. Judith saw something move in the depths of his eyes, and his body tensed. She was reminded of the tell-tale twitch of a stalking tiger's tail, precursor to the kill. He was a seething mass of feelings, and the first emotion to erupt was anger.

'Because the man is a sadist and a murderer. He enjoys

hurting people weaker than himself. He is also totally corrupt and stands accused of colluding with the Thugs— professional stranglers, their ranks consisting of thieves and brigands.' He glanced at Judith. 'You will have heard of them.'

Judith nodded. Yes, she knew all about the incredible secret society that roamed India in gangs in the guise of pilgrims and merchants. It was a murder organisation which befriended travellers before strangling them with a cloth, in one corner of which was knotted a silver coin consecrated by the Kali, the goddess of destruction— which gave a religious backing to their activities, although they were not above making a profit out of the proceedings.

'Then you will know that local rulers sometimes protect this fanatical sect, and share their ill-gotten gains, overflowing their coffers with jewels and rupees beyond price. Minton was one of them, and he made my life as a soldier trying to track down these murderers—to make it safe for travellers to go about their business—almost impossible. His greed knew no bounds.' His voice became low and trembled slightly. 'I also hold him responsible for the death of the Rajah's eldest daughter. To me, this was the blackest of all his crimes.'

'Why?'

'She was married to Chandu's son when she was just fifteen. At sixteen he died and she was to become suttee.'

A chill stole over Judith and she shuddered. Suttee, belonging to the higher castes of Hinduism, was the custom of burning widows alive on the funeral pyres of their husbands. It was a holy practice, one which Judith thought hideous and cruel. The widow had to die painfully, and should she escape the flames, she could expect no pity from her own people, who would push her back onto the pyre. It was a practice the English sought hard to abolish, but it still went on.

'At the earnest request of the Rajah, who considered suttee a hateful business despite it being an accepted part of his religion, my superiors sent me to Prince Chandu to prevent it.'

'And did you?' Judith asked in a small, hopeful voice.

He nodded, his expression grim. 'On the whole I respect the customs of India, and I understand why the English are slow to interfere with a custom sanctioned by religion, but the practice of condemning widows to a fiery hell cannot be right. If it has to be, then the act must be voluntary, and there are widows who love their husbands so much they choose to burn with them of their own free will. But nine times out of ten they go to the flames in terror.'

'I know. I have heard of the practice, but I've never witnessed it. It's suicide.'

'Which is not a crime to the Hindus—but murder is, and I consider it murder forcibly to burn widows. I knew the Rajah's daughter. Her name was Anjali. She was full of laughter, kind and gentle, and her father adored her. When her husband lay dying, she wrote to her father, begging him to come for her. Prince Chandu would not allow it, so I went in his place. When I arrived Anjali's husband was already dead. I appealed to Chandu to allow Anjali to return to her father, but he refused my request.

'I sought out Minton, but he had the ear of Prince Chandu and would do nothing. He had power in the district and he could have halted the suttee—had he wished. He chose not to do so. I already knew what little regard he had for honour and fair play when a generous bribe was being dangled beneath his nose like a carrot to a donkey. I have no doubt Chandu rewarded him hand-

somely for his co-operation. That was the moment the
matter became personal.'

Jordan's voice, so flat a moment before, shook with a
restrained fury. 'With no time to spare I had to act
quickly, and on the night before the funeral, myself and
two of my most experienced soldiers stole into Chandu's
palace and rescued Anjali and took her back to her father.

'Nothing was heard from Chandu, and as the months
went by everyone thought the matter was ended. But
Chandu was like a sleeping tiger. He believed it was his
duty to his dead son to see that his widow died. By her
pain she would release her husband from the burdens of
his earthly sins, earning him aeons of blessedness in
heaven. When the Rajah left his palace to seek enlight-
enment on a pilgrimage to the holy places, Chandu sent
men to capture her. They succeeded and took her back.'

Judith felt herself trembling, and gooseflesh lifted the
hairs on the back of her neck.

'The distraught Ranee sent for me and I went after
Anjali, but I was too late.' A fine sweat had broken out
on his temples and his fists were clenched. His mouth
closed tight for a moment, until he found the strength to
go on.

'I will never forget it. I will never forget the swaying
crowd, the chanting of the holy men—the lonely figure
of a young girl, half crazed with terror as she was bound
and forced onto the pyre. I still hear her screams. There
was nothing I could do but watch as the fire consumed
her, feeding avariciously on that small thing in its midst,
the noise it made sounding so much like the roaring in
my ears. I couldn't even get near her to put a bullet in
her heart to hasten her death.

'I watched until her screams died with her, when her
spirit had begun its journey on a road to heavenly beat-

itude, to lie beside that of her husband, beyond the reach
of man's cruelty. Beside the pyre I saw Minton and
Chandu seated on gilded chairs. Chandu was attired in
flowing robes of crimson and gold and decked in rubies.
They were gloating—laughing.'

Momentarily falling silent, Jordan recalled that the
hard look he had given Minton had only been a small
measure of the fury that had possessed him—fury at
Minton for allowing the burning of Prince Chandu's
beautiful, sixteen-year-old daughter-in-law to take place,
and his own inability to prevent it.

'Half mad with fury, I wanted to kill Minton,' he continued at length, 'to throw him into the flames, and I
couldn't for the life of me remember why I couldn't,
beyond the fact that he was an Englishman like myself.'

Sick and outraged by what he had told her, Judith had
been holding her breath and now let it out. She slowly
began to understand his hatred of Lord Minton, and the
look of strain on his face. Not knowing what to say, she
squeezed his hand, feeling the tension going out of him
with the end of the story. He smiled briefly, then put an
arm round her and pulled her towards him.

'So you too have your demons—like me,' she murmured, meeting his gaze quietly. 'What happened to me
is in my memory like the ache of an unhealed wound—
as it is with you. I'm sorry, Jordan. I wish I could say
something to make it easier. But I can't. Nothing can alter
what has happened—or bring Anjali back. People say
that time is a great healer. They are usually right but not
always.'

Jordan looked down at her. The sheer intensity of his
feelings seemed to resonate along the empty shore. Her
eyes and the quiet, unblinking way she had of looking at
a person reminded him of some ancient mystic—as

though she could see a good deal farther than most people. Her face was calm and full of understanding. It was also looking at him with an expression that made him lower his head without conscious thought. The kiss he placed on her lips was brief and tender, yet as remarkable in its impact as though they had just plighted their troth.

He raised his head, but the warmth of it lingered on Judith's lips, so that she could still feel it. She breathed in the taste of it, seeking to hold on to it. The moment was interrupted by the raucous cry of a gull swooping overhead.

'Come back with me to London,' Jordan said. 'I want you with me—so I'll know that you're safe.'

'As much as I would like to, I can't go with you, Jordan. Not just now. I would like to spend a little time in Brighton with Aunt Cynthia. She is to be married soon and will be moving to Chichester.' She smiled, standing on her toes and planting a light kiss on Jordan's lips in an attempt to alleviate his concern. 'I'll be all right. Don't worry about me.'

'But I do. My darling girl,' he said softly. 'You gave me all of yourself, and held nothing back. You give me honesty when I ask for it—it isn't in you to lie and I thank God for it. I won't lose you now I've found you, Judith.'

She frowned, looking at him steadily. 'You speak as if you are afraid something will happen?'

'I don't know. I hope not.' His voice was just as fast as the possessive tightening of his arm round her waist once more. 'We are bound, you and I, and nothing is going to part us. We will be married very soon. I promise.'

'I would like that,' Judith whispered, her eyes shining with happiness.

Chapter Sixteen

When Jordan had left Brighton, later that day, with the sun sinking in a blaze of crimson on the horizon and still basking in the glow of his embrace, Judith returned to the beach to mull over everything that had happened.

On meeting Jordan, her aunt had been impressed, telling Judith as she watched his splendid carriage drive away that he was a fine-looking man. When he had said farewell to the woman he intended to wed, it was more than interest that had lingered in his eyes, and her aunt had curiously enquired as to his reason for coming to Brighton. Judith had calmly told her it was to collect the necklace, but her aunt had not been deceived.

Swallowing her disappointment over the loss of the precious necklace, Cynthia had cautiously asked if there was anything in their relationship. Judith had merely smiled secretly, not yet ready to share her confidence with anyone. The future that had looked so bleak and meaningless without the man she loved was suddenly filled with hope.

In the dying light of the setting sun she returned to the house, taking no notice of the carriage standing close by. All the windows were dark, and then she remembered that her aunt was visiting a friend a few streets away. The first thing she heard on opening the door was someone moving about in the drawing-room.

'Aunt Cynthia!' she called, thinking the maker of the noise must be her aunt, having come home early. 'I didn't expect you—'

The words died on her lips as she pushed the drawing-room door open. The fading light revealed a man searching through the drawers of a large dresser and carelessly discarding things onto the floor, his huge frame seeming to fill the whole room as he worked. She stopped dead at the sight of the intruder and choked back a scream, every instinct telling her even before he turned that it was Lord Minton.

The shock of recognition when he greeted her with a profoundly mocking bow was mingled with incredulity.

'You are alone?'

She nodded.

The sharp eyes flickered back and forth between her and the door, as if assessing her truthfulness. Instinctively Judith knew why he had come. He must suspect her of having the necklace—although how he had come by the knowledge was quite beyond her just then. Trying not to show her fear, she threw him a cold glance.

'What are you doing here?' she asked, struggling with the nervous tension that was sapping the strength from her quaking limbs. 'You have no right to be in this house. How did you get in?'

With a flick of his eyes he indicated the window her aunt had left unlatched. 'It wasn't difficult,' he said in his deep baritone voice. 'Pardon me for not bothering to knock,' he drawled, 'but there was no one at home to let me in.'

'What are you looking for? There is nothing here that could possibly belong to you. Please go away.'

He laughed, and under the drooping lids the pupils of his eyes seemed to burn. 'No, lady. You'll have to put up with me for a bit. I stay until I have what I came for.'

'There is nothing here that could possibly interest you,' she seethed. Her voice was shaking and her hands were clenched in the folds of her skirt, the fabric clutched between her fingers. 'I have nothing to give you.'

'Ah, Miss Wyatt, that is where you are quite wrong,' he countered, feeling his jaded senses coming to life as he watched the tiny pulse throbbing just above her collarbone. In her anger she was so young and fragile, and wary. 'You have two things that interest me.'

The lurid smile that stretched his lips as he looked her over left Judith in no doubt about his meaning. Fear began to claw at her stomach, and a spark that forbade acquiescence appeared like heat at the back of her eyes.

The sight of it filled Lord Minton with anticipation. 'I told you at the ball that we had something to discuss,' he went on, 'and I see you are at liberty to be of assistance to me now.'

His threat combined with the physical bulk of the man—the sheer power of him—made Judith tremble. Out of the corner of her eye she glimpsed her aunt's long, silver paper knife on her desk where she wrote her letters. She grabbed for it and brought it to bear in front of her. 'Stay away from me,' she hissed, mustering firmness through her fear.

Lord Minton's face remained calm when he looked at her. Her opposition was the most piquant thing he had felt in months. His laughter was brutally mocking. 'Your hand trembles. I do not think you have the strength to hold the knife, let alone use it.' Slowly, confidently, he walked towards her. She backed away and he laughed again.

An onrush of panic was loosed within Judith's mind. She turned to flee, but Lord Minton's arm shot out, knocking the paper knife from her hand. Suddenly she was caught and held fast in an iron grip. Holding her with one hand, he produced a thin cord from his jacket pocket and quickly bound her wrists firmly together behind her.

Her cry of pain echoed hollowly in the room. 'How dare you!' she cried, appalled and angered by the ferocity of his assault. 'Let me go.'

His eyes glittering with a singular malice, he took her arm and yanked her towards him, twisting his fingers in her hair, forcing her head back, and kissed her with a deliberate brutality that made her squirm. His hands pressed the fabric over her breasts and her horrified gasp only provoked more laughter.

He spoke harshly into her ear. 'You little bitch. Did you think I would let you escape me—especially now when I know that *he* wants you?' The *he* he referred to being Jordan, which Judith understood. 'Even in temper you're a pleasing sight.'

With an acrobatic litheness that amazed him, Judith writhed away from him and spat in his leering face. He struck her with the speed of a snake, catching her across the mouth with the back of his hand. She tumbled to her knees at his feet, blood welling from her bruised lips.

Her hair awry, tears streamed down her cheeks, but she glared at him without blinking, her eyes snapping up at him with a promise of vengeance, letting the stinging pain serve to feed her anger. 'You'll pay for that,' she seethed. 'I swear it.'

Lord Minton jerked her back to her feet by a fist in

her hair, the cocksure smile acquiring a malevolent twist. 'I think not, lady.'

'What are you proposing to do with me?'

'Since you ask, unless you produce the necklace—which I know Grant gave to you—I intend to enjoy myself with that soft little body of yours until you're black and blue, before wringing that pretty neck. In fact,' he murmured, the evil in his eyes plain for her to see, even though they were half shuttered, 'I have a mind to do that in any case. It would be worth eliminating you in order to get at Grant—to punish him for past slights, and destroy him for ever.' The young woman's tear-stained face was a real mask of terror, and he savoured her panic.

Her lips throbbing from the blow, Judith was certain that Lord Minton's clear, ruthless mind, which had done nothing to halt the burning of a terrified young widow, would not hesitate to end her own life. She was in the clutches of a depraved and dangerous man, and she could see no way of escape. 'And if I tell you that I don't have the necklace?'

'I wouldn't believe you.'

She swallowed nervously. 'How is it that you are so well-informed?'

'In my position it is a matter of life or death to know as much as possible—about friends and foes—and it is often in my best interest to make the acquaintance of the friends of my foes.'

'You talk in riddles, Lord Minton,' Judith scoffed, her watchful eyes shining like stars in the dim light. 'I think what you are saying is that someone has betrayed Jordan to you.'

'Shall we say a certain lady was none too pleased about being passed over by Grant for you.'

'Alicia!' Judith gasped, remembering seeing the two

of them together at the ball, and the camaraderie that had sprung up between them. 'So—she has acted from sheer spite.'

Lord Minton's smile was chilling. 'Exactly. A typical example of a woman scorned, you might say. Now, tell me where you have hidden the necklace. As you see, I have searched the house from top to bottom.' His eyes narrowed, fastening on her bosom. 'Maybe it's not so far away from me, after all.'

With a sudden jerk, he ripped the fabric of her gown and shift to her waist, revealing her exquisite flesh.

Reacting instinctively, Judith kicked him hard on the shin. 'How dare you,' she shrieked, her voice trembling with outrage rather than fear. 'You loathsome animal. I no longer have the necklace, I tell you. I gave it to Jordan when he came earlier. You're too late!'

Lord Minton stiffened, his eyes gleaming like twin daggers. The full force of his rage was ready to explode. 'Grant? He's been here?'

'Yes,' she flung at him, wishing her hands were free so she could cover her partially exposed breasts. 'He has taken the necklace back to London.'

Again Lord Minton yanked her hair, pulling her close. She uttered a yelp of pain as the roots dragged at her scalp, and he laughed fiendishly. 'So, this changes things. He has the necklace. I have you. It will be interesting to see just how valuable you are to him.'

'Jordan will never yield to the demands of a blackmailer,' she spat, giving him a scalding glare.

'He will, if he wants you back alive. A valuable hostage against the release of the diamond? Oh, yes. I am sure he will consider my demands very seriously when he receives my note. I made a serious mistake in thinking you were of no consequence to him when I took you the first time.'

'So it was you who abducted me.'

'And let you go. I can see now that I should have held onto you.'

'And Mr Khan? Was he a party to it?' She had no wish to bandy words with him, and yet she could not help but be curious.

'Khan?' His lips twisted scornfully. 'No. He thinks as ill of me as I do of him—just like Grant and me.' His face darkened with a malevolent frown, hatred leaping from his close set eyes. 'Now there's a man I'd take pleasure in killing—slowly. Every slight, every time he gave orders and expected me to obey, every time that bastard looked down his nose at me, I remember—and he'll pay for it. I would like to see all that arrogant power brought to its knees and humbled.

'Khan and I are only together out of necessity. He's a fool and also expendable. He wants to retrieve the necklace for no other reason than to secure his own position at the court of Prince Chandu—a man I am certain Grant has told you about. Khan has been sent to England not only to retrieve the annexed state of Ranjipur for Chandu, but also the diamond, and Chandu will not care to hear of two failures. Unless one of his missions is accomplished, Khan will die.'

'Perhaps he will remain in London.'

'Chandu's arm is far-reaching. It is one or the other— the state of Ranjipur, or the diamond.'

'Whereas you want the diamond for yourself.'

'Exactly.'

'Even though it will mean you leaving England for good.'

'If I have the diamond, when I have turned such a

treasure into money, the gain to myself will be well worth the sacrifice. The British and the charges hanging over me can go to hell. Where I am going they will never find me.'

'Jordan was right about you. I believe you would sell your soul to the devil for the right amount of money. You said yourself that Prince Chandu's arm is far-reaching,' she reminded him coldly, her look one of profound disgust. 'If that is so then I would advise you to find a very deep hole in which to hide.'

Lord Minton shrugged his shoulders, unperturbed by this. 'I know the east. There are places I know of where not even Chandu will be able to find me.'

'And Mr Khan has no idea of your nefarious plot, and that you have come to Brighton?'

'None.'

'I see. What was he doing in Greenwich on the day I encountered him?'

Lord Minton shrugged. 'Curiosity, mainly. He wanted to see where Grant lived, hoping to search the house. He soon gave up on the idea.'

'And were you behind the assault on Jordan that day at Blackwall?'

'I was,' he admitted coolly, seeing no reason to deny it. 'Unfortunately I hired a pair of bungling, incompetent fools to do the work, and one of them ended up dead.'

'I know. I was there. And the night he was drugged.'

'That was Khan and myself. We suspected he might be carrying the necklace on his person, and we would have succeeded in searching him had not a group of his friends turned up and taken him home.'

'What are you going to do with me?'

His laugh was cruel. She was looking round the room like a cornered animal, obviously thinking of escape and calculating her chances. She was intelligent, and he sensed she would not give up easily. 'Why—I shall take you on board the boat I've hired that's waiting to take me to France. Unfortunately things have not gone as planned and I do not yet have the jewel I have long coveted. But with you to barter with, I don't believe I shall have long to wait. Now come along. We are wasting time.'

Taking her arm, he dragged her towards the door. Judith struggled and screamed deliberately, hoping to attract someone's attention.

'Screaming's useless,' Lord Minton hissed into her ear. 'There's no one to hear you, and the man on the box of my coach is my own servant. You will learn to keep your mouth shut, for there will be no other to help or protect you, save me.'

He pulled a gag across her mouth against further outcry and flung his iron-thewed arm around her. Lifting her off her feet, he carried her outside into the darkened street and shoved her into the waiting coach, where she fell upon the seat. Ordering the driver to take him to the boat, he climbed in after her and pulled down the shades.

Judith continued to struggle, to lash out with her feet, kicking him wherever she could, until a broad fist struck out, hitting her hard on the side of the jaw. Abruptly his accompanying words reverberated hollowly down that long final plummet and she slipped into total blackness.

On his return journey to Greenwich, Jordan indulged himself in the pleasurable occupation of dwelling on his future wife. Just thinking of her caused his chest to constrict with emotion, and there was an unfamiliar lump in his throat.

Closing his eyes, he leaned his head back, harbouring

not the slightest doubt of what he felt for Judith. He loved her with a passion that was deeply rooted within his soul. She filled him with a feeling that was a mixture of awe, joy, and reverence, and he could not believe she had been the one who had sent him to unparalleled heights of desire and unequalled depths of satisfaction on that one night they had shared. The mere thought that already a child of his might be growing within her womb filled him with a feeling so intense, so profoundly proud, that he almost burst with it—although he did realise that for proprieties' sake, it would be best for their first child not to be born too soon into their marriage.

With regret, he realised that he had not made the depth of his feelings clear to her, and that he had failed to explain that he'd never known there were feelings like this, that he could neither see nor touch her without wanting to satisfy his craving for her. He also realised that he had not told her the most important thing of all—that he loved her.

He was a quarter of his way to London when the occupants of a carriage coming towards him caught his attention. The turbaned Indian was sitting ramrod straight and looking impassively ahead, his two servants facing him. Immediately all Jordan's senses were alert. It was Jehan Khan, and he was heading for Brighton. Why? And where was Minton? He had an acute premonition of danger—that Minton might already be in Brighton, seeking out Judith.

Ordering his driver to turn the carriage around, he tensed, his mind recklessly leaping ahead and climbing mountains before he'd reached the foothills. A vision of Judith completely at the mercy of Minton set his mind on fire. She could no more stand against him than a child.

It was dark when he arrived back at the house he had left just a short while ago.

'Oh, Lord Grant,' Cynthia said, letting him in. 'Thank goodness you're here. I really do not know what to do next.'

Her apparent distress and the state of the ransacked house sent a chill through Jordan. 'Miss Wyatt, please calm down and tell me what has happened.'

'Oh, dear! How I wish I knew.'

'Where is Judith?'

Cynthia slowly shook her head in absolute bewilderment. 'I really do not know. I've just arrived home after visiting a friend, and I find—this—and no sign of my niece. Who can have done this? What can it mean? Judith has completely disappeared.'

Pain lanced through Jordan. It was so sharp that he could scarce keep himself from shaking the woman in front of him. 'Disappeared? Are you certain? Have you looked for her?'

'No—I—I haven't had time.'

'When did you last see her?' Jordan demanded, clenching his hands in frustration.

'The last I saw of her was at about six o'clock. When I left the house she was getting ready to go for a walk on the promenade—which she does every evening when she comes to Brighton.'

'Could she have called on anyone—friends, perhaps?'

Cynthia shook her head. 'No. She never visits anyone unless I am with her.'

'What about the servants?'

'I—I only have the one, and she doesn't live in.'

'And when you left the house, did you see anyone loitering outside—a carriage, perhaps? Anything suspicious?'

'No, I don't recall seeing anything of a suspicious nature,' she answered, feeling uncomfortable beneath Lord Grant's probing stare, as if he thought it was her fault that Judith had gone missing. Suddenly he turned on his heel and strode towards the door. 'Where are you going?' she asked in alarm, having no wish to be left by herself in case the intruder returned.

'To look for her.'

'Oh, dear! Lord Grant, do you think she has been kidnapped—or worse?'

Jordan spun round, his manner abrupt. Then he saw the woman standing in the middle of the room wringing her hands, her eyes clouded with anxiety. Going back to her he laid a calming hand on her arm and forced his expression into less severe lines. 'You are jumping to conclusions. We do not yet know she has been harmed.'

'But—the person who did this,' she said, indicating the shambles all around her. 'Perhaps Judith interrupted him and he's taken her with him—or murdered her. Perhaps she is lying injured or dead somewhere. Oh, dear!' She placed her hands to her cheeks at the sheer horror of such a dreadful thing happening to her niece.

'I beg you do not distress yourself, Miss Wyatt. I am almost certain that I know the identity of the person who did this, and if I am right then I can assure you that it has nothing whatsoever to do with you. He came here to look for something he believed was in your niece's possession, and when he didn't find what he wanted he will have taken Judith. I fully expect him to communicate with me in some way.'

'Do you mean he will demand a ransom?'

Jordan stared at her wordlessly, his eyes a pale, misted grey.

'Dear God,' she cried, her voice vibrating about the

room, in danger of being overcome by her emotions as her anxiety grew. 'Where can she be? Where can he have taken her?' Her eyes appealed to the man in front of her. His face looked grim. Gone was the softness she had seen earlier, and the charm she had found so appealing. In its place was a steely determination of a battle-hardened soldier.

'I do not know. But I will find her,' he said, with determination. 'I promise you that.' And he had to do it before Jehan Khan got to Minton.

Jordan was striding down the path to speak to his driver when a youth carrying a lantern appeared in front of him. His eyes narrowed with suspicion. 'Who are you, and what is your business with Miss Wyatt?'

'Name's Freddie Scales, sir,' the youth supplied, holding something out to him that looked like a letter. 'Gentleman gave me this half an hour ago and told me to deliver it to Miss Wyatt.'

Jordan took it. 'Who was this gentleman?'

'Dunno, sir,' Freddie replied, fidgeting awkwardly on his feet beneath the penetrating stare.

'What is it?' Cynthia asked, coming out of the house.

'A letter addressed to you—although I suspect there are instructions inside asking you to have the letter forwarded to me in London.'

'Then please open it quickly,' Cynthia whispered, her voice frantic. 'I couldn't.'

Jordan ripped it open. He was right. The missive was meant to be forwarded to him at Greenwich. After scanning what was written he shoved it into his pocket, his expression grim. 'I was right. She is being taken to Dieppe.'

'France?' Cynthia gasped, horrified. 'Is she in danger?'

'Probably.' Jordan knew Judith would be feeling terrified, and the thought of her in Minton's power knifed through his heart and was enough to make him forget the necklace secure in his inside breast pocket.

Cynthia glanced at him as a thought occurred her. 'Lord Grant, why did you come back to Brighton?'

'It's a long story, Miss Wyatt. Under the circumstances I think an explanation will have to wait. I must go after Judith.' His expression was one of gravity when he looked at her. 'I will instruct my driver to remain at your house until I return, but for your own safety it might be advisable for you to seek the hospitality of one of your friends—for tonight, at least. There is someone else in Brighton who may call on you, and it would be best for you not to be here.'

She nodded. 'Yes,' she whispered. 'I will take your advice.'

Jordan looked at the youth. 'Freddie, where can I get a boat?'

Freddie looked vague. 'Nowhere I can think of. Not at this time o' night.'

'Think, lad,' Jordan said insistently. 'What does your father do?'

'Nothin'. He's dead—lost at sea in a squall, he was. I live wi' Rory—me brother.'

'And what does your brother do?' Jordan asked, trying hard not to show his frustration and impatience with the lad.

Freddie shuffled his feet uncomfortably. 'He's a fisherman.'

Jordan let out a long sigh of relief. At last he thought he was getting somewhere. 'And is your brother at home?'

'No, sir. He's wettin' his whistle at the Ship, and he'll not take kindly to being interrupted in his drinkin' after finishin' his day's work,' he informed the gentleman, intent on saving his own skin. Rory might treat the womenfolk in his house with something little short of reverence, but when it came to his young brother, he was not averse to giving him a cuff on the ear if he disturbed his hour at the Ship after a hard day's fishing.

'He will,' Jordan said with firm conviction, 'when faced with an offer he can't refuse. Come on, lad, take me to him.'

Cynthia went back inside the house, shaken and deeply shocked by Judith's disappearance, and she fervently hoped that whoever had taken her would let her go unharmed. However, she decided against leaving the house. She wanted to be on hand should Lord Grant find her and bring her back.

In her own way she had become fond of her niece, and had begun to look forward to her visits to Brighton. This was the main reason why she had informed her of her early return from the Continent, in the hope that she would find the time to come down—although she would never confess to it.

To openly display affection was something Cynthia found awkward, and it had been much easier to play on the gastric ailment that was troubling her at the time. It had not been serious and it had had the desired effect— although now she was beginning to regret ever having written to Judith. If she hadn't she would be safe and well in Greenwich with her friend Charlotte.

Chapter Seventeen

There was no shortage of taverns in Brighton, and Freddie took Jordan to one close to the front that catered for fishermen. Pushing open the low door they went inside, being met by a reek of alcohol, human sweat, and a babble of voices. Freddie took Jordan towards a table where a big man with skin like leather and piercing blue eyes beneath bushy black brows was sitting. He had a mug of ale in front of him, and was contentedly smoking a clay pipe. Immediately Jordan took the chair opposite.

'You are Rory Scales?'

'Aye,' Rory replied, quietly taking stock of the stranger. Humble fisherman he might be, but he was not unobservant. Neither was he a poor judge of men, and there was no mistaking the imposing, vigorous bearing of the man facing him, who carried himself with all the confidence of a seasoned soldier.

'Your brother tells me you have a boat.'

The man glanced at him dubiously and nodded. 'What of it?'

'I need one immediately to take me to sea. Can you help me?'

Rory shook his head, puffing thoughtfully at his pipe.

'You're the second man to approach me in the last three hours—and I'll tell you what I told him. Not tonight.'

'And why didn't you take him? Wasn't he generous enough?'

'Not generous enough for the risks involved. I wanted the money all right—but France?' He shook his head slowly. 'Didn't like the look of him, either.'

Jordan grinned thinly. 'I applaud your judgement. Still, someone must have been tempted by his offer?'

'Aye—a ne'er-do-well by the name of Jed Taylor—a drunk who beats his wife and anyone else who gets in his way when he's that way out. Mention of gold is always enough to make him prick his ears up. He'll do anythin' when he hears the jangle of coins.'

Jordan leaned forward, lowering his voice. 'Listen, Rory, it is imperative that I go after that boat. I must catch up with it before it reaches Dieppe. I am not without means, and I will more than double what the man offered. Will you take me? He has a woman with him—and I will tell you that she is not his sweetheart. She will not have gone willingly. I am obliged to go after her. It could be a matter of life or death.'

For a moment interest mingled with anger flickered in Rory's eyes. Cherishing the memory of his dead mother, being blessed with two little girls who were the apples of his eye, and a love for his wife, Letty, that verged on worship, he had no time for men who showed no respect for their womenfolk.

Fine and dandy the man was who had approached him earlier, but there had been something ugly beneath his skin, and the prospect of finding himself alone with him at sea made him shudder. He was certain the man had no scruples and would have sold his own mother for the right price, and killed her for a bit more. Leaning heavily across the table he thrust his face close to Jordan's.

'You're in luck. I'm a great respecter of women and don't like to hear of them being ill-treated, so I'll take you. But it depends.'

'On what?'

'Whether or not you pay half now.'

Jordan nodded, glad he'd had the presence of mind to bring some coins with him. Taking a purse from his pocket he discreetly passed it across to the fisherman. 'There's twenty guineas in there.'

Rory took it and pocketed it. 'Just so that's understood. And the rest?'

'Unfortunately I don't have any more money with me. I am Lord Grant, and I give you my word that I will have an equal amount sent to you as soon as I return to London—and more if we succeed.'

'And why should I trust your word, Lord Grant?' Rory allowed considerable scepticism to show in his voice.

Jordan arched his brows and fixed him with a level gaze across the table top. 'No one has ever had cause to doubt my word, Mr Scales.'

Rory sat for a moment, contemplating the other man, and then he nodded. 'Aye, I'll trust you. Just one more thing. Whatever you and that other chap are involved in is something that's no concern of mine. I reckon they've nearly an hour start on us, but the state Jed and his mate were in when they left here, they'll not be making good time so we should catch up with them in mid-Channel.' He turned to Freddie, who had been watching the proceedings with wide-eyed interest. 'Go home, lad. Tell Letty where I am and that she's not to worry.'

When Freddie had scampered out of the inn, Jordan turned to Rory. 'Did anyone see them leave?' he asked, wondering if anyone might have tried to stop Minton bundling a struggling woman into a boat—his mind refused to contemplate the thought that Minton might have rendered her incapable of fight.

'Shouldn't think so.'

'Is there anyone else we can recruit? Another man at the oars will make all the difference.'

'I can do better than that. Wait here.'

Rory returned accompanied by three more fishermen, tall and broad-shouldered, all eager to supplement their meagre incomes any way they could, and without question. With no need for conversation they hastened towards the beach, where boats were drawn up on the shingle above the high-water mark. Fortunately the tide had just turned and it didn't take them long to drag the boat into the water. Climbing in, they pushed it clear of the shore with their oars. It was a clear night. The moon's gleam painted the water in a silver sheen, and the stars were like a million eyes looking down on them.

'Shall we light the lantern?' Rory asked.

'No,' Jordan answered. 'The moon will provide us with enough light. Our friends in the other boat will have no idea they are being pursued, and I have no wish to alert them until it's too late for them to escape. Double your pace, lads, and I'll make it worth your while.'

With the creak and splash of the oars they put out to sea, rowing rhythmically and with precision, moving their whole bodies with every stroke. With nothing to see but the blackness of the water against the sky, Jordan scoured ahead for a light. Fortunately the sea was calm, with only the slightest swell.

There was a time when crossing the Channel at night would have been a risky business—when smuggling had been in its heyday, with contraband being brought across from the Continent on every tide. Now there was little chance of meeting the revenue cutters. The crime had declined since the end of the Napoleonic wars—not because the preventative system worked, but because the customs duties imposed no longer made it profitable.

It was close to midnight when Jordan saw the dull glow of a light bobbing in the far distance, alerting all his senses. 'Row, men—harder,' he said, speaking through gritted teeth. 'If that's our quarry we're gaining on them.' He took out his pistol and primed it.

'God in heaven! Is there to be shooting?' someone gasped in a horrified voice.

'I hope not, but I know what I'm dealing with.'

When Judith regained consciousness there was a searing pain inside her head. Mercifully her wrists were no longer bound. Bruised and shaken by her rough handling, she found herself lying on the bottom of a boat, the stench of fish and bilge water turning her stomach. Hearing the gentle slap of water against the hull and the splash of oars, she knew she was at sea and drifting off into the unknown. Her heart sank with despair.

Someone was sitting close by speaking in low tones to the oarsmen. Lord Minton was no more than a silhouette, black against the lantern's glow. The close proximity of her kidnapper made her shiver, and she felt a sudden sense of panic sweep over her, and a premonition of the dangers that lay ahead of her in France.

As if sensing her scrutiny, Lord Minton turned his head. He observed the whiteness of her face, and how lifeless she was, and as always when he was in the presence of someone smaller and weaker than himself, her distress acted pleasurably upon him. It brought a vicious tang to his excitement when he thought of the pain and fury that would consume Grant when he discovered his intended bride had been abducted yet again.

'Sit there and be quiet,' he growled, her presence losing its flavour as he got to wondering if the lad he'd hired to deliver the note to the girl's aunt had done so.

His coach driver—who was also his personal servant and had been with him throughout his time in India—could have taken the letter direct to Grant at Greenwich, but wanting to stall for time until he was safely in France, and knowing it would take a little longer if he sent the letter via the girl's aunt, he'd decided to use the lad and instructed his servant to lie low for a few weeks, for it was vital that he avoided coming into contact with Jehan Khan.

Judith heard Lord Minton's words through a haze of exhaustion. With throbbing head and smarting eyes she saw the two oarsmen facing her, although with their backs against the moon it was impossible for her to make out their features. Who were they? she wondered. Fishermen, most likely, she decided, who had taken Lord Minton's money in return for the Channel crossing with no questions asked—which was why they totally ignored the existence of a helpless female aboard their boat.

She shrank closer to the side of the boat, away from the nearness of her abductor, resigning herself to the movement of the swaying boat. Looking up, she gazed with passionate intensity at the stars shining brightly in the sky. How she longed to escape from this hell Lord Minton was inflicting on her. It was a time of great peril and she felt like a frightened child without protection, drained of courage and all capacity for thought, helpless and without the smallest hope.

Her fatigue was such that she fell into a light doze, which gave her a moment's respite from her terror, in which she dreamed she was being held close in Jordan's arms, and that he was whispering tender words of endearment from his lips. But the dream faded when noises penetrated the night air, the sound dragging her back to the world.

Suddenly something seemed to be happening. A voice shouted for them to heave to, causing Lord Minton to swear comprehensively. He stood up and ordered the two men to row harder, but already a boat was drawing alongside. The men stopped rowing and the boat began to rock to and fro as someone clambered aboard.

Judith's eyes became riveted on the figure, her thundering heart drowning out every other sound. She was able to distinguish his features in the light, and for a moment she thought she must be dreaming, but that keen, fine-boned face and firm lips, the unruly black hair being ruffled by the salt wind, were indelibly printed on her mind. Her heart gave a joyful leap and cried out his name long before her lips framed the word. 'Jordan!'

Suddenly a pistol exploded, shattering the night. Jordan fell to his knees beside Judith and let the ball pass harmlessly close to his ear, and he felt the breath of its passing upon his cheek. He cursed softly and fired his own pistol. There was a grunt as the ball hit its target, but Lord Minton was not sufficiently injured to give up without a fight. He was on his enemy like a flash, but despite his muscular bulk, in his weakened state and with a fire burning in his shoulder, he was no match for the other's might.

There was little room for manoeuvre in the small boat. It rocked madly as Jordan struck Minton in the ribs, the other fist coming down in a numbing blow on the point of his shoulder. Winded, Lord Minton's broad, vigorous body lay slumped down in the boat. There was a look of intense surprise on his face, and a spreading rosette of blood on the front of his coat from his injured right shoulder.

'Move, and you're a dead man,' Jordan said through clenched teeth.

Jed Taylor and his companion, resting on their oars, shuffled back on their seats, staring at the newcomer with wide-eyed alarm. His black hair, curling in a thick mass above his fierce silver eyes, was brushed back with an impatient hand. His uncompromising jaw was set as hard as granite, and his shoulders were hunched powerfully beneath his jacket.

Rory had climbed aboard and Jordan handed him a pistol. 'Watch him,' he growled, indicating the injured man, 'and if he moves shoot him.' Jordan then turned and glanced at the small, dejected figure huddled in the bottom of the boat. It was the one he loved and sought. 'Judith!' he whispered, going down on one knee beside her. With aching gentleness he pulled her into his arms.

'Thank God you are safe!' Threading his fingers through her sweet-scented hair, he framed her face between his hands and gazed at her. 'If anything had happened to you I would never have forgiven myself for leaving you alone in Brighton. I love you,' he whispered hoarsely. 'Dear God, Judith! How I love you. I love you so much I would gladly give up my life for you. Your face might have eluded me that night, but you stole my heart and gave me yours. I know you did. I could see it in your eyes when you looked at me that day at Landsdowne when we parted.'

The naked anguish in his voice brought tears to Judith's eyes as she looked adoringly at him, and the shattering sincerity and tenderness of his words sent a jolting tremor up her spine. Happiness began to spread through her until it was so intense she ached from it. She tried to speak, to express her joy, her love, but everything that had happened to her in the last two hours at Lord Minton's hands had used up all her resistance. She allowed him to draw her back into his arms, and they clung to each other in silence, too relieved and deeply moved for speech, seeming to forget the fishermen conversing noisily among themselves existed.

After a moment, Jordan gently held her away from him, tenderly smoothing back the hair from her face. 'It's all right, my love. It's all over,' he said.

'How frightened I have been,' she whispered, drawing a long, shaky breath. 'Thank goodness you came after me—but I never expected you quite so soon.'

Briefly Jordan explained how he came to be there. Anger blazed in his eyes when he saw the evidence of Minton's brutal viciousness—her swollen lips and torn dress, and the feeble attempt she had made to draw it together for modesty's sake. How could one slender girl endure such cruelty? 'If that blackguard has hurt you I might just change my mind and kill him now,' he seethed.

'I may be shaky-kneed with fright, but I'm not hurt, Jordan,' she said quickly, a wobbly smile curving her lips. She noticed how strained he looked, as if he, too, had gone through a great ordeal in the past few hours. 'A few scratches and bruises—you can see for yourself— but basically I'm sound.'

Jordan put a gentle hand beneath her chin and tilted up her face. He traced the bruise on her chin with his finger, and when she winced he drew in his breath, and cursed softly. 'I could have spared you this. I should have known when I left you that I was putting your life at risk. When I found you gone—I thought—I feared—' His arms were round her once more. 'The villain set a pretty trap for me and I'm lucky to get you back. We both know what Minton was doing in Brighton. He must have been disappointed when he found you didn't have the necklace. But how did he know you had it in the first place?'

'Alicia told him,' Judith informed him simply.

The truth hit him then, and all the things that had puzzled him clicked neatly into place. The unspeakable depths of Alicia's treachery made him tremble with rage. 'When I told her I would not marry her and sent her back to her father, I never realised what vengeance she harboured, or the lengths she would go to to appease that vengeance. But perhaps even Alicia would have thought twice about approaching Minton, had she known the power of evil that inhabits the man.' Becoming aware of the others around them, he got to his feet. 'Come, we will speak of this later. Let me help you into the other boat.'

A terrible, consuming hatred flared in Lord Minton's eyes when he looked up at his powerful assailant etched against the pale light. Defeat had come as a crushing blow. 'Why don't you finish me?' he hissed, breathing shortly. The answer was a hard, bright silver stare that seared him to the backbone.

'I'm sorely tempted, Minton—and had I any sense I would. For too long you have escaped your fate—and you have been a burden on my flesh from the moment I first set eyes on you. You took the woman I am to marry with no other cause but to make me surrender that which you seek to possess.' Removing the necklace from his breast pocket, after removing the handkerchief still wrapped round it, he let the diamond pendant dangle loosely though his fingers, his smile one of savagery when Lord Minton's eyes feasted on it greedily.

Jordan watched his adversary shift his gaze, from the jewel he'd sought so fiercely to obtain, to him, the round buttons of his eyes watchful, like those of a cornered rat. 'Take a good look at it, Minton, for it will be your last. This is what it has all been about—this diamond that belongs to the Ranee of Ranjipur, which I intend delivering to her in person.'

Nothing moved in the boat or beyond but the shimmer of moonlight on water. The face above the wounded man was a blur, but he could feel the spasm of hatred and disgust, the revulsion, that rose from the man's core, radiating through his flesh. Unable to blink, to break the hard silver gaze that held him frozen, Lord Minton felt his body shrink.

Replacing the necklace in his pocket, Jordan went on, very, very softly, to list Minton's crimes, each word enunciated. The first two were against the Rajah of Ranjipur, his third directed against himself. 'It was your henchmen who assaulted me at the docks that day, and when that failed you had me drugged in an attempt to secure the diamond for yourself.

'Your final crime is your abduction and assault of Miss Wyatt—twice. That, Minton, is quite a list. Your luck turned when you were summoned back to England to face charges of corruption. But still with your eye on the main chance, you saw there was something worth the taking, something that could set you up for life if only you could lay your thieving hands on it. But the game's up. You've run your course—had your day—and if I don't kill you, Chandu will.

'Unfortunately you will live—for now. I cannot, in all honour, kill you in cold blood. You will see a surgeon in Brighton to tend your wound, and at a date that is convenient to me we will settle what is between us on a personal basis.'

Jordan's voice lacked nothing in conviction, quiet as it was. There was a moment's silence, broken only by the lap of the water against the hull, when no one in either boat seemed to breathe. 'Follow us,' he told Jed Taylor. 'And don't even think about trying to escape. Minton will be charged with Miss Wyatt's abduction— and you two of aiding him in his nefarious plot. You became accessories when you took his money and agreed to take him to France.'

'But we had nothing to do with it,' Jed spluttered objectionably.

'I'm afraid you will find it hard to make any judge believe that.'

Having put the house to rights, Cynthia was pacing the carpet in a state of extreme anxiety when Jordan arrived with an exhausted Judith. She gave a start when they entered.

'Heaven be praised!' she ejaculated. 'It is you, Judith, and me half out of my mind with worry. Why, anything might have happened to you.'

'I am back safe and unharmed, Aunt Cynthia,' Judith said, managing a tremulous smile.

Cynthia shook her head, unconvinced by such dishevelment. 'But—your poor face is bruised—and your dress… Oh, my dear!' she gasped in distress, taking her hand in both her own. 'You—you weren't—'

'I wasn't ravished. I suffered nothing worse than a little rough handling,' she assured her aunt quietly, deeply touched by the older woman's genuine concern and obvious relief that she had returned. She was warmed by it, and hoped that after four years of resentment, she was beginning to see some redeeming features in her one remaining relative at last. 'I'm so sorry about the mess, but I see you've managed to put everything back.'

'The truth is, having to remain here and wait, I was glad to have something to do. The dragging inactivity was worse than being out there looking for you,' she said, ushering her niece to a comfortable chair by the fire before turning her attention to Lord Grant. 'You will both be glad of a little brandy, I think, after your ordeal. And then I would like an explanation.'

'Thank you, but no brandy for me,' Jordan said. 'I will leave you to put Judith to bed where she belongs. Explanations will have to wait, I'm afraid. I must get back to the beach.'

'But—must you go now?' Judith asked in a small voice, when her aunt had disappeared into the kitchen.

'I have to. There is much yet to be settled. What has happened is serious and must be reported to the proper authorities.'

'Does it have to be?'

Jordan's eyes narrowed. 'Are you saying you don't want Minton to be charged with your abduction?'

Judith heard the astonishment in his tone and sighed resignedly. 'You must do what you think is right. What I want is to forget. I am safe now, and so are you—and that is all I care about.'

With aching gentleness Jordan took her in his arms, his gaze probing with flaming warmth into hers. Bending his head, he caressed her lips lightly with his own. 'You echo my thoughts entirely, my love. Nothing matters to me but you. I love you, Judith, and my desire for you is hard driven. But I have not forgotten that Jehan Khan is at liberty in Brighton. It cannot be ignored, so I will leave my coachman here for your protection until I return.'

She looked at him in alarm. 'You will be careful? Promise me.'

His eyes held hers as he tenderly brushed a tangled curl from her cheek. 'I will. I promise.'

'Well!' Cynthia exclaimed in astonishment when he'd gone. 'So that's the way of things!'

Judith smiled. 'Yes, Aunt. It is.'

'And has he asked you to marry him?' she asked, seating herself opposite.

Judith nodded. 'I am sure he will speak to you about it in due course, Aunt.'

Cynthia perched excitedly on the edge of the chair opposite, trying to imagine what it would mean to her personally, having a niece married into such a prestigious family as the Grants of Greenwich. 'I never expected a gentleman of Lord Grant's means to offer for you.' She looked directly at her niece, her expression one of gravity. 'You would be very foolish to refuse him, Judith.'

'I have no intention of doing any such thing.'

'I am glad to hear it. I confess I was concerned that you were upset about me having to sell the house, but this makes me feel a whole lot better. Are you sure it's what you want?'

Judith nodded, settling back into the chair. Secure in the knowledge that Jordan loved her, she felt certain that there was no other man in the whole world for her. 'It's everything. I love him so much. Sometimes, what I feel frightens me. When I came to England, I could never imagine another world for myself and thanked God I was successful in the one allotted to me. But Jordan changed all that.'

Suddenly she recalled what her mother had once told her, that there had been a gentleman in her aunt's life whom everyone had thought she would marry. But he had left her for someone else. Apparently, it had been a rather tragic business at the time, leaving her aunt broken-hearted and bitterly disappointed. But she had bottled up her feelings and got on with her life.

Judith glanced across at her, wondering how much she had suffered because of it. 'H—have you ever loved very deeply, Aunt Cynthia?' she dared to ask quietly. Her aunt's eyes misted, and for a moment her life seemed to be suspended by memory of a tragic love. Drawing a deep breath, she half-turned her face away, and Judith was struck by its mournful look.

'Yes,' she replied at length. 'Once. Its loss is too painful and its presence too demanding. I swore when he left me for another that I had done with love—and I kept my word to myself. That way life is more straightforward. It suits me. Mr Wakeman is quiet and uncomplicated and will suit me well enough,' she said with quiet resignation.

'I'm glad of that, Aunt,' Judith murmured, looking at her as if seeing her for the first time, realising there was an underlying sensitivity and fragility about her, which until now she had not been aware of. At last she was able to understand her aunt a little, and to think of her with a kind of tenderness. The small revelation of what was in her heart had won her affection, too. However, if their relationship was going to improve, they would have to ease into it.

'Will you return to London with Lord Grant, Judith?'

'Would you mind if I remain here in Brighton with you for a while, Aunt? I want to make the most of it—before you marry Mr Wakeman and move to Chichester.'

'I would like that,' she smiled.

'Then I shall—and when Jordan and I are married, you and Mr Wakeman must visit us in London. I must also write to Miss Powell at the academy and inform her of all that has transpired.'

'At least your marriage will take care of that problem. You will no longer have the need to take up employment to support yourself.'

'I may not need to, Aunt, but I am determined to remain involved with the academy in some capacity.'

Her aunt glanced at her sceptically. 'You may find that your husband will object most strongly to that.'

'He won't,' Judith replied with a smile of confidence when she recalled the conversation at the dinner table on her first evening at Landsdowne, when she had made her opinions plain to everyone and seen the spark of admiration in Jordan's eyes. He had told her afterwards that he was by no means prejudiced against females with brains, adding that she had taught him something new, and he was beginning to think that there was no substitute for a clear-sighted, intelligent woman. She hoped he would still feel that way when she was his wife.

Chapter Eighteen

The beach was a long, pale ribbon of light against the black sea, and dawn was breaking on the horizon when Jordan strode to the water's edge and helped Jed Taylor and his companion pull the boat carrying Jeremy Minton up onto the shingle. After securing a promise from Jordan that the remainder of what he owed would be forthcoming, Rory and the others had already gone to their homes. Jordan stood aside as Jed helped Minton from the small craft. His face was a hardened mask of icy wrath as his eyes blazed at his enemy, and the air between them was filled with hate and hostility.

Without a word they turned to leave the beach, when Jehan Khan, dressed in white robes and an extravagant turban, appeared before them like an apparition. His carriage was drawn up on the promenade, his two servants standing like statues a few paces behind him. Jehan Khan's unexpected arrival and princely bearing, set against the backdrop of the Prince Regent's Royal Pavilion, with its eastern domes and minarets, brought the two gaping fishermen to a halt.

Khan's hooded eyes were fixed and unblinking. His stare did not waver from Lord Minton's stumbling form.

They came face to face. The Indian's black eyes narrowed and glittered dangerously.

'Welcome back,' he said smoothly, his voice of a thin, high-pitched timbre. 'Your sudden departure was not without reason. I had almost begun to fear I would have to go to France in search of you.'

'So,' Lord Minton hissed, 'you set your bloodhounds onto me, Khan.'

'I didn't need to. In your haste to reach Brighton you carelessly left the letter sent to you by Miss Paxton in the top drawer of your desk. It didn't take me long to find it.' The dislike and distrust Khan felt for Minton had turned into a consuming hatred at this latest treachery, and it showed in the deadly glitter in his coal-black eyes.

'You will regret this, Lord Minton. You have not only gone against me, but Prince Chandu, also. I always knew you would bite his hand when your luck turned. I've seen it coming for a long time. You have played a double game with the wrong man, and you will find it hasn't paid you. Of course, I knew you wanted the diamond, but the desperate measures you have gone to to obtain it I cannot allow to pass. You are wounded, I see. Your work, I suspect, Grant-sahib.'

Khan's eyes lingered briefly on Jordan, reminding him of a cobra's eyes beneath its hood—staring and malevolent. They shifted back to Lord Minton.

'I promise you I will not wound you, Lord Minton. I shall do myself the honour of killing you.' His voice was flat and deadly, and Minton stared at him with frustrated anger and pain.

Jordan was too far away to prevent Khan from driving a knife to the hilt into Minton's chest. It was done swiftly and cleanly, which was the case in all Khan's dealings. Minton fell on his hands and knees, but succeeded in staggering to his feet and lurching towards Khan, hands outstretched, with a sleepwalker's face.

He knew the folly of trying to double cross Prince Chandu, and retribution had come quickly in the form of Jehan Khan. Khan slowly backed out of his reach as Minton tripped, and with a final convulsion that fixed a grin in a hideous rictus upon his face, he coughed up an amazing quantity of bright red frothing blood, and fell dead at his feet.

With his blank face, his white robes and the blood on the hand still holding the thin-bladed knife, Khan truly resembled some demon cast up out of the pit. Jordan knew the kind of creature Chandu's envoy was. He knew what depths of evil and sadistic cruelty lay behind that face. Minton's death would not lie heavy on his conscience. He lifted his eyes to Jordan.

'It is done, Grant-sahib. I grew weary of his presence, his treachery and his lies, and so—as one would do to a scorpion about to strike—I killed him. It must have occurred to you that he was in the pay of Prince Chandu.'

'There is little that escapes me, Khan.'

'My master made him rich, but his palm itched for more. He wanted the diamond of Ranjipur for himself.'

'I know that, too. But this is not the frontier region of India, where you indulge in tribal warfare. This is England, and you have just murdered a man. You will be called to account for your crime.'

'I think not, and please—do not try to apprehend me,' Khan said on a warning note, indicating his servants hovering close, clutching weapons of their own which they kept concealed in the folds of their robes. 'I realise it is now dangerous for me to stay here, so I shall simply disappear. Now the government has made it plain that they will not grant Prince Chandu the state of Ranjipur—

and since you are to give the Ranee the necklace my master sought to possess, there is nothing to keep me here. It is time for me to return to India.'

He bowed his head ceremoniously, his face taking on a neutral expression. The huge black pearl in his turban caught the light of the rising sun as he turned and walked slowly back to his carriage, and as he did so the white silk of his robe billowed out behind him, so that for a moment it seemed to Jordan that he was looking at a departing ghost. A sudden chill descended on the three men left on the beach, and no one spoke until the carriage had disappeared along the empty promenade.

When Jordan arrived at Miss Wyatt's house in mid-morning, he found Judith alone. Without moving, she looked across the room at him, her face pale, her eyes questioning.

'Is it over?'

'Yes, it's over.' His voice was solemn. Wearily he moved towards her. 'It's good news—or bad, depending on how you take it. Minton is dead, Judith. He can do no more harm.'

She was stricken. 'You—you killed him?'

'No. Jehan Khan did. I lost no time in reporting your abduction and Minton's murder to the local magistrate. I disclosed the identity of the murderer, but I know there is little hope of Jehan Khan being apprehended and arrested. He's as cunning as a fox, and will disappear without trace.'

A moan of relief, of torment, tore from Judith's chest. She came wordlessly into his arms, kissing him with a silent desperation that matched his own, pressing herself to him, crushing her soft mouth to his. The passing of carriages out in the street brought them back to reality and they stood, arms still entwined, gazing at each other.

'I can't believe it's over, Jordan. I can't believe you're here, holding me at last,' she whispered. 'Just a few hours ago everything seemed so—so—'

'Futile?' he provided in the deep, compelling voice that never failed to wreak havoc on her body, her soul, and her heart.

She nodded. 'And hopeless. Dear Lord, when I regained consciousness and found myself in that boat with Lord Minton, I was already missing you so much.'

Jordan answered her with his mouth, his warm lips moving fiercely on hers, as he kissed her with a raw, urgent hunger that made her feel helpless. Her hands crept up his muscular male chest, fastening around his neck, allowing her lips to yield to his kiss, parting beneath the sensual pressure. The sensation of his hardening body crushed against hers was all so achingly, poignantly familiar to her, because she had experienced it before and lived it in her dreams a million times.

Dragging his mouth from hers, Jordan gazed down at her flushed face, at the half-moons of her dark lashes, her unselfish ardour having a devastating effect on his starved body.

'Open your eyes, little one,' he whispered.

She obeyed and found herself meeting his half-shuttered eyes, seeing in them the changes that passion had made in him. A muscle moved spasmodically in his throat, his face was hard and dark, his lips sensual, his voice low.

'We will be married just as soon as it can be arranged.'

His eyes gazed into hers, plumbing their innermost depths, and Judith was overwhelmed at the passionate desire she read in them. She rested her hand against his

shaven cheek. 'By your side I will happily stand, Jordan,
if you want me there. But my marriage to you must not
stop my work. I would still like to be involved in some
kind of employment at the academy. I cannot do as convention demands—a lady of leisure, with nothing to do
but run a house. It is important to me that I am involved
in something productive. You do understand, don't you?'
She lifted her eyes to his pleadingly, watching with a
mixture of anxiety and hope for his reaction.

A wry smile touched his mouth, and he gave in without
a struggle. 'You're always so practical, my love, and of
course I wouldn't stand in your way if you want to involve yourself in matters at the academy,' he said decisively, 'but my mind is on productivity of a different
kind—a process that might be in motion already, don't
forget.'

The intensity of his gaze ploughed through her composure. 'I haven't forgotten,' she could not resist teasing.
Then she became serious. 'But if I'm not—'

He raised his brows in amused challenge. 'You very
soon will be.'

'Jordan—there is something I have to tell you.'

'What?' he queried.

'I—what I mean to say is—there is no baby.'

'You are certain of this?'

She nodded. 'As certain as a woman can be about such
things.'

His face remained expressionless. 'Are you disappointed?'

'Relieved,' she confessed.

'But you do want my baby?'

'Desperately. I was simply worried about the timing.'
she whispered, pressing a kiss against his throat.

Grinning wickedly, Jordan cupped her face between

his hands, brushing his thumbs over her smooth cheeks. 'Keep doing that and you could find yourself with child sooner than is decent,' he murmured. 'As soon as you are my wife, I intend to spend every night in the pleasurable occupation of siring my heir. If I don't succeed, it won't be for want of trying. I'm terribly selfish, my love, and I want us to be married without delay.'

Judith's cheeks turned scarlet, but an answering sparkle lit her eyes. 'So do I. But won't everyone think that is highly irregular?'

'I don't give a damn about what everyone else thinks. Besides, everything about our relationship has been highly irregular, in every way.'

'I fear the news that we are to marry will cause a terrible scandal.'

'A few eyebrows are bound to be raised, of course.'

'I am prepared for gossip—even to be cut, but I am far too happy to care.'

'That's the kind of spirit I expect from you. And we will be happy, my love. I promise. As soon as the wedding is over I must leave for India on Company business. We will go together and make it our honeymoon. I intend showing you the beauty of the foothills as well as the serenity and quiet beauty of the distant Himalayas. We will stay in Delhi, where we can watch the magic of the moonflowers opening together—and press some more in a book to remember our time there. Does that appeal to you?'

Judith stared at him, unable to comprehend what he had said. 'India?' she whispered, swallowing hard and looking at him warily. 'Jordan—you do not jest with me?'

'I would not jest about something which I know means

a great deal to you. Come, what do you say? I know you would like to return.'

Unable to put her thoughts into words or to stem her feelings, she threw her arms about his neck and wept tears of absolute joy. India was hundreds of miles away, but already she could feel her life stretching away to unimaginable horizons. She could smell the bazaars, the sweet flowering orange blossoms, jasmine and frangipani—the smell of home.

'Am I to understand from this outpouring of emotion that you are happy with the arrangement?' Jordan asked softly.

When she raised her tear bright eyes to his she smiled broadly. 'I'm very happy. I don't know what to say—except thank you, Jordan—with all my heart. I am just so happy I could die.'

He grinned, placing a kiss on her brow. 'Don't you dare. I can't get married without you,' he teased. 'Now, can't I persuade you to return to London with me?'

'I will stay in Brighton for a little while, if you don't mind. I know Aunt Cynthia would like me to.'

His brows arched quizzically. 'You and your aunt seem to be getting on remarkably well, all of a sudden. Do I detect a softening in your attitudes towards each other?'

'Yes. Which is why I would like to remain a little longer. Perhaps two weeks. You don't mind, do you, Jordan?'

'Mind? Of course I mind,' he said, his arms going round her once more, his breath sending vibrant warmth spilling through her veins. 'I can't bear being apart from you. But you corrupt me with your delightful distractions, my love. I've been idle for two days, and I'll have to work twice as hard when I return to London to make up for it.'

When it was time for Judith to leave Brighton, Jordan sent the carriage for her, refusing even to consider allowing her to use the Brighton to London stagecoach as she had done previously. As he was unable to come himself, Charlotte arrived with Emily, and after partaking of Aunt Cynthia's hospitality—she was absolutely delighted to entertain two such distinguished ladies—the four of them went for a stroll along the promenade.

After bidding her aunt farewell—with a fondness always absent on their previous partings, Judith set off for London with her two companions, the entire conversation from Brighton to Greenwich being about the arrangements to be made for her wedding to Jordan.

Like everyone else, Charlotte had been horrified when, on his return to Landsdowne, Jordan had told them of the unfortunate events that had shadowed him since his return to England, and how Judith had become innocently drawn into the dastardly Lord Minton's web of treachery, and the brutal treatment she had received at his hands when he had abducted her again. However, she was ecstatic at the way things had turned out, and that her dear friend was to be her sister-in-law—but then, she said with a haughty toss of her blonde curls, she had always known she would be.

On reaching Landsdowne they were met by Lady Grant, who was highly delighted to receive her future daughter-in-law safe and well, and she sincerely hoped the whole unfortunate episode concerning Lord Minton was well and truly behind them. Judith was a remarkable young woman, who would make her son a far more fitting wife than Alicia ever could, and since he had returned from Brighton, she had never seen him so relaxed and happy.

'Where is Jordan? Can I see him?' Judith asked, unable to contain her impatience.

'Of course you can, just as soon as he returns.'

Judith had a sudden sense of disappointment. For days now she had been living with the one thought of seeing him and being with him for ever—sharing their lives together—and now she found she must wait a little longer. So great was her disappointment that it came as something of a shock to hear Lady Grant laugh.

'Don't worry, my dear. He is not far away. He arrived from town early, and so impatient was he to see you, he has gone to work his frustration out on his poor horse and is riding in the park.'

Judith relaxed, her face breaking out into a smile. 'Oh, is that all? Then out of pity for his poor horse, I feel I must go and find him.'

The sky being overcast, there were few people in the park. She hadn't been walking very long when the sound of galloping hoofbeats made itself heard, and she paused, seeing a horse and rider coming towards her. The noise grew louder, nearer, and in a moment they were upon her. In danger of being ridden down, she stepped back. So still was she standing in the shade of the trees that it was likely Jordan had not seen her.

Held spellbound by the wildness of horse and rider, and the sheer beauty of the gallop and the man in the saddle, she gasped—a tide of love rolling over her and almost drowning her, a torrent that, had she had any doubts about marrying this man, would have swept them away.

When she stepped out of the trees the great horse reared back, its slender legs pawing the air, then dropped them to the ground and stood quiet, while its master sprang to the ground with athletic ease. He strode towards her, his eyes smiling, and swept her up into his arms.

'I've missed you,' Judith said quietly, looking up at him, loving him, the mere sight of him and the way his dark hair fell carelessly over his brow twisting her insides into hot, tight knots of yearning.

'And I you,' he murmured, looking at her with adoration in his eyes. 'I love you wholeheartedly and without reserve. You are my future, Judith. Without you my life is incomplete. I have arranged for us to be married a month from now. Miss Powell has suggested that you stay with her until the wedding. Do you have any objections to that?'

'Only one.' Her smile was impish.

He frowned. 'Oh?'

'Why do we have to wait so long? Couldn't you have arranged it sooner?'

'Minx,' he said, catching her up into his arms once more and spinning her round, their laughter drawing the attention of a group of people strolling close by.

Slipping his arm about her waist and taking the reins, together they made their way slowly out of the park.

'Have you heard anything of Alicia, Jordan?' Judith asked on a more serious note. 'Do you know if she's still in Kent?'

He nodded. 'And expected to remain so. Indefinitely.'

'Oh? You surprise me. I thought she disliked the country intensely.'

'So she does. It was unfortunate for Alicia that Emily informed their father of her unacceptable behaviour while she was our guest here at Landsdowne, and the devious methods she used to entrap me into wedlock. It was like pouring oil over red-hot coals,' he chuckled softly.

'What do you mean?'

'That moral, hugely respected man erupted like a volcano. During Alicia's absence he learned of her affair with his steward, Philip Mason, from the wife of an acquaintance—who probably told him for some spiteful reason of her own. According to Edmund, this, combined with her disgraceful antics here in London, motivated that usually mild-mannered man into action. He was outraged, his temper unrestrained.'

'Why, what on earth did he do?'

Jordan grinned down at her. 'Determined to curb his daughter's wild ways once and for all—to punish her, to teach her a lesson she will never forget—he insists she will wed his steward before the month is out.'

Judith stared at him incredulously. 'Alicia will never agree to that. She is far too proud, too arrogant, ever to submit to marrying a man of such low social standing.'

'Oh, she ranted and railed against it, but even Alicia cannot stand against her father when his mind is made up. It is hardly the expedient marriage he had planned for his daughter, you understand, but her affair with Philip Mason has become common gossip and Alicia's reputation is in ruins. Her father is determined that she will pay for the shame she has brought upon the family, that nothing will impede the marriage—and his steward is highly delighted with the arrangement.'

'Then, despite their affair, he cannot be aware of the true nature of the woman he is marrying.'

'I doubt anyone will ever know the true workings of Alicia's mind, but however you look at it, Philip Mason stands to gain from the marriage in a material sense. All her life Alicia has been a sore trial to her father. He called her wanton—accusing her of inheriting bad blood from an uncle on her mother's side—and bad blood will always out in the end. I doubt Alicia will ever get over the humiliation and shame of being forced to marry one of her father's employees. She'll never be able to hold her head up in society again, so I doubt she will venture far from home—at least, not in the foreseeable future.'

Judith felt a stirring of exultation and overwhelming relief that she wouldn't have to face Alicia again if she didn't want to, leaving her thankful. She waited for the pang of sadness she might feel when a woman is forced into a marriage against her will, but none was forthcoming.

'Speaking of Alicia brings to mind one other who has tried to harm you,' she said. 'Jehan Khan! Have you heard what has become of him?'

'No. Although I suspect he will be on his way to India by now. The Ranee of Ranjipur has arrived in London with her daughter. I will take you to meet her.'

'I would like that. Is she to remain in London indefinitely?'

'No. She intends to return to India and seek asylum in her brother's domain, where she should be safe from Chandu's evil machinations.'

'Will it be granted?'

'Yes. Her brother owes loyalty to the Ranee's husband, and will make her welcome.'

'You have given her the necklace?'

He nodded. 'To be perfectly honest, it was a relief to be rid of it—although she did offer to loan it to you to wear with your wedding gown.'

'She did? Oh—I don't know what to say,' Judith said, looking away, not wishing to give offence by refusing such a generous offer; but in truth, she never wanted to see that particular treasure ever again.

Jordan smiled, reading her thoughts exactly. 'Don't

worry, my love. I took the liberty of refusing on your behalf.' He grinned when she raised her eyes to his. 'I have jewels of my own to adorn the neck of my bride on her wedding day—but no jewel on earth is as exquisite as you. To me, my love, you are a rare gem indeed—a jewel beyond price.'

For Judith her wedding day had a distinct aura of unreality. Never had she believed she could be so happy. In a church aglow with candlelight and perfumed with lavish blooms, among a sea of smiling faces and a vicar waiting with the marriage book open in his hands, on Edmund's arm and with Charlotte in attendance, it was with a sense of quiet joy that she walked down the aisle to take her place beside Jordan.

Turning, Jordan felt as if his chest would burst at the sight that greeted him. Holding a spray of white lilies, Judith was a vision of ethereal loveliness in cream and white. A special kind of radiance was gathered into her face beneath the dawn mist of her veil. She was glowing, but it was her smile that tugged his heart the most. So filled with peace and contentment, it was the most beautiful smile he had ever seen, and in her eyes he saw all the love in the world, the promise of unborn children, and a lifetime of happiness and love together.

After speaking their vows they were pronounced husband and wife. A grand banquet and reception followed, which to the happy couple seemed like an eternity of smiling and being polite, until they found the opportunity to slip away.

In no time at all Judith fell under the spell of her husband's heavy-lidded gaze and inviting smile. Fuelled by weeks of abstinence, desire began to beat fiercely in Jordan's veins and he pulled her close, his mouth opening over hers with sudden urgency. They kissed deeply, almost savagely, pausing only long enough to cast off their clothes, before falling onto the bed, their bodies melting feverishly, entwining at last. Waves of pure, physical pleasure washed over them. Lost in the physical bliss of their union, of giving to the other and finding everything and much more in return, they each knew that theirs was a special kind of love.

Later, sated and spent, entwined in the afterglow of passion, the quiet of the bedroom was wafted by sighs. After a while of being wrapped in each other's arms, Jordan raised himself so that he could look down at Judith's sleeping face, unable to believe that she belonged to him at last. He was much enamoured of this adorable young wife of his, and there was much more to her than he had ever realised. Bending his head, he placed a lingering kiss on her parted lips, breathing in the delicious fragrance of her. She opened her eyes and he smiled.

'Welcome home, my love,' he said softly, for he knew without doubt that this was not the first time he had made love to his wife, and that the mysterious woman who had shared his bed on the night of the ball had returned to him. What they had was meant to be. It was like the fish in the sea, the ever-changing seasons, and the moon and the stars in the sky. It was eternal, and should the earth cease to exist, they would still go on.

Judith was the woman he would love to the end of his life, and beyond.

* * * * *

A Penniless Prospect
by
by Joanna Maitland

For Frances

Joanna Maitland was born and educated in Scotland though she has spent most of her adult life in England or abroad. She has been a systems analyst, an accountant, a civil servant, and director of a charity. Now that her two children have left home, she and her husband have moved from Hampshire to the Welsh Marches, where she is revelling in the more rugged country and the wealth of medieval locations. When she is not writing or climbing through ruined castles, she devotes her time to trying to tame her new house and garden, both of which are determined to resist any suggestion of order.

Readers are invited to visit Joanna's website at www.joannamaitland.com

Chapter One

'It's Cinderella, all over again. Who says fairy tales don't come true? The only difference is, I'm a mite short of fairy godmothers.' With a heartfelt sigh, Jessamyne sank into a hard, straight-backed chair, the only one in her spartan bedroom.

'Oh, miss, you mustn't take on so. If my lady should hear you—'

'The wicked stepmother? Come now, Biddy dear, she knows precisely what I think of her, as you are well aware. But she also knows there is nothing I can do about it, since she has my father's ear as well as control of the purse-strings. Papa will not help me. And without money, I cannot help myself. Now, if you were but a fairy godmother, Biddy...'

'Oh, give over, Miss Jamie, do. Them things only happen in fairy stories. There ain't no Prince Charmings in the real world. P'raps if you was to make more of an effort to please her ladyship—'

'I've tried that, Biddy. You know I have. It doesn't work. She simply walks all over me. But if I stand up to her, she has to acknowledge I exist, however

little good it may do me.' She glanced at the empty
grate and the layer of crazed ice on the inside of the
window pane. Drawing her threadbare shawl more
closely round her shoulders, she smiled bravely at her
old nurse. 'At least she doesn't make me scrub floors
and sweep cinders.'

'No,' agreed Biddy, 'but it would make little difference if she did. Your hands are little better than a
scullery maid's, with all that gardening you do. In the
depths of winter, too! If only you would—'

She was interrupted by a scratching at the door—
a maid with a message summoning Miss Jessamyne
to her stepmother's dressing-room.

Jamie swallowed hard. Such a summons always
boded ill. Sometimes she would simply be berated,
belittled for her looks or her behaviour. Sometimes
she would hear of punishments to come, for real or
imagined transgressions. And sometimes both. Never,
in all Lady Calderwood's time in the house, had she
spoken a single kind or loving word to her stepdaughter. There was no reason to suppose that this summons would be any different.

Although Jamie entered those stern precincts with
head held high, she could not wholly conceal the uncertainty she felt. Lady Calderwood was seated at her
dressing table while her abigail put the finishing
touches to her hair. Jamie was left standing by the
door, unacknowledged, for several minutes. Her uncertainty was soon replaced by indignation. How
dared that woman treat her so?

At length, her ladyship was satisfied, and her
woman was dismissed. She turned slowly to look at

her stepdaughter, scrutinising her from head to toe with ill-concealed dislike. Her lip curled slightly. 'Well, Jessamyne, you may guess why I have sent for you.'

'No, ma'am,' replied Jamie evenly, 'I have not the least idea.' She noted, without surprise, that she was not invited to sit. She was deliberately being left to stand like a disobedient child awaiting punishment. Well, she would not help her stepmother to play her little games. Jamie lifted her chin a fraction. She would not say anything more.

After a moment, Lady Calderwood continued grimly, 'Very well, I shall tell you, since you do not wish to venture an opinion.' She gave a very nasty smile at which Jamie shivered a little, in spite of all her efforts at self-control. She felt so helpless when she was in the power of this woman.

Her ladyship's smile broadened. 'You are past twenty already, Jessamyne. It is high time you were married and ceased to be such a charge on your poor papa.'

Jamie bit her lip in frustration. She was precious little charge on 'poor papa', considering how little was spent on her. She could not remember when she had last had a new gown or anything becoming to wear, even at second hand. But marriage—did that mean a season in London, *at last*? And perhaps even a few new gowns? For if they did not garb her becomingly, who would be found to offer for her?

'Of course, there can be no question of a season for you,' announced her ladyship sharply, watching her stepdaughter's face fall. 'Your papa could not

countenance the expense. And it would be a waste of
money, for who would choose to offer for a girl like
you? No looks and no portion? No. Even *I* could not
fire you off successfully.'

Jamie could feel the colour draining from her face.
She clamped her lips tightly together in an effort to
control their trembling. No doubt her ladyship was
pleased with the effect.

'I see you have grasped my meaning. There is only
one solution for a girl like you. And you should be
grateful to your papa for all the trouble he has taken
to find you a husband who is prepared to have you,
in spite of all your shortcomings. What have you to
say to that, my girl?'

She smiles like a snake, thought Jamie, a snake
who is about to swallow me up. Oh, God! What am
I to do? She is waiting for me to ask who has been
found to take me off their hands.

She compressed her lips even more tightly and
stared brazenly at her stepmother, refusing to give her
the satisfaction of a response. She was pleased to see
her stepmother's frown. Jamie's defiance had turned
self-satisfaction to anger. Good—even if it did turn
on her.

'You think to defy me, girl? But not for long, I
assure you, not for long.' Lady Calderwood paused
to rearrange the generous folds of her amber silk
gown. 'You will be married within the month. And I
shall warn your husband about the need to curb your
rebellious nature, be sure of that. He will see that you
abide by your vows of obedience.'

Jamie remained motionless, but her brain was

churning. Who was this man who had agreed to marry her, a plain girl with no dowry? And why? She shivered again, but then she forced herself to straighten her back and stiffen her wobbly knees. Clearly her stepmother was determined not to give her a name until she asked for it. So be it. There would be a battle of wills.

For long moments, the two women stared at each other—one young, shabbily dressed but proud, the other somewhat past her prime and indulged in every way. The older woman broke first. 'Insolent chit!' she hissed. 'Go to your room. I shall deal with you later.'

Head held high, Jamie left the room and returned to her own freezing chamber, where she threw herself on to the bed and thumped her clenched fists into the pillow. 'The old witch,' she muttered. 'May she rot in hell!'

Much as she tried, Jamie was not able to prevent a few tears from squeezing their way out on to her cheeks. She despised her own weakness. But the thought of marriage to some unknown man—chosen by her stepmother, so bound to be utterly hateful— was horrifying. She would be completely in his power, forced to submit to his will in everything— until the day she died.

Not for the first time, Jamie was left alone in her room for hours with neither food nor company. She had known it would be so. However frightened she might be of the fate which awaited her, she refused to yield to her stepmother's petty tortures. Dumb insolence was her only weapon and she was quite prepared to use it, at whatever personal cost. In this case, she knew she would win eventually, for she would have to be given the name of the lucky bridegroom sooner or later, even if only on the day of her wedding.

She huddled herself into a ball on the bed, wrapping every scrap of blanket around her in an effort to stop herself from freezing. Eventually, in spite of cold and hunger, she fell into a troubled sleep.

It must have been the sound of the door which woke her. Biddy was standing in the centre of the room with a gown draped over her plump arm. She looked uncomfortable. 'Her ladyship sent me to warn you that your betrothed is arriving later today. You are to be ready to receive him.'

Jamie sat up immediately, her eyes wide with shock. She was still freezing cold, in spite of the blankets, but at least she was not shivering. She refused to appear as a quivering wreck in front of her old nurse.

But she was not too proud to ask Biddy for the man's name.

'I'm sorry, miss, but I'm afraid I don't know. Nobody does—except her ladyship, and your papa.' Biddy moved towards the bed. 'Her ladyship sent this gown for you to wear to dinner this evening.' Biddy sounded more confident now, moving on to practical matters.

It was a plain white muslin gown such as might be worn by a debutante from a family of modest means. 'White,' breathed Jamie bitterly, 'as becomes the virgin sacrifice. How very appropriate. With my colouring, I shall certainly look the part.'

Her irony was lost on old Biddy. 'White is the proper colour for a young girl such as you, miss. I'll admit you do look better in colours, being as you're so pale-complexioned, but you have no choice tonight. You have no other decent gown to your name. It'll have to be this white muslin.'

Jamie got up, pulling the blankets from the bed and wrapping them round her shoulders. 'When is he due to arrive, Biddy?'

'Nobody is sure. He may be delayed by the weather, o' course. It's difficult travelling at this time of year.' Biddy seemed to be trying to avoid the subject of Jamie's future.

Jamie was not really surprised. Old Biddy had served the family for over twenty years as, first, Jamie's nurse, then as her half-brother's, and now Jamie's three half-sisters'. Biddy would not dare to risk her place with the Calderwood family by taking Jamie's part against the formidable mistress of the house.

Jamie forced a smile. She still had her pride. 'Thank you, Biddy. I shan't need you this evening. Go back to your little ones. They'll be fretting for you.' Biddy hurried away to the nursery where it was warm and cosy.

As Jamie began to change into the thin muslin gown, she heard the sound of wheels crunching across the drive. He was here! The ice on the window blurred her view, but she could just make out a gentleman's travelling carriage and four horses. Her betrothed travelled in style to acquire his reluctant bride, it seemed. He must be wealthy—which might explain how he could afford to marry a girl with no dowry. What else might it mean?

She felt an overpowering desire to see what this man was like. Would she recognise him? Would he be one of her father's gambling cronies? Hastily throwing her shawl around her bare shoulders, she crept down the stairs to find a safe vantage point on the landing. Kneeling behind the balusters, she peered through to get a glimpse of her fate when he was admitted through the great doors of Calderwood Hall.

But the gentleman who stood in the entrance hall to be relieved of his travelling coat was like no man she had ever met. Although he was dressed in deep mourning, to Jamie's untutored eye he was tall, dark and unbelievably handsome.

She drew in a sharp breath and held it, waiting for him to speak.

'My name is Hardinge,' he said, in a deep, well-modulated voice that sent a shiver all the way down to her toes. She was transfixed by the sound. It set her mind spinning so much that, for several moments, she could not make out a word that was being said.

She came to her senses as the gentleman stopped speaking. The butler was glancing surreptitiously at the card in his hand. 'Certainly, my lord. If you would kindly step into the saloon.'

Jamie watched as the noble visitor was bowed into the crimson saloon. The door closed on him, but his image remained before her. How could it be that such a man—a man whose mere presence could make her skin tingle and her heart race—should arrive at Calderwood now? He could not be her betrothed.

Could he?

Chapter Two

'My name is Hardinge.' Richard, Earl Hardinge, proffered his card to the butler. 'Be so good as to take my card up to your master and beg him for the favour of a few minutes of his time, with my apologies for having arrived unannounced. It is a matter of some importance.'

Richard was content to wait in the saloon while his message was delivered. He looked carefully at his surroundings. So much for the rumour that the family was deep in debt. This elegant room was fairly recently refurbished, as far as he could judge from the sumptuous hangings. A pity the family's extravagance did not extend to more than a tiny fire—the room was absolutely freezing. He was not altogether surprised, for he had heard nothing but ill about this family of wastrels. He would be glad when his business was concluded—provided, of course, that he was successful. He could not afford to fail.

Richard stood with his back to the fireplace, trying to get some warmth into his limbs after the long journey. He hoped his servants were receiving better hospitality in the kitchen than he was, for they must by now be frozen to the marrow.

Barely five minutes after the door had closed behind the butler, Lady Calderwood entered the saloon and extended her hand politely to her visitor. 'Lord Hardinge,' she said, with a hint of enquiry in her voice, 'you have come on a matter of some urgency?'

'Lady Calderwood.' Damn the woman! The last thing he wanted was to discuss his business with Calderwood's wife. Surely the man was not too cowardly to meet him? Richard managed to conceal his annoyance as he bowed over her immaculate white hand. 'How kind of you to receive me, ma'am. I hope Sir John is not indisposed? I shall not take up much of his time, I assure you.'

Lady Calderwood took her seat in a wing chair near the fire and motioned her guest to sit opposite. 'I am afraid my husband is suffering from a severe chill,' she said silkily. 'His doctor has forbidden him to leave his room—or to receive visitors. It seems you have had a wasted journey.' She smiled. 'But you must be cold after your hours on the road. Perhaps I can offer you some refreshment before you leave?'

Richard shook his head, returning her false smile. He had not the least intention of leaving empty-handed. If Calderwood did not dare to face him, then he would have no choice but to get to the man via his wife. She was just one more calculating society woman—he would put the fear of God into her, if he had to. By the looks of her—he could tell at a glance exactly how much had been spent on her lavish attire—she was deeply involved in her husband's spendthrift habits. He was going to enjoy putting her in her place.

He relaxed slightly into his chair and lifted his chin. The smile still played around his firm mouth. 'You must be wondering about my errand, ma'am,' he began. 'It is a matter of business, you understand.' He paused. 'Normally, I would not dream of discussing business matters with a lady…so few men confide in their wives. And yet…yet I feel somehow certain that Sir John is one of those rare men who knows how to value a shrewd and intelligent helpmeet. I cannot doubt that you are in your husband's confidence.' Lady Calderwood was smiling broadly now. Excellent. Just a little flattery and she had given herself away. Her husband would have been more on his guard, Richard was sure. Perhaps it was as well that the man was indisposed, after all. 'It is a matter of some delicacy, I fear, ma'am, but I am sure I may rely on your discretion.'

Lady Calderwood inclined her head graciously.

Good. Now he had her. 'I should explain, ma'am, knowing that I may speak in complete confidence to you, that I am in the process of settling my father's affairs following his recent death.'

Lady Calderwood murmured condolences.

'Thank you, ma'am.' Richard looked innocently at Lady Calderwood, keeping his expression unreadable. 'You will be aware that my late father lent a very large sum of money to your husband,' he said bluntly. 'I have come to collect that debt.' Lady Calderwood had become suddenly paler. He bent forward so that his face was near hers. In a low voice, but with every syllable absolutely clear, he said, 'The debt is repayable on demand.'

Lady Calderwood flushed. 'How can you possibly know that? Your father had no—' She stopped and bit her lip.

He held her gaze for several seconds without speaking. 'No papers?' he said gently.

He gave her time to speak, but she did not. He found he was not really surprised. 'The debt is, none the less, due. And I intend to collect. Every last penny. You may tell your husband that he has fourteen days, otherwise…' He let the threat hang in the air. Without written evidence of the debt, Richard had very few legal avenues open to him, but the Calderwoods might not be aware of that. And there were other ways.

Lady Calderwood had been outmanoeuvred and she probably knew it—but if she felt any chagrin, she did not allow it to show. 'My dear sir, I shall naturally convey your message to my husband, though I am not sure… I cannot say what his reaction will be. He has never mentioned to me any financial transactions with the Hardinge family. Indeed,' she added with a titter, 'as far as I am aware, the only dealings we have had were in the matter of references for my present abigail. She was previously employed by your lady mother, I collect.'

'Ah, yes,' said Richard vaguely. He was not surprised by her ladyship's attempt to turn the conversation. 'A tall woman, I recall, though I do not remember her name.'

'Smithers,' said Lady Calderwood.

'Ah, yes,' said Richard again. 'I believe she was
with my mother for some years. A first-class dresser,
I think my mother said, but really only suitable for a
lady who is prepared to spend a fortune on her back
every season.' He looked her up and down apprais-
ingly. It was a studied insult. 'No doubt Sir John
makes you a very handsome allowance, ma'am.' He
was being incredibly rude, but he was determined to
shock this woman into some kind of action which
might prove useful to him. Otherwise he might indeed
leave empty-handed.

Lady Calderwood's eyes flashed dangerously as
she rose abruptly and started for the door. 'I do not
think my financial arrangements can be of any interest
to a stranger, sir,' she said icily. 'If you will excuse
me, I shall go and tell my husband of your visit—and
give him your message.' With the faintest bow, she
passed through the door he was holding for her.

Richard smiled faintly as he closed it on her. He
had struck a spark, right enough, but would the tinder
catch?

The butler soon returned with a decanter of madeira
and some biscuits. Richard was glad to see that he
added some wood to the pitifully small fire in the
grate, but it was still far from generous. Her ladyship
obviously practised strict economy in her household—especially on unwelcome visitors. Richard was
still pondering the inconsistency between the mean
fire and her ladyship's extravagant attire, when the
door opened once more. It was the abigail, Smithers.
Now, why on earth…?

Richard took a few moments to scrutinise the

young woman. He had barely noticed her when she
had been part of his mother's household. She was
about thirty, tall and slightly angular, with rather wiry,
dark red hair and a host of freckles across her nose
and cheeks, but she was dressed with the quiet elegance of a top-class lady's maid.

Smithers returned his gaze for a moment before
making a quick curtsy. Richard fancied she looked
uncomfortable. 'Her ladyship's compliments, my
lord. She…she has asked me to tell you that, since
Sir John is likely to be convalescing from his illness
for some time, it would not be…advisable for you to
make another visit. She will write to you when Sir
John is recovered enough to receive visitors.'

So neither of the Calderwoods would dare to face
him now. Damn them! Richard fixed the abigail with
a hard stare. She coloured slightly. Obviously she was
embarrassed at having to tell such downright lies, especially to the son of a previous employer. He should
feel sorry for her. It was not her fault, after all. 'My
mother will be glad to know that I have seen you,
Smithers,' he said, adopting an affable tone. 'I hope
you are well?'

The abigail visibly relaxed. 'Yes, my lord—and
thank you for your enquiry. Her ladyship was kind
enough to write that she hopes I am well settled here.
I admit I did not expect to receive such a mark of
attention.'

Richard refrained from asking whether the woman
was happy in her new position. It was none of his
concern. On the other hand, she might be a useful
source of information about this appalling household.

She might even know some detail of her master's financial dealings. With an engaging smile, Richard deliberately set about exercising his charm on the abigail.

He did not succeed. It seemed that Smithers was too clever to let fall anything really helpful. Eventually, he gave up.

'I am keeping you from your duties, Smithers. My apologies to your mistress—and my thanks for her hospitality.'

Smithers curtsied herself out, looking somewhat relieved to escape.

Richard sat quietly sipping his madeira while he reviewed his meagre store of information. Precious little so far. In fact, almost a wasted journey. Almost.

Chapter Three

Watching the comings and goings had been more than a little confusing for Jamie. Her stepmother's speedy arrival, and smug smile, had led Jamie to believe for a few minutes that this was indeed the man who had been chosen for her. Perhaps he was not as stern as he looked. Perhaps he might eventually come to value her, especially if she made every effort to be a good wife. Perhaps…

Doubts were sown by Lady Calderwood's sudden departure. It was obvious from the set of her shoulders that she was in a boiling rage. And Jamie's father did not appear at all. Jamie knew then. Whoever the visitor was, he was not for her. What a simpleton she was, to imagine for a moment that her betrothed would be young, or handsome. It was time to go back to her attic.

Just as Jamie made to rise, her stepmother's abigail appeared in the hall and went into the crimson saloon. No doubt she must be delivering some message from Lady Calderwood. But as the minutes passed and Smithers did not reappear, Jamie began to wonder what on earth the visitor and a mere servant could be talking about for so long. It was very strange. Jamie resolved to stay where she was.

The sound of Lady Calderwood's door opening made Jamie shrink down behind the polished balusters. But her precautions were unnecessary. Her ladyship strode downstairs without a sideways glance, reaching the hall just as her abigail came out of the saloon.

From her vantage point above, Jamie could hear every venomous word. 'And just what, pray, have you been discussing with his lordship all this time?'

The abigail blushed. 'Why, nothing, my lady. His lordship was merely asking how I did and…and telling me about the Countess.'

Lady Calderwood's eyebrows rose. 'Was he, indeed? How very…how very kind of him, to be sure.' She turned away and put her hand on the doorknob. 'Wait for me in my dressing-room.'

Jamie recognised that voice. Lady Calderwood always used it when she planned to inflict some kind of punishment on her underlings. And, judging by the way the abigail hurried off, she knew it too. Poor woman.

Barely five minutes later, her stepmother reemerged and marched up the stairs towards her dressing-room. She looked even angrier than before. And the deep frown and tight lips suggested that she might have been bested in her discussion with her visitor. Heaven help them all if that were so.

Jamie was freezing now—and so stiff that she could hardly move. She needed to return to her room before someone noticed her. But in spite of the risk, she found she could not resist waiting for one last look at what might have been—even if only in her imaginings. It would give her something to dream about, something to cling on to, when she was faced with the reality of the man her parents had chosen.

The butler had returned as soon as Lady Calderwood was out of sight, but it was nearly fifteen minutes before the visitor was back in the hall, preparing to don his travelling coat. His lordship stood frowning into the middle distance, apparently oblivious of the service being rendered by the butler. But then he turned to smile his thanks, and Jamie saw that his face was transformed. The butler was flattered by the attention. Jamie was thunderstruck.

Then the door closed on the visitor with an ominous thud, bringing Jamie back to earth and to the reality of her situation. The dream was over. Her true betrothed might arrive at any moment. Faced with the prospect of her parents' choice, she now found she wanted to postpone any sight of him for as long as possible. She rose, shivering, to return to her room.

'Why, Miss Jessamyne, you have dirt on the hem of your gown.'

'What? Oh, Smithers, I did not see you. What did you…? Oh, dear. Mama will be furious.' Although such fury would be nothing new, Jamie felt a moment of hopelessness. Who would help her now?

'Let me help you, miss,' said Smithers briskly, taking Jamie's arm and guiding her up the stairs and into her room. Smithers surveyed the extent of the damage, then whisked the dress over Jamie's head. 'You had best put something round you, miss, while I sponge this, or you'll be half-frozen before I've done.'

Huddled in her shawl, Jamie sat silently on the edge of her bed, watching Smithers' expert hands at work on the soiled dress. In next to no time, the marks had disappeared.

As she helped Jamie into the gown once more, Smithers commented, 'Have you a coloured sash, or shawl, or perhaps some flowers to wear with this, miss? Unrelieved white is very difficult to bring off, especially for someone so fair-skinned.'

Jamie grimaced. 'I have nothing of that kind, I'm afraid. Mama might be able to lend me something, since she has so many. But I don't think she would be likely to agree if I were to ask her myself. I don't suppose... Could you perhaps ask her?'

Smithers' face became suddenly hard, her expression set. 'I am sorry, I am unable to help you there, miss,' she began tightly. 'Lady Calderwood has turned me off.' Jamie gasped. 'I leave in the morning.'

'Oh, Smithers, how dreadful for you. Why has she done it? Will she give you a character?' Jamie's concern was real. She knew her own position was desperate, but, whatever happened, she would not starve. A lady's maid dismissed without a reference might never find employment again.

Smiling weakly, Smithers explained that the situation, though difficult, was not quite as catastrophic as that. Lady Calderwood would give her a character, of sorts, since she had no direct evidence of wrongdoing. Her ladyship had, however, made it clear that, should any potential employer apply to her for additional information, she would feel obliged to hint at something unsavoury in the abigail's past.

'And is there?' burst out Jamie, without stopping to think.

Smithers looked at her severely, and Jamie could feel the beginnings of a flush of embarrassment. Why could she never think before she spoke?

Smithers forestalled Jamie's apology by saying, 'You know you should not have asked such a thing, miss. But it's understandable, perhaps, with her ladyship's fine manners as an example to follow.' By now, Jamie was almost scarlet. 'Don't worry, I haven't taken offence. And, no, there is no murky past. Nor have I betrayed the confidences of this house to my previous employer. Her ladyship has been misinformed.'

'By that gentleman who just left?'

'Possibly.'

'How wicked of him! Why should he do such a thing? It is monstrous!' Jamie was quite ready to do battle on the abigail's behalf. For the moment, her own troubles were forgotten in her concern to right this manifest injustice.

Smithers shrugged. 'It is water under the bridge now, miss. You must get ready to meet your betrothed. And I must go and pack my things. Her ladyship has ordered the gig at first light to take me to the inn for the stage to Bath.' If she felt bitter, she was managing to conceal it well.

'What will you do there?'

'Bath has a number of reputable agencies for the placing of domestic servants, like abigails and governesses. If I am not successful there, I shall try again in London. Now, if you will excuse me, miss, I'll say goodbye. And good luck.'

Jamie did not hear those final generous words. She was too much struck by what had just been said about agencies for governesses and the possible escape route which they might provide. No such post, she firmly believed, could be worse than her present situation with Lady Calderwood and the prospect of a forced marriage. If she could become a governess, or a companion (under an assumed name, naturally) she could at least choose her own tormentors. But first she would have to get away from Calderwood Hall.

Jamie sat down on the bed, gazing abstractedly into the middle distance. The shawl fell unnoticed from her shoulders. She was no longer conscious of the cold as she concentrated on planning her escape, exploring and then dismissing various options—the prospect of freedom had given her back all her normal courage and resolve.

Then she was summoned to her father's study.

'Ah, come in, child, come in.' His voice was tired, prematurely aged like the rest of him. Though he was not beyond middle age, his hair was thin and white, and his hands shook slightly. In spite of his neglect of her, Jamie found she pitied him, even though she had long ago lost all trace of love for him. He was just a poor old man, broken by a strong-willed second wife and by his own addiction to the gaming tables.

'Mama has told you about the marriage which has

been arranged for you, I understand? Good, good,' he finished, without giving Jamie time to reply. 'I hope you realise how lucky you are, my child. It is not every man who would take you, you know, but luckily, Cousin Ralph is rich enough not to object to your lack of dowry.'

Jamie's blood seemed to stop in her veins. Ralph Graves—a distant relation of Lady Calderwood—was old enough to be her grandfather. She went cold all over at the very thought of him, with his twisted and wizened body, and his tiny black eyes. She remembered how those leering eyes had followed her round the room, how he had sought every opportunity to touch her, how clammy was the feel of his hand. Everything about him had made her flesh crawl.

'No!' Her protest burst out before she could think what she was saying.

Her father slowly raised his eyes to meet hers. Under his increasingly stern gaze, she flushed but held her ground. 'What did you say?' he asked ominously.

Jamie took a deep breath. 'I said I will not marry Ralph Graves, Papa.'

Her father ignored her protests. She should have known he would. 'Your betrothed is due to arrive at any moment. You will receive him graciously and accept his formal proposal when he makes it tomorrow. And then you will be wed as soon as the banns have been read.'

'No, Papa,' said Jamie again, in the most reasonable tones she could muster, 'I will not marry Ralph Graves.'

He looked sharply at her then. 'You are my daughter and you will obey me. Graves and I have settled on this arrangement, and I will not permit you to undermine my position with him. I say you will marry him.' She could see that her obstinacy was fuelling his rising anger. His face and neck were turning an alarming shade of purple. 'No other man would take you, plain and penniless as you are. Take him, or by God, I'll disown you and cast you out!' His hands were shaking even more now.

Play for time, said Jamie's inner voice. Let him calm down a little or he will throw you out this very day.

Jamie forced a tiny smile. 'Papa, please, do not be angry with me! I do not mean to vex you. I know you mean to do what is best for me and I *am* grateful, truly I am.' Behind her back, she crossed her fingers. 'But Cousin Ralph is so much older than me, besides having buried two wives already. I just…I need a little time to accustom myself to the idea of marriage to him. All I ask is a little time. Please, Papa!'

She could see not the slightest sign of softening in his face. Nothing she could say would ever sway him. He expected her to submit without a murmur—to become Ralph Graves' property, his dumb, downtrodden chattel. She refused to contemplate being so completely in the power of such a man.

'You have until this evening,' her father said flatly, without looking at her. 'Cousin Ralph is expected for dinner. And you will comport yourself as you have been taught. Or else.'

She was dismissed. There was nothing more to be

said. Slowly she climbed the stairs to her freezing refuge. Inside, she leaned thankfully against the door, closing her eyes in an effort to shut out the image of Ralph Graves. It all felt like a wicked joke. Ralph Graves might be rich, but generous he most certainly was not. From what little Jamie knew of him, he was rich because he was a miser, a miser who grudged every penny he spent. If she married him, Jamie would be exchanging one freezing garret for another—and, in addition…

No! She had never allowed herself to dwell on her sufferings. Now was definitely not the time to start.

She found herself wondering why Graves would agree to wed her without a dowry. It hardly seemed in character for such a miserly old man. She could not understand how her father could have persuaded Graves to offer for her without some kind of financial incentive. Yet she was penniless.

Jamie shook her head impatiently. She had picked a strange moment to worry over impossible riddles. She had been prepared to escape before, when she did not know who had been chosen for her.

Now, she had far more reason to flee.

Chapter Four

When Jamie entered the drawing-room, the shrivelled figure of Ralph Graves uncoiled itself from the
chair by the blazing fire and came to greet her. Taking
both her icy hands in his, he leaned forward to place
a kiss on her cheek. Jamie was enveloped in the
musty smell of his clothes. Then, at the touch of his
wet mouth on her skin, she could no longer stop the
nausea from rising in her throat. She closed her eyes
and willed herself to conquer it.

'I knew you should not mind a betrothal kiss, my
dear,' he said in a rather high-pitched voice which
cracked occasionally in the most disconcerting way.
He turned her to face him so that he could view her
properly.

He needs to examine the goods, Jamie concluded,
conscious of his bright little eyes and his damp hand
on hers. And he thinks he owns me already. She bore
his scrutiny with dignity for a moment, then said, 'Ah,
but you are a little previous, Cousin Ralph, I believe.'
She forced herself to smile flirtatiously at him, subduing the temptation to pull her hand away and rub

it clean on the muslin dress. 'Papa told me that we should meet this evening and I might then expect your formal proposal tomorrow. Do you tell me you do not intend to make one?' she teased, trying to hide her disgust behind a mask of archness.

It worked. Cousin Ralph laughed, an odd croaking sound. 'By Gad, she has grown up, as you said, Sir John. I think I may yet have the best of our bargain.' He turned back to Jamie. 'Very well. Tomorrow it shall be.'

With as genuine a smile as she could manage, Jamie enquired about their guest's journey. She was rewarded with a detailed recital of the horrors between Bathinghurst and Calderwood, where the roads alternated between slush and sticky mud.

Cousin Ralph had, he affirmed, put up with the cold and discomfort quite willingly. The warm welcome which awaited him at Calderwood—and here he paused to look meaningfully at Jamie and to pat her trapped hand again—was compensation for any hardships.

Jamie suddenly knew she had conquered all her fears—for she wanted to laugh. If Cousin Ralph had been plagued by cold and draughts, he ought to spend more of his hidden wealth on improving the comfort of his carriage. He probably even begrudged the cost of a hot brick for his feet! No real gentleman would travel in such a way. The gentleman who had called earlier, for example…

Jamie was nodding absently, apparently in agreement with what Graves was saying, and he beamed at her. But her thoughts were dangerously far away, with an elegant gentleman dressed in black. If only—

Jamie was saved by the announcement of dinner.

Graves naturally offered his arm to escort Lady Calderwood to the dining-room, where he took his seat in the place of honour on her immediate right. Jamie breathed a sigh of relief to find that she had been placed on her father's right, at the opposite end of the long mahogany dining table.

The dinner which her ladyship had ordered, though not lavish by the standards of the *ton*, was much more extravagant than the normal fare at Calderwood Hall. As the dishes of the first course were being served, Lady Calderwood turned brightly to her guest. 'Do have a little of this buttered crab, cousin. It is difficult to come by crab at this season, of course, but I re-called that it was a favourite with you.'

Graves helped himself liberally. There would be little or none left for the host or his daughter, but Jamie had been denied food for so long that she did not care. Indeed, if she partook of too many unac-customed dishes, her stomach might rebel at the un-wonted richness. She must guard against that at all costs. So, she ate a little soup and some plainly cooked fish and vegetables, refusing the beef. If Cousin Ralph noted how abstemious she was, he would be congratulating himself. His wife-to-be would not cost much to feed.

During the first course, Sir John addressed barely a word to his daughter. He preferred to address him-self to his wine, consuming copious amounts with every dish. The second course included several delicacies, together with a Rhenish cream, another of Cousin Ralph's favourites. But Jamie's eyes were fixed on a dish of gleaming oranges, piled high on a nest of green leaves. It was many years since she had been permitted to taste one, and her mouth watered at the thought of their delicious juices.

As the butler moved to offer the dish to Jamie, Lady Calderwood intervened. 'Leave them here, if you please,' she said sharply, adding, as the butler replaced the dish in front of her, 'Sir John never touches oranges at dinner, cousin. He maintains that they spoil the wine.'

Graves cast a shrewd glance at his host who was now well into his third bottle. 'There may be something in that, cousin, indeed. I do not grow oranges myself. A very ordinary fruit, in my opinion, given the shocking cost of maintaining an orangery. Do you not find it so?'

Lady Calderwood tittered. 'Oh, these were not grown here, cousin, certainly not. The expense, as you say, is not to be thought of. No, these were procured from town for your visit. I should not have done it else, I do assure you.'

Graves smiled smugly and helped himself to the finest specimen on the plate.

The knot of tension in Jamie's stomach grew tighter once more as she looked down the table at the odious cousins. She tried to concentrate on her apple but could not. Eyes fixed on her plate, she heard her father signal to the butler to refill his glass yet again. Sir John was, as usual, becoming very much the worse for his wine. By the time Lady Calderwood rose to signal the ladies' departure, her husband's occasional words had become noticeably slurred.

As soon as the gentlemen rejoined them, Lady Calderwood moved rapidly to the bell-pull by the fireplace to order the tea tray. A great wave of relief flowed over Jamie as the butler received his instructions. Not long now, surely? She bent almost eagerly to her stitchery, trying to shut out the sound of Cousin Ralph's voice.

'Jessamyne.' Jamie raised her head at the sharp voice. 'What are you about? Come and help me to serve tea to our guest.'

Jamie rose obediently from her place. She took the teacup to Graves, who was sitting in the best chair by the fire. 'Cream and sugar, cousin?' she asked politely, trying to avoid his sharp little eyes.

He took the cup awkwardly from her, trying to touch her fingers as he did so, but only succeeding in spilling the tea into the saucer.

Jamie's sharp intake of breath was drowned by a gasp of outrage from her stepmother. 'Jessamyne! How can you be so clumsy? Fetch a clean cup for Cousin Ralph. At once!' she commanded sharply.

Holding grimly to the thought that this ordeal must soon be over, Jamie did as she was bid without uttering a single word and then retreated to her dark corner once more.

Some fifteen minutes later, Lady Calderwood rose, glancing anxiously at her husband, who seemed to be half-asleep in his chair. 'If you will forgive us, cousin, I think we shall retire now. I am sure you agree that it is wise to keep early hours, especially in winter. The cost of candles is quite outrageous these days.'

Cousin Ralph rose to take his hostess's hand. 'You are only too right, dear lady. A very wise proceeding, which I also adhere to in my own establishments, particularly in the servants' hall. They are quite profligate with candles if one does not supervise them most strictly. As I am sure you do, cousin,' he added, relinquishing her hand and turning to Jamie.

He took Jamie's hand in both of his, pressing it with his clammy fingers. 'Good night, my dear Jessamyne. Sleep well. I shall see you tomorrow, as we agreed. After breakfast, do you not think?' He raised her hand to his lips.

She managed to overcome the urge to pull away from him, but she could not suppress a shiver of loathing as his lips touched her skin once more. He looked up sharply into her face.

Jamie's mind was racing. She must find a way of reassuring him. Oh, why did her body insist on betraying her so? She forced a rather wobbly smile. Maidenly modesty, she prayed, would be blamed for a little quiver of excitement at the thought of his proposal on the morrow.

'Until tomorrow, then, my dear,' he said again, letting go of her hand at last.

Jamie succeeded in waiting until she was back in her own chamber before rubbing the offended hand vigorously on the white muslin gown. She did not stop to wash. She had far more important things to do.

* * *

Jamie's preparations were swift and methodical. First, she collected together her pitifully small store of money and a bare minimum of clothes and other necessities, which she stowed under her bed. Next, she removed the awful muslin dress and her petticoats, replacing them with her nightgown over her underthings. Finally, she lay down on her bed, extinguished her candle and drew the bedclothes up to her chin.

Then, in the darkness, she waited.

She had known that waiting would be the worst part. It seemed the threat was all around her, hovering in the gloom like an evil spirit. She closed her eyes, forcing herself to focus on practical, positive things. In her mind's eye, she began to design a wondrous garden...

It seemed to take hours before the house was finally quiet. Lying on her bed, Jamie watched the moon flood the landscape with ethereal light. She breathed a silent prayer of thanks to some ancient virgin goddess for the help it would provide. Surely this was a sign that her plan would succeed?

Cautiously she slipped out of bed and across to the door. She listened carefully—there was no sound of life in the house. A quick peep into the corridor confirmed that everyone must be in bed, for no lights were to be seen.

Without lighting her candle, Jamie crept downstairs to her half-brother's room.

Less than ten minutes later she was back with her booty, completing her preparations. The bundle was retrieved from under the bed and tied up for travelling. Her nightgown was cast aside and replaced by outdoor clothes. Wrapping Edmund's worn cloak over the whole, she made her way down the back stairs and out, by the garden door, to the stables.

Her mare greeted her with a soft whinny and allowed herself to be led quietly out of the yard with only a rope halter.

'Bless you, Cara,' whispered Jamie, stroking the velvet muzzle as they reached the shadow of the outside wall. 'I hope we can both remember the way of this. It's been a very long time.' Without further ado, Jamie jumped up on to a convenient outcrop and mounted, tying her bundle into the small of her back with the strings which bound it. Edmund's old cloak covered her almost to her feet, hiding both the bundle and the fact that she rode bareback.

Holding lightly to Cara's black mane, Jamie walked her quietly away from Calderwood Hall.

Jamie was in no hurry, since she had all the hours of night to complete less than five miles. Besides, she would not for all the world have risked her beloved old mare by travelling too fast at night.

They made good speed until they came to the edge of the wood and the end of Calderwood land. Now Jamie was grateful for the moonlight, since she had to follow less familiar paths and bridleways, some of them perilously ill-kept. 'Only another mile down the lane, my Cara,' she whispered. 'Not long now.' The mare's ears twitched at the sound of her mistress's voice, but she did not pause in her gentle walk.

When Jamie reached her destination, she slid down from the bay's back and led her through the hedge and into the shelter of a belt of trees. 'Oh, I shall miss you so much, Cara,' she whispered, wrapping her arms round the mare's neck. Cara whickered softly in response, nuzzling Jamie's shoulder, then stood calmly watching her mistress as she made her final preparations.

Jamie extracted a small spade from her bundle and dug a hole under a leafless beech tree. Then she used a pair of shears to hack off much of her curly titian hair, cursing softly when she realised she had forgotten to bring anything to serve as a mirror. The hanks of hair went into the hole, followed by the shears and the spade.

As she was tying back her shoulder-length hair with a piece of black ribbon from her pack, she was surprised into a giggle by the look of interest on her mare's face. 'Well, Cara, what do you think of your new master?' Cara blinked slowly. 'Not very complimentary, are you? I admit I've probably made a poor fist of the haircut, but I can tidy it up later, if I can find a mirror and some scissors.' She patted her hair self-consciously. 'But, at least, Edmund's clothes are a reasonable fit. Don't you think I make a fine boy?' She twirled. Cara edged uneasily as the cloak billowed.

'Now we must wait.'

Dawn came slowly, a half-hearted winter light.

Still they waited.

After what seemed a very long time, the sound of hooves was heard in the nearby lane. Jamie crept forward to crouch behind the hedge. Yes, it was the Calderwood gig, driven by the old groom, with

Smithers sitting very upright in her place, staring straight in front of her.

Jamie returned to her mare. 'Now, the only risk is that old Timothy will decide to stop to wet his whistle at the inn instead of going straight back to Calderwood, as he ought.' She continued to wait, listening intently. Some fifteen minutes later, she was rewarded by the sound of the returning gig. If Timothy had slaked his thirst, he had not stayed long to do it. Jamie watched with satisfaction as the gig passed out of sight.

'And now it really is goodbye, Cara,' whispered Jamie, releasing the mare, removing the rope halter and throwing it into the hole which she then filled in with her bare hands, allowing the dirt to get under her fingernails and into her skin.

She turned to stroke the mare once more. 'Go home, Cara. Back to your warm stable.' Then she picked up her bundle and made her way down to the lane. Behind her, the horse pulled idly at a few tufts of thin grass. There was almost nothing to eat at this time of year. Soon she would be hungry enough to find her way back to Calderwood.

Jamie did not look back. Adopting the easy stride of a boy, she walked on to the village, whistling.

At the inn, all was bustle. No one took any notice of a slightly grubby boy, anxiously looking around as if in search of something. Jamie ventured into the inn, keeping her hat pulled low over her face. In the taproom, she found Smithers alone, seated primly on a bench by the wall. Jamie sat down beside her.

'What, may I ask, do you want, young man?' asked Smithers crisply, though her voice was not hostile.

'I need your help, Smithers,' pleaded Jamie softly, looking up at her. 'Please don't give me away.'

'Good God! Miss Jessamyne! What on earth are you about?' Luckily, Smithers did not have a carrying voice.

'Please, Smithers! Help me! I need to escape. I cannot marry that terrible man. All I need is a few weeks. Then I shall be safe.'

'What do you mean about "a few weeks", miss?' the abigail asked, in a low voice.

'Don't call me that. Someone will hear. Just call me "Jamie".' Jamie searched the maid's face for a sign that she might relent, but there was none. Jamie swallowed hard. 'In a few weeks, I shall be twenty-one. Then, no one can force me into marriage with him. All I have to do is stay in hiding until I come of age. Please help me, Smithers!'

Jamie felt the woman's slow scrutiny. Surely the proposed bridegroom made even Smithers' flesh creep?

The abigail lifted one of Jamie's grubby hands and brushed it across Jamie's cheek so that it left a dirty streak. 'You'd better start calling me "Annie", don't you think?' she smiled.

'Oh, bless you!' cried Jamie, hugging the older woman impetuously.

'Hey! That's enough of that,' cried Smithers, pushing her away. 'I haven't said I'll help you yet.' She paused. 'It will depend on precisely what you want from me. Well?'

Jamie launched into her prepared speech. 'You said you were going to Bath on the stage…er…Annie. I only want you to help me to get a seat too. I have the money to pay, don't worry. And, once we reach Bath, I can look after myself.'

'Oh?'

'Yes. I plan to… But perhaps it would be better for both of us if I kept my plans to myself. Then, if anyone should ask, you can truthfully say you don't know, can't you?' She beamed innocently at the abigail.

'It sounds pretty rum to me, I must say. And, if I help you to get on the stage, I *will* be involved, whatever you choose to do about telling me your plans. How am I to explain that away?'

'No one will be looking for a *boy*, Annie, I promise you. These clothes belong to Edmund. He won't be back from Harrow for weeks and weeks, so nobody will notice they are missing. And all the clothes in my pack are my own, so when they discover I am gone, they will be searching for a girl.'

'Hmph. And what if they discover that the lady's maid from Calderwood Hall was suddenly to be found in the company of a young lad?'

'They won't. I don't want us to be *together*. I just want you to tell me how I go about obtaining a seat on the Bath stage. Then I'll do it myself.'

Annie Smithers seemed to be wavering. 'It won't do, Miss Jamie, I'm afraid. A young lad travelling by himself and buying his own seat at the last minute would be bound to attract attention. They'd wonder if you were running away from school.' Jamie's suddenly despondent expression must have shocked her. 'Don't take on so, miss. Look, I can help a little. I'll go and see if I can buy an extra seat on the stage for you. Give me the money. Right. Now, you stay here. I don't want them to know it's for you.' Pocketing Jamie's coins, Smithers left the taproom.

In five minutes, she was back. 'I'm sorry, Miss Jamie. It can't be done. Mine was the last place on the stage. There's no way he'll take you, I'm afraid.'

Jamie sat down heavily on the wooden bench. She had tried to plan for every eventuality, but she had not foreseen this. She dared not hang around the inn waiting for the next stage in hopes of getting a seat. Too many people from Calderwood and the nearby villages used the Boar's Head. She would very likely be recognised by someone.

Jamie groaned in anguish, clenching her fists. Then she slumped dejectedly against the wall. It had all been for nothing.

A cool voice from the doorway interrupted them. 'Why, it's Smithers, is it not? And in some difficulty, if I am not mistaken. How tiresome!'

Chapter Five

At the sound of that deep authoritative voice, Jamie felt a shudder run through her body. She knew exactly who had uttered those deceptively simple words. But, now that she was finally to meet the man whose image had been haunting her, she did not dare to turn round to look at him. What if he saw through her disguise? What if…? She shrank further into her boy's clothes, trying to make herself as inconspicuous as possible. Why did his arrival affect her so? He could not recognise her, for he had never set eyes on her, but somehow there was something incredibly threatening about his very presence. She sat staring at the floor, her hands clasped tightly together, as if in supplication.

Smithers, by contrast, was facing up to this unexpected arrival who seemed to find their presence so tiresome. She dropped a quick curtsy and then, without any kind of warning, cuffed Jamie lightly round the ear. 'Stand up at once, Jamie, and make your bow to Lord Hardinge.'

Jamie rapidly obeyed, trying her best to bow as

Edmund did and to conceal her dismay as she did so. What on earth was Smithers going to say? And do?

'I beg your pardon for my brother's want of manners, my lord,' continued Smithers quickly. 'He's worried, you see, because there's no room for him on the stage. They must have made a mistake up at the Hall and booked only one seat instead of two.' She shrugged. 'We'll just have to wait, I suppose.'

Lord Hardinge looked inquiringly at the abigail. 'A sudden departure, I collect?'

Smithers swallowed. 'Urgent family business, my lord. I have to get Jamie to Bath quickly. He's been…er…with me more or less since Mother died, you see, and now there's a chance of a situation for him in Bath. But I need to be sure he's settled. I promised my mother I would.'

'Ah yes, very laudable, Smithers, very.' He looked hard at Jamie. 'And how old are you, my lad?'

Jamie found she could not speak. She looked appealingly at Smithers.

'He don't talk much, I'm afraid, my lord. He's a little…well…backward. But he understands everything you say to him, I assure you, and he has the sweetest nature, too.'

Jamie gulped. Smithers was getting carried away. 'I be thirteen,' she croaked. 'Gardener I be, sir.'

His lordship laughed, but not unkindly. 'I could have guessed that from the state of your hands, Jamie, though not perhaps from your fine clothes. Are you a good gardener?'

Jamie nodded vigorously.

'He has a wonderful way with growing things, to

be sure,' added Smithers, 'though he's not been a gardener, in the ordinary way.'

Lord Hardinge raised an eyebrow.

'What I mean,' continued Smithers hastily, improvising around the truth, 'is that Jamie wasn't exactly *employed* at Calderwood, just allowed to stay there. Charitable of her ladyship, really, to give him bed and board. The gardening was his attempt to pay his way. He's not much good at household duties, I'm afraid.'

Jamie kept her head down, trying to hide her face from his lordship's penetrating gaze. She knew she was blushing. That did not seem appropriate for a thirteen-year-old boy, even a backward one.

'So, you have found him a proper situation as a gardener's boy, have you, Smithers? That sounds hopeful.'

Jamie groaned inwardly. Smithers was beginning to struggle in the complications of her own story. If she claimed there was a position for Jamie, his lordship would probably enquire as to the employer's name, and then what could Smithers say? Jamie held her breath.

'No, not precisely, my lord.' Smithers started to move towards the far end of the room. 'Sit down there, Jamie,' she called back. 'Would you mind, my lord?' she continued in a low voice. 'I don't like to discuss this in front of Jamie.'

Jamie swallowed a gasp. She wanted to stop them, but she could not step out of the part she was playing. No backward boy would understand what was being discussed, far less insist on being part of it. She must just put her trust in Annie Smithers. At least it would give her time to school her features into blankness— and a chance to strain her ears to hear what was being said.

'I thank you kindly for your interest in my brother, my lord. In fact, there is no definite situation for him yet, but I am most hopeful. One of the Bath agencies believes he can be placed. There are many openings for bootboys and the like.'

'But you said he has no bent for indoor work,' he returned sharply.

Jamie saw that Smithers was flushing, caught by the twists of her own tale. 'Not *real* indoor work, like a page boy,' the abigail said hurriedly, 'but even he can black boots.'

His lordship smiled coldly. 'You would not say that to my valet, Smithers,' he said caustically. 'However, we are wandering from the point. Now, the stage is due in about ten minutes. Do you take your seat on it, and I will take the boy on the box of my carriage. You may find him at the coach office when you reach Bath.'

Smithers' reply came out in a rush. 'How very kind you are, my lord. But, no, I'm afraid I cannot accept your offer. Jamie's never been on his own, you see, especially in a big city. I couldn't think of letting him travel all that way by himself or having him wait at the coach station for such a long time on his own.' She lowered her voice a little. 'People sometimes take advantage, make fun of him. They can be very cruel.'

Fixing the abigail with a hard glare, his lordship pronounced on her fate. 'Your sisterly concern does you credit, Smithers. Very well. Since you will not

leave him to me, you had better come along as well.
Get the lad to load your bags into my carriage. I am
leaving immediately. I hope you do not object to travelling forward?' He walked out with an indifferent
nod, not waiting for her reply.

Smithers hurried back to Jamie. 'Did you hear what
we said?' At Jamie's rapid nod, the abigail continued,
'Remember you must act the part of a boy, Miss
Jamie. You're to travel on the box with the coachman,
which means you won't have his lordship's eye on
you. He's altogether too sharp, that one, for my liking.'

'For goodness' sake,' hissed Jamie, 'you *must* stop
saying ''Miss Jamie''! Remember, I am ''Jamie'' and
you are ''Annie''. What if he heard you?'

'Yes, yes, very well,' agreed Smithers, shooing her
to the door. 'Now, go and load the luggage. Quickly.
You don't want to draw his lordship's attention to you
by being tardy.'

Jamie grabbed her pack and the abigail's bulky
travelling bags and hurried out to the carriage, trying
not to think about the risks of what was happening.
Keep out of his way, she told herself sternly, and act
simple.

But her eyes were still drawn to him, like a moth
to flame. Lord Hardinge was standing by the steps,
giving crisp instructions to his coachman. The grooms
were stationed by the horses, ready to whip the cloths
off their backs as soon as he gave the word. He ex-
uded authority. And he was watching her!

'Jamie!' he called sharply as he mounted into the

carriage. 'Tell that sister of yours to get a move on. Quickly now!'

Jamie nodded obediently and trotted off into the taproom where Smithers was waiting, looking rather more composed than before. 'Come on, Annie! He's becoming impatient! Now, do be careful what you say to him. Don't spin any more stories, *please*. I shan't be able to keep up with them.'

'Yes, you will. Just stick to your character—backward, without many words. If you don't know what to say, say nothing. And look simple.' She turned to go.

'Annie.' The abigail turned back. 'Thank you, dear Annie. Some day—'

'Oh, stuff! Now, let's be going. He'll expect you to help me into the carriage.'

Up on the box beside the old coachman, Jamie was soon inwardly rejoicing at her escape. In just a few hours, they would reach Bath, and then she would be free. Her heart was singing. But no amount of joy could prevent her from gradually freezing. Edmund's clothes were not thick enough for winter wear and his cloak, though long, was thin, affording little protection against the bitingly sharp wind. Jamie glanced enviously at the thick greatcoat, mufflers and gloves of the coachman. Her own hands were becoming blue with cold and so numb she could barely feel them. She was sure there was a drip on the end of her nose. With grim determination, she ignored it and concentrated on mastering the chattering of her teeth. She refused to give up now. Only a few hours more…

* * *

Once Smithers was settled, Richard studiously ignored her. He relaxed in the corner of his opulent carriage, a fur rug over his knees, and closed his eyes to indicate that he did not propose to converse during the journey. He waited until the abigail fell asleep, lulled by the rhythmic rocking of the carriage. As her breathing slowed, he opened his eyes once more. And he fixed his gaze on her, thoughtfully examining every aspect of her person.

He had been surprised to find that he felt sorry for a simple lad, in spite of his suspicions of the sister's lame explanations. The boy had looked so uncomfortable in his fine clothes, obviously charity cast-offs from someone in the Calderwood family. And he would be vulnerable without his sister, if he were indeed taking a situation on his own. Richard sighed. His conscience would not allow him to draw back, when a simpleton needed his help. Besides, there might be profit in this encounter. Smithers knew more about the Calderwood household than any agent he had yet been able to employ.

Richard had noted the attempt at masculine panache as the boy slung his sister's bags into the carriage. But it was not so much the awkwardness of Jamie's movements which had attracted his attention, as the size of the abigail's baggage. Strange, if she were indeed travelling to Bath for a few days only. If she were leaving for good, on the other hand...

He smiled to himself. Things were beginning to work out rather better than he had hoped, and might yet be turned even more to his advantage. He would consider further during the journey. There was no rush, now that he had the woman under his eye.

At length, the carriage turned into a posting inn for a change of horses. The grooms were quickly about their business, unhitching the team and assessing the quality of the replacements. Nobody was paying any attention to Jamie. She sat immobile, too cold to move a muscle.

Lord Hardinge lowered the glass on his side of the carriage and poked his head out. 'Jamie! Down from there! Go and fetch me a tankard of ale. Look sharp, now!'

Jamie hurried to climb down. She made a pretty poor showing, for her fingers were so cold she could barely grip the handholds. Seeing a waiter coming towards the carriage with a tray of tankards, she rushed to grab one and immediately dropped it. The ale splashed all over the waiter's boots.

'Why, you young—' began the waiter, incensed, raising his free hand to strike Jamie.

'That will do!' commanded Lord Hardinge, flinging open the door and jumping down. 'If my servants are to be chastised, I shall do it.'

The waiter began to stammer an apology, but his lordship simply took a full tankard from the tray, threw down some coppers and turned away.

'Come here, Jamie.'

Jamie's first reaction was to run, but her frozen limbs would never have moved fast enough. Keeping her eyes lowered, she approached her intimidating benefactor. He sounded much less angry now than when he had shouted at the waiter, but still…

'Show me your hands.'

Jamie did so. They were thin and blue. The filthy fingernails stood out starkly.

'Have you no gloves?'

Jamie shook her head, still gazing at the ground.

His lordship put a hand on her frozen cheek. Suddenly it seemed as if all the blood in Jamie's body had rushed to that spot. She felt sure that the outline of his fingers was impressed in brightest scarlet on her burning skin. And that same quivering of all her body had returned.

'Why, you're frozen to the marrow, lad. No wonder you dropped that tankard. I should have known. You're much too thin—and as for these clothes… Well, you'd better come inside with your sister, before I have your death on my conscience.'

Jamie did not move. She was still trying to come to terms with the strange effects this man had on her.

'Don't just stand there, boy.' It sounded as if the Earl was beginning to regret his generosity. 'Come, jump in.' He gave Jamie a hearty push towards the carriage.

As Jamie climbed in, she registered the shock on the abigail's face. No wonder. Spending hours under the eagle eye of Lord Hardinge might well lead to discovery. Jamie dared not utter a sound. Annie busied herself with chafing Jamie's hands and clucking over her like an anxious mother hen.

'Enough, Smithers, enough!' snapped Lord Hardinge. 'I have no objection to your helping your brother to get warm but, for heaven's sake, do it without all this gabblemongering!'

Looking chastened, Smithers lapsed into silence. Eventually, she drifted off to sleep again.

Jamie soon found herself the only one awake. Cautiously, she sat up in her corner, pushing her hat back from her eyes and flexing her fingers, which tingled painfully as the sensation returned. She felt in her pocket for a handkerchief to deal with the drip on her nose. She did not have one, which reminded her that boys like simple Jamie never used them, so she experimented with wiping her nose on her sleeve instead. Ugh!

But what did that matter? She had escaped! She might never again live the life of a gentlewoman, but her future was now her own to decide. She paused to savour the luxury of the carriage, its deeply cushioned seats and the pervasive smell of rich leather. Nothing at Calderwood was half so splendid. And if Lady Calderwood had owned such an equipage, she would never have allowed her hated stepdaughter to set foot in it. Jamie sank back in her seat, longing to shout with exultant laughter.

Opposite her, Lord Hardinge moved in his sleep. He had removed his hat, presumably so that he might doze more comfortably. Jamie found herself gazing at him. It was such a handsome face in repose—thick, arched black brows, a finely chiselled nose, perhaps a little long, a generous mouth made for smiling, and a strong chin, slightly cleft. His thick dark hair became him, even in disarray. Jamie found herself wondering about the colour of his eyes. Dark, she supposed, like the rest of him, unconsciously raising her eyes to look again at his face.

Cobalt blue eyes bored into hers! Lord Hardinge had been watching her, just when she thought she was safe. And his eyes seemed to be able to see into the depths of her being! She shuddered visibly.

Glancing at the still-sleeping abigail, the Earl frowned across at Jamie, his face very stern. 'Satisfied, are you, lad?' he asked in a menacing whisper.

Jamie shuddered again.

Lord Hardinge's expression softened slightly. 'Don't worry, Jamie. I am not angry.' His voice seemed less hostile now. 'But you really must not stare at your betters in that insolent way. It could earn you a beating in some houses.'

Jamie began to stammer an incoherent apology.

'Forget it,' interrupted his lordship sharply, closing his eyes once more.

Jamie held her breath for a long time, trying to control her racing pulse and fearing another onslaught from the powerful man sitting opposite her.

The carriage remained silent. It seemed that Lord Hardinge had had enough of the boy Jamie, at least for the present.

Jamie looked enviously at the abigail, sleeping peacefully alongside her. If only she dared to close her eyes too. She was so tired—and the growing warmth inside the carriage was making her eyelids droop. But it was too great a risk. She dug her fingernails into the palm of her hand. She must not sleep where he might watch her. She must not.

At the next change, the Earl allowed them both a

bite to eat and a mug of ale. It tasted foul, and much too strong, but Jamie could find no reason to refuse it. Ten minutes after they had moved off, she began to succumb to the effects of the alcohol and her sleepless night. Her eyes closed, but still she struggled to stay alert.

'I am glad your brother is asleep, Smithers, for I want to talk to you about him.'

'Yes, my lord?'

'From what you have told me, he would make a pretty poor bootboy. Much better to place him as apprentice gardener on a large estate.'

'Yes, my lord. I intend to do so, if such a situation can be found. But—'

'It can be. I need just such a boy on my own estate. I shall take him.'

'I thank you for your offer, but we can't accept it. You see...' The abigail's voice trailed off. She seemed to be fast running out of excuses.

'Why don't you tell me the truth, Smithers?'

His slightly raised voice penetrated Jamie's half-slumber. At the sound of the word 'truth', her eyes snapped open.

'I don't understand...' began Smithers.

'Gammon. You know very well. No woman of your station carries all her worldly goods with her on a three-day trip to Bath. You have been dismissed from your post, I collect, and are hoping to find another in Bath. Well?'

'It is true, my lord,' agreed Smithers in a whisper. 'Lady Calderwood would not keep me at the Hall after your visit. She decided...she believed...' Her voice tailed off miserably.

'Indeed? And so both of you are turned out into the world again? I must say it makes me wonder why you will not accept my offer for Jamie.' There was an edge of irritation in his deep voice as he stared suspiciously at the abigail. The handsomeness of his face in repose had been replaced by a frown which drew his black brows together in a hard line.

Smithers began to stammer a little. 'I...I was hoping to find a situation where we could be together, so that I could look after him. You know what I mean, I think.'

'Yes, I do know. There is no need to elaborate. I assure you, he will come to no harm under my roof.' He paused to look directly at Jamie, who shrank a little under his stern gaze. 'Very well, Smithers. If I can persuade my mother to re-engage you as her abigail, will you then agree to my proposal for Jamie?'

'I don't know.' She turned to consult Jamie, who nodded quickly, taking no notice of the silent warning in the older woman's eyes. 'Since Jamie seems willing—then, yes, if we can stay together, we accept.'

'Good,' said the Earl crisply, settling back in his seat. 'I have no doubt Lady Hardinge will be delighted to have you back in her service. We should be at Harding in about an hour.' He closed his eyes once more.

Jamie looked anxiously at the abigail, who shrugged impotently. It was now clear to Jamie that his lordship never had intended to take them to Bath, but straight to Harding, his own estate. Jamie felt a prickle of alarm. What did he have in mind for them now?

Chapter Six

'What on earth possessed you to agree to his offer?' snapped Annie in exasperation, sinking on to the bed. The attic chamber was small, but better furnished than the average for servants. There were still some privileges attached to the position of lady's maid.

Before Jamie could reply, they were interrupted by the noise of heavy footsteps on the stairs. 'That will be the truckle bed for you, I suppose. Open the door and help them with it, Jamie.'

Jamie did as she was bidden, biting back the retort which had risen automatically to her lips. Annie really was beginning to treat her like a younger brother, rather than as a lady. And if she wanted to be safe, she would just have to become accustomed to it.

'Can't understand why you wants a lad like him in here, Miss Smithers,' grumbled the young footman, dragging the bed through the narrow doorway. 'He could just as easy sleep out by the stables.'

'No, thank you, Tom. Lady Hardinge has agreed that he should be with me until he's settled.' She was unbending a little more than she normally would to an inferior. 'Will you keep an eye on him, when you can, Tom? You know better than I who might be unkind to him.' The smile she gave him transformed her normally stern countenance.

Flattered by such a show of confidence from one of the highest servants in the household, Tom grudgingly agreed to look out for Jamie when he could. 'But out in the gardens he'll be on his own, for I'll not be able to go out there much. He'll be all right with old Mr Jennings. He wouldn't hurt a fly. Caleb, now, is a different kettle o' fish. Nasty piece o' work. Got a vicious temper, he has. Jamie'll need to keep out o' his way.'

'Who is Caleb?' asked Annie.

'Undergardener. Came after you left. Mr Jennings is getting too old for all the work, so his lordship wanted someone younger, ready to take over when the old man retires. Mind you,' he added with a chuckle, 'Mr Jennings ain't the kind who'll give up easily. Yon garden is his pride an' joy an' he's like to rule it 'til he drops.'

'Thank you for the warning, Tom. I'll try to make sure Jamie keeps out of Caleb's way as much as possible.'

As the door closed behind Tom, Annie set about unpacking Jamie's belongings. Jamie watched helplessly as Annie inspected her few clothes with pursed lips.

'We must sort out some more boy's clothes for you. You can't possibly work in the garden in those you have on. As for these'—she picked up a plain green gown and held it disdainfully at arm's length between finger and thumb—'I'll put them among my things. Though how anyone could think I would demean myself to wear such a monstrosity, I cannot imagine.' She dropped the offending garment on the chair.

It was that single gesture that brought home to Jamie just how impossible her situation had become. She had fully intended to revert to being a girl as soon as she reached Bath, but now she was buried on a private estate, miles from anywhere, and irrevocably cast as a gardener's boy. Could she carry it off? What if she were discovered?

Looking down at her filthy hands and travel-stained clothes, Jamie concluded that, even if she were found to be a girl, no one would ever guess she was a lady. She had needed a hiding place for a few weeks, until she came of age. What could be better?

As Annie continued to scrutinise Jamie's meagre wardrobe, muttering darkly, Jamie began to giggle. The giggle grew uncontrollably until she was laughing in great gusty whoops, gripping her aching sides. In the face of such infectious hilarity, Annie too began to laugh until they both collapsed in a helpless heap on the bed, wiping tears from their eyes.

'Oh, Annie,' gasped Jamie at last, 'however did we get into this? And how shall we ever get out of it again?'

'I don't know, I'm sure. I doubt if I shall ever find another place after this, that I do know.'

'Of course you will. If I were rich, I'd take you like a shot. Perhaps when I come of age—'

'If you were rich, Jamie, we wouldn't be in this

fix. And what self-respecting abigail would have anything to do with a lady who looks like a—'

'A dirty little scarecrow? Yes, well, perhaps with the right sort of dresser I could be improved.' Jamie made a face. 'What do you think?'

'I think that it's high time I found some more boy's clothes for you, so that you can start your apprenticeship. Let's see how happy you are with this silly playacting after a week's hard work.' Annie's sharpness failed to conceal her real concern.

'Annie, dear, don't worry. No matter what they give me to do, I won't give myself away, I promise you.'

Annie grunted. 'Well, see that you don't.' She made for the door, warning Jamie not to leave the room until she returned.

While Annie was gone, Jamie reassessed her own position with some care. She must not be discovered, for that would mean disaster for her—and the workhouse, or worse, for Annie Smithers.

Jamie refused to dwell on the risks they ran. Instead, she thought hard about the handsome Earl, in an attempt to identify what it was about him that affected her so. She could not decide. He was an enigma. She found it impossible to reconcile his relative kindness to her with his behaviour to poor Annie. He must have given Lady Calderwood reason to believe that Annie was not fit for a position of trust, considering how rapidly she had been dismissed. It was monstrous! She said as much, yawning widely, when Annie came back into the room with a large pile of worn, but serviceable, working clothes.

'I don't want to talk about it,' retorted Annie flatly. 'I have no way of knowing what he might have said to Lady Calderwood and, since he has seen fit to re-engage me at Harding, I really have very little to complain about. It could have been much, much worse. As for you, young lady—' Jamie yawned again '—you need to go to bed. Did you not sleep last night?' Jamie shook her head. Annie made to turn down the covers on the bed.

'I can't sleep there, Annie. That's your bed.'

'It wouldn't be right for a lady to sleep on that little truckle there,' protested Annie, tight-lipped. 'It will do very well for me.'

'And how will you explain it to anyone who happens to come in and finds you there, while your little brother lies in luxury? Come, Annie, you know it won't do. I shall be perfectly comfortable here.' With that, she lay down on the truckle bed and closed her eyes. In less than a minute, she was asleep.

Countess Hardinge closed the book-room door quietly behind her.

Her son strode across the room to embrace her and place an affectionate kiss on her cheek. 'That was remarkably swift, my dear,' he said. 'I take it they are settled? Thank you. I'm only sorry I could not explain properly when we arrived, but with both of them listening…'

He relaxed as she nodded, lingering for a moment in his embrace.

'I understand now why you brought them, Richard—or Smithers, at least—but it seems such an unlikely route to recovering our losses. Can we really afford to spend our time on a mere abigail—situated as we are?'

He stood back slightly to look more carefully into her face, noting her worried frown and the anxiety in her eyes. 'It is nothing like as bad as you fear, my dear,' he said gently. 'We are still comfortable enough. And we shall come about.' Gently he drew her to the best chair by the fire. 'Come, sit down,' he murmured. 'Let me fetch you a glass of madeira.'

Lady Hardinge let out a long sigh as she sank into the chair. Her son could feel her eyes on him as he filled a single glass from the crystal decanter.

'I should pour one for yourself too, Richard,' she advised, before he had even turned round.

That sounded ominous. He looked questioningly at her, but her eyes had closed. Something really serious was on her mind, but surely it couldn't be money this time? They already knew exactly how much was missing. And now that he had given up his gambling and his opera dancers, they should be able to manage—just—on the income from the estate.

That left only one other possibility—another impassioned plea that he set about finding himself the wife that they had long ago agreed he must have.

As he placed her glass on the little table by her elbow, he attempted to deflect what might be coming. 'I have been thinking about what we said before, Mama, and I have concluded that you are right. I do need to marry soon. So, I have decided to offer for Emma Fitzwilliam. After all, we have known each other for nearly twenty years, so there would be few surprises. She may not be witty or clever, but she is nothing like as fickle and flighty as most of her sex. I imagine we could rub along pretty well together.'

His mother sighed again. Her features registered some inner turmoil, but she did not respond to his sweeping slight on womankind.

Richard realised he was making a poor fist of his explanations, but he was in too deep now to withdraw. And besides, his mother was the very one who constantly urged him to marry. She…no, that was not quite fair. His mother wanted him to fall in love and *then* marry. On that count, Emma Fitzwilliam most definitely did not qualify.

He swallowed hard. 'May I take it that you approve my choice, Mama? After all, the Fitzwilliam estates march with ours, and she will inherit them some day. Her dowry will be handsome. She has, besides, all the attributes a man must seek in a wife: beauty, breeding, a conformable nature—'

'She may have all the required qualities, Richard,' interrupted Lady Hardinge at last, 'but you do not!' She ignored her son's gasp of protest. 'Family tradition requires that you give the Hardinge betrothal ring to your bride as a token of your deep love for her—'

'Oh, tosh, Mama! Forgive me—but people like us do not marry for love, especially nowadays. Marriage is a matter of business. It would be a union between two families—the Hardinge title and the Fitzwilliam wealth. You're not still hoping for a love match, are you, my dear?' He softened his words by smiling warmly at her.

'The head of this family *must* marry for love,' she replied firmly. 'That rule has held true for all the Hardinges, for centuries. Your father believed in it— and so do I. You know that. And you know, too, that disaster struck on the only two occasions when the tradition was flouted.'

Richard did not reply.

'Richard?'

'Yes, Mama,' he said softly, 'I do know what happened to them, but I don't believe in the curse for a moment. It was just coincidence that both of them died, without an heir, before they reached forty. It happens in other families too. And they don't have a curse to blame it on.' He sat down and tossed off his glass of madeira in a single swallow. 'Clearly, there is only one solution—I must instantly fall head over ears in love with a lady of vast fortune. It is the obvious way to reconcile the needs of the estate with the family tradition.' He laughed bitterly. 'If only life were so simple.'

She turned slightly, looking him full in the face. 'I am sorry, Richard.'

He shook his head. 'It's not your fault, Mama. Papa was taken in by that blackguard, Calderwood, when he was too ill to know what he was doing. You could not have prevented it—even if you had known.'

He sat for some moments, grimly contemplating the dregs of wine in his glass. 'Well,' he returned at length, 'if I am to abide by your rules, I must have earned a temporary reprieve. I cannot guarantee to fall in love with an heiress, so marriage will have to wait—until the money has been recovered!' He smiled impudently. 'Every cloud has a silver lining.'

His mother could not conceal a slight twitch of her lips at his words. But there was no amusement in her voice. 'If you take that attitude, you'll make no match at all, far less a love match. I know that, after Celia, you feel—'

Richard allowed his stony expression to show her how little he appreciated any mention of that name from his past.

His mother rapidly changed tack. 'Think, Richard. You are already one-and-thirty. You have no brothers. You really must marry soon.'

She was beginning to wring her hands. Gently, he enclosed them in his own, letting her gain strength from his warmth. 'Does my marrying for love mean so much to you, my dear?'

'Not just to me. To all of us. Especially to you.'

A taut silence fell. Richard could see the strain on his mother's face, but he was not prepared to pursue this subject further, even with her. 'Come, my love. Let me take you upstairs. You will wish to rest and change before dinner.'

Lady Hardinge gave her son a smile of silent understanding as he led her out of the study and up the staircase to her bedchamber.

When Richard returned to his desk, he remained some moments toying with his pen and staring into space. So much of his ordered world turned upside-down by those few words from his mother. Words he had long tried to avoid—the Hardinge family's love matches. A fairy story, surely? And out of the question for a man like him. Yet he knew it would now be impossible for him to carry out his hastily devised plan of offering for Emma Fitzwilliam. Fate? He could not decide whether the luck was for good or ill.

Next morning Jamie rose with the lark, ravenous. She was astonished to discover that she had slept for fifteen hours.

'I am ever so hungry, Annie,' she said, as she gave herself a perfunctory wash and began to change her clothes. This was her first day of freedom, and she meant to enjoy every moment of it.

Annie eyed her balefully. 'There will be plenty to eat downstairs. But first, we must see to your appearance.' She forcibly removed the garments Jamie was holding. 'No, not those. Breeches and gaiters, a smock and an undershirt. Here.'

Jamie wrinkled her nose at the thick, rough smock. It looked thoroughly uncomfortable. Just touching it made her itch.

'It can't be helped, Jamie. You chose to be the gardener's boy. It's a good thing you're a bit thin. Boys of that age usually are. But we'll need to bind your breasts, just the same.'

Jamie blushed scarlet, but it seemed to make no impression on Annie, who was busily rummaging in the clothes press. Jamie gasped a protest as her old calico petticoat was pulled out and efficiently ripped into bandages.

'Not fit for a lady anyway,' Annie pronounced. 'If you ever become a lady again, I can provide you with better than this and with gowns more becoming than yours.'

Annie seemed to be in her element. She certainly knew how to manage a young lady, even a slightly unwilling one. In no time, she was wrapping the strips tightly round Jamie's upper body.

'Now, put on the rest of the clothes and let us see how you look.'

There was no point in protesting any more. Annie was right. Jamie had to be able to pass muster as a boy. They were both at risk if she failed.

She stood in the centre of the room while Annie inspected her minutely. 'Not bad,' the abigail conceded, 'but why did you do that to your hair? Boys don't wear it like that nowadays—it's much too long.'

'I was trying to leave myself enough so that I could be a girl again. It's just about long enough to be put up.'

'I'll tidy it up a little, at least.' Annie fetched her comb and scissors. As she freed Jamie's hair from the restraining ribbon, the dark red curls fell forward, framing Jamie's pale face. 'Why, how different you look, miss, much prettier than that severe bun you always wore at Calderwood.'

Jamie smiled shyly up at her, surprised by the half-compliment. 'Mama always insisted I wore it so, in order to tame my ''appalling red mop'', as she called it. She never permitted me to cut it.'

'She never permitted anything which would make the best of your looks, if truth were told.'

Jamie laughed. 'But I have none. I've always known I'm plain.'

'Oh? Look here.' Annie forced Jamie to sit down in front of the brown-speckled mirror and then arranged her curls becomingly around her heart-shaped face. 'Now, tell me you're plain.'

Jamie was astonished. Annie really sounded as if she meant it. But then, when Jamie did look, she suddenly saw herself through new eyes. Against the frame of titian hair, her pale complexion glowed and her deep green eyes sparkled. The plain pasty-faced dowd had disappeared. In her place, there was a pretty, red-haired—boy!

'Good grief!' Jamie hastily began to drag her hair back from her face to tie it up again. 'They'll never believe I'm a boy if I look like that,' she said, unconsciously immodest.

'True,' said Annie, with a short laugh. 'Here, I'll tidy it up for you. Then you'll do, I think.'

Annie trimmed the ends of Jamie's hair and combed it back severely from her face, tying it very tightly with a piece of twine. 'Gardener's boys don't use ribbon,' she observed sagely.

The winter sun was dipping low in the sky when Jamie finished her first day's work. She sat on her heels, stretching her aching back and looking ruefully at her grime-encrusted hands. Her body might ache, but her heart was singing. She was safe from the Calderwoods now, and surely she could remain hidden at Harding for the few weeks she needed?

She finished tidying the bed, packing all the weeds into her buckets for the compost heap and the bonfire. Mr Jennings would have no cause to complain about her ability to sort out the perennial weeds from the rest.

It was only as she passed the gardener's hut on her way to the compost heaps that she heard the raised voices. She herself was the subject of a heated discussion between Mr Jennings and another man. She allowed herself to dawdle a little.

'But this bit o' the garden's always been left ter me,' protested the unknown voice vehemently. 'B'ain't no call for nobody else, least of all a witless boy. No knowing what harm he might do.'

'The boy knows what he's about,' commented Mr Jennings calmly. 'He'll do no harm. And we can be doing with another pair of hands here, what with spring planting coming.'

'Don't need no extra hands here,' said the unknown. 'I've allus done it all m'self, ever since I been here. Why change it now? For a half-wit?'

'That's for me to decide, Caleb, not you.'

Caleb! Jamie shivered. The man was obviously angry about her arrival, even though he had never set eyes on her. It made no sense at all—for what threat was a garden boy to him? Still, she had been warned about his vicious temper. He sounded like the kind of man who would enjoy bullying a simpleton. She must keep out of his way.

The heated voices were still audible as Jamie moved slowly away. 'Let me have the minding of the boy, at least. I can't be a-running of the garden if'n I dunno what he might do next.'

'No.' Mr Jennings' voice was curt and decisive.

'I'll be responsible for the lad myself. If you want him to do work for you, you must come to me.'

'But that's—'

'That's the way it'll be, Caleb, an' no buts. That's the way his lordship wants it. You should know better by now than to cross him.'

'But—'

'Let it be, Caleb. That's the last word.'

Jamie hurried away. The men would come out of the hut in a few moments and must not find her hanging around.

From the comparative safety of the compost area, she watched the hut door. It was fully five minutes before it opened and Caleb emerged. She crouched down a little, busying herself with her work.

Caleb was a huge man, almost as tall as Lord Hardinge, but of much heavier build. He had immensely broad shoulders with massive arms and hands. He seemed to be carrying a lot of surplus weight—he had the belly of a drinker and a nose to match, its purplish colour easily distinguishable even in the fading light.

Jamie tried not to think about how she could handle a confrontation with this brute of a man. He—and his temper—must be avoided at all costs. She must make herself indispensable to Mr Jennings and perhaps allow him to see that she was afraid of Caleb. Given Lord Hardinge's explicit orders, that might serve to keep her apart from the undergardener. She prayed that it would.

Chapter Seven

The next morning, while Jamie was weeding around the parsnips, she was dumbfounded to see Lord Hardinge come into the kitchen garden with a lady on his arm. Jamie felt herself flushing bright red at the thought that he would be scrutinising her yet again. He seemed to see so much. And the more often she came under his eye, the more likely he was to penetrate her disguise.

She tried to make herself as small and inconspicuous as possible, hoping her dun-coloured smock would help her to hide among the vegetable beds.

It was not to be. Mr Jennings hurried out of his lair to meet his master and wasted no time in commenting on the skill of the new apprentice. At his summons, Jamie rose reluctantly to her feet and stood staring bashfully at the ground. She dared not look up to see what Lord Hardinge's reaction might be.

'Yer cap, Jamie,' whispered Mr Jennings out of the corner of his mouth.

Jamie looked up then, bewildered.

'Mr Jennings thinks you should remove your cap

in the presence of a lady,' said his lordship laconically, with a sidelong glance at the lady on his arm.

Jamie blushed furiously as she pulled off the offending cap, murmuring an apology.

'You will know next time, I am sure,' said a soft female voice. 'Jamie, is it not? I am glad you are doing so well in our garden.'

The kind undertones prompted Jamie to glance briefly at the speaker. She was tall for a lady, taller than Jamie, and, judging from her delicate bone structure, she had been very beautiful in her youth. Now, though still beautiful in a faded way, she was a middle-aged lady with greying hair. Her figure remained trim and her carriage erect, but there was a look of sadness about her deep blue eyes. The likeness between the lady and the Earl was very strong. Jamie could tell at a glance that the lady was his lordship's mother.

In her guise of simpleton, Jamie felt it was necessary to speak. 'Thank you, mum,' she said in a low voice, rather hesitantly.

Mr Jennings made to intervene. 'Not "mum", m'lad—'

'I am sure he is doing his best, Jennings,' interrupted the lady smoothly, in her soft voice. 'But he does not know who I am, so why should he be expected to know how to address me?'

Mr Jennings nodded.

'Now Jamie,' continued the lady, 'you must know that I am Lady Hardinge, your master's mother. You must address me as "my lady". Can you remember that, do you think?' She smiled warmly as she spoke.

'Yes, my la-dy,' said Jamie slowly, articulating every syllable as if the expression were totally new to her.

'Excellent,' said the Countess. 'And this gentleman is Lord Hardinge, as I think you know. You should address him as "my lord".' The lord in question was looking indulgently down at his mother as she spoke.

'Yes, mum—my lady,' said Jamie again, correcting herself laboriously. The Countess must be in no doubt about the boy's want of wits.

'I think that is enough learning for one day, my dear.' The Earl laid his free hand gently on his mother's gloved one where it rested on his arm. 'We should let Jamie get on with his work. Eh, Jennings?'

'Aye, m'lord. There's a tidy bit to do afore dusk, I'll grant ye.' He gestured to Jamie to return to her weeding. 'Not that I've any concerns about the lad, though. He works hard, whether I'm watching or no. Born to it, I'd say, m'lord, even though he don't have many wits.'

'Good,' agreed the Earl. 'He must earn his keep, of course. But I do not want him to be the butt of jokes and pranks here, Jennings, pray understand that. He is too much of a weakling to defend himself— even if he understood such things, which I doubt. You will see to it?'

'Aye, m'lord,' affirmed Mr Jennings with a slight bow. 'Ye can trust me.'

With a nod of acknowledgement, Lord Hardinge led his mother out of the walled garden towards the shrubbery to finish their winter constitutional.

Out of the corner of her eye, Jamie watched them

go. She continued to work diligently, apparently oblivious of everything else, but in the silence she could feel Mr Jennings' eyes on her back. He was probably thinking over what his lordship had said.

A blackbird's sudden alarm call echoed round the garden. 'Jamie,' called Mr Jennings. 'That's enough for this morning. Be off to yer dinner now.'

In the afternoon, Jamie was set to her first task outside the walled garden—weeding the beds by the side of the house. She bent to her work, nimbly picking out the young weed seedlings, while inwardly she smiled, dreaming of what it would be like when she was finally free of the threat from the Calderwoods.

The sound of a horse interrupted her search for an appropriately damning curse to call down on her stepmother's head. It was Lord Hardinge, astride the most beautiful black stallion Jamie had ever beheld.

She sat up to gaze at it. The stallion was truly magnificent—he had an arched neck and a fine aristocratic head with flaring nostrils. Strength and speed were written in every line of his glossy, glowing body. He seemed to be more than a little spirited too, for he was doing his best to unseat his rider.

The horse whinnied as she watched and then started to buck in an attempt to rid himself of his unwanted burden. Jamie gasped aloud, which drew his lordship's attention to her for just a split second.

The stallion reared. For a moment it seemed as if the rider would be unseated. Jamie's heart was in her mouth as she watched. But no. Lord Hardinge was much too good a horseman to lose to such an obvious trick. He lay along the horse's straining neck and brought him under control with knees and hands.

Jamie could hear him speaking softly to the big animal, though she could not make out his words. The effect seemed almost miraculous, for in less than a minute the horse was totally calm. Jamie watched in admiration, forgetting the role she should be playing and the chores she was neglecting.

Then Lord Hardinge turned towards her, fixing her with an enquiring stare. She noted the beginnings of a frown creasing his brow. She could not move, impaled by that stern gaze.

'Have you no work to do, boy?' His lordship's voice was not loud, but the unmistakable thread of authority carried easily across the distance between them. 'Well?' His irritation was manifest.

Still Jamie could not move. She felt a blush start at her neck and rise rapidly to her hairline. She knew she should stand up when the master addressed her, but her limbs would not obey her. She tried to speak. Her lips moved but there was no sound.

Lord Hardinge's frown eased suddenly. 'There is no harm done, Jamie. Now, get on with your work.' Without waiting to see whether she obeyed, he turned the stallion and gave it its head.

Jamie allowed herself the luxury of watching the superb beast as it galloped down the drive. Horse and rider were well matched, she decided. Only a very fine horseman could control such an animal. Or a horsewoman…

She forced herself to return to her weeding, but her thoughts kept returning to the horse and rider as she mechanically pulled the weeds and dropped them in her bucket. *She* could ride that stallion. Of course she could. There had never been a horse she could not ride. He'd be a handful, but her hands and heels itched at the very thought of him. If only...

Jamie rose from her weeding as the sun was dropping behind the top of the avenue of limes. She straightened her weary back, trying to ease her stiffness, and started towards the compost heaps with her buckets of weeds.

This part of the garden was deserted. In the gathering silence, the sound of horses carried easily from the nearby stables. She found she could not ignore them. It seemed as if the beautiful animals were calling to her, offering her friendship and comfort in her isolation.

In the space of a few moments, she had emptied her buckets and crept into the stable yard. It seemed to be empty. Jamie stood for a moment, her practised eye admiring the order and cleanliness of the place. A horse whickered nervously from one of the stables, perhaps a little disturbed by her unfamiliar scent. Without another thought, she moved towards the sound. The animal must be gentled, settled with hand and voice. She unbolted the door to slip inside, momentarily blind in the gloom.

The horse snorted uncertainly at her unexpected arrival, turning to face her. It was the black stallion! Close to, he was huge and powerful. He did not seem best pleased to see an intruder.

Jamie stood very still, allowing him to get used to her presence and her scent. Then she began to croon softly to him, encouraging him towards her out-stretched hand. After a few seconds, he took one rather hesitant pace towards her, then another. Soon she was blowing her scent into his nostrils, and he was allowing her to stroke his velvet muzzle.

Her head was laid gently against his glossy neck when she felt, rather than heard, the stable door open behind her. The big horse shifted nervously, but she stilled him quickly with a soft murmur, before glancing round to see the newcomer who had caught her where she had no business to be.

'Well, now. And what might you be doing here?'

Jamie closed her eyes in momentary panic. Lord Hardinge—again. Where had he appeared from this time? He sounded more surprised than angry, but still…

Jamie was torn between the need to calm the highly strung horse and the need to maintain her disguise. She stroked the stallion's neck reassuringly and crooned again, wordlessly. Then she blew gently into his nostrils once more. His ears twitched and relaxed, as she continued her stroking and crooning. Let his lordship make of her what he would. He was too good a horseman, she was sure, to lose his temper in front of such a nervous animal.

Richard had no intention of losing his temper. His initial shock at finding the stable door unbolted had been quickly replaced by concern. Othello was unpredictable and potentially dangerous. No one but himself had really been able to handle him. Until now, that is. For here was a skinny stripling who could barely string two words together, yet had reached a level of understanding with Othello which nobody else could match. Richard stood and—against his will—he marvelled. The boy had a most amazing gift, however backward he might be.

'Jamie?' he said softly, at last. The boy half turned. He ventured an uncertain half-smile. 'All right, lad,' Richard murmured. 'I can see you're doing no harm. Do you like horses?'

Jamie nodded vigorously. ''Osses,' he said eagerly. It sounded as if that single word was as much as the boy could manage.

At that moment, the head groom appeared round the corner of the stable block and hurried over to join his master. He looked shocked when he saw Jamie stroking the temperamental black stallion.

Richard ignored the new arrival. 'Good,' he said. Then his voice became stern. 'But you should not be neglecting your work, should you? Back to the garden with you now.' He watched thoughtfully as the boy trotted out of the stable yard.

The groom gulped guiltily. 'M'lord! I were just—'

'Easy, Weaver, easy. I'm glad you were not here to turn the boy away, for I should have missed something well worth seeing. Especially with Othello.'

Weaver gulped again, reddening noticeably as he made to speak.

'Save it, Weaver.' Richard paused. 'I wonder… Seems to me that boy is wasted in the garden. Could you use him here?'

'Aye, milord. Surely. Wi' a gift like that…'

Richard smiled pensively. 'Leave it to me, then. And, meanwhile, let the lad come to the stables whenever he wants.'

The groom was still nodding in wonder, as Richard turned and strode away.

The next few weeks were among the happiest that Jamie could remember. She worked in the garden from dawn till dusk, under the benevolent eye of old Mr Jennings, preparing the ground for spring planting. She was even permitted, under strict supervision, to help in the stovehouse where the tender plants were overwintered. Every night, she fell into her little bed to sleep the sleep of physical exhaustion and dream the dreams of contentment. Her nightmarish visions of incarceration by Ralph Graves faded into the background. For the first time in her life, she was truly well-fed. Her thin frame was beginning to fill out, so much so that Annie now teased her openly about the need for her bandages.

The idyll was marred only by the louring presence of Caleb. Jamie often felt his eyes boring into her defenceless back. The hatred was almost palpable, though she could not begin to account for it, for what threat was a simpleton to him? On the few occasions when Jamie dared to turn round to look at Caleb, he made no attempt to disguise his hostility. Once, he drew his forefinger across his throat in an unmistakably threatening gesture. Jamie began to go to enormous lengths to keep out of his way.

Her luck did not last. One blustery March day, Jamie was on her knees, using a hand trowel she had picked up, when Caleb's huge shadow fell across her. Looking up, she saw that his face was contorted into a predatory grin—and that there was nobody else within earshot. Her heart began to pound.

'So,' snarled Caleb, 'old Jennings' little pet sees fit to steal my tools, does he?' He dragged Jamie to her feet by the collar of her shirt. 'Ain't nobody learned you what happens to thieves, boy, eh?' He pulled the collar tight around Jamie's neck until she could hardly breathe. 'They gets hanged, boy, hanged by the neck 'til they be dead. An' then left on the gibbet to rot.' He tore the trowel out of Jamie's hand. 'That's what'll happen to you, lad, I'll see to that. One day soon, just you wait.' He released the collar and dealt Jamie a ringing box on the ear which felled her to the ground. By the time she had regained her wits, Caleb was gone, though his evil presence still seemed to be all around her.

She sat on the bare earth, massaging her neck as she tried to overcome the wave of panic which had engulfed her. Why was he so intent on being rid of her? What was she to do? She dared not run away from Harding, for she had nowhere else to hide. And yet, it would not take many blows from Caleb's huge hands to break her bones. She swallowed hard, refusing to dwell on such images—she was determined not to give in to her darkest fears. She would need to be much more vigilant, that was all. She must make sure she was always working within sight of one of the other gardeners. And if Caleb did catch her on her own, she must simply take to her heels.

* * *

Lord Hardinge chose that afternoon to make one of his increasingly frequent visits to the garden. Although he rarely spoke to Jamie directly, she knew he watched her and that he often asked after her progress. It seemed a strange sort of behaviour for a gentleman—in Jamie's limited experience. The more he watched her, the more she was overcome by the strangest feelings. Her body seemed to go hot and cold all over, both at the same time. And whenever he came near, her thoughts turned into a jumbled, tangled mess so that it became ever more difficult for her to maintain her role as Jamie, the simpleton.

Lord Hardinge had paused to speak to the head gardener, but Jamie was too far away to hear what was said. In any case, she had no reason to suppose they were talking about her.

After a moment or two, Mr Jennings called Jamie from her digging.

Taking a deep breath, she trotted over, wiping her hands on her smock and smiling as innocently as she could. But her heart was racing, and she was praying that she would not blush under the Earl's scrutiny as she always seemed to do.

'Jamie, Mr Jennings tells me you're doing very well here,' began Lord Hardinge with an encouraging smile. 'He would like you to stay.'

Jamie beamed at Mr Jennings.

'On the other hand,' continued his lordship, 'I have a fancy you could be better employed elsewhere.'

Jamie felt a wave of anxiety wash over her. Surely he would not dismiss her? She was so close to her goal.

'What do you say to working with my horses instead?'

Mr Jennings hurriedly began to reassure Jamie that no harm to her was intended. Jamie knew his motives were kind, but she barely heard him. She was desperately trying to work out the risks of discovery if she accepted his lordship's offer. It would get her away from Caleb; but it would put her even more in the master's way. Nothing was worth the risk that that entailed. She dared not take the chance that he might discover what she was. She shook her head.

Lord Hardinge smiled. 'You were right, Jennings.' Turning back to Jamie, he added, 'Don't worry, lad. I mean you no harm. Knowing how much you love horses, I thought you might like to help take care of mine. If you change your mind, just tell Mr Jennings here. And now, back to work with you.'

Jamie ran back to her task, leaving his lordship talking to the head gardener. He had not raised his voice but, even from the far side of the walled garden, Jamie could tell that he was now furiously angry.

Chapter Eight

'Where did Jamie get those bruises on his neck, Jennings?'

'I'm sure I don't know, m'lord. Some silly accident, probably. Something he shouldn't have been doing, I'll warrant. I'll make sure he gets into no more trouble.'

'See that you do, Jennings. See that you do.' With that, Richard strode back to the house.

He marched into his book-room, trying to keep a rein on his temper which was threatening to explode at any moment. Accident, indeed! Those bruises were surely no accident. Somebody in his household had injured a backward lad, probably deliberately. So much for his pledged word that no harm would come to Jamie under his roof! An attack on Jamie was an attack on his master's honour, too.

He would not allow his fury to get out of control, however, but paused to consider dispassionately who might be the culprit. If it were one of the gardeners—not Jennings, he was a gentle old man, if a bit of a stickler—the solution might indeed be to put the lad with the horses. But it could just as easily have been one of the grooms. Or someone in the house, even Smithers?

His anger had simmered down to more manageable proportions by the time the abigail appeared in answer to his summons. She was plainly nervous. Richard surveyed her slowly. Yes, she was a big woman, and strong, much stronger than Jamie. She could easily have done it.

'Smithers, I have just come from the kitchen garden. Have you seen your brother today?'

'Not since breakfast, my lord. Is something wrong? Oh, dear, what has he done now?' The words tumbled out in a rush.

'I think you had better see for yourself.' He pulled the bell once more and gave instructions that Jamie be sent for immediately. They had to wait fully five minutes for the boy's arrival, during which Richard sat silently behind his desk, mercilessly scrutinising the abigail. She wilted a little under his stern gaze.

Jamie entered shyly, head down. Richard noticed that the boy smiled a little when he saw that he was not alone with the master of the house. But Richard made no acknowledgement of Jamie's arrival. He continued to stare at Smithers without a word.

The woman's nerve broke first. 'Oh, Jamie,' she cried, 'what have you done this time?'

The boy's head came up, a militant glint in his eye. The bruises were livid on his bare neck.

Smithers gasped. 'Good God, who has done that to you? If I get my hands on…' She broke off. Jamie looked bewildered. 'I beg your pardon, m'lord. I should not have spoken so. But just look at those bruises.'

Richard was now satisfied. Smithers was not responsible for Jamie's injuries. 'Smithers, I should like you to take care of your brother's hurts, if you please. And then I want you to find out from him how they came about. I will have no such cruelty on the Harding estate. The culprit will be punished. I expect you to bring me a name—by tomorrow at the latest.' He looked down at the papers on his desk. 'That is all. You may go now. See what you can do for the boy.'

Annie hustled Jamie upstairs to their room to begin applying witch hazel to her bruises. She paid no attention when Jamie winced at the cold liquid on her tender skin. 'Tell me what happened,' she demanded sternly.

'Nothing,' croaked Jamie. It was the first word she had tried to utter since her encounter with Caleb. It hurt.

'Jamie, I wasn't born yesterday. Bruises like these don't appear by themselves.'

'It was an accident. It's nothing.' Jamie's brain was in a whirl. Although her throat was very sore and she could barely swallow, it had not occurred to her until now that there might be visible evidence of her encounter with Caleb. She must not name him. It would only give the bully more reason to attack her. 'I caught my collar on a low branch, and it almost choked me before I could get free. I was clumsy, that's all.'

'Do you expect me to believe that? His lordship certainly will not.'

'He will if you tell it properly. And why should he concern himself anyway?'

'You heard him. He thinks someone did it deliberately, and he will not tolerate it. He's a fair man—'

'Fair? What's fair about his treatment of you? He had you turned off from Calderwood and—'

'He's a fair man, Jamie, as I said, particularly to someone as vulnerable as my baby brother. Why don't you tell the truth?'

'I've told you what happened, Annie. There's nothing more to say.' She paused for a moment, seeing the real worry on the abigail's face. 'Even if there were someone else involved—and I have told you there was not—it would only make matters worse for me. He would just make sure there were no visible marks, next time. Now, I must get back to work, Annie.' She forced herself to smile. It wobbled a little, but she did not think Annie had noticed. 'See you at supper.' With that, she hurried out.

Barely fifteen minutes after she had left it, the abigail was again in the book-room, recounting Jamie's tale. Richard sat impassively behind his desk. He let the woman see that he did not believe a word of it. 'That's all he said?' His voice was quiet, but full of suppressed anger, as he glared fiercely at the servant.

Smithers nodded.

'And did you believe him?'

'He doesn't say much, my lord, and it's sometimes

difficult to follow his meaning, but when I suggested someone else had been involved, he denied it, vehemently. It *could* have happened as he described,' she finished lamely.

'In other words, you don't believe him. And neither do I. Little good it will do us, though, without knowing the identity of the villain.' He was talking more to himself than to the abigail for a moment, but then he turned back to her with a frown. 'As his sister, you should surely have been able to extract the truth from the boy. I do not accept his explanation for a moment. You will set about identifying the true culprit at once, if you please. I leave it to you to decide how, but the moment you find out anything more, Smithers, you are to come to me immediately. Do you understand?' At her rapid nod, he dismissed her and returned to his papers.

Richard spent the rest of the afternoon reading reports from his agents in London and elsewhere, his frown deepening as the day wore on. All the money and effort he was expending in an attempt to recover the missing loans was bringing scant return. There was plenty of information about the Calderwood household, which seemed to have been in uproar since his visit—apparently as the result of some domestic crisis or other—but there was nothing about the money. Thus far, unfortunately, Calderwood had won the day.

Richard needed a new strategy but, for the moment, ideas eluded him. At length, his patience exhausted, he stuffed the papers into his desk and mounted the stairs to his mother's sitting-room.

She welcomed him with a smile of concern. 'You look tired, Richard, and worried too. Come and sit down. May I help in any way?'

'It's frustration as much as anything else, Mama,' he admitted, dropping a kiss on her cheek. 'I need to be doing something, but until I can find some lever to use against Calderwood, I can't begin to act. None of my enquiries has come up with anything yet. And now, to make matters worse, I appear to have a child-beater on my estate.'

Lady Hardinge looked puzzled.

'That backward brother of Smithers is clearly being abused by someone at Harding, but I cannot find out who it is.'

'How unfortunate.' She paused, thoughtfully. 'You know, it's not like you to take so much interest in waifs and strays, Richard. Why are you doing so with this lad?'

'To be honest, I am not sure. Oh, at the outset, it was perfectly straightforward—I wanted to have Smithers here so that I could use her to find out more about the Calderwoods. Offering a place to the boy was a means of snaring his sister. And it worked. But now, I'm rather taken with him, I admit. He's an engaging lad, very willing and hard-working, and extremely talented when it comes to growing things, as we have both seen. He seems to have a way with horses, too.'

'You shouldn't be so surprised, my dear. Very often the simpletons who find it so hard to communicate with people seem to have a natural understanding of plants and beasts.'

Richard nodded. 'What about Smithers herself, Mama? Has she let fall any clue that might help us?'

'Absolutely none. She does her work very well, as always, even though I no longer require an abigail of her talents, as you know. But she says nothing to that. No doubt she is keen to stay where her brother is.'

'No doubt,' Richard echoed grimly, staring into the fire.

His mother watched him silently for several minutes.

Richard rose abruptly. 'I must *do* something, Mama. The waiting is beginning to drive me mad. I shall go to London to see my agents and to find out whether any of their leads is even vaguely promising. They say not, of course. But perhaps I can spot something they have overlooked. At least I shall be *doing* something.'

As the days passed, Jamie continued to work contentedly in the garden, though she had become even more careful than before. There were no more attacks from Caleb. But at night, in their room, Annie continued to pester her about what had happened.

'For goodness' sake, Annie, stop this. Every time you see me, you go on and on about those bruises. I have told you all there is to tell. The bruises have gone. Do leave it now.'

'His lordship did not believe that story. He—'

'Damn his lordship!' exploded Jamie, momentarily forgetting the manners of a lady. 'What right has he to interfere?'

'Jamie! Keep your voice down, or someone will

hear you. Lord Hardinge has every right, as you know very well. He is the master here. Would you be any less concerned if it were one of your own servants?'

'No,' Jamie agreed reluctantly, 'but this is different.'

'Oh? Why?'

Jamie was in real difficulty now. She could not find words to explain the strange effects Lord Hardinge had on her, intimidating and exciting all at once. She did not understand it herself. 'It's…it's not normal for a gentleman to pay so much attention to a gardener's boy,' she managed at last, which sounded pretty feeble even to her own ears.

Annie looked hard at her wayward charge, but merely said, 'He won't be doing so for a while. He left for London four days ago.'

'Oh, so that is why he hasn't—' Jamie shut her mouth abruptly, silently cursing herself. No one must suspect that she watched for the master's frequent walks in the garden and had been disappointed every day since his departure.

Annie seemed not to notice Jamie's gaffe. 'How much longer now till you come of age, Jamie? And what do you plan to do then?'

'March the twenty-sixth. After that, well…I should tell you, I suppose, Annie. I know I can trust you.' She rose and fetched her pelisse from among Annie's clothes. Then she slit open one of the seams to extract what was inside.

'These were my mother's pearls, Annie,' she said simply, showing her the single strand. 'They are the sum total of my inheritance from her. I believe they are very fine and very valuable.'

Annie nodded.

'Once I come of age, I shall be able to sell them and go back to being a girl again. Then I shall look for a situation as a governess or a companion, so that I can support myself. The pearls will pay for my keep until I find a position.' Jamie saw that Annie's expression was registering concern. 'I thought I might use one of the Bath agencies you spoke of, Annie,' she continued.

Annie took both the callused hands in hers and sat beside Jamie on the bed. 'Oh, Miss Jamie,' she said gently, 'it won't do. To be sure, it won't. First of all, if you were to try to sell those pearls now, as you are, you would be had up on suspicion of theft, sure as eggs is eggs.'

'I'll go as a girl, then,' protested Jamie. 'I may not be richly dressed, but I do *sound* like a lady.'

'And secondly,' continued Annie, without a pause, 'no agency will even consider you without references.'

'I should have thought of that,' admitted Jamie in a small, crushed voice. Annie put a comforting arm round her shoulders. 'But I shall find a way, never fear. Somehow I shall achieve my independence. Even if I have to write my references myself.' Her face brightened. 'Yes! That's what I shall do. Miss Jessamyne Calderwood of Calderwood Hall shall provide an impeccable reference for her erstwhile companion, Miss…er…Jemima Crane!'

Annie gasped. 'You cannot!'

Jamie cocked a saucy eyebrow. 'What choice do I have? And it will harm no one. I myself shall sign it, so it is no forgery. I shall just…embroider the truth a little. It will appear that I am an elderly spinster, somewhat ailing, who employed a young companion to brighten her life.'

'Hmph!' Annie did not sound convinced. 'And why, pray, did this paragon of virtue, Miss Jemima Crane, leave her place with so kind an employer?'

Jamie thought for a moment. 'Miss Calderwood is to go abroad, for her health. Jemima will not go, not for any price. She is afraid of the sea!'

Annie had to laugh. 'You are beyond redemption, Miss Jamie. What if—?'

Jamie refused to listen. 'I have no choice, Annie, so I had better make the best of it. Oh!' Her face fell. 'But I have no Calderwood notepaper. It will not do.'

Annie sat silent for a while, studying Jamie's face. 'I have some,' she said simply. Jamie beamed. 'Honestly come by, I promise you. I was planning to write to my old mistress in London, the day Lady Calderwood turned me off. I think I still have the sheet.'

Jamie flung her arms round Annie's neck and kissed her on the cheek. 'You are wonderful, Annie Smithers. Can we do it now? Please?'

The abigail fetched the sheet of writing paper from her case and, together, they began to compose the all-important reference for Miss Jemima Crane, spinster companion.

Chapter Nine

Mr Jennings had taken to sending Jamie every morning to cut a bunch of daffodils as a gift for Lady Hardinge. Although he never explained, Jamie knew the flowers were a token of sympathy for the widowed mistress he had served ever since her marriage to the late Earl.

It was a delightful time to be out of doors. The mornings were crisp and clear and, although there was often frost on the ground, it soon melted in the early spring sunshine. The swathes of daffodils lifted Jamie's spirits with their glorious golden colour, reminding her of the rapidly passing days. Soon it would be her birthday and she would—somehow—attain her freedom!

One morning, very much later than usual, while Jamie was picking the daffodils, she came upon a tiny plant of late snowdrops, hidden among the drifts of gold. They were quite beautiful, white overlaid with green. Jamie put the cut daffodils in the trug while she fetched her trowel and a small clay pot. The snowdrops would make a delightful gift for her ladyship. It did not matter that they would soon wilt indoors.

Jamie knelt among the daffodils to dig up the tiny flowers. It took some strength to do so, for the daffodil bed was firm and stony and her trowel had to be eased through it to get under the tiny bulbs without damaging their roots. At last they were free. She laid the little clump on the grass and began to remove some of the earth and stones from underneath, before putting the flowers into the pot.

'What the hell do you think ye're at?' cried a harsh voice.

Jamie half turned, to see the towering figure of Caleb, his face purple with fury, his arm upraised with a thin stake in his hand. Before she could move, he brought it down across her back, knocking her flat on to the earth and then pinning her there with his boot. A hail of blows followed. Jamie could not stir. Her face was driven into the flower-bed so that she could not scream aloud. At every gasp, she inhaled fine soil which threatened to choke her.

On the curious thought that she had so nearly made it to freedom, she passed out.

Caleb was raining furious blows on Jamie's inert body when he was wrenched aside by a strong arm. A sharp right to the jaw knocked him backwards to the ground, where he lay moaning and bleeding from a deeply split lip.

'I shall deal with you later,' snarled Richard, lifting Jamie's senseless body and striding back towards the house. He looked anxiously for signs of life. The boy would not die from a whipping, surely? But if he had suffocated?

No—the boy was breathing, thank God. Although still quite deeply unconscious, Jamie seemed somehow aware that the terror was over and that he was safe. Richard was reminded of a trusting child, as Jamie snuggled deeper into the safety of his encircling arms, moaning a little.

Spurred on by the sound, which seemed to suggest serious injury, Richard increased his pace. As he strode rapidly through the hallway to his book-room, he threw an order over his shoulder for Smithers to be fetched at once. A moment later, he was laying Jamie gently on the sofa and throwing off his own dust-stained coat.

The boy was breathing fairly easily now. That much was obvious from a first cursory examination. The state of his back would be another matter.

Very gently, and silently cursing the delay in Smithers' arrival, Richard turned Jamie over so that he could attend to the boy's back. Lifting the heavy smock, he pulled the undershirt out of Jamie's breeches. To his surprise, he found, instead of broken and bleeding skin, thick bandages covering most of the boy's back. A few weals were visible on his shoulders, but the skin there was not broken.

Without further thought, Richard crossed to his desk for some scissors. Then he cut through the bandages from waist to shoulder, peeling them back to see what injuries lay beneath. He was more than a little relieved to find that the bandages and the heavy smock seemed to have absorbed most of the force of the blows. A few fine red lines were the only sign of the beating Jamie had received at the hands of the appalling Caleb.

Satisfied, Richard let out the breath he had been holding. Gently he turned Jamie on to his back to make him more comfortable. The bandages fell away. To Richard's astonishment, he found that his hands were cradling, not the body of a thirteen-year-old boy, but the delectable breasts of a fully-formed girl.

Richard's mind was spinning. He was remembering everything that had happened since Jamie had come into his life and discovering new perspectives on both her reactions and his own. All the strange attractions he had felt towards a simpleton boy... As he tried to gather his tumbling thoughts, his hands continued to cup her breasts, his thumbs unconsciously massaging the reddened ridges where the bandages had cut into her tender flesh.

And at that moment, Jamie's eyes opened and she looked up into his. She seemed half-dazed. But she appeared to recognise him. And then she smiled.

For what seemed an eternity, he felt he was drowning in those slumberous green eyes, responding to the invitation they contained. But when she lapsed back into insensibility, his sanity returned. He was caressing an unconscious woman. No matter what he had read in her eyes, he was taking advantage of her by touching her so. He snatched his hands away as if he had been burnt.

'Lord Hardinge!'

Suddenly, Smithers was there beside him. He had

not heard her come in. He hastily pulled down Jamie's smock, knowing very well it was too late.

Smithers was looking daggers at him.

'You had better see to your brother, Smithers,' he said curtly. 'Or should I say "sister"? Never mind. What matters at present is Jamie. You must know that I found him being severely beaten by Caleb. The bandages seem to have saved him—or rather her—from serious hurt. But you will wish to see for yourself.' He turned his back in recognition of Jamie's need for privacy, as Smithers knelt down by the inert body.

Richard pulled the bell with a grim smile. 'Doubtless you would welcome an opportunity to concoct yet another of your fairy tales. You have such a vivid imagination, as I have good reason to know. But I fear you will be disappointed there. I have no intention of leaving you alone together now, not until I have got to the root of this business!'

The butler appeared in answer to Richard's summons. 'Ah, Digby. Be so good as to ask Mrs Peters to come to the study and remain here with Smithers and Jamie until I return. And ask Tom to remain outside in the hall. Neither Smithers nor Jamie is to leave this room until I say they may.'

The butler turned to go. By not the flicker of an eyelid had he betrayed any surprise at Richard's unexpected manner of returning from London.

'Ah, yes,' Richard murmured. 'One moment, Digby.' He returned to his desk to pen a short note, which he folded and gave to the butler. 'Deliver that to Lady Hardinge before she leaves for Bath, if you please,' he ordered. 'And send one of the maids to attend on her ladyship while her abigail is…otherwise occupied.'

As the butler left to carry out his various instructions, Richard turned back to Smithers. 'Now,' he began, in a marginally less harsh voice, 'take care of Jamie. Whatever you have both done, nothing can excuse what that brute was doing to her.' He came to stand over Jamie, looking down at her pale face. An ironic smile twisted one corner of his mouth, as he thought about these past weeks and the strange part Jamie had begun to play in his life. He had felt such sympathy for an innocent, backward lad—who had turned out to be no boy, and was probably neither backward nor innocent. Remembering how she had smiled up at him when he was caressing her, he was now sure of it. How completely he had been gulled!

As soon as the housekeeper arrived, he left the room without another glance, pausing only in the hallway to ensure Tom understood his instructions. Then he mounted the stairs to the top floor of the house, to begin a systematic search of the room shared by Smithers and her so-called brother.

Standing in the doorway, he surveyed the neat attic room. A bed and a truckle, a chest of drawers and a small clothes press, and nothing else. Not many hiding places here, surely? But he did not know what he was looking for. The main evidence of their wrongdoing was Jamie herself. What else might he find?

Richard chose to be very careful and methodical. He examined every item in every drawer. He pulled out the drawers to search behind and beneath them.

He moved furniture and bedding so that he could search every inch of the room.

When he found what he was looking for in the clothes press, he was tempted to return immediately to confront the women, but something stayed him. There might be more. He would remain until his painstaking search was complete.

It was some two hours before he returned to the study, dismissing Tom and Mrs Peters from their posts.

As the door closed, Richard surveyed the two women slowly. Jamie had apparently recovered from her ordeal and was sitting on the end of the sofa where he had laid her earlier. Smithers was standing behind. He noticed that Jamie had not risen from her seat as he entered the room. Indeed, she seemed remarkably composed, considering her situation. Smithers, by contrast, was twisting a handkerchief in her fingers and almost ripping it in her agitation. Good, he would start with her.

'Smithers. First, you will be good enough to explain why you perpetrated this disgraceful fraud on my household.' It was a statement, not a question.

'Jamie had to get away. She was being persecuted. It…it seemed the only way.' Her words petered out.

'Is Jamie your sister?' he demanded.

'Yes—' began Smithers.

'No,' interrupted Jamie in clear, resolute tones.

That single word was spoken in a remarkably educated voice which the woman was making no attempt to disguise. Who on earth could she be?

'No, I am not,' Jamie repeated. 'Nor am I backward, my lord. I myself am responsible for everything that has happened. Annie's only crime is that she took pity on me. Vent your anger on me, if you please.'

She might be a fraud, and she might even be a harlot, but there was no mistaking the dignity and courage with which she faced him. For a split second, and against his better judgement, he felt like applauding.

'Who are you?' he asked sharply, refusing to be ensnared by her dangerous wiles.

'I cannot tell you.' She closed her lips tightly. From her mulish expression, Richard knew she was determined to resist his questioning.

'Do you really expect me to accept that?' he asked with withering scorn. 'Come, come. Remember, I have all the power of the law at my back. And I will use it, if I have to. Now—I ask you again—what is your name?'

Jamie returned his hostile glare. 'I cannot tell you, my lord,' she replied with quiet composure. 'Since you choose not to accept that, there is nothing more to be said.' She clasped her hands lightly in her lap and stared down at them.

Richard exploded. 'By God, I shall have the truth out of you, one way or the other. Do not doubt it.'

But he did not succeed. In spite of continuing to question them for nearly an hour, he discovered nothing more. What little patience he had was totally exhausted. 'Very well,' he said, in a low menacing voice, 'since you choose to defy me, we shall adopt a different approach, an approach which you will not enjoy, I promise you. But first, I shall give you time to meditate upon your transgressions. Both of you.'

With that, he gave orders for Smithers and Jamie to be locked in separate rooms for the night. He was resolved there would be no opportunity for collusion between them, before he had got to the bottom of the mystery. He was not sure what kind of approach might be successful, but he hoped that his vague threat would prey on their minds in their isolation and help to bring them to confess.

Richard dined alone and then returned to his book-room, where he remained until almost all the household was abed. Thank God his mother had gone to stay with her sister in Bath and would not return for a few days. He did not yet feel equal to explaining matters to her.

He leaned back in his leather chair, gazing vacantly into the middle distance. His mind was preoccupied with the puzzle of the items he had brought away from his search of Smithers' room. He just did not know what to make of them. Jamie might possibly make sense of them, if she could be persuaded to speak, but somehow he doubted it. Whoever, and whatever she was, her courage was extraordinary. She was likely to outface him, however he tried to coerce her.

Thoughts of coercion brought the brutal figure of Caleb back into his mind for the first time since the encounter in the garden. The undergardener needed to be dealt with for his mindless cruelty to Jamie. In spite of the lateness of the hour, Richard sent for Caleb.

But Caleb was not to be found. He had not waited to be subjected to Richard's wrath. He had not even paused to collect his belongings. It appeared that, as soon as he had recovered his breath, he had set about putting a safe distance between himself and the powerful master of Harding.

For Richard, it was the very last straw. Frustrated at every turn, his temper again got the better of him. No insolent chit was going to defy him in his own house. He would have the truth out of her. Now! Before the night was over!

Although Richard knew perfectly well that his wisest course would be to tackle Jamie and Smithers separately in the morning, when he was fresh and better able to question them effectively, his logical mind was overridden by his now ungovernable temper. His feet led him to the attics instead of to his own chamber.

He stopped outside Jamie's room. The key was in the lock, and there was no sound from inside. Transferring his candle to his left hand, he quietly unlocked the door and went in. Once inside, he locked the door again and pocketed the key.

That single candle lit only part of the room. Beyond its range he could make out the shadowy shape of a small bed and a low chest. The room contained nothing else, not even a chair.

He moved across the room, lifting his candle so that its light fell on the bed where Jamie was sleeping. Her titian hair, freed from its daytime straitjacket, surrounded her pale face in a riot of tumbled curls. Her long dark lashes—why had he never noticed them before?—rested on slightly flushed cheeks. Was she a little feverish?

Without thinking, he stretched out his hand and laid it gently on her forehead. It was cool to his touch, the skin as soft as a petal in spite of her weeks in the open air.

Her eyes fluttered open. She seemed to register the fact of his presence in the gloom and of his cool hand on her brow. As before, she smiled at him, an otherworldly smile which almost touched his heart.

'No, Jamie,' he said sharply. 'No, I am not so easily manipulated. I have come for the truth.'

The harshness in his voice jerked her into wakefulness. Her smile vanished as she realised she was alone with the master of the house in the middle of the night—and he appeared to be in no mood to humour her if she defied him.

In a flash, Jamie was out of the bed and across the room to the door. Behind her, his lordship laughed quietly. The sound seemed very menacing in the oppressive silence of the dark house.

'A waste of time, my dear. The door is locked.'

Jamie turned to face him then, her back against the door. 'What are you doing here, my lord?' she asked, trying to control the trembling of her voice.

She put him in mind of a mythical nymph, all in white, fleeing from some marauding satyr. The image inflamed his temper even further. 'What do you think I am doing, Jamie?' he responded cynically, seeking for the most effective means of putting her under pressure. 'This afternoon, in the book-room, you made me an offer with your eyes. Did you not think I would come to collect?'

She cowered away from him. What had become of the honourable man who had taken pity on a simple lad? He had even shown kindness to the boy Jamie. How could it have come to this?

His lordship set the candle carefully on the chest and came towards her, pinning her against the door with a hand on either side of her head. 'Now, my girl, are you going to tell me what I want to know? Or do I have to force you?'

Her whole body was shaking. She tried to turn her head away, but he gripped her by the chin, forcing her to look up at him. In his eyes, she saw anger, frustration—and dawning desire. And the merest touch of his hand on her face had started that same strange quivering in her limbs that she had experienced every time he touched her. She could barely stand.

It was the fear in her eyes which first penetrated the red mist of his anger. Whatever she had done, she was now helpless—and terrified of him. Then, behind her fear, he glimpsed something deeper, reaching out to him, urging him to respond.

Suddenly, both his hands were cupping her face. His mouth descended hungrily on hers, demanding that she yield to him.

Jamie was powerless to resist the pull of that first kiss. Somehow, her arms were around his neck, her fingers threading through his thick hair, her lips opening beneath the pressure of his.

Kissing her less urgently now, teasing at her lus-

cious mouth, he picked her up and carried her back
to the bed. Questions were long since forgotten as he
stretched out beside her, caressing her soft cheek. She
moaned softly when his lips moved to her neck, nuzzling gently.

'Ah, Jamie, my beauty. Soon, I promise you, soon.'

Jamie had lost all sense of who and where she was.
Everything was pure sensation—the tingling of her
skin wherever he touched her, the magic of holding
his powerful body in her arms, the longing in her
innermost being as she responded to his ardent kisses.

Chapter Ten

It was the pull of the coarse lacing of her nightgown which brought Jamie back to sordid reality. This was not the joining of two souls in pure love. She was lying in bed with Lord Hardinge *who thought she was a servant and a fraud.* Lord Hardinge was going to ravish her. This was not love, but lust. Oh, no matter that she had encouraged him, that—if she were honest with herself—she wanted him as much as he wanted her. It was wrong, despicable, base. He must not be allowed to do this. She would never forgive him—or herself—if he did.

She caught his hand and pushed it away with all her strength. 'No, please, my lord, I beg of you. Please let me go. I cannot do this.'

Richard sat up abruptly, recalled to his senses by the renewed fear in her voice. For all his reservations about womankind, he had never in his life taken any woman against her will. But this one—for this one, he was sorely tempted. She was a tease, had led him on, and now she spurned him? Surely she deserved to be taken in anger?

'Do not do this, I beg of you,' she repeated, more urgently now. 'You will never forgive yourself if you do. I have never yet known a man.' In spite of all her attempts at self-control, hot tears had begun to flow.

The last remnants of Richard's anger melted away at the sight of those tears. He passed his hand across his brow, trying to recover his composure. 'God help me! What am I doing?' he cried, anguish in his deep voice. He rose from the bed. 'Go to sleep, Jamie. I give you my word I shall not touch you again. Go to sleep now.' Then, taking up the candle, he unlocked the door and was gone, leaving her in total darkness.

Jamie could not move, not even to find out whether he had locked her in again. She lay with tears pouring down her face, trying to understand what had happened between them—and why she had denied him when she wanted him so much. The memory of his mouth on hers sent flushes of desire coursing through her veins, making her limbs at once burning and boneless. She was unable to control the longing which filled her.

Her head told her he would have taken her in anger, and as a servant, not as a lover. Who knows, he might afterwards have delivered her up to the constable and even to the gallows?

But, in spite of that knowledge, and the self-loathing which accompanied it, she knew that, if he had persisted, she would not have denied him. Only his honourable response to her pleas had spared her. If he had kissed her again, nothing else would have mattered.

* * *

On the other side of the door, Richard was standing with his hand still on the knob, trying in his turn to come to terms with what he had so nearly done. It did not matter that she was only a servant. His behaviour had been despicable. The hand which held the candle was a little unsteady, and the tiny flame cast strange flickering shadows as it moved.

'My lord? Is there something I can do for you?'

He turned to see the housekeeper emerge from the shadows behind him. He cursed inwardly. Not only had he allowed his impossible temper to lead him to the verge of doing something contemptible, he had also been caught in the act. No matter that he had not seduced the girl. The whole household would soon believe that he had. Damn, damn, damn!

'My lord?' said Mrs Peters again.

He was not about to make any sort of apology or excuse to his housekeeper. He fixed her with an aristocratic glare and said evenly, 'This young woman is locked in her room on my instructions. She is to be kept there. And she is not to be allowed to have any dealings with Smithers. Do I make myself clear?' He extracted the key from his pocket and locked the door.

Mrs Peters still looked more than a little shocked. She shook her head unhappily as he turned and made for the stairs.

Downstairs in his study once more, Richard quickly consumed four very large brandies and poured himself a fifth. He was at a loss to account for his own behaviour. Never, in all his adult life, had he lost control in such a way. That girl—Jamie—must be part witch.

But no witch had eyes like tropical pools—or a mouth like ripe fruit, waiting to be plucked. At the memory of their kisses, he shifted uncomfortably in his chair. Even the thought of her stirred his desire.

He tried to re-ignite his anger in an attempt to control his body's responses. She had pretended to be a boy to obtain a situation in his household. And she had no explanation to offer. She had yet to attempt to explain away the evidence he had uncovered during his search earlier. He would be surprised if she succeeded there, either!

But still, somehow, he was not fully persuaded of her guilt. The vision of her, as he had seen her upstairs, rose again in his mind, her eyes opening to smile up at him. When she looked at him in just that way...

He downed his brandy in a single swallow and slammed the empty goblet on to the table. Action, as ever, was the answer, so he returned to his desk and read yet again the document he had brought down from Smithers' room. With a decisive nod, he drew a fresh sheet of paper towards him and penned a crisp but careful letter. Then he sealed it with a wafer, before inscribing the address in a firm hand and franking it with his signature.

Without pausing for further reflection on the wisdom of what he had done, he rose from the table with the letter in his hand, hesitating for only a moment over the brandy decanter. No. No more tonight. In the hallway, he dropped the letter on the tray where the servants would find and despatch it first thing in the morning. Then, drowsy from the effects of the brandy, he made his way to bed.

Having gone very late—and a little foxed—to his bed, Richard slept very long into the next day. Gregg, the valet, who had naturally waited up to see his master to bed, knew better than to disturb him, so it was well after noon before he stirred.

When Richard awoke, refreshed in spite of the excesses of the night before, he recalled with satisfaction that he had had the presence of mind to despatch that letter. Then he remembered the detail of his encounter with Jamie, which gave him no satisfaction at all, only guilt. He had no wish to confront her again until absolutely necessary. If he were honest with himself, he was not sure how well he could handle such a meeting.

Instead, Smithers was summoned back to the study in mid-afternoon. She was pale and drawn.

'You look unwell, Smithers,' he commented coolly. 'Troubled sleep, perhaps?'

'Lack of sleep is not the problem, my lord,' countered the abigail quickly, bristling at the innuendo. 'Rather, lack of food.'

'What?'

'I was released from my room barely five minutes ago, my lord. No one has come near me since last night. I fancy they do not dare.' She sounded angry and bitter. Clearly, she did not care if it showed.

'And Jamie?'

'I do not know. But if you gave no express orders...'

In spite of his justifiable anger, Richard was mortified by his own stupid oversight. 'I apologise, Smithers. Go down to the kitchen now and have something to eat. I shall see you again in half an hour. And send someone up to Jamie's room with a tray.'

Smithers looked surprised at his sudden change of tone.

It did not last. 'One moment, Smithers. You realise, of course, that someone other than you must take up the tray?'

'Of course,' she repeated, with heavy emphasis, and left for the kitchen.

Half an hour later, the interview was resumed, but it proved singularly unproductive. Smithers still refused to answer any of his lordship's questions even when, in exasperation, he threatened to turn her off without a character.

'You could end up on the parish, or worse,' he thundered. 'For God's sake, woman, tell me the truth.'

Smithers would not do so. Her mouth had assumed the same mulish expression that he had noted on Jamie's face the previous day. 'It is not for me to say, my lord,' was her only answer. 'You must ask Jamie. She must decide. I cannot help you.'

Richard ran his hand through his thick hair. 'Go back to your room. I will deal with you later—once I have dealt with Jamie.'

He had finally decided that the confrontation with

Jamie could no longer be delayed, however uncomfortable it might prove to be. As he waited for her to be fetched, he repeated the resolutions he had already made. He would not touch her. He would not allow her to provoke him—until her arrival in his life, he had prided himself on his ability to control his temper in almost any situation. And he would not frighten her. The image of her cowering away from him filled him with shame. He pushed it guiltily to the back of his mind.

This time he would be calm and persistent in ferreting out the truth. No threats, no temper, no violence.

Jamie had no sooner entered the book-room than most of his resolutions were broken. 'Good God, woman, have you no shame?' His voice was almost a shout. 'How dare you persist in dressing so improperly?' His eyes raked her figure mercilessly, finally resting on her close-fitting breeches.

Bristling with anger, she looked straight at him. 'You gave me no choice, my lord,' she countered, flushing under his angry gaze. 'Everything but my nightgown is locked away with Annie. I thought you would not wish to see me in that. Would you have me go and change?'

Richard swallowed, trying yet again to master his temper and to ignore her provocative impudence. She was clever and manipulative, this one, and might well best him if he did not remain calm. He forced a thin smile. 'No, Jamie. As you well know, it would not serve my purposes to have you and Smithers back together. We will remain as we are.'

He saw that Jamie continued to stare at him without the least acknowledgement of his undoubted power over her. He could have her carted off to gaol at a word, as she must be well aware, but she showed no sign of fear. A remarkable woman indeed. Or foolhardy in the extreme.

He sat back in his chair, forcing himself to breathe slowly and deeply until his self-control had returned. 'We will start with what happened yesterday, if you please, Jamie. Tell me about it.'

'I have been thinking about that all day, my lord. Heavens knows, I have had little opportunity for any other activity since yesterday.' That little barb hit home, and his jaw clenched. He was ashamed to be reminded of his treatment of her.

Richard sat forward in his chair, watching her intently. Everything in her manner suggested honesty and openness, but he must remain on the watch for the slightest flicker of deceit.

'You must know that Caleb has been threatening simple Jamie ever since we arrived,' she began. 'I cannot see what threat a simpleton could be to the undergardener, but he clearly wanted to be rid of me. You suspected that no accident was responsible for my bruises last week.' Richard remained impassive as she looked defiantly at him. 'You were right. It was Caleb. Then, yesterday—' She swallowed hard. 'Yesterday,' she began again, in a slightly wobbly voice, 'I went to cut daffodils for her ladyship, as I have been doing for some time now. I found a tiny group of snowdrops buried among the taller daffodils. I imagine Caleb must have planted them.

'I decided to dig up the snowdrops for Lady Hardinge. But Caleb caught me just as I was tidying up the clump to put it in the pot. The rest, my lord, you know.' She clasped her hands loosely in front of her and rested her open, direct gaze on his face.

Under that calm gaze, Richard felt himself flushing. He had been a fool not to secure Caleb from the first. Now he could see that he had been obsessed with Jamie to the exclusion of all else. He did not dare pause to wonder why that should be so, saying merely, 'I shall speak to him in due course. It is clear he has much to answer for, not least his attacks on you, for which I am sorry.'

Jamie seemed to relax a little at his words. Good. Now was the time to find out the real truth about who she was.

'Let us turn to other matters now, Jamie. I want explanations for your presence here and for this blatant fraud.' He waved a hand in the direction of her rough male clothes. 'And I want an explanation for this,' he added sharply, holding out a sheet of paper.

A single glance was sufficient to show her what the paper was. 'How came you by this?' snapped Jamie, all remaining signs of deference gone.

Richard smiled with satisfaction. He had her on the defensive now, and he meant to follow up his advantage ruthlessly. 'That is of no importance. I am waiting for your explanation.'

For a moment, judging by her tight-lipped expression, he thought she would take refuge in silence.

'That is my reference, my lord, from my previous

employer, Miss Jessamyne Calderwood. You will have seen that she speaks very highly of me.'

He raised an eyebrow. 'She speaks very highly of Miss Jemima Crane,' he said, pointedly staring at her trousered figure.

'I am Jemima Crane,' said Jamie, sounding remarkably composed.

Both brows shot up. 'Are you, indeed? Then why, pray, did you not say so yesterday? Why this disreputable imposture? How comes it that such a woman'—he paused, reading from the paper—'"honest, reliable, well-educated in the ways of society"—should stoop to such impropriety?'

'I had to leave because Miss Calderwood was going abroad for the sake of her health. And for my own protection. Lady Calderwood has a distant cousin—his name is Graves—who was becoming very persistent in his attentions, which were not honourable. He gave every indication of being ready to follow me wherever I went, perhaps even to possess himself of my person by force. I admit I was very frightened.'

She shuddered—very realistically, Richard thought.

'Lady Calderwood would do nothing to help me. But Miss Jessamyne was more than kind. She procured boy's clothes for me and helped me plan my escape. We thought that, if I could lie concealed for a few months, Ralph Graves would lose interest. That is why I could not tell anyone who I was.

'I had intended to leave on my own. But, following your visit, when her ladyship dismissed Smithers, Miss Jessamyne suggested we might go together and, out of the kindness of her heart, Smithers agreed. Now, see what ill fortune it has brought her!'

'Ill fortune?' He reached into the drawer of his desk to bring out the string of pearls, which he placed carefully on the desk in front of Jamie. 'I should have said, rather, good fortune. Would not you?'

Jamie blanched. 'Those pearls, my lord, are mine, not Annie's.'

'And may I ask how you came by them?' he asked silkily.

'They were given to me,' she said unhelpfully.

His eyes bored into hers, demanding that she say more. He thought she looked guilty.

'They belonged to Miss Jessamyne. They were a parting gift to me, before I left Calderwood Hall.'

'I see. What a very generous lady she must be, as well as—shall we say—a little eccentric in her dealings with her servants?' He was anything but convinced and he wanted her to know it. Suddenly he smiled. 'No doubt Lady Calderwood will be able to substantiate your story. I expect her reply to my letter any day. We shall return to this matter then.'

He had the satisfaction of seeing her turn dead white then. So she *was* lying! About the necklace—and probably much more. His tactics were working. The waiting would give her time to dwell on her transgressions, provided she had no further opportunity to escape.

He leaned back in his chair. 'That is all for the present, Jemima. You may go.'

As she turned to leave, he added, 'And I do not wish to see you improperly dressed again. Return to your old room and see to it. You and Smithers will have the freedom of the house, for the present. But that is all. I intend to get to the bottom of all this and to ensure that the guilty are punished. So, until I am satisfied on that head, you will not be permitted to leave Harding.'

Jamie fled from the room.

Chapter Eleven

It was a great relief not to be locked into the bare attic room. Jamie mechanically folded her nightgown as her mind ranged over her options. She must get away before Lady Calderwood found her. It was that—or forced marriage to Ralph Graves. How long would she be able to resist him? And how would she live with herself if she did not? No—it must be escape. And it must be now!

Jamie knew that it would be very wrong to involve Annie this time. The abigail had already suffered quite enough as a result of her kind-hearted espousal of Jamie's cause. Lord Hardinge would expect them to try to escape together, probably after dark. Well, she would surprise him. She would go immediately. Alone.

Taking up the folded nightgown, she went back to the room that she and Annie had shared. Annie was still locked in.

'Jamie!' she gasped as the younger woman entered alone. 'What has happened?'

Jamie sat down on the bed. 'His lordship has decreed that we need no longer be separated,' she said bitterly, 'since he has discovered my imposture.'

'I don't understand.'

'He searched this room yesterday. He found the reference we wrote for Jemima Crane. And my pearls.'

'Oh, God!'

Jamie paused. It would not do to tell Annie that his lordship had written to Lady Calderwood. 'We are not to leave the house for the present, but he has *kindly* said that we need not remain locked up,' she continued, staring fixedly ahead. 'And I am not to wear boy's clothes any more.'

'That's one good thing, then,' said Annie. 'With a little work with our needles, I am sure we can make you quite presentable.'

'That will take too long. He is insistent that I change immediately,' Jamie lied, 'but I have nothing of my own to wear. I shouldn't have allowed you to send that green gown to the orphanage. If I had kept it—'

Annie shook her head. 'It was only fit for the fire.'

'I have an idea,' cried Jamie innocently. 'The second parlour maid is about the same size as I am. Perhaps we could borrow something from her. Just for today.'

'Well...'

'If *you* went to Mrs Peters and asked her, I am sure she would help. Especially if you tell her that it's on his lordship's instructions. Please, Annie!'

Annie did not stop to question why Jamie was suddenly so keen to please his lordship. 'Oh, very well. I'll go and see her now.'

The moment the door closed, Jamie flew to retrieve her store of money. Surprisingly, it was still there. No doubt his lordship would not deign to touch such a pitifully small sum. Stuffing the money in her breeches pocket, she grabbed an old woollen scarf and gloves and made for the door. There was no time to leave a note for Annie. She would be hurt, but at least she would not be implicated—and she would be sure to understand, once she found out about the letter to Calderwood.

Jamie crept down the back stairs. There seemed to be no one about. She supposed most of the kitchen servants were making ready to serve his lordship's dinner. The others would be in the servants' hall.

She paused at the bottom of the stairs to decide on her escape route. She dared not go through the kitchens, for she would certainly be seen there. The front door was impossible. And the side door was much too risky—too near his lordship's study. She would have to find a window instead. The breakfast parlour would be a good choice. Nobody used it at this time of the day. And from that side of the house, she could easily make her way through the gardens without being seen.

The breakfast parlour was deserted. She crossed to the window and lifted the sash. It squeaked in protest and stuck halfway. Jamie cursed. But there was enough room for her to squeeze through into the welcoming gloom beyond. She would just be able to see her way for a while, but it would soon be pitch dark.

She would need to get as far away as she could, before finding somewhere to bed down for the night.

Standing in the soft flower-bed, she reached up to close the window behind her. She cursed again as it refused to budge. She knew she was wasting precious seconds in trying to cover her escape route.

'Perhaps I may help with that?'

Lord Hardinge! Jamie spun round in horror, blanching at the sight of his sardonic smile.

'We shall return by a more conventional route, I think,' he said, taking her by the arm to pull her on to the path. 'Come, Jamie.' Without another word, he marched her into his study and slammed the door behind them.

'Now,' he began grimly, 'an explanation.'

Jamie glared back at him. In spite of everything, she was not afraid.

'I am waiting. Or perhaps I should summon Smithers?'

'No,' Jamie bit out. 'She knows nothing of this. I slipped out while she was with Mrs Peters.'

'Leaving her alone to face me? I see. There is indeed no honour among thieves.'

'I am not a thief!' cried Jamie hotly. 'I have taken nothing from you!'

'Indeed? Empty your pockets.' When Jamie made no move to obey, he came towards her menacingly. 'Do as I bid you, or I shall do it myself!'

With a final shrug of defiance, Jamie obeyed.

She dropped her little heap of coins on to the desk. There was also some string and a few pins. Nothing of value. Watching Lord Harding gazing at his meagre haul, Jamie wondered what he had expected. It must be obvious now that she was desperate to escape, since she had been prepared to run away with little more than the clothes on her back, in spite of the harsh March weather.

What would he do to her now?

'It seems I have no choice but to lock you in your room,' he said flatly.

'No, please,' begged Jamie instinctively.

'How else am I to be sure you will not leave Harding?' he countered sharply.

'I will give you my word—'

His sudden laughter cut her short. 'Are you really suggesting that I should accept *your* word? By God, your impudence is beyond belief!'

Jamie knew she had turned scarlet. With as much quiet dignity as she could muster, she said, 'I offer it to you, none the less, my lord. Since I have so little time left, I should rather spend it with Annie Smithers than locked in solitary confinement.'

He raised an incredulous eyebrow. Perhaps he had expected tears or tantrums.

'Very well,' he agreed at length. 'Will you give me your word not to try to run away from Harding for...shall we say, three days?'

Jamie looked sharply up at him, making no attempt to conceal her surprise at his offer. There was a very strange expression on his face, half-stern, half-indulgent. 'You have my word, my lord.' Then greatly daring, she added, 'I take it I may run away at first light on the fourth day with your good will?'

Her riposte shocked him into laughter once again,

but this time she knew it contained no malice. 'You do not want for courage, Jamie, I grant you that. Now—be off upstairs before I change my mind.'

She smiled at him then, and left the room without haste.

'If you are to be a girl, we may as well make you presentable.' Annie was obviously delighted at the chance of using her talents on Jamie. The attempted escape was behind them now. 'Mrs Peters was no help, so—'

'It's the future we should be thinking about, not appearances, Annie. He has written to Mama! They will know where to find me. And I have given him my word to stay here for three days. My only hope is that the time will be up before he hears from her. Then I can still escape.'

'But his lordship is determined you shall not do so, Miss Jamie. Besides, time is on your side. Just consider—today is March the twenty-fourth. Her ladyship probably will not have his letter until tomorrow at the earliest, so she cannot be expected to arrive before the twenty-sixth. You will be of age by the time she comes. She will have no power to coerce you.'

Jamie brightened. She had become so obsessed by the encounters with Lord Hardinge that she had lost count of the days. 'Oh, Annie, thank you. Of course, you are right. Only two more days.'

'And then you will be able to tell Lord Hardinge the truth. Once he knows you are a lady, he will surely lose his suspicions of you, even if he don't approve of your conduct.

'Now let us see whether any of my fine gowns can be made over for you.' Annie began to pull out the silk and muslin gowns she had been given over the years by past employers. It would be a difficult task to adapt any of them to fit Jamie's shorter, fuller-bosomed figure. Two gowns were immediately discarded. One was much too matronly for a lady of Jamie's age. The other could not be altered to fit.

'That leaves the green silk,' said Annie. 'It always was my favourite—'

'Then you must not dream—'

'—my favourite,' repeated Annie, 'but this particular shade of green does not suit me. For you, however'—she held it against Jamie—'it will be perfect.'

'Oh, Annie!' breathed Jamie, touched.

'Enough of that, Miss Jamie. We'd better get to work on this gown. And when we have done that, I shall dress your hair for you. I've been itching to do that for months, so don't try to stop me. I promise you will be pleased with what I can do. Even Lady Calderwood appreciated the styles I created, and *she* was never one to give praise lightly. If you'll just allow me to—'

'I give in, Annie, truly I do. After all the trouble I have brought you, that is the least I can do. I have nothing else to offer.' Her voice cracked a little as she spoke.

Annie began to busy herself with unpicking a seam. 'We had best get started, don't you think?' she said briskly. 'The light will soon be gone.'

By the time their work was completed, next day, Jamie had been transformed from a grubby boy into an elegant young lady. She twirled round in the green silk gown, revelling in its luxurious softness and flowing lines. 'His lordship will not doubt that I am a proper lady's companion now, Annie.'

'No, he will not. Though I am sure he was convinced as soon as he heard you speak. As long as he does not think you are the lady herself. Then there would be the devil to pay.'

Jamie's agitated response was interrupted by a knock at the door. 'Miss is to come down to the drawing-room at once, his lordship says,' reported the little maid. 'A lady and gentleman have arrived,' she added helpfully.

'Oh, God! It is Papa and Mama! What am I to do?'

Annie looked steadily at her young charge, her eyes full of pity. 'Miss Jamie—'

'There is nothing I can do, for he is bound to learn the truth now,' continued Jamie, more resolutely now. 'I shall go down and face him.' She straightened her shoulders, threw a nervous smile at Annie and followed the maid downstairs.

'Ah, come in, Jamie.' Richard had forgotten, in his shock at the sight of her transformation, that she claimed to be Miss Jemima Crane. For she *was* transformed. Gone was the awkward boy whose apparent gawkiness was emphasised by overlarge smock and breeches. In his place, Richard saw a svelte, elegantly clad young woman with titian curls and an elfin face, dominated by huge—and terrified—green eyes.

'Pray be seated, Lady Calderwood. And you, Mr

Graves,' Richard began politely. He was determined that he would not betray his inner feelings by so much as a look or a gesture.

For a moment, Jamie seemed to be transfixed by the menacing glare from Lady Calderwood who was standing in the centre of the room, looking as if she were about to take charge. Then Jamie put her hand on the arm of the nearest chair and sank into it—strangely forward behaviour from a paid servant, Richard thought. But the girl's skin was ashen—and she seemed to be about to faint.

Richard was not a man to allow Lady Calderwood to take the initiative from him. He continued to look after his guests as though nothing untoward were happening, forcing an exchange of empty pleasantries on to Lady Calderwood while the butler served refreshments. Meanwhile, he watched Jamie out of the corner of his eye. Only when he saw that her colour was returning a little did he turn his full attention back to his guests. He was determined to maintain complete control over this unexpected encounter.

The woman was a harridan—that was crystal clear. God help her poor benighted husband! Even Calderwood deserved better. The man Graves? A singularly appropriate name, he felt, for someone who looked as if he belonged among the stench of death and decay. No wonder Jamie had fled from him. In spite of what she was, the thought of her in the power of such a disgusting creature made his blood run cold.

As soon as the door closed behind the butler, Lady Calderwood began her attack. 'You wrote that you had in your household a young woman bearing a reference from Miss Jessamyne Calderwood, my lord. You understood that Miss Calderwood was an elderly relative who had gone abroad for her health.'

Richard did not move a muscle.

'I must tell you, sir, that you have been grievously misled. No Jemima Crane has ever worked in my household.' Lady Calderwood seemed to be enjoying the play of anxiety and dismay on Jamie's face. 'Nor has there ever been any elderly spinster at Calderwood. Besides my husband, my children and myself, there is only one other member of the family—my stepdaughter, Jessamyne Calderwood.'

She turned in her chair to level an accusing finger at Jamie. 'And there she sits, the wicked undutiful daughter who ran away from her home, rather than fulfil her obligations to her family.'

Lady Calderwood's eyes were fixed on Jamie, who was now clutching desperately to the arm of her chair.

Richard quickly masked his shock with an expression of polite concern. 'May I ask, ma'am, what obligation it was from which your stepdaughter fled?'

Lady Calderwood turned back to her host. She ploughed on, obviously secure in the power of her position.

'Marriage,' she spat venomously. 'Her father had gone to considerable lengths to arrange an advantageous match for her—she has no dowry, you must understand, and is singularly lacking in accomplishments—as I said, a most advantageous match. But Jessamyne refused, positively refused to comply with Sir John's wishes. I have come to take her back and to ensure that she does her duty.'

She glared at Richard, daring him to defy her.

Richard was well aware that all the might of the law and all the rules of polite society were on her side. No one could refuse to yield up a girl to her rightful guardians. 'Let us be perfectly clear about this, Lady Calderwood.' His voice was measured and reasonable, if a little clipped. 'Your stepdaughter ran away from you in order to avoid a marriage which was—shall we say?—distasteful to her? May I ask the name of the bridegroom?'

Before Lady Calderwood could reply, the whining voice of Ralph Graves intervened. 'She is betrothed to me, sir! I am here to reclaim what is owed to me!'

'Indeed?' Richard's tone was suddenly icy. 'I had not noticed any betrothal announcement.'

'The engagement is understood between the families,' said her ladyship soothingly, 'but no public announcement will be possible until my stepdaughter is safely back at Calderwood. Engagement visits and the like, you understand.'

'Oh, yes, I do understand. Believe me, I do.' He favoured his guests with a tight smile, as he reviewed the situation. He had no choice, in honour. None at all. He knew now exactly what he must do.

Lady Calderwood was also smiling, in expectation of imminent triumph, it seemed. 'We are most grateful to you, sir. We shall all, I hope, endeavour to forget that she was ever here. No one at Calderwood will ever speak of it. And the wedding will take place without delay.'

'One moment, ma'am, if you please. You were speaking of duty, of your stepdaughter's obligations to her family. Far be it from me to disagree with you. I shudder to think that any member of my family might ever be guilty of such unnatural conduct as you have described.' He glanced briefly towards where Jamie sat, apparently on the point of collapse. 'But do you not agree that there is a yet higher duty, owed by a woman to her husband?'

'Well, yes, of course,' replied Lady Calderwood, sounding perplexed at this new turn of the conversation. 'Jessamyne will certainly owe her first duty to Mr Graves, once she is married. But—'

'I am glad we are agreed on that point, Lady Calderwood. I do *so* want to avoid any unpleasantness here. As you say, a wife's first duty is to her husband. And so you will agree that your stepdaughter's first duty must be to me, her husband?'

'What?' shrieked Lady Calderwood, springing up from her chair.

'Impossible!' screamed Ralph Graves. 'Such a marriage could not be legal. She is under age.'

Richard rose slowly from his seat to confront his visitors, drawing all their attention on to himself and away from Jamie, who was sitting in stunned silence. His eyes narrowed menacingly and his voice made clear that he would brook no opposition. 'As my wife, she has the protection of my name and of my position in society. I suggest to you, sir, that it would be most unwise in you to meddle further in this matter.'

Mr Graves did not reply, but his jaw worked unconsciously. The grinding of his teeth could be heard in the sudden silence.

Lady Calderwood's shock had temporarily deprived her of the power of speech. She stood gasping for breath, turning redder and redder, like a broiling lobster.

'Do, pray, resume your seat, ma'am,' invited Richard smoothly. 'You will wish to rest, I am sure, before you start back to Calderwood. I shall arrange for a nuncheon to be sent in.'

He smiled tightly. 'Now, if you will excuse us, my wife and I must attend to some urgent business which will, I fear, prevent us from returning to bid you farewell. So we shall take our leave of you now.'

He bowed politely to Lady Calderwood and, with barest civility, to Mr Graves. Then he crossed the room to take Jamie's trembling hand and raise her from her chair.

'Come, my dear,' he said, smiling gently down at her as he led her swiftly from the room.

As the doors closed behind them, Jamie tried to find her voice.

'Say nothing now,' Richard warned in a low voice, squeezing her hand meaningfully. 'Come.' He led her downstairs, pausing only to ensure the butler understood his instructions about the prompt despatch of the visitors and the need for absolute discretion. 'We shall be in the book-room,' he added. 'We are on no account to be disturbed.'

With studied politeness, Richard then ensured Jamie was comfortably installed in the privacy of his library. He pressed a glass of brandy into her hand.

'Oh, no, my lord, please!' she protested.

'Drink it,' he instructed. 'I promise it will do you good. You have been through an dreadful ordeal these last few days, mostly at my hands. Come, humour me, Jamie.' He smiled again, trying for a semblance of the irresistible smile which had melted so many hearts, and was rewarded when she sipped gingerly at the fiery liquid.

She spluttered a little, as the brandy burned its way down to her stomach.

'Good,' he said. 'Now, a little more, Jamie.' He watched approvingly as she sipped again.

He took his seat beside her on the leather sofa, but not close enough to make her feel in any way threatened. He knew he must handle this interview with kid gloves. 'First, you must tell me what I should call you. "Jamie" reminds me too much of grubby gardener's boys.'

Jamie was beginning to feel the warming effects of the brandy. Coupled with Lord Hardinge's apparently light-hearted approach, it was exactly what was needed to enable her to respond lucidly to him. 'My name, as you will have collected, sir, is Jessamyne. It was my father's choice, I'm afraid. I have never liked it. Neither did my mother. Indeed, it was she who took to calling me "Jamie". It really is my name, you see.'

'Your mother?'

'She died when I was six.'

'I am sorry. It must have been very hard for you, especially when your father remarried.' He did not add 'to that woman' but it was easily inferred from his tone. He laughed suddenly. 'Well—"Jamie" it shall be, if that is your wish. I shall soon become accustomed to "Jamie the elegant lady" instead of

''Jamie the backward garden boy''. Now, tomorrow—'

Jamie was almost ecstatic and, in her relief, burst out, 'Tomorrow, I come of age, at last. My lord, I shall never be able to thank you enough for what you have done in saving me today. I only pray the damage to your reputation will not be irreparable. It was the most chivalrous action I have ever known and oh!— I thank you!'

His lordship seemed to be avoiding her gaze. He continued briskly, 'Chivalry had nothing to do with it, Jamie. It was the only possible solution for both of us. I admit I had not reckoned on your being under age but, thankfully, that difficulty will be resolved by tomorrow. I shall be able to get a special licence and then—'

'But you cannot!' cried Jamie.

'Have a little more faith, my dear,' he drawled laconically. 'Of course I can. An Earl, even newly made, does have some influence, you know.'

'But, I meant... You cannot intend to go on with this?'

'Why not?' he asked baldly. 'It is the obvious solution.'

'But you cannot want to marry me. Why, I am a nobody, penniless, and my reputation must be in shreds. I am no fit bride for you, my lord.'

He took both her trembling hands in his. 'Jamie, you are the daughter of a baronet and a perfectly suitable wife for an earl. I have not the slightest need of a dowry. And as to your reputation'—he laughed bitterly—'*I* brought you to Harding. *I* forcibly parted you from Smithers. And if your reputation now lies in ruins, it is because *I* tried to take advantage of you, when I had promised you would be safe here.'

Jamie could not tear her eyes away from his and from the anguish and guilt she saw there.

'Jamie,' he continued earnestly, 'there is no other way to protect you, to restore you in the eyes of the world. You *must* agree to accept my name. You must! You have nothing to fear from me. I shall not force my attentions on you again, you have my word on that.'

Jamie gulped back a sob at this evidence of his unselfish regard for her honour above his own desires. 'My lord, I cannot allow you to do this. It is not necessary, believe me,' she pleaded, trying unsuccessfully to free her hands from his grasp. 'From tomorrow, I shall be a free agent. I shall find a situation and make my own way in life. That is, if you will return my pearls to me, so that I may sell them,' she added, with the merest hint of a smile.

He smiled a little sadly in response. 'Your pearls shall be returned. Were they your mother's?'

'Yes,' she admitted shyly, 'they are all I have from her—my dowry, you might say.'

'Then you must keep them, Jamie. It would be a crime to part with them.'

Jamie felt an overpowering need to make him laugh, to lighten the intense atmosphere a little. He was thinking too much about his own guilt. And overlooking hers. 'You thought that I had already committed a crime to get them, did you not, my lord?' she ventured.

His smile widened a little. Clearly, he had not expected wit. 'I did. And I humbly beg your pardon, ma'am. May I hope for forgiveness?'

'After what you have done today, I believe I could forgive you anything, my lord.'

'Richard.'

'No, my lord. It would not be right for a mere servant—'

'But perfectly right for my wife. Jamie, listen to me! You really do not understand what risks you run. Consider, for a moment, what could happen if you find paid employment as you intend—which, I have to tell you, will be difficult, if not impossible. However elevated you may be, you will still be a servant, with no protection against your stepmother's machinations or against the odious Graves. No one would lift a finger to take the part of a paid companion against a gentleman. You could be abducted, forced into marriage—or worse.

'Jamie! Do you understand what I am saying? Marriage is the only way of protecting you. You have no other choice.'

Jamie sat very still and silent for a long time. She had ceased trying to free her hands from his. She gazed at them now, her reddened, callused hands lying within Richard's elegant white ones. Then she raised her eyes to his. 'I cannot answer you, my lord, not now. So much has happened in these last few days that I must have time to think. Will you allow me a little time?'

'I will. On one condition.'

'And that is?'

'Jamie, I have not forgotten that tomorrow you will be twenty-one, and free, and that you believe you do not need my protection. I know otherwise. At first light tomorrow, I shall leave to procure a special licence, which will then be perfectly legal since you will be of age. I should be back the following day. *Then* you can tell me what you have decided. I shall not try to force you. I ask only that you remain until I return.'

'But how will you explain the licence? Surely it is not done for an earl—'

'It is perfectly normal, when a family is in mourning, for marriages to be small, private affairs. No one will raise an eyebrow. The announcement will be made later, once the wedding is safely over. Now, Jamie, what do you say?'

Jamie could not read the expression in his eyes, but his voice betrayed his growing tension. She answered as calmly as she could. 'I shall be here when you return, my lord. You still have my word.'

Richard's answering smile was a mixture of triumph and pleasure. It lit up his face. He lifted Jamie's hand to his lips and kissed it gently.

'Now, my dear,' he said briskly, rising from his seat, 'do you remain here until we are sure those vultures are safely on their way. No one shall disturb you. And, in the meantime, I shall make arrangements for your new accommodation.'

Jamie began to protest.

'It will not do, you know, for a lady to be sleeping in a bare attic,' he said teasingly. 'But, if it will put your mind at rest, Smithers shall be given a bed in your dressing-room, at least for the present. Will that content you?'

Jamie nodded. Her heart was too full to speak.

'Good. I shall send Smithers to you directly. I leave it to you to decide how much you tell her.'

Chapter Twelve

Richard paused for a moment outside his mother's sitting-room, trying to collect his thoughts. How was he going to tell her what he had done? And how would she react? He had had no opportunity to speak to her since her return from Bath. She knew nothing about the revelation of Jamie's real identity. And his terse note, before his mother left, had simply warned her that he was detaining Smithers while he investigated her suspicious behaviour.

He reached for the handle, still hesitant. He would look in quietly, he decided, and if Lady Hardinge were resting after her journey back from her sister's, he could return later. Without knocking, he silently opened the door.

Lady Hardinge was seated in a chair in the window bay, staring vacantly at the park. His brain registered that, in profile, she was still a beautiful woman, in spite of her years. A single sheet of paper lay in her lap.

'Forgive me for disturbing you, Mama,' he said

quietly, closing the door and crossing to where she sat.

She turned to smile up at him, with a little frown of puzzlement on her brow. Lifting his scrawled note, she said simply, 'I hope you have come to explain this, Richard. I admit to being intrigued and, I am afraid, a little saddened. I had not thought it of Smithers.'

'Nor were you wrong, my dear,' he confirmed quickly, pulling up a chair to sit at her side. 'I have a great deal more to tell you now.' He explained in very matter-of-fact terms about Caleb's assault on Jamie and the discovery that she was a girl.

Lady Hardinge was aghast. 'I cannot understand what on earth Smithers was about, to embroil herself in such a disgraceful imposture. I had thought her so honest—so trustworthy.'

'There is more to it than that, Mama. I must tell you—Jamie is a lady.'

The Countess was shocked into silence for fully half a minute. When she found her voice again, she fastened on the key word in what her son had just said. 'A *lady*? Surely not?'

'She is Miss Jessamyne Calderwood, Mama, only child of Sir John Calderwood and his first wife.' When his mother made no response to that staggering revelation, he continued, 'She ran away from home because she was being forced into marriage with an old man who is, it appears, both a miser and a lecher. Forgive my plain speaking, Mama, but I must have you understand the way of this. You see, I...' he cleared his throat '...I have compromised her, Mama. In all honour, I must marry her.'

'Dear God,' breathed Lady Hardinge. 'Oh, my dear, surely not? You cannot marry a girl who has behaved in such a shockingly improper way. It was she who compromised herself, by coming here dressed as a boy. Why should you rescue her from her own folly? Oh, Richard, no!'

Her son took a deep breath and looked into his mother's sad eyes. 'It is worse than you know, Mama. Until two days ago, she had taken great care never to be in a compromising position in spite of her masquerade. But after I found them out, I locked Jamie and Smithers into separate rooms. I wanted to prevent any further collusion between them. That was my only motive, I promise you.'

He put his hand to his brow and ran his fingers through his hair.

'Two nights ago...' He stopped and tried again. 'Two nights ago, I went to Jamie's room. I...' Guilt overcame him then. He found he could not continue.

'You seduced her?' whispered his mother in horror.

'No,' he replied flatly. 'No. I admit I tried to, but she repulsed me.' He could not hide the self-loathing in his voice as he acknowledged his despicable behaviour in the starkest terms.

A long, painful silence ensued.

Then Lady Hardinge began to explore possible avenues of escape for her son. Richard half-expected her to raise the question of the family curse once more, but his mother was much too practical for that. 'If you did not seduce her, then I do not see that you must marry her. I am sure something can be arranged. If I—'

'No, Mama, the die is cast. I have ruined her. And there is yet more to this sorry tale.' He had recovered some of his normal composure now. 'This morning I received a visit from the present Lady Calderwood and Ralph Graves, the man to whom Jamie was to have been forcibly betrothed. He is quite the most repulsive man I have ever met. He made even my flesh crawl. I could not see her sacrificed to him, Mama. When Lady Calderwood insisted on taking Jamie away, I told her she could not, because Jamie was already married to me.'

'Good God!' cried Lady Hardinge. 'Whatever possessed you to do such a thing?'

'The expression on Jamie's face when she first recognised the visitors,' he admitted, with the tiniest hint of a smile. 'Horror, and innocence, mixed together. And then a look of such hopeless resignation that I could not do otherwise than save her. Truly, I could not.'

'I see,' said his mother meditatively.

Richard was quite sure that she did not see.

'What is her dowry, do you know?' asked Lady Hardinge, after a pause.

'She has none, Mama,' he replied in a flat voice. Before she could speak, he continued, 'It is of no moment, in any case. This marriage is a matter of honour—and honour only.'

'I see,' said his mother again. 'And when is the wedding to be?'

'As soon as I can procure a special licence. Tomorrow, Jamie comes of age and so—'

'A minor!' gasped Lady Hardinge. 'Richard, for heaven's sake—'

'She will be twenty-one tomorrow. All will be well once I have married her. If she will have me, that is.'

This last information clearly put a new complexion on the matter for Lady Hardinge. 'You mean she has refused you?' she asked incredulously.

'She has certainly tried to do so. I wish you will see her, Mama, and convince her that she has no choice.' As his mother stared at him in disbelief, he added, 'She thinks she can earn her own living once she is of age. As a governess, or some such. It is madness. No one would employ her without references. And I fear Graves would seek to revenge the insults she has heaped upon him. Will you not see her, Mama, and persuade her?'

'I will see her, certainly. As to the rest—we shall see.'

When Richard rose to leave, his mother smiled anxiously up at him. 'It is a dreadful coil, Richard, I admit, but there may yet be another way. Send her to me, and I shall see what may be done.'

Jamie's approach to the Countess's sitting-room was very hesitant indeed. She had known the Countess for a kind, rather sad lady who had taken a real interest in the progress of a backward garden boy. But Lady Hardinge was most certainly a great lady. Having discovered how Jamie had imposed upon her by perpetrating such a shocking fraud, the Countess must be expected to be haughty and unforgiving. She probably intended to read Jamie a stern lecture on the proper conduct for a lady. Perhaps even to insist that she return to Calderwood and Ralph Graves?

At that point, if she had dared, Jamie might have fled, but it was already too late. Digby had thrown open the door. 'Miss Calderwood, my lady,' he intoned.

Jamie stood transfixed on the threshold as the butler closed the door behind her. Her head was bowed. She could not find any words to say.

Lady Hardinge turned in her chair and surveyed her visitor with careful calculation for a long time. 'Miss Calderwood,' she said at last.

Jamie raised her eyes to the Countess's face, but could not speak. She felt she was just a tangle of emotions—misgivings, principally, mixed with contrition. But she must meet this trial with courage, for that was all she had to fall back on.

'Miss Calderwood. Will you not be seated?' said Lady Hardinge formally.

From her position by the door, Jamie curtsied, but did not move to sit down. 'Lady Hardinge, I do not deserve your kindness. I have imposed upon you and your son in the most shocking way imaginable. There is no possible apology which I can make for the wrongs I have done you both, although I would make amends if I could.' She was twisting her hands together as she spoke. 'It is my intention to leave Harding, ma'am, so that you may be free of me. There can be no question of pardon, I know, but oh!— I am sorry!'

The Countess seemed to be much affected by this emotional little speech. 'Do come and sit down, Miss Calderwood,' she said again, more gently now. 'My son has told me something of your history, but I should prefer to hear it all from your own lips, if you are prepared to tell me. You need hold nothing back, I assure you. I am not easily shocked. And my son has told me what happened when he came to your room.'

Jamie blushed fierily to the roots of her hair. 'Oh, ma'am, he did not—'

'I think it best if you start from the beginning,' intervened Lady Hardinge calmly. 'Don't be afraid. Just tell me the truth.'

Jamie looked wonderingly at her, trying to decide what to do. The Countess did not seem particularly stern, though not particularly friendly either. She still had that same sad look in her eyes, perhaps even more intense than usual. Jamie hesitated a little before deciding that a simple recital of the facts would do no harm. Not now.

She sat stiffly on the edge of the chair opposite the Countess, clasping her hands tightly in her lap to hide her nervousness. 'My name is Jessamyne Calderwood, ma'am. My father is Sir John Calderwood, of Calderwood Hall in Hampshire. I am twenty years old.' Her voice was strained and her delivery stilted, but she forced herself to continue. 'The present Lady Calderwood, whom I think you know, is my father's second wife. My own mother died when I was six.'

Lady Hardinge nodded slightly.

'I have a half-brother and three half-sisters at Calderwood which is…not a rich holding. There was no possibility of a London season for me, on account of the expense, and unfortunately I have no dowry. So my parents sought elsewhere for a husband for me. They chose a Mr Ralph Graves, who is a distant cousin of Lady Calderwood.' Her staccato delivery faltered at that point. She could not go on, because she did not know how to describe Graves without straying into improper criticism of her parents in the process.

'Is he so dreadful, this Mr Graves, that you could not face him squarely and simply refuse him?' asked Lady Hardinge softly.

Jamie's chin came up. 'It would have changed nothing, ma'am. The betrothal announcement was about to be made, whether I refused him or no. If I had then cried off at the altar, I should have been branded a jilt before all the world, and any marriage for me would have become impossible. My only hope was to prevent the announcement from being made. There was no one to help me. So I fled.'

'Why did you choose Harding? And as a boy?'

'Oh, ma'am, please don't blame Smithers for my deception. She simply took pity on me when I could not buy a seat on the stage.' Jamie gulped. 'You see, it had been my intention to seek work as a governess or companion through the agencies in Bath, but…it became clear that it would not serve. I had been dressed as a boy for the journey only, but when Lord Hardinge offered to take me as a gardener's boy, it seemed such a heaven-sent opportunity that I… The truth, ma'am, is that I was so desperate that I seized upon his offer without thought for the harm I might do. Especially to Annie Smithers. Afterwards, it was too late to retreat.'

'And may I ask when you proposed to confess your deception to us, if it had not been discovered?' asked the Countess sharply.

Jamie stared at her clenched hands. 'To be honest, ma'am, I hoped to avoid doing so altogether. I intended to leave Harding in such a way that there would be no concerns about the boy Jamie or trouble for Smithers either.' The Countess's frankly disbelieving look prompted her to explain rather more than she had intended about her plans to make her own way in life. 'I should have taken care to contrive that simple Jamie was seen to have left Harding for a better position elsewhere,' she concluded, biting her lip.

'You did not think to trust us with the truth, my dear?' asked Lady Hardinge in a suddenly softer tone.

That voice, coupled with the unexpected endearment, was Jamie's undoing. Her carefully erected defences crumbled. Tears stood in her eyes. 'Since my mama died,' she said simply, 'there has been no one I could trust. Except—these last weeks—Annie Smithers.' She dropped her head into her hand to hide the tears that were threatening to overpower her.

'Miss Calderwood, my son tells me he has offered you marriage, but that you have refused him.'

Jamie nodded but did not speak.

Lady Hardinge hesitated. 'Will you tell me why?' she asked at last.

Jamie swallowed hard and raised her head, blinking

back her tears. 'Lord Hardinge saved me from being forcibly married, by telling Lady Calderwood that I was already married to him. That lie was successful. There is no need to make it a reality.'

'Do you not wish for marriage? For children of your own?'

'Oh, yes,' breathed Jamie, without stopping to think, 'but that is not what Lord Hardinge has offered.'

'I do not understand. Pray explain, Miss Calderwood.'

'Oh, dear,' said Jamie, biting her lip once more and cursing her too ready tongue. 'Your son, ma'am, feels he is honour bound to save my reputation by making me his wife. In that, he is…mistaken. I myself am responsible for everything that has taken place since I left Calderwood, and I alone must bear the consequences. Lord Hardinge must marry some day, no doubt, but it cannot be a marriage in name only to a woman like me, whom he does not love and cannot respect. He deserves better than that,' she added hotly.

Lady Hardinge looked shocked. Eventually, she said, 'You have much courage, Miss Calderwood. Few women would choose as you have done. I honour you for it.' Then she added, 'But I should not be too hasty in making my decision, if I were you. Perhaps you should sleep on it.'

Jamie looked at her in consternation. It sounded as if Lady Hardinge were urging her to reconsider Richard's offer. Surely that was impossible? Surely she must have imagined it? But no, Lady Hardinge was gazing steadily at her, with a half-smile on her lips and a not-unfriendly gleam in her eye.

Giving herself a mental shake, Jamie begged leave to retire to reflect on the Countess's advice. 'Thank you, ma'am, for receiving me with such kindness,' she said, as she curtsied herself out. 'It is much more than I have deserved.'

The Countess sat long after Jamie's departure, pondering the inwardnesses of what she had learned. The girl was unquestionably a lady, and a lady of spirit and courage. She was Richard's equal by birth, without a doubt. And, since she was certainly not indifferent to him, there seemed to be no rational explanation for her refusal. Nor, to be honest, was there any sound reason for Richard's having proposed in the first place. In the past, he had gloried in his affairs, and in his ability to abandon them without a backward glance. But now... The man Jamie had described sounded less and less like the son she knew—except for his determination to challenge the Hardinge curse head on. That, she felt, was very much her son.

Lady Hardinge decided to let matters take their course for a little longer yet, before she chose which side of the scales should receive her two penn'orth. She smiled to herself. It would all be really rather entertaining, if it were not quite so serious.

'She seems determined not to have you, Richard,' said Lady Hardinge later, sitting alone with her son in the drawing-room. Jamie had been persuaded, with difficulty, to join them for dinner, but she had retired to her room immediately afterwards.

'Hardly surprising,' he answered bitterly, 'considering my behaviour towards her. But she has no choice, Mama. I shall convince her, never fear.'

Lady Hardinge let that pass. 'But a marriage in name only, Richard? Is that wise, do you think? Forgive me'—she blushed slightly—'but could you abide by it, if she did agree?'

'Of course,' he replied tersely. 'I have given her my word.'

Lady Hardinge tried another approach. 'I believe Miss Calderwood may have a romantic soul, Richard,' she said slowly.

He threw her a sharply questioning glance, which she ignored.

'She will look for love in marriage. I had hoped that you would do the same. I have not forgotten the Hardinge tradition, even if you have.'

'If love is what it takes to persuade her,' he replied, after a moment's thought, 'then love there must be. God knows I have been told often enough about my ability to attract the female of the species. Obviously I must set about wooing this one, and quickly.'

His mother was aghast. 'Richard! Surely you could not be so wicked?'

His set expression gave the lie to that.

'Oh, Richard, do not, I beg you. Love is a *mutual* passion. Love which is not shared turns to hate, and despair. You know that. You must remember what Celia made you suffer when she jilted you. You may make Jamie love you now, to win her consent, but later, when she finds you do not care for her…I predict you would both be very unhappy. Better to let her go, Richard, as she wishes.'

He turned a bleak face to her. 'No, Mama, it cannot be. This marriage touches my honour. I have pledged my word that Jamie will be my wife. But I promise you that I shall try to avoid causing her the unhappiness you fear. After all, she need not know her love is not returned. Surely that is not so hard to do?'

His mother was of the opinion that such a deception was not merely hard, it was impossible. But her son would not listen. He was adamant that it was his duty to marry Jamie. He would not be moved. He would make just one concession—in deference to his mother's misgivings, he would not give Jamie the Hardinge betrothal ring, since family tradition required it to be given as a token of love.

When the door closed behind her beloved but impossible son, Lady Hardinge sighed. Richard would go to any lengths, perhaps even coercion, to enforce his will. As a result of her careless words, he had seen that he could have his way by making Jamie fall in love with him. And now, quite cynically and deliberately, he would set about winning her love. No doubt he would succeed, too. He was famous for his address. Poor, poor girl.

And yet, she thought suddenly, perhaps he may not have his way in this in quite the manner he supposes. He would never have offered marriage to any of the simpering, empty-headed females he so despises, no matter what the circumstances. There must be something more behind his willingness to do so now. Jamie Calderwood is not like any other woman he has known. And it may be that he feels more for her than he yet knows. He will woo her, certainly, but I fancy she may have more than a little say in the outcome of this strange courtship. Yes. I think it may do very well. In more ways than one.

Chapter Thirteen

Jamie lay on her back, staring up at the rose pink canopy of the great bed. She could not sleep. Her brain was churning with the extraordinary events of an extraordinary day.

Richard, Earl Hardinge, had proposed marriage to her! And he seemed intent on going through with it, even though he could not possibly love her. He desired her, that was certain. She had had ample proof of that. But was desire any basis for wedlock?

Lady Hardinge's attitude, too, was a riddle. She had received Jamie more than graciously, once Richard had explained how matters stood. She might even be favourably disposed to Jamie, to judge by the way she had treated an ex-servant. But there was something hidden beneath Lady Hardinge's outward calm, something which Jamie could not quite identify.

As for Jamie's own feelings, she was afraid to probe them too deeply. She did not love him. Of course not. How could she? She barely knew him—and only as a servant knows a master.

A picture of him rose in her mind. She felt her body

tremble at the mere thought of him. What was it about him that affected her so? His image so easily dominated her to the exclusion of all else. It was not fear, she was certain. Fear was what she felt at the prospect of being married to Ralph Graves. If she married Richard instead, she would be just as completely in his power, yet…it was not the same.

She forced herself to begin to think rationally, to banish his beguiling presence. She valued him for all his finer qualities—his kindness, his honesty, his charity. Above all, for the honourable way he had treated her. Even when he was trying to force explanations out of her, he had never been other than fair. The only exception was the episode in her bedroom, when his passions had momentarily overcome his reason—and for that she must be as culpable as he. It shamed her to admit it, even to herself, but she knew she desired Richard Hardinge quite as much as he desired her.

None of this seemed to be helping her to reach a decision on his proposal. She knew in her heart of hearts that he was right about marriage—it *was* the only solution which could guarantee her safety—but the idea of a loveless marriage appalled her. She had spent too many years as a spectator of her father's. She could not inflict that on a man like Richard.

Besides, Richard had said that it would be a marriage in name only. That would be grossly unfair on him, not least because it was his duty to beget an heir. And as for her—she was not sure whether marriage and motherhood would ever be offered to her now, but she did not think she was ready, at the tender age of twenty-one, to sacrifice all hopes of having her own children at her knee.

She shook her head helplessly as she tossed around on the pillows. Nowhere was there a spot of cool relief for her fevered cheek. Her thoughts continued to wander round and round the arguments. One single idea kept recurring—it would be absolutely wrong to accept Richard and to force him into a loveless, childless sham of a marriage. She could find no way to counter that thought. Beside it, her own situation paled into insignificance.

So—the decision had made itself. Even at some personal risk, she would not accept him. However much she might be tempted, she would go her own road, and do her best to escape from Harding and all its works for ever. It was the only honourable solution open to her. She would just have to be resolute in withstanding him.

What would Annie say? Oh, dear! Annie's reaction to the day's events—for Jamie had told her everything—had been ecstatic. She had a simple vision of a comfortable married life for the future Lord and Lady Hardinge—with the new Countess ably served by her faithful abigail, naturally! She had roundly castigated Miss Jamie for even considering refusal of his lordship's offer.

Jamie sighed. To Annie, it all seemed straightforward. She had seen many *ton* marriages based on far less mutual regard than existed between Jamie and the Earl. Annie had no time for missish notions about loveless marriages. She had a vested interest too for, as Countess Hardinge, Jamie would be sure to employ her. Whereas if Jamie left, Annie might well have to leave too.

Jamie tried not to think about that. She must not allow sympathy for Annie to sway her decision. It would be difficult to cling to it in any event, she knew, especially when faced with Richard's overpowering presence.

She burrowed deeper into her soft pillows, trying to compose her mind for sleep and watching the play of the moonlight on the wall opposite the window. At long last, she was just beginning to drift off when the shaft of moonlight disappeared. Pity, she thought drowsily, that it had clouded over. It was so beautiful.

The shadow moved across the wall. That could not be the effect of clouds, surely? Jamie tensed, listening, all thought of sleep now banished from her mind. There must be someone in the room! Without pausing to wonder whether it might be Richard, Jamie screamed at the top of her voice.

'Gawd!' muttered a man's voice from somewhere near the window. 'It's all up now! I'm off!'

Then there came a separate sound—a movement somewhere nearer the bed. At the same moment, the door to the dressing-room was thrown open to reveal Annie Smithers, clad only in her nightgown, but armed with a heavy candlestick in one hand and a pair of curling tongs in the other.

The obstruction at the window disappeared, allowing the moonlight to flood the room once more. It showed a man rushing towards the window in an attempt to escape. Annie did not hesitate for a moment. She ran across the room, arm raised, and brought the brass candlestick down on the head of the intruder. He crumpled to the floor, where he lay motionless, with Annie standing over him like a hunting dog over its prey.

Jamie reached the window just in time to see a dark figure sprint across the garden and disappear into the shrubbery. All that remained was the wooden ladder, propped up against the window sill.

'Jamie!' Richard stood at the open door to the dressing-room from where he could take in the situation at a glance. 'Fetch something to bind him, Smithers!'

Annie hesitated, looking first at the motionless body on the floor and then at Jamie in her thin nightgown.

'Quickly now! I'll look after things here.' Annie dared not disobey that sharp instruction. Richard knelt to feel for a pulse on the fallen figure.

'There was another man too,' whispered Jamie a little shakily, turning back from the window. 'He was on the ladder outside the window. But he has escaped across the grounds. You will never catch him.'

Richard swiftly bound the man's hands with the scarf which Annie had brought from the dressing-room and rose to face Jamie. 'Go back to bed, my dear,' he said in reassuring tones. 'I shall take this visitor downstairs for a while and *enquire* as to his business here. I doubt it will take long to unravel this mysterious little episode. Don't worry. You are safe now.' He hefted the inert body over his shoulder and made for the door.

'Richard.'

In spite of his burden, he turned quickly, looking both surprised and pleased.

Jamie was intent on telling him of her suspicions. 'I heard the second man's voice, the one who escaped. He was outside the window on the ladder. I think it was Caleb.'

At the mention of Caleb's name, a shadow of fury crossed Richard's face and his lips tightened in disgust. He did not attempt to argue with Jamie. But then the anger disappeared, and he smiled at her reassuringly.

'Go to bed, my dear,' he said again. 'I shall be back soon, I promise. And, in the meantime, Smithers shall remain here with you. With her candlestick!' He smiled warmly at the abigail. 'Thank you. I shall not forget this.'

With Richard gone, Jamie could not be persuaded to return to bed. How could she ever sleep now? She paced the room in her agitation. Why had Caleb and his accomplice broken into her chamber?

Richard tried to collect his thoughts as he carried the intruder down to the cellars. For that single second when Jamie had used his given name, he had thought she was warming to him. But one look at her face had confirmed that she was using it quite unwittingly. A twinge of something like disappointment had intruded on him. Now, why was that? Of course, he was on the look-out for signs that he was succeeding in his campaign to make her love him—he had to be—but he should be noting those changes coldly and rationally. The surge of emotion he had felt when she spoke his name was not in the least bit rational.

Richard pushed this riddle to the back of his mind. He needed to concentrate on his prisoner—and the identity of the second man. Could it have been Caleb? It was, after all, quite plausible, especially as Caleb had been allowed to give him the slip. Richard cursed himself yet again for that mistake but dared not dwell on it. He forced himself to focus on the task before him.

Richard's interrogation of the second man produced results surprisingly quickly. By the time he returned to Jamie's bedroom, he was very grave.

'Jamie!' he cried. 'You should be in bed!' He signalled to Smithers to withdraw, but she stubbornly ignored him. Her expressive face registered her strong disapproval—a man should not be here in the middle of the night, especially when her mistress was dressed in only a fine lawn nightgown!

Richard's eyes narrowed angrily. He was about to utter a very sharp rebuke when Jamie forestalled him.

'Thank you, Annie,' she said firmly, nodding towards the door. The abigail withdrew unwillingly into the dressing-room.

'She will still be listening, I expect,' smiled Richard, opening his arms encouragingly to Jamie.

Without further thought, she went to him, breathing in the scent of his warm body and allowing his strength to enfold her. She felt so safe now, leaning her head against his chest and closing her eyes thankfully. Only then did she realise that, under his thin silk dressing gown, he was practically naked!

'My lord!' she cried, all the years of her proper upbringing automatically asserting themselves as she tried to pull away from his dangerous embrace.

Richard held her tightly so that she could not break free until he chose to let her go. She must be made to begin to trust him. 'Don't be afraid, Jamie. I shall not attack you again. I have given you my word. Come.'

He sat her on the bed and looked down at her. How lovely she was! The cold fire of moonlight glowed with a pearly lustre on her pale complexion in its frame of titian curls. Most of all, her eyes—huge and shining, dominating her beautiful face—seemed to gaze hauntingly into his. For a brief moment, thoughts of Caleb were forgotten as he drank in the vision before him.

Then cold sanity returned. His face assumed a stern cast.

Jamie shivered a little under his scrutiny.

'I have not learned very much from the man in the cellars,' he began. 'You *were* right about Caleb, I think. He may have been trying to steal from us as some kind of revenge. But that was certainly not the prime motive.' He sat down beside her, taking her cold hand in his.

She did not attempt to pull away. She knew this was a gesture of reassurance, not of desire.

'Jamie—I am sorry—their object was *you*. They were paid, by someone who seemed to be a gentleman's servant, to carry you off.'

'Who?' whispered Jamie through a constricted

throat. She could not begin to understand this impossible nightmare.

'I have no name, nor any proof. But can there be any doubt about it? Who but someone from Calderwood could have any reason to try such a thing?'

It was all too much—fantastic, horrible, unbelievable. Jamie bit back a sob.

Richard enfolded her in his arms once more. He kept his touch gentle, though his taut voice betrayed the anxiety he too was feeling. 'Jamie, you really do *not* have a choice. Lady Calderwood—or Graves—is determined to seize you. If they would dare to break into Harding itself, then there is nowhere you could be safe. Don't you see?' His voice had risen a little, as he attempted to convince his unwilling charge. He sensed that his moment had come.

Jamie nodded slightly, thoroughly bewildered. She no longer had the strength of mind to think straight, particularly when Richard's arms were round her. What was happening to her? None of it made any sense, least of all Richard's steadfast determination to sacrifice himself to save her.

'Then you do agree? You *will* marry me? Answer me, Jamie!'

There was a long pause. Jamie felt the strength and comfort which flowed from him, as he held her cradled gently against him. She knew she wanted to hold on forever to this glorious feeling of warmth and belonging. Maybe, just maybe, theirs could become a real marriage, a union of love, instead of a marriage of convenience? After all, he had shown her that he was a passionate man. And he seemed to care, at least a little…

She must stop this wishful thinking. She had resolved to refuse him. Why couldn't she just tell him so? But he was still waiting expectantly for her response, smiling warmly at her, in a way that touched her heart.

It was no contest. 'Yes.' Her whispered response was barely audible.

His arms tightened round her for a moment, his eyes closed, and he placed a tender kiss on her titian curls. 'Thank you,' he breathed into her hair. After a moment, he straightened and said briskly, 'I promise you will not regret it. We shall be married before Graves learns his plot has failed. The ceremony can be performed as soon as I return.

'And in the meantime, my dear, I beg you will take no risks. Stay indoors. Go nowhere without escort. And make yourself beautiful for your wedding day!'

A strangled sound escaped Jamie, half-laugh, half-sob. No chance for second thoughts now. She knew he would not allow her to retreat.

Richard kissed her softly on the lips, laid her back on the bed and pulled the bedclothes over her. 'Sleep now, little one,' he said, stroking her hair. 'I shall send Smithers back to you. You will be safe now.'

As he started to open the dressing-room door, he turned back for a second to smile generously at his betrothed. 'Happy birthday. Sleep well.'

Jamie glanced down at her wedding band as Richard led her back from the chapel to the house. It was done! They were married!

It seemed strange to be entering the house by the main door. The butler stood rigidly to attention, holding open the door for the Earl and his new Countess. Jamie wondered what was going on behind that expressionless face. What could he possibly think of her?

'Thank you, Digby,' said the Earl affably. 'We shall be in the blue drawing-room. Bring some refreshments.'

'Certainly, milord.'

To Jamie's horror, he brought not tea, but champagne! 'Excellent, Digby,' commended his lordship. 'Will you take a glass with us, Mama?' He seemed to take it for granted that Jamie would not refuse to join the celebration.

'I shall propose a toast,' announced Lady Hardinge, taking her glass. 'To Jamie and Richard—long life, love, and happiness.' She sipped her wine, watching the faces of the newly-weds over the rim of her champagne flute.

Jamie was embarrassed by her words, especially the mention of love.

Richard seemed to conceal his feelings rather better. He merely smiled inscrutably.

'The second toast is mine, I think,' Richard responded. 'To the new Countess Hardinge, my beautiful wife.' Jamie averted her gaze. 'I couple that with another toast,' he added mischievously, 'to the other Lady Hardinge, my beautiful mother, the Dowager Countess.'

His mother spluttered a little over her wine. 'Oh, dear,' she murmured. 'Yes, I suppose I am now. I imagine I shall become accustomed to it after a while.' Her expression of chagrin caused the others to smile. Soon all three were laughing gaily.

'We had better change for dinner soon, I think,' warned the Dowager. 'No doubt something rather special has been prepared below stairs. I hope it has not spoiled as a result of the delay.'

'Oh dear.' Jamie could not hide her concern. 'I have no evening gown, I am afraid—'

'You look delightful just as you are, Jamie,' interrupted the Dowager, smiling with approval at the cream silk gown which she had pressed on her prospective daughter-in-law for the ceremony. 'In any case, a bride should sit down to her wedding breakfast in her wedding gown, however late it may be. Let Richard change. You and I shall sit here comfortably until he returns.'

Their waiting was not comfortable, however, for Jamie was very awkward in her new position. She felt more of an impostor now than she had ever done as Jamie the simpleton. A lady she might be—by birth— but she felt she had long ago forfeited that status. How could she ever attempt to regain it?

The two ladies were sitting in silence when his lordship returned. He took in the scene at a glance. Then, in an attempt to break the ice, he ordered a fresh bottle of champagne.

'Richard! What are you about?' cried his mother, the moment the door closed behind Digby.

'Celebrating,' he replied simply, refilling his empty glass.

Dinner might have been a difficult occasion without Richard's careful planning. He knew that his mother must be expected to yield up her place to Jamie. He was sure, too, that Jamie would not wish to oust his mother from the foot of the table. In other circumstances, he would have watched in amusement as two women jockeyed for position. But these were not any two women—these were his mother and his wife. So he solved the problem by putting Jamie on his right at the head of the table and his mother on his left. Both were too surprised to make any kind of fuss.

The meal was indeed sumptuous. They marvelled at how so much had been done in so little time. Where had the lobsters appeared from, for instance, and the ducklings? Someone had worked miracles for Jamie's wedding day.

Richard rose from the table with the ladies, refusing to remain drinking port in solitary state. He preferred, he said, the company of the two ladies in his life.

'Do you play, Jamie?' asked Lady Hardinge, nodding towards the piano, when they were back in the drawing-room once more.

'I was used to, ma'am, but of course I have not done so since I came to Harding. I was going to ask you if I might—'

'Of course you may practise here, if that is what you wish. Remember, you are mistress of Harding now, not I. You may do just as you like.'

'Within reason, Mama,' added Richard, with a grin,

'for a wife must still defer to her husband, must she not?'

The Dowager threw him an eloquent look. Intercepting it, Jamie giggled uneasily, wishing Richard had not pressed quite so much champagne on her. She was feeling really rather strange.

'If you will excuse me,' said the Dowager, rising from her seat, 'it has been a very long day, and I should prefer to retire now. Jamie will deal with the tea tray, Richard, I am sure. Goodnight, my dears.' She kissed each in turn. 'Bless you both.'

As he closed the door behind his mother, Richard smiled across at his bride. 'A model of diplomacy, do you not agree, Jamie?'

'Yes, indeed,' agreed Jamie, too eagerly, then lapsed into silence. Heavens, where were her wits? She was behaving like a green girl just out of the schoolroom. Surely she could think of something to say?

No words came. The only thoughts swirling in her mind were of Richard Hardinge—who was now her husband!

Richard came slowly across to where she sat and took her hand. Raising it to his lips for a whisper of a kiss, he took his place at her side. 'You are bemused by all that has happened, I fancy, my dear. Do not let it worry you. You have all the time in the world to learn your new role. And you are safe here, I promise you that.'

Jamie nodded, her gratitude visibly written in her beautiful eyes.

'Come, my dear,' he said then, raising her to her

feet. 'You too are tired. Let us retire.' He led his blushing bride into the hall.

Too late for regrets now, thought Jamie, as they made their way up the main staircase to the suite of rooms which had always been occupied by the Earl and Countess Hardinge. She glanced at the powerful man at her side, immaculate in his evening dress. She shivered, unaccountably, for she did not fear him, of that she was certain, even while she hesitated to delve too deeply into what her feelings really were.

When at last they stood alone together in the splendid sitting-room which lay between the two bedchambers, she raised her eyes shyly to his and found that he was gazing at her in a most disconcerting way.

'My lord,' Jamie began uncertainly, 'I—'

'Ah, yes,' interrupted Richard, recalled to the present by her words and trying to bring his own ragged thoughts into some sort of order, 'that reminds me—did you, or did you not, just promise to obey me, wife?'

What was she to make of an ominous statement like that? She nodded apprehensively, unable to tear her eyes away from his strange expression.

'I do not expect to be much in the habit of issuing orders, but when I do, I shall expect them to be obeyed. Always,' he added sternly, glaring down at her. 'And my first—and only—order for this, your wedding day, is that you cease to address me as "my lord". Or else!' All of a sudden, he was openly grinning at her.

'Why, you…!' She burst out laughing. All the earlier tension between them was dispelled. 'Or else what, *my lord*?' she demanded impudently, echoing his mood.

'Or else I may be forced to tan your delectable backside, you witch. I mean it, you know.'

'Really?'

'Really. Now—say it, Jamie.' His tone was suddenly very serious indeed.

She looked up into his eyes which seemed more black than blue in the shadowy room. She could not read his expression. The pressure of his hands on her shoulders was strong. 'If it is truly your wish, I shall call you by name. Richard,' she said caressingly, making the single word sound almost like an endearment.

He held her to him for a few seconds. Her defences seemed to be crumbling, but it would not do to go too fast. 'Thank you,' he whispered into her hair. 'And now, I suggest we go to bed. You need your rest, my dear.'

The new Lady Hardinge blushed to the roots of her hair.

'No. I have not forgotten my promise.' He moved to open one of the doors off the sitting-room. 'Your chamber is here, and you will not be disturbed. Mine is on the other side.' He indicated a door in the opposite wall. 'Goodnight, Jamie.' Richard pushed his hesitant wife gently into her bedchamber and closed the door on her before retreating to his own room and the decanter of brandy which awaited him.

Then, for the very first time, he began to review his position dispassionately.

Jamie Calderwood was his wife—in name at least.

He had given her his word that he would not force himself on her, so he could not bed her, not unless *she* released him from his bond. But if he did not bed her, she could *still* be at the mercy of the Calderwood clan—for if they regained control of Jamie, the marriage could be forcibly annulled. Dear God, this solution of his might be no solution at all!

Why had it mattered so much to him? Why had he risked so much for a red-haired waif who had it in her power, now, to deny him both comfort and children? He shook his head in bewilderment, sipping abstractedly at his brandy. Truly, he did not know. He had done it, but he did not really know why, except that he had felt an overpowering need to atone for his earlier dishonourable treatment of her and to protect her from her appalling family. Jamie affected him strangely, as no other woman had ever done. Was it her indomitable spirit that made him want to stand between her and all the world? She had rare courage—and beauty besides. She was fit to be a queen, not just a countess.

But she was his Countess now. And if he wanted a true marriage—which he was at last prepared to admit that he did—he would have to gain Jamie's trust, and overcome the disgust he had surely engendered on that fateful night, so that *she* would agree to release him from his vow. He was not sure whether she would ever do so. She had repulsed him when they were alone in her room two nights ago, even though his only desire had been to reassure her. And today she had seemed to be afraid of him, shivering at the merest touch.

For a man who was famous for his ability to charm women, he had been singularly unsuccessful so far with the one who was now his wife. Had it not been for the attempted abduction, she would probably have continued to refuse him. He knew he had taken advantage of her when she was at her most vulnerable. And he had given her no chance to withdraw. Now honour was satisfied—but in a loveless union. His mother's concern about a one-sided passion seemed laughable in the circumstances. Jamie certainly did not love him.

It would not be an easy task to win her, nor quickly achieved. But now that they were married, they could spend a lot of time together. He would be able to keep her safe from her terrible family. And she would come to know him better without feeling threatened. Perhaps eventually she would be charmed into trusting, even loving him?

Chapter Fourteen

Jamie lay awake a long time, her thoughts full of the enigmatic man who was now her husband. Eventually she slept, but she could not escape him even there. Her wedding night was disturbed by erotic dreams she did not fully understand.

When Annie eventually drew the curtains, the sun was already well up. 'You must make haste, my lady,' she chided, proudly reminding her charge of her new status. 'His lordship went down to breakfast some time ago. Will you not want to join him?'

Jamie allowed herself to be persuaded and made haste to dress. As Lady Hardinge, she should now be in mourning like the rest of the family, but she possessed no blacks. Indeed, she had only two presentable gowns to her name—the cream silk in which she had been married and the green gown which Annie had made over earlier. She would have to create an opportunity to ask her husband's permission to order mourning gowns, or she would disgrace him in public. She swallowed hard. Richard could be very intimidating, and she did not relish the thought of applying to him for money on the very first day of their marriage. But what choice did she have?

The butler greeted her warmly at the bottom of the staircase, pointedly ignoring her inappropriate green gown. 'Good morning, my lady. You will find his lordship in the breakfast parlour.'

'Thank you, Digby,' answered Jamie with a winning smile. 'And Lady Hardinge too?'

'No, my lady. The Dowager Countess is taking a tray in her room this morning.'

Jamie paused a moment to reflect on that interesting snippet of information. Richard's mama had always made a point of breakfasting downstairs, having made clear to all that she did not believe in assuming die-away airs. This careful absence was yet further evidence of her tact and consideration where her new daughter-in-law was concerned. Jamie felt herself warming even more to the older woman, and hoping very much that they could become friends for, in all her twenty-one years, Jamie had never been permitted a real friend from her own station in life. She felt the beginnings of a glow of happiness.

Digby showed her into the breakfast parlour and discreetly withdrew. Richard, sitting at the head of the table, looked up, smiled and sprang to his feet. 'Jamie! I had not expected you to come down.' He came round to help her into her seat, placing a gentle kiss on her cheek as he did so. 'You look a little pale, my dear. Are you quite well?'

How considerate he was. 'I am very well. Truly, I am.' She smiled reassuringly at him and was rewarded when his anxious frown disappeared. 'Idleness is my problem, more like. You must remember that I am not used to such luxury. I had to earn my keep at Calderwood. And when I was employed by the fearsome Lord Hardinge,' she added impudently, 'I had to work like a slave from morn 'til night. Just look at my hands!'

Richard laughed, resuming his seat. 'You are a minx, madam. With the hands of a scullery maid!' He sipped his coffee meditatively. 'We shall have to do something about them, you know. They really are not fit to be seen, and you cannot always be wearing gloves. Still, there are bound to be remedies. I imagine Mama will be able to give you some cream to make them presentable.'

'About that… It's not just the state of my hands. I am afraid I am not in the least presentable. I have no mourning clothes. Do you think—?'

'You have no clothes at all, as far as I can see,' he responded quickly, coming immediately to the nub of her problem. 'But don't worry about that. I have already arranged for Mama's dressmaker from Bath to wait on you, later today. You should order whatever you need from her.'

'Oh, but—'

'And not only blacks,' he continued. 'You will need half-mourning soon too, and eventually society wear. I should like you, if you will, to order something in green now, to match your eyes.' He smiled conspiratorially. 'You can wear it here at Harding, so that I can admire you in secret. No one else need know.'

Richard's smile was captivating. But on this occasion, it did not exercise its usual charm on Jamie's vulnerable heart. She was merely surprised into a chuckle at his swift resolution of her problem. And now she had to face another. 'I have very little experience of modistes, I'm afraid. Mama—Lady Calderwood, I mean—never allowed me new gowns.'

Jamie was glad to find that Richard could stick to practicalities when it mattered. And that he had a ready solution to offer. 'If you would like it, Mama would be very willing to assist you. You may trust her judgement too, for she has exquisite taste.'

Jamie agreed gratefully. She could not do better than the combination of Lady Hardinge and Annie. Apart from welcoming Lady Hardinge's advice, she would be glad of an opportunity to know her mother-in-law better.

'You should know that I have sent the announcement to the *Gazette* and to the *Morning Post*. It should appear tomorrow, so, in a day or two, our marriage will be common knowledge and there need be no more worries about the odious Graves.' He sipped his coffee slowly, watching Jamie as she toyed with a slice of bread and butter. 'And, just in case that does not suffice, I have also written to your father.'

Jamie began to relax a little, soothed by his deep voice and his apparent mastery of all eventualities. She felt so secure with Richard around. Surely no one could harm her now?

Before she had a chance to speak again, he put his cup down and moved to take the chair next to hers. 'One more thing, my dear. I omitted to give you a gift for your coming of age. Happy birthday, Jamie.'

'Oh,' breathed Jamie, as he laid a flat leather case by her plate.

'Open it.'

Jamie did so, to reveal a beautiful square-cut emerald pendant on a gold collar set with tiny diamonds. Matching emerald ear studs, on a slightly smaller scale, completed the set.

'These are not Hardinge family jewels—though you will have those too, of course, as soon as we are out of mourning. Mama will tell you all about them, and the history of the family too, if you let her. But these emeralds are just for you. For your green eyes.'

'But how…? There has not been time.'

Richard grinned impishly, almost like a schoolboy. 'There are ways of beating time, if one puts one's mind to it. I happened on them in London yesterday, and I knew I had to buy them for you. A messenger brought them this morning.'

Jamie could not take her eyes from his fabulous gift. Or her mind from his thoughtfulness. 'Thank you, Richard,' she whispered in awe. 'They are quite beautiful.'

He rose and made for the door. 'Forgive me, Jamie,' he explained in a serious voice. 'I must leave now. I have to deliver our unexpected visitor to Bristol so that he may face his trial. I am hoping that, once he is confronted with the full panoply of the law, he will tell us more than he did three nights ago. It is *just* possible, I suppose, though I am not very confident.

'He came from Bristol, too, so there are one or two

leads I may be able to follow up. Who knows, I may even find the elusive Caleb.'

'Please take care, Richard,' Jamie whispered.

'Have no fears, my dear. I shall not be alone with our friend. And besides, I go armed.' He patted the pocket of his coat reassuringly. 'I am counted an adequate shot, you know,' he added modestly.

'I shall try to be back before dinner,' he promised, 'but do not wait if I am late. And make sure you enjoy yourselves with the dressmaker. I expect you to be quite ravishingly gowned by the time I return.'

'Oh, but—' began Jamie, in protest. Too late. Her husband had already gone.

The Dowager and the new Lady Hardinge prepared to spend a very pleasant and expensive day with Madame Françoise, the modiste from Bath. She was, according to the Dowager, more than competent to provide a wardrobe for Jamie while the family was in mourning.

'But, when you go to London, I advise you to have your gowns from Célestine,' said Lady Hardinge. 'There really is no one to equal her. Do you not agree, Smithers?' Annie did.

Jamie was more than happy to learn from their experience. For what did she, a penniless country mouse, know of such things?

Madame Françoise brought with her a number of part-finished gowns and two of her seamstresses to work on them. By the time the consultation was over, Jamie would have both a day dress and an evening dress fit for a countess.

Encouraged by the Dowager, Jamie ordered a bewildering array of gowns and accessories. She had never thought to own so many clothes in all her life. She was even persuaded to a grey velvet riding habit, so that she might begin to ride again as soon as the family was out of full mourning. Just the thought of being on horseback again made her want to shout for joy.

Madame Françoise was beginning to pack away her samples by the time Jamie mustered the courage to broach the subject of that other dress. 'Have you any green among your samples, *madame*?'

Lady Hardinge looked up sharply but said nothing.

'Why, yes, *madame*. I shall fetch zem on ze instant.' She bustled out.

Jamie looked guiltily at her mother-in-law. 'Forgive me, ma'am. I do not mean to shock you. You see, Richard wants—'

Lady Hardinge smiled indulgently. 'No need to explain. I understand very well. Let us order exactly the kind of creation Richard has asked you to wear. Green—to match your eyes, of course. He always did have good taste. I am sure we can create something to please him.'

How well she understands her son, Jamie thought. If only I could read him half as well.

Madame Françoise returned with her samples. Both ladies lit immediately on the same glowing silk and on the same style from the many drawings. 'Simplicity is the key,' said Lady Hardinge knowledgeably. 'Let the gown enhance your youth and beauty without drawing attention to itself.'

Jamie blushed but agreed. Her new wardrobe was complete. But would Richard approve?

When Jamie was finally gowned in her new black-silk day dress—which was finer than anything she had ever before possessed—she felt more than a little self-conscious. But Lady Hardinge welcomed her warmly when she returned to the sitting-room. 'Ah, my dear, that is splendid, especially now that Smithers has re-done your hair in just that way. Those loose curls do become you. She is a treasure, is she not?'

'I owe her a great deal, ma'am.'

'So I believe, though I have only the sketchiest notion of how you came to be together in the first place. I hope you will do me the honour of confiding in me some day. I am not really an ogre, you know!'

'Oh, Lady Hardinge, I never for one moment thought that you were!'

Lady Hardinge's eyes twinkled mischievously. 'My dear, you really must try to call me "Mama". What would Richard say if he heard you?'

Like mother, like son, thought Jamie, recalling how Richard had teased her into dropping all formality with him. She felt as if she were being surrounded by a warm protecting cocoon. How could she deserve all this?

'I shall try to remember, Mama,' responded Jamie with a shy smile.

'Excellent, my dear. That sounded almost natural!' She beamed at her daughter-in-law. 'Now, about Smithers. It is clear that your need of her talents is much greater than mine, and so I shall not even suggest taking her to the dower house with me. Besides, she would not come, not if it meant leaving you, of that I am sure.'

'But surely, ma'am—Mama—you do not mean to leave Harding?'

'Of course I do—though not immediately. The dower house is not yet ready, even though the work was begun months ago. It was so very neglected. Richard—bless him!—had the work put in hand not long after his father died, for he knew how much needed to be done, and we had agreed it would be best if I were to remove there as soon as his marriage had taken place.' Lady Hardinge stopped suddenly, a slight flush rising up her neck. 'You see, Jamie…' she began uncertainly.

Jamie felt all her hopes tumbling around her. 'Marriage? But—'

Lady Hardinge bit her lip. She hesitated uncharacteristically. 'Er—he is an only son, you see. He accepted, some time before his father died, that he needed to marry to…to secure the succession.'

Now Jamie was absolutely mortified. She had considered many aspects of her marriage to Richard, but never this. Still, it had to be faced. She continued as bravely as she could. 'Did he…did he have anyone particular in mind?'

Lady Hardinge hesitated even more, as if desperately searching for words. 'It was a matter of duty rather than of inclination, I am sure,' she said.

If Lady Hardinge expected that platitude to satisfy Jamie, she would be disappointed. Jamie gazed directly at her, waiting patiently for a name.

'I believe he had settled on Emma Fitzwilliam,'

said Lady Hardinge at last. She looked very flushed. 'Her father's estate marches with ours.'

Jamie felt as if all the breath had been knocked from her body. Dear God, what had she done?

Richard had already chosen a bride and had sacrificed her—and his own inclinations, no doubt—for Jamie's honour. How could she ever hope to make a true marriage based on such infamy? She had been wicked to accept him, when all her better instincts had prompted her to refuse. Now what was she to do?

She dimly perceived that Lady Hardinge was still speaking, but she did not understand a word of it, as she fought to regain control of her whirling thoughts.

'...as soon as it is finished. Will that be convenient, my dear?'

Jamie forced a smile. 'Whatever you wish, ma'am,' she said evenly. Heavens! What had she just agreed to? She needed some time by herself to sort out what to do now.

But the Dowager would not allow Jamie to escape. 'Splendid,' she said, sounding totally confident again. 'Now, will you pull the bell, my dear, and order us some tea?'

Over tea, Jamie gradually recovered a little from her shock, as she was skilfully drawn out by her mother-in-law's gentle questioning. By the end of an hour, Jamie had given Lady Hardinge all the important details of her life at Calderwood and of her subsequent flight.

Lady Hardinge was looking at Jamie with a mixture of envy and admiration. 'You have great courage, my dear. Have you told all this to Richard?'

'No, not all,' admitted Jamie. In truth, she had told her husband very little. For when could she have done so?

'You should. Or, if you prefer, I could do it for you?'

Jamie shook her head. 'I shall tell him myself—when the moment is right.' Seeing her mother-in-law's knowing smile, she changed the subject abruptly. 'Will you tell me more about the family history, Mama? Richard said I should ask you.'

'You do surprise me. Do you tell me he did not warn you against my superstitious nonsense?' As Jamie looked at her blankly, she said, 'I see that he did not, which is something of a surprise. In any case, you shall judge for yourself.'

She sipped her tea delicately. 'The Hardinges have served the kings of England for centuries—ever since the Conqueror, we believe.' She laughed gently. 'And they have almost always managed to be on the winning side too, which must have required a remarkable amount of luck, especially during the Wars of the Roses.'

Jamie nodded, fascinated. At Calderwood, she had read all the histories she could lay her hands on. Almost every noble family had found itself in disgrace at some time or other during that period.

'I like to think that the family has prospered because of the tradition that the head of the house must marry for love. It has been upheld for centuries. In fact, it goes back so far that we do not really know how it came about. All we know is that, when the rule is flouted, a curse descends on us.'

Jamie listened in increasing wonder. She did not dare to think what such a curse might mean for her—and for Richard. She held her breath, waiting for her mother-in-law to continue.

'At least, that is how it appears,' added Lady Hardinge. 'There have been only two occasions when the head of the house did not marry for love. Twice they flouted the tradition—and twice they died without an heir.'

Jamie felt the blood draining from her face. She swallowed hard. This could not be real.

'And then there was the Hardinge diamond,' continued Lady Hardinge with a mischievous smile. 'It was given to Major Richard Harding for his services to an Indian prince. You must understand that the major belonged to a cadet branch of the Hardinge family—he did not even have the "e"!'

'I beg your pardon, ma'am? I am afraid I do not quite understand.'

'Goodness. Richard has been remiss!' chuckled Lady Hardinge. 'When the first Earl Hardinge was created, for services to Charles II, there was a mistake in the letters patent—an "e" was added to the end of the name. Of course, it had to remain. One does not cavil at the gift of an earldom. Only the main branch of the family took to using that spelling, though. The rest remained plain "Harding" without an "e". That is why this estate, which predates the earldom, is also "Harding" without an "e".

'But, to return to Major Harding—there were probably well-nigh twenty people between him and the earldom, yet in the five years following the gift of the stone, every single one of them died. The title fell into his lap.

'And there have been similar happenings since. The diamond brings luck—but it cannot undo the curse. It did not help the Earl who married a woman he detested, purely for her money. He was crippled shortly after, by a fall from his horse, and died in agony. He had no son. The title went to his cousin.'

Jamie nodded, fascinated—and more than a little unnerved. Was the curse the reason for Lady Hardinge's underlying sadness about Richard's marriage to her? What would happen to Richard, she wondered, to punish him for marrying where he did not love? And to her, for accepting him?

Chapter Fifteen

Jamie determined to wait up for her husband, however late he might be. She needed to know whether his enquiries had produced any result. But she dare not allow herself to be idle, for then her thoughts would stray towards Emma Fitzwilliam or the Hardinge family curse. Instead, she explored the glories of the Harding library, finding that it included just the sort of novels and frivolous books which had never been permitted to cross the threshold of Calderwood Hall.

To her surprise, she soon found herself absorbed in *Sense and Sensibility* in spite of the questions nagging in the back of her mind, and the evening passed swiftly until a soft tap sounded on the door of their sitting room. That would be the butler, summoning her to meet her husband. She rose and smoothed her gown, trying to look totally composed.

The door opened to reveal, not the butler, but Richard, looking a little damp from his travels.

'Digby said you were waiting up for me, Jamie. But you should be in bed, my dear. It is very late.'

He smiled wearily down at his wife, and found himself thinking how well black became her. He felt a sudden desire to take her in his arms, just to hold her against his travel-worn body, but he managed to resist the impulse. He was not sure he would be able to control what might happen afterwards.

'Digby was supposed to fetch me down to you,' Jamie began anxiously. She had hoped for a little longer to prepare herself.

'He did try, I promise you.'

Although he was tired, there was mischief in his eyes, but his wife did not respond to it. 'I see,' she returned seriously.

They sat down side by side on the sofa, not touching. He thought she seemed a little wary of him. It hurt to think that she could not be at ease with him, though he was not sure why it mattered so much to him.

He raised one of her hands to his lips and dropped a feather-light kiss on her palm. Then he repeated the gesture with the other, gazing deep into her glorious eyes and recognising how truly troubled she was. 'You have no need for concern, Jamie,' he said in a soft, but serious voice. 'You are my wife, remember?'

She looked away, unable to hold his gaze. His words shamed her, for she knew she was no true wife. Unconsciously, she withdrew her hands and clasped them in her lap.

Richard's jaw tightened at the thought that Jamie was repelled by his simple reminder that she was his wife. The fact that he had intended it as a reassurance made it worse. Clearly he had been wrong to believe he was making progress with her. Even a kiss on the hand was too much, too soon, apparently.

Swallowing his defeat, he smiled at her. 'I have to admit that I have achieved little today, in spite of all my efforts. Our intruder has been delivered to the Bridewell but, even there, I could get nothing more out of him. To be honest, I think he has told all he knows. My search for Caleb has been equally fruitless.' The smile was a little rueful now. 'That is my account of myself. A thoroughgoing failure, I'd say. So, if you have any more thoughts on what we might do, let me have them, I beg you, for I am at a stand.'

How weary he is, Jamie thought, trying to resist the urge to touch his furrowed brow and smooth away his cares. 'I do have one thought,' she ventured, ruthlessly subduing her softer feelings. 'My father has an agent in London. I think Ralph Graves may use him too.'

Richard slapped his open hand down on his thigh with a loud crack. 'Good God, where are my wits? I should have guessed as much. I shall start for London in the morning.' He smiled broadly at his wife. 'Well done, my dear. In fact, if you—' He broke off in mid-sentence, apparently embarrassed.

Jamie could not imagine what might be in his mind, but, encouraged by that generous smile, she allowed herself to voice her own thoughts. 'Might I come with you, Richard?' At the look of astonishment which crossed his face, her precarious composure shattered. She found herself beginning to stammer apologetically. 'I'm sorry. I did not mean... Please, do not—'

'I should be delighted if you would accompany me, my dear. In fact, I was just about to ask if you would agree to come. I cannot imagine a better partner in this adventure than my quick-witted wife.' This unexpected compliment provoked a rosy blush from his now thoroughly confused wife. 'Good. That's settled then,' he said quickly, keeping his tone light and practical. 'Can you be ready early tomorrow?'

'You forget, my lord,' she returned archly, trying to regain some vestige of her earlier self-control, 'that, until recently, I was wont to rise with the dawn.'

'Witch!' he laughed, getting up from his seat and dropping a kiss on her titian curls. 'Now, get thee to thy rest, wife, for we have much to do tomorrow.'

Jamie listened as he descended the stairs, probably to return to his study. She sighed wistfully, wondering why she made such a mull of every encounter they had.

Back in his book-room, Richard forced his mind on to practicalities. Summoning Digby, he gave instructions for their early departure for London in the morning. In view of the chilly weather, and the presence of his wife, they would travel in his carriage, rather than by curricle. A messenger must be sent ahead immediately to warn the staff at Hardinge House to prepare for their master's arrival. And his valet and her ladyship's abigail must follow with all speed, together with the baggage.

'Does your lordship expect to make a long stay?' The butler was responsible for calculating quantities of baggage and allocating packing duties.

'A week, perhaps two, I should think. We shall not

be going into society, of course, so there will be little need for baggage. We can always send back for anything more we need, if we decide to extend our visit.' The butler bowed himself out to set about rousing the household to meet this sudden change of plan.

Richard had turned meanwhile to penning a long explanatory note to his mother, in case she was not awake before they left on the morrow. He paused to wonder about the wisdom of taking Jamie with him. In London, they would be thrown together much more than at Harding. Could he resist the temptation she presented?

Her lovely face, framed by her glorious hair, seemed to appear before him, tantalisingly. Dear God, how he wanted her! What was it about her that stirred him so? He could not tell. Nor when and how his feelings had begun to change towards her. But he knew now that he felt something for his wife which he had never experienced before in all his dealings with womankind. And that he did not dare to put a name to it. Not yet.

Very early next morning, Lady Hardinge entered the cheery breakfast room where her daughter-in-law was calmly pouring coffee for her husband. Richard was dressed for travelling. Jamie had put on her black silk again, since it was the only appropriate day gown she now possessed.

Richard rose in surprise to greet his mother. 'What are you doing down at this hour, Mama? I had left a note for you explaining everything.'

'I am quite well aware that you think I am in my

dotage, Richard, but you are mistaken if you think me incapable of rising early. I have come to ensure that Jamie is properly taken care of, before this mad escapade gets under way. Your note of explanation'— she waved a sheet of paper in his direction—'says much, but it does not say that.'

Richard grinned, a little sheepishly, and politely helped his mother to her seat. He threw Jamie a look suggestive of the persecuted fugitive.

'If you have your way,' continued Lady Hardinge, without allowing either of them to say a word, 'this poor child will freeze to death. Have you no conscience?'

Jamie tried to suppress a giggle. 'Oh, Mama, you really are most kind to worry so about me, but truly there is no need. Only think—on my last journey in Richard's carriage, I was left to freeze to death on the box! I am sure this trip will be most comfortable by comparison.'

Lady Hardinge interrupted her son as he made to defend himself. 'That is nothing at all to the point, Jamie. Your husband has a duty to look to your well-being and, in my opinion, he is failing in it. What, for example, did you plan to wear over that thin silk gown you have on?' There was no response, except for a muffled choking noise from Richard's end of the table. 'Quite. However, there is a solution. After breakfast, you shall come upstairs to my dressing-room and we shall make a selection from what I have there. I have, for example, a black sable cloak and muff which will be just right for you.' She glared at her son. 'I take it you do not object, Richard?'

'Not in the least, Mama,' he admitted, grinning cheerfully at her. 'Against such a formidable combination as my mother and my wife, how should I dare to say a word?'

Jamie gasped with laughter.

'Stuff!' exclaimed Lady Hardinge inelegantly. 'You, my son, are bound for a bad end—unless a good woman can save you.'

'I recognise it might be a tall order,' quipped her son, glancing towards his wife for a split second.

Lady Hardinge sipped at her coffee and turned to Jamie. 'Do go to Célestine's while you are in London, my dear, and order your half-mourning. You will need it quite soon.'

'But, Mama, I have already spent a fortune on my wardrobe here. I cannot…' She broke off, looking guiltily towards her husband.

'Why not?' demanded Lady Hardinge. 'It is surely up to you how you spend your allowance. Why, what on earth is the matter, my dear? I did not mean to embarrass you—'

Richard's deep voice intervened. 'Jamie is embarrassed for me, I collect, Mama. She has no allowance—not yet. With all the other events happening around us, I am afraid I overlooked it. But no matter.' He turned to Jamie. 'How much do you think you will need, my dear?'

'I—'

'Richard! How is Jamie supposed to know the answer to that? Really, men are quite witless sometimes, I do believe!'

Jamie was again trying not to laugh. She dared not look at Richard's face.

'Why don't you start with the same allowance I had from your father and see whether it is enough? But you will need to be prepared to increase it, I warn you. A young bride's needs are bound to be much more than those of an old woman in her dotage.' Lady Hardinge finished her coffee and rose to leave. 'I shall expect you upstairs in five minutes, Jamie.'

As the door closed behind her, Jamie dared at last to look directly at Richard, whose eyes were brimming with laughter. In a matter of seconds, both of them were convulsed, trying vainly to muffle the sounds of their mirth.

'What on earth came over Mama?' chuckled Richard, as soon as he could speak. 'I have never seen the like.'

'I think she feels I need a champion. And she was splendid, quite splendid. If you had seen your face when she said men were witless…' Jamie succumbed to another peal of laughter which she stifled as best she could with her now damp and crumpled handkerchief.

'What could I say?' pleaded Richard. 'A man may not contradict his mama, after all.'

'Oh!' If there had been a loose cushion on her chair, Jamie would have thrown it at him. 'How outrageous you are, my lord!'

'And how beautiful you are when you laugh, my lady,' countered Richard, with a hint of deeper meaning in his voice. Too much, he realised immediately. She looked like a frightened doe again. His recover was very swift this time. 'However,' he continued smoothly, 'your first duty now, ma'am, is to attend on my mother, before she demands my head on a charger for dereliction of duty! If you would save me, I beg you, go!'

Good humour restored, Jamie did as she was bid.

His laughing voice followed her as she made for the stairs. 'But delay at your peril, my lady. After fifteen minutes, I depart, with you or without you.'

Jamie picked up her skirts to run nimbly up the stairs to Lady Hardinge's dressing-room, and was still smiling broadly as she entered.

'I am delighted to see you in such spirits, Jamie, my dear. And Richard too. He has not laughed like that in a long time.'

'I do believe you provoked him deliberately,' said Jamie suspiciously, spying the twinkle in Lady Hardinge's eye. 'If I may say so without giving offence, Mama, I think I know from whom he has his wicked sense of humour.'

Her mother-in-law seemed pleased at this. 'I take it from that, my dear, that my son has been showing you at least a little of his lighter side. Good. In my opinion, that is what you both need.'

Before Jamie could reply, the Dowager turned to the cupboard and began pulling out clothes, all of which she tossed to the protesting Jamie. 'Come, Jamie, you need them, at least until your own wardrobe is delivered, whereas I have no need of them now. Humour me, if you will.'

In the end, all was agreed. Jamie would wear the sables, and the matching hat. The other clothes would be packed up immediately and loaded into the second carriage with Smithers and Gregg. Honour was satisfied.

Precisely fourteen minutes later, Jamie arrived back in the hall, swathed in sables, just as Richard came out of the study with some papers in his hand. 'Well!' he said, admiring the picture she made. 'You lost, I see!' He grinned. 'But you had the good sense to take your fall quickly. Most commendable! What a wonder you are, my dear.' With an exaggerated bow, he offered her his arm. 'May I see you to your carriage, my lady?'

In less than five minutes, they were under way. Jamie sank back into her corner, relishing the comfort of her sables, the fur rug across her lap and the hot brick under her feet. Even as Miss Calderwood, she had never dreamt of treatment like this. It seemed... unreal.

Richard, too, sat back in his corner, idly watching the play of expression on his wife's face. She was sometimes very easy to read. And at the moment, her childlike pleasure in her surroundings was evident. Good. So far. He would try to keep the journey lighthearted. And he would not touch her. He knew well enough the mistakes he had to avoid.

'How are we going to set about finding my father's agent, Richard?' Her practical question broke into his careful calculations, dispelling his increasingly dark mood.

'Ah, now, there I do have some ideas. I daren't let my wife do all the thinking, lest she, too, conclude I am witless.'

Jamie chuckled, as he had known she would. He found himself thinking again how beautiful she had grown since her unmasking, like a flower blooming under a dedicated gardener's careful nurturing. But he pushed such delicious thoughts to the back of his mind. He was nowhere near ready for such temptations, especially now, with the prospect of many hours alone in her company.

'I shall go, first of all, to my own agents. They should be able to furnish some names, which will give us a start.'

As he spoke, the carriage lurched, throwing Jamie towards him. Their hands touched. Even through their gloves, Jamie felt as if a bolt of lightning had shot up her arm. She felt herself flushing with embarrassment and pulled her hand away sharply. Why could she not control her reactions to him? What on earth would he think of her behaviour? She clasped her hands in her lap, trying to concentrate on counting the tiny stitches in her kid gloves.

Richard looked steadily at her and cursed silently. So lovely, so desirable—and so afraid of him! How was he ever going to win her trust?

Chapter Sixteen

A slightly uncomfortable silence prevailed for several miles. Jamie had suddenly become conscious that she was truly alone with her husband for the first time since their wedding ceremony. On other occasions, there had always been the likelihood of imminent interruption—or it had been clear that Richard had no intention of prolonging their tête-à-tête. But now…his presence seemed to fill the carriage. The scent of him was all around her, preventing her more rational self from functioning. And after that single touch, she could think of nothing but Richard, of how close he was, of how much she wanted to be in his arms.

Jamie transferred her gaze to the sable muff. She sensed that her husband was watching her, but she felt unable to raise her eyes to look at him. She focused instead on the lustrous black hairs of the beautiful fur. How thick and soft it was.

Richard shifted deliberately in his seat, but his tactic did not succeed—Jamie still would not look at him. He frowned, racking his brains for some way of putting her at her ease again. Why did she recoil from him so? Was she still suffering as a result of his attempt to seduce her? Then why had she agreed to marry him? Had he really coerced her?

He shook his head a little, trying to clear his thoughts. It really would not do to continue along this 'if only' road. Nothing could be undone. They had to go forward from where they were.

He smiled across at her tense figure. 'I hope you are more comfortable today than on the last occasion when we shared this carriage,' he said lightly.

She looked up briefly, a slight flush rising on her neck. 'Thank you, it is most comfortable,' she said in a rather strangled voice, before lapsing into silence once more.

He groaned inwardly. This was not going to be easy. But still—their first encounter was as good a topic as any. He continued in a bantering tone, 'I wonder you did not think to take some gloves when you fled from Calderwood. But then—perhaps better not, for I should not have known you were freezing. I could not tell how thin your clothes were.' She must say something now, surely?

'It was kind in you to notice. Many a master would have left me to freeze on the box.'

That was true. Richard had surprised himself when he had taken the boy inside. 'I wonder I did not. It must have been the effect of your soulful eyes, my dear. You looked so helpless, so lost.'

Jamie thought back to that incident. She remembered every second of it, especially the burning touch of his hand on her cheek. She could feel it still. And now he was waiting for her to continue the conversation, but no words would come. In desperation, she turned to the window, rubbing the mist from the pane with her black kid glove. 'Where are we now? We seem to be making very good speed. Shall we reach London tonight?'

Richard sighed. Still, it was better than silence. He began to describe the route they would take. With luck and good horses at every change, they should make London in the day. The important thing was to make progress while the light lasted, for once darkness fell, their speed would be very limited.

'I hope you will not mind, Jamie, but I do not propose to stop to eat. Mrs Peters has provided a basket of provisions which—if it is up to her usual standard—would feed an army for a week. We can eat as we go. We should be able to get some coffee or a glass of wine while the horses are being changed.' He looked towards her for some sign of acquiescence.

'That will suit me very well,' she nodded. 'Thank you. I…I must say I am rather too excited to eat in any case. I have never been to London before.'

'Truly?' queried Richard. This was too good an opportunity to miss! 'Then I hope you will allow me to show you some of the capital, my dear.'

Jamie looked uncertain.

'It would be my pleasure to do so,' he added with his most charming smile.

'Oh, I should like that above all things, Richard, only… Would it be proper to do so while we are in mourning?'

Richard cursed silently. She was quite right. He did not try to hide his chagrin as he admitted his fault.

'But some few amusements may be possible, none the less,' he added. 'Even in mourning, we may visit Westminster Abbey and St Paul's. If you would like to go, that is.'

'Oh yes, very much,' she began eagerly. She was about to launch into a description of all the things she wished to see in the Abbey—like Queen Elizabeth's tomb and the Coronation chair—when she remembered that her father had called her a 'bluestocking' for just such a display of erudition. She lapsed into sudden silence.

Richard threw her a wondering look. 'It sounds as if you know about them already, Jamie,' he began, with a smile. 'Are there particular places you wish to visit? The City?' His smile broadened. 'Or the London gardens, perhaps?'

'Well—yes.' Jamie tentatively began to describe things she longed to see. Hesitant at first, she soon became animated, as she warmed to her subject and forgot all her father's strictures. She spoke knowledgeably of historic buildings and described London's gardens in the spring as if she already knew and loved them.

Richard was entranced. Not only was his wife courageous and beautiful, she was also well read and displayed a fine intellect for one so young. With nods and smiles, he encouraged her to talk, so successfully that the miles flew by. He was on the point of suggesting that she might like to redesign some of the gardens at Harding when the slowing of the horses brought Jamie up short.

'Goodness,' she exclaimed, flushing, 'how I have been rattling on!'

'Nothing of the sort. It was most interesting. I am delighted to discover we have so many tastes in common, my dear. Clearly you must be given free rein in all my gardens. And given your obvious love of history and of books, we shall never want for a topic of conversation.'

Jamie felt her blush deepen. Was he roasting her?

'Now, this is Marlborough, Jamie. May I order you some refreshment? You must be thirsty.'

Jamie could not deny it. 'A cup of coffee would be very welcome,' she admitted. 'If it will not delay us.'

'It shall be done forthwith, madam, if you will excuse me a moment. And I shall get you another hot brick too. The drive through the Savernake Forest can be cold and gloomy.'

So it proved to be, but they made good speed, none the less. It began to look as if they would certainly reach London in the day. And then, in the afternoon, in the Maidenhead thicket, the mist came down. The carriage slowed to a bare walking pace, as the coachman eased his team through the murk.

Richard's face bore a set expression. There was nothing to be done. If they came through the other side of the mist, they might still make London. Otherwise…

It was Jamie who first voiced a doubt. 'If we cannot go faster than this, we shall never make London tonight, surely? Do you know where we are, Richard?'

'Aye. Just outside Maidenhead. If the mist does not lift soon, we shall have to rack up somewhere for the night. Don't worry. There are some quite tolerable inns hereabouts.'

'Oh, I have no worries,' exclaimed Jamie blithely. But she had. She was still alone with Richard—and anything might happen at a strange inn.

When the coachman dared drive his team no farther, they stopped at the Castle Inn, a small but high-class hostelry, hard by Maidenhead. Unfortunately for the Hardinges, they were neither the first nor the only travellers to seek shelter there.

The landlady was wringing her hands as she apologised to her high-ranking new guests. 'I have but the one chamber left, milord, milady. We've so many guests arrived unforeseen this evening, and I couldn't be turning them out, milord, not in this weather. You see—'

'I see exactly your dilemma, my good woman. Do not fret over it. We shall be quite comfortable in the chamber you have, I am sure. Now, if you would take my wife upstairs...'

The landlady bustled up the staircase, apologising volubly all the time. She flung open the door at the end of the passage. 'Please to go in, milady. The fire is lit, as you see, but I'll send up hot water in two shakes.'

'Is there a private parlour?'

'Well, no, milady, I'm afraid not. I only have the one and some earlier guests have taken that. I could ask them—'

'No, indeed,' said Jamie quickly. 'We shall be quite comfortable here, if you could send up some supper.'

The landlady agreed at once. 'Your ladyship's abigail…' She let the question hang in the air.

'I have no idea where she may be. Or my husband's valet either. The second carriage was some time behind us. We must suppose that they have stopped somewhere. Would you…?'

'Have no worries on that score, your ladyship,' responded the landlady promptly. 'If they do arrive, I can find them a bed somewhere. And my daughter can wait on your ladyship, if you wish.'

'That is most kind,' said Jamie gratefully. 'What is her name?'

'Annie, your ladyship.'

Jamie grinned. 'How appropriate. I am sure we shall do very well. Pray send her up to me.'

As the door closed behind the landlady, Jamie surveyed the room. Although the chamber was large, it was dominated by a huge, curtained bed. There were two easy chairs by the fireplace and a small table at which they would no doubt sup. There was a washstand in the corner. And there was plenty of hanging space for clothing. But there was no dressing-room. And there was nowhere else to sleep but that one great bed.

Jamie swallowed nervously when the door opened, but it was not Richard. It was Annie, the landlady's daughter, much flustered at being asked to serve such a great lady. 'Will you change your gown, milady?' she asked shyly, moving to unpack Jamie's travelling portmanteau.

Jamie knew a moment of panic. Where was Richard? Surely he might walk in on her at any moment? Trying to control her voice, she gave the maid to understand that she thought it unnecessary to change. She washed and tidied herself, rather more hurriedly than was her wont. She tried to hide her relief as Annie refastened the last hook of her gown and began to redress her hair.

'Shall I tell his lordship he may come up now, milady?' asked Annie, when she had finished.

Jamie lifted her chin at such impertinence. 'His lordship will come up when he is ready,' she said icily.

'Oh, no, milady. Beggin' your pardon, but his lordship asked me to tell him when you had finished your toilet. He is waiting in the coffee-room.'

How thoughtful he was! And all her haste for no reason!

'Thank you, Annie,' she said, with an apologetic smile. 'Pray tell him so. And bring up some more hot water too.'

Moments later, a soft knock announced Richard's arrival. Jamie rose uncertainly from her chair. His powerful presence seemed to fill the chamber. Richard—and the huge double bed.

Richard was not slow to read the situation. He crossed to where his wife stood by the fire. 'You look much refreshed, Jamie. Is that hot water over there? I should like to be rid of my dirt.'

'I have ordered some more for you. It will be here directly.'

He smiled at her. 'How thoughtful. Thank you.' He began to strip off his coat and waistcoat, then paused.

'Forgive me, Jamie, but as there is no dressing-room…'

She shook her head, trying to smile confidently at him. 'No matter,' she said quietly, resuming her seat so that her back was towards the washstand.

As soon as the hot water arrived, Richard stripped to the waist and began to wash. In the little mirror on the wall, he could see his wife sitting rigidly in her chair. But as he began to shave, she moved. It was a barely perceptible shift of position but just enough, he fancied, for her to watch him out of the corner of her eye. Even curiosity was better than nothing, he decided. He chuckled to himself, but continued to ply his razor as if nothing untoward were happening.

Jamie had failed to resist the temptation to take just one look. She consoled herself with the knowledge that he could not see what she was doing and, since they were bound to share that bed, she might as well know something of what lay in store. But one single look was not enough, she found, for his broad shoulders and smooth skin drew her eyes like a magnet. She had seen him in a dressing gown, but somehow his naked skin was different, making her long to stretch out to touch him.

He put his razor aside and began to wash the traces of shaving soap from his face, reaching for a towel. Jamie edged back into her earlier position, her face flaming. What would he think if he caught her? Luckily, he did not turn. By the time he had put on a fresh shirt and neckcloth, she knew her flush had subsided.

In deference to Jamie, who unaccountably had not

changed her dress, Richard resumed the same coat and waistcoat, even if they would not have been acceptable to Gregg's critical eye. Then he relaxed into the chair opposite his wife with a long sigh. 'You must be tired, Jamie, after all those hours cooped up in the carriage. I am sorry I insisted we should try to make London in the day. It was foolhardy. I should have arranged for us to break our journey at somewhere more comfortable than this. Forgive me.'

She looked up at him then, surprised by his apparent seriousness. His eyes smiled warmly at her, though there was a little hint of annoyance there too. 'You should have organised the mist better,' she ventured and was rewarded by his rich chuckle.

'Indeed I should, madam. But next time, I beg that you will remind me of it *before* we set out.'

That was too much. In a moment, both were laughing merrily. The gay mood, carefully nurtured by Richard, lasted throughout the wholesome supper which the landlady served for them, even though Jamie declined to share Richard's wine.

Jamie pushed her plate away. 'I could not eat another bite. The landlady must believe her guests are starved, I fancy.'

Richard smiled at her across the top of his wine-glass. 'Probably. And she has a reputation to maintain. The Castle is small, but well known for the quality it offers its guests. I must say that the claret is excellent.' He sipped it approvingly.

'Shall you ring for some brandy?' asked Jamie a little hesitantly. It was so difficult to know what to do in a shared room doubling as both bedchamber and supper room.

He cocked an impudent eyebrow. '*And* cigars, do you think?'

'Oh!' She gasped with laughter. 'Pray smoke, my lord, if you wish. I should not for the world spoil your enjoyment of your meal.' She made to rise to ring the bell.

'Jamie, don't you dare!' he warned dramatically.

She turned back and gave him an arched look.

He slowly finished his wine and replaced the glass on the supper table. 'I shall take a glass of brandy downstairs, madam wife, as a gentleman should. Shall I send the maid up to you, once the covers are cleared? You are tired, I know, and will wish to make ready for bed.'

Suddenly all the good humour left her face, and he kicked himself for his lack of tact. How thoughtless to remind her now...

'Thank you,' she said in that familiar strained voice. 'You are very good. I am a little tired, I admit.'

He made his way to the door. 'Go you to bed then, my dear. I shall try not to disturb you when I come up.'

Jamie did not know what to make of that last remark, but she decided there was no point in fussing over it. She would go to bed, as he had suggested, and wait to see what happened. Perhaps she would be able to sleep, in spite of not knowing... Perhaps he really would not wake her...

Two hours later she still lay awake, alone in the great bed, wondering how much longer he would wait before coming up. He would have consumed a considerable amount of brandy by now, surely? She did not know whether that would make matters worse, or better.

The flickering shadows on the wall betrayed the draught from the opening door. She closed her eyes and lay still. She heard the tiny fizz as he snuffed his candle and then the soft sound of his steps as he approached the bed to look at her in the glow of the firelight. She knew he was gazing down at her. And she knew she could no longer pretend. She opened her eyes:

'You should be asleep, wife,' he smiled softly at her.

'I c-could not,' she stammered in a whisper.

'No, I can see that.' He moved round to the other side of the great bed and began to pull back the covers.

Jamie stiffened.

'Since there is no sofa, it will have to be "bundling", I am afraid.' He smoothed the top sheet up and under the pillows on his side of the bed. Then he looked across at his wife. 'If you do not let out that breath you are holding, Jamie, you will surely expire, you know.'

Jamie gasped and turned the colour of the glowing embers in the hearth. 'I don't understand,' she managed at last.

'About "bundling"? It's an old country custom, my dear, for courting couples who have nowhere to go in winter but the…er…family bed. They are put into bed together but with the sheet between them so that they cannot…er…' He coughed. 'I believe that, in medieval days, the knights used a sword for the same purpose—but as I do not happen to have a sword by me this evening, I thought the sheet might serve instead.' He smiled mischievously at her and sat down on the bed, waiting for her embarrassment to subside.

It was some moments before she was able to look at him.

'That's better. You have nothing to fear, Jamie. We shall share the bed to sleep, that is all. Now, close your eyes, my dear.'

Obediently, she did so. She could hear him moving about as he removed his clothing to make ready for bed. She dared not look. Even when he came round to close the bedcurtains, she dared not look.

Presently, the bed dipped as his weight descended on it. He pulled the remaining bedcovers over himself and closed the curtains. Inside the great bed, it was quite dark. She began to feel the warmth from his body stealing through the thin sheet which separated them. She lay totally motionless, hardly daring to breathe.

'Goodnight, my dear,' he said gently. 'Sleep well.' Then he turned on his side and said no more. In less that five minutes, his breathing had become deep and regular. He was asleep!

What a fool she was! She should have known he would find a way. He always did. He had told her he would keep his word. She should have trusted him.

She continued to reproach herself for quite some

time, lying in the dark with her sleeping husband by her side. But at last, exhausted, she too fell asleep.

When she eventually awoke, it was broad day, and Richard was gone from the bed. Annie, the little maid, was drawing aside the bedcurtains and offering her a cup of chocolate.

'His lordship is out in the stables, milady,' supplied the girl helpfully. 'Not that it'll do much good, I'm afraid, seeing as how the mist is worse than ever this mornin'.'

It was mid-afternoon before it lifted. Richard hesitated before deciding to drive on to London. The mist might easily descend again. On the other hand, it would be better to take the risk. Jamie needed to be properly installed in Hardinge House as soon as possible. 'Bundling' was a temptation best not repeated!

Chapter Seventeen

It was very late indeed by the time they reached Hardinge House in Hanover Square. Although the remaining distance had not been great, there had been further patches of mist to delay them. But, by dint of perseverance and some good luck, they had eventually reached their goal.

For Richard, this final part of the journey had been very instructive. Although Jamie had been quite reluctant to speak, he had eventually acquired a tolerably good understanding of what her past life had been like.

Her father had treated her abominably. Her stepmother was quite unspeakable. No wonder Jamie had been so shocked to find Lady Calderwood at Harding.

And yet, in spite of everything, Jamie had emerged without bitterness from their shadow. His wife was—he now knew—quite as strong and courageous as he had believed. But she was also much more vulnerable. In all her one-and-twenty years, no one had really cared for her, except perhaps her long-dead mama. She needed to be loved and cherished, of that he was sure, but she was afraid to lower her guard in order to let it happen.

Hardly surprising, considering what had been done to her. He wondered whether he could succeed against such odds—and what it would mean to him if he did. To be sure, he had never before been daunted by a female's defences—the stronger they were, the greater the satisfaction in breaching them. He had never failed. But now… He could not be sure. Jamie was so different from his society women. All he could do was to work on her defences, slowly and carefully, in hopes that, eventually, they would crumble.

As the carriage pulled up, Richard looked down at his wife, who was sleeping peacefully with her head on his shoulder. He felt again a great yearning for her, but he managed to master his desire to touch her. 'Jamie,' he said softly. 'Wake up, my dear, we have arrived.'

'Oh!' Jamie came suddenly awake, blushing to find how she had slept. 'Oh, dear! I beg your pardon, Richard. How very uncomfortable for you.' She drew away from him, busying herself with her hat.

'My pleasure, ma'am. After all, we witless men have to have some uses, do we not?'

She smiled uncertainly, but at least her flush had subsided. A moment later, he was helping her down from the carriage.

Jamie was surprised, next morning, to find Annie opening her curtains and offering her a cup of chocolate. The abigail did not even look especially tired.

'Oh, it was nothing, my lady,' she responded airily to Jamie's question. 'We just plodded on until we got here, about five o'clock this morning. What will you wear today, m'lady?'

'The black silk again, I suppose. I have no choice. Lady Hardinge's gowns will need to be altered for me.'

'Beg pardon, my lady, but you do have a choice. Three gowns from Madame Françoise were delivered just before we left. I have taken the liberty of pressing one of them for you this morning.'

As Annie moved aside, Jamie saw that a new gown was hanging on the dressing-room door. Like the first, it was black and demure in style, with a high neckline and long sleeves, but this one was lightened by a little ruff of lace around the collar and some rather fine beaded embroidery. Jamie was delighted with it, and with Annie's ability to work such miracles.

Jamie was not in time to join her husband in the breakfast parlour. Instead, she had to content herself with exploring the house and interviewing the house-keeper.

It was well after mid-day when Richard returned.

'I have seen my people this morning,' he said, 'and set them to finding your father's agent in London. I have also arranged to offer a reward—discreetly—for information on Caleb. If he has gone to ground in the rookeries—'

'Rookeries?'

'I beg your pardon, Jamie, for my language. It means those parts of the city where the poor are crowded together in the most abject squalor, where no gentleman would dare to go alone. Many of the people there are totally honest, I'm sure, but a great many of them are villains—thieves, burglars, coiners—and worse. If Caleb is in hiding in London, that is probably where he will be. We shall have to trust to the greed of his neighbours to discover him.'

Jamie looked unconvinced. 'He may not be in London.'

'That is true, though London is certainly the best place to hide. I suppose he might have gone to your father's estate…'

'Or to Ralph Graves' estate at Bathinghurst,' Jamie put in, her voice almost a whisper.

'True, but in either place he would be much more difficult to conceal. Country people always know what is going on, I find.'

Jamie nodded. Calderwood had been just the same.

'If we have no news of Caleb in a few days, I will go to Calderwood myself,' said Richard decisively. He saw that all the colour had drained from Jamie's face. 'Don't worry, Jamie. I am quite capable of dealing with your father myself—and with Lady Calderwood, too, if it should come to that. If Caleb is there, I shall find him. And it is time I paid another visit to Calderwood. I have some unfinished business to discuss with your father.'

Jamie looked truly puzzled, but she said nothing.

Richard smiled down at her, admiring her tact. 'Now that you are my wife, Jamie, I should not conceal this from you, but it is not an edifying story. You see…my father… Towards the end of his life, my father was severely ill—not physically, you understand, but in his mind. His memory was…uncertain. Sometimes he did not recognise his own family. And he had unpredictable changes of mood. At times, he would be in a violent temper—even towards Mama. It was very…distressing.'

Jamie nodded, her eyes full of concern.

'At some time during those last months, my father made a very large loan to yours.'

Jamie gasped.

'There must have been some kind of document, of course, but I have not been able to find it. I think your father may have it.' He was looking increasingly grim. 'Without the evidence of that contract, I have been unable to recover the money.'

Jamie closed her eyes in mortification. Her father…yes, it was all very much in character. He would have borrowed the money to finance his gambling. And he would have had no qualms about imposing on a sick, old man to do it.

'I am so sorry, Richard,' she said, after a moment. 'If only I could…' A sudden, horrifying thought struck her. 'And yet you married me, his daughter— without a penny of a dowry.' She felt like crawling away to hide.

Richard could read his wife's emotions from her expressive face. Gently, he took both her hands in his. 'Jamie, you are in no way responsible for what your father may have done. And I told you once before— I have no need of a dowry. Oh, I admit that I will be glad when I have recovered the loan money—I have plans for extensive changes to the estate, which I cannot fund easily without that capital—but I am not yet running from my creditors, I promise you.' He smiled mischievously. 'Believe me, the estate is still wealthy—your mantua maker's bill will be paid.'

Jamie smiled back at him, but her guilt remained. What about the bill for those emeralds?

'Now, this afternoon,' continued Richard briskly, 'I plan to enquire in the clubs about your father's contacts in London. And Graves', too, for that matter. I'm afraid I shall have to do that by myself, Jamie.' He grinned. 'Unless you would like to dress as a boy again?'

Jamie burst out laughing. 'My lord,' she said, trying to look severe, 'you are quite incorrigible.'

'How true! How true!' He was still grinning, delighted that he had diverted her mind from her appalling family. 'Oh, by the bye, I forgot to mention... I met an old friend in the City this morning—Sir Edward Fitzwilliam.'

Jamie looked down, trying desperately to conceal her dismay.

'He is a very old friend of the Hardinges. I hope to introduce him to you, one day soon. And his daughter, Emma.' He laughed at some fleeting memory. 'She and I lived in each other's pockets when we were younger. She was a little urchin then, though, seeing her now, no one would believe that. She was the toast of London, last season. Blondes were all the crack.'

Jamie managed to mutter an appropriate, but non-committal reply. She had long ago determined to avoid Miss Fitzwilliam's company if she possibly could.

'It was a happy coincidence that we should meet,' Richard continued. 'I have been wishing to find you some congenial female company, and I can think of no one more suitable than Emma. She is a delightful girl, and most accomplished. And she has exquisite dress sense too. You could perhaps take her with you, when you go to visit Célestine, do you not think?'

Jamie did *not* think—but she could hardly admit to the fact, especially to him.

'Are you all right, Jamie?' asked Richard, seeing her strained expression, but unable to guess its cause.

'I have the headache a little,' admitted Jamie, not untruthfully, for a pain had begun to nag behind her eyes.

Richard was all polite concern. 'It's the after-effects of our dreadful journey, I expect.' He immediately summoned Smithers and insisted that Jamie rest in her chamber.

Soon Jamie lay on her bed, frustrated in her desires and in her curiosity, wondering what to do next.

She began to review her situation, overcoming her earlier emotional reactions and forcing herself to think logically. Emma Fitzwilliam could indeed have been the ideal bride for Richard. But, although he must have had many opportunities to offer for her, he had never taken any of them. For whatever reason, he had not married Emma. Had he really wished to? If so, why had he waited so long? It made no sense, except in the light of his mother's words that he had chosen Emma out of duty, not inclination.

In the end, he had married Jamie, not Emma. A little voice murmured that he had offered for her, too, out of duty not inclination, but she resisted its siren call towards dark despair. She would have none of it. Richard was married to her and, somehow, she was going to make their marriage a success.

When Jamie woke again it was evening. The headache was gone. She felt refreshed and renewed. The emotional turmoil over Emma Fitzwilliam was a distant memory, as if it belonged to another world.

'What time is it, Annie?' she asked brightly.

'It wants about an hour until dinner, my lady.'

'Excellent. I should like to take a bath first. Have you pressed my black evening gown?'

'Yes, my lady, and also the green one, in case you felt like wearing it this evening.' She bustled to the door. 'I'll go and see to the hot water now.'

Annie's words had conjured up the memory of Richard's tantalising smile as he had asked Jamie to order it. A shiver ran down her spine. Intrigued, and a little fearful, Jamie made for Annie's sanctum. The black silk evening dress, much adorned with beading and ruffles, hung just inside the door. On the far side, the green gown caught her eye, and she let out a little gasp of surprise.

She had chosen the sea-green silk and the pattern under Lady Hardinge's expert guidance, but she had not thought it could be quite so lovely. The style was simple enough—a ruched bodice, cut very low and edged with matching satin ribbon, a slim draped skirt, totally plain, to show the rippling silk to advantage, and short tucked sleeves, again edged with ribbon. Jamie reached out to touch it, relishing the luxurious feel of the delicate fabric in her fingers. As the skirt moved, the colour seemed to shimmer in the half-light.

'You are pleased, my lady?' Annie was a little out of breath from having run upstairs from the kitchen. 'Your bath water will be here directly.' She hurried into the bedchamber to make ready for its arrival.

Jamie stood transfixed, gazing at the glorious green gown. Richard had asked her to order it, and it was he who had suggested she wear it when they were alone, instead of black. Did she dare? Now? Tonight?

Her wandering thoughts were recalled to reality by the clank of copper water cans being carried in for her bath. She could decide while she bathed, she concluded, wavering uncharacteristically. After all, she did not know whether the dress would become her. It might be better to settle for the safe, black gown. Still, she might just try the green, to see how it looked, before resuming her mourning. Yes, that would be best. For, if she wore the green, what would Richard think—and do?

She settled back into the scented water, allowing the warmth to relax her muscles and the perfume of jasmine to invade her senses. She had never known such luxury. It seemed like a delicious dream. And she definitely did not want to wake up.

In no time at all, it seemed, Jamie was dressed, all but her gown, and her hair was arranged in a riotous tumble of loose curls. 'Better than that horrid bun, my lady?' asked Annie impudently, regarding her handiwork with satisfaction.

Jamie had to concede. While she still found her complexion overly pale and her hair colour unbecoming, she was forced to admit that, under Annie's skilful fingers, she had become just about presentable.

The abigail fetched the sea-green gown and slipped it carefully over her mistress's head before fastening the back. 'That does look well, m'lady, very well indeed,' she beamed. 'Now, if I was to add a green ribbon to your curls, it would be quite perfect.'

'Oh, but I am not going to wear this gown, Annie. I just wanted to try it on, to see whether it fitted properly, that's all. I shall, of course, wear the black.'

Annie snorted. 'Why?' she asked sharply, reverting for a second to her previous role of elder sister. 'You look beautiful in it, and his lordship specifically asked you to wear it. You told me so! Do you not wish to please your husband?'

'Annie! How dare you?' If Annie had forgotten their present relationship, Jamie had not. Annie blushed and looked away, mumbling an apology. 'It is for me to decide when I am ready to leave off my blacks, Annie, not you, nor even his lordship. What I told you about my conversation with his lordship was in confidence. I did not expect you, of all people, to abuse my trust. Oh, don't take on so,' she added more gently, patting the older woman's hand. 'I didn't intend to fly up into the boughs. It's just that…I am not ready yet.' On that unfathomable statement, she proceeded to remove the green dress.

Standing before the glass once more, Jamie admitted to herself that the sea-green gown had been much more flattering than the safe, black silk. For a second, she even toyed with the idea of changing again, but quickly overcame the impulse. She had no idea how Richard would react if she wore it, or what he might read into her choice. She did not yet know her husband well enough to be able to deal confidently with him. Until she was better prepared, she did not dare to make herself even more vulnerable than she already was. Squaring her shoulders, she left the room.

Richard was waiting in the saloon when she appeared. 'How splendid you look, my dear,' he smiled appreciatively. 'With your colouring, you make black seem the colour of choice, rather than of convention. Many women would envy you.'

Jamie blushed rosily, wondering traitorously whether his compliments were sincere. Black could look just as good on blue-eyed blondes, she would have thought.

He drew her to a seat and brought her a glass of sherry. As he took his place beside her, the faint fragrance of jasmine filled his senses for a second, temporarily halting his practised flow of words. She is like an exotic flower, he thought idly, so fragile, so easily crushed.

Just then, dinner was announced. He rose and offered her his arm.

Apprehensively, Jamie rested her fingertips lightly on his immaculate black sleeve, waiting for the jolt of electricity which happened every time she touched him. But, this time, it was different. As he smiled down into her eyes, a great feeling of warmth spread through her body, making all her nerves tingle expectantly, and heightening all her senses. It was not frightening, nor unpleasant. It was a feeling difficult to describe in words. All she knew was that she was waiting for something to happen, something beyond her wildest imaginings, something somehow magical.

Her husband stood quite still, looking down into her eyes and trying to unravel the emotions he saw there. He could have sworn that there was no hint of fear, even if there was not yet trust. But there was something else, hidden behind a misty veil which he could not penetrate.

Richard was recalled to himself by the butler's discreet cough from the doorway. 'Are you ready, my lady?' Richard said softly, covering her hand with his.

Jamie jumped. *Now* she had the bolt of lightning again. Her body quivered slightly. 'Oh, forgive me, my lord,' she said quickly, trying to make a recover. 'I was miles away for a moment.' She forced a warm smile for her husband, who had not removed his hand from hers. 'Shall we go in?'

Dinner was a light-hearted affair. Richard had taken the unusual step of having both places laid at one end of the long dining table, 'so that we do not have to be forever shouting to each other'. He set out deliberately to exercise all his considerable charm on her, regaling her with amusing tales of his childhood at Harding and of his less reprehensible adventures at Oxford.

Jamie allowed the warmth of his presence to envelop her like a cloak and smiled indulgently at his more madcap escapades. She hardly noticed that he refilled her champagne glass more than once, or that she drank it. It was all part of the dreamlike quality of the evening, which she attributed to their closeness and harmony, as her husband wove his potent spell around her.

'And now you must tell me more about you, my dear,' he said, topping up her glass once more and signalling to the servants to withdraw. 'Tell me about your escape from Calderwood. I've never understood quite how you managed to get away without being caught.'

Jamie was now beginning to feel more than a little light-headed, but she set about explaining, as best she could, trying to overcome her natural embarrassment about 'borrowing' her brother's clothes and stealing out at dead of night.

'How did you manage the horse? It's a wonder you weren't heard in the stable.'

'I was not in the stable long, just a moment to put a halter on Cara and lead her out. She's very good.'

'Just a halter?' repeated Richard, amazed.

'I… Yes, well, it was too dangerous to spend time saddling her. And besides, they would have known then that I was dressed as a boy. So I rode bareback and let Cara find her own way home. I hoped they would think she had got loose by accident.'

Richard was gazing at his wife with new respect. 'You can ride bareback?'

With a slightly giggly laugh, Jamie admitted that she could. 'Astride too, I'm afraid,' she added guiltily, 'but only on Cara. At least, I have never tried on any other horse.'

'Cara. Is she your horse?'

'Not exactly. She belonged to my mother, and I sort of adopted her. Strictly speaking, she belongs to my father, I suppose, though no one else would want to ride such an old horse.'

Richard rose to escort his wife to the saloon, happy to forgo the solitary splendour of port or brandy for her increasingly fascinating company. Life with Jamie would never be dull. As he offered her his arm, he said softly, 'As soon as we are out of mourning, I must see you properly mounted. There is a mare at Harding that might suit... Or should you like me to try to buy Cara for you?'

'Richard!' gasped Jamie, her eyes shining. 'Oh, Richard, would you? Oh, thank you so much!' She was so overjoyed at his generous offer that she forgot all remaining constraint and, throwing her arms round her husband's neck, hugged him impulsively. No one had ever been so kind to her before.

For a second, Richard's hands hovered over her back, but then he forced them to his sides again. Like an endearing child, he thought, as she pulled away from him, looking a little sheepish. But the lady in her soon returned. Her hands went automatically to her hair.

'No, it's perfect, believe me,' he said with a warm smile. 'Not a curl out of place.' As he spoke, he reached out to touch the single ringlet which hung down on to her bare shoulder and moved it an infinitesimal distance to the right. 'Absolutely perfect,' he repeated, not quite succeeding in his attempts to keep his voice light and playful.

Jamie had managed not to shiver this time, perhaps because his fingers had not actually touched her skin, but she felt again that weird tingling of every nerve. She could not read his expression either. He seemed to be admiring *her*, of all people, when he could have had any number of beautiful women, like Emma Fitzwilliam. And he was going out of his way to be gentle and amusing. Oh, she did not understand it, even as she basked in it.

'How are your hands coming along?' he asked, when they sat once more in the saloon. He reached out to lift her right hand for examination in a very practical way. 'Those calluses will take a while, I suppose, but at least the skin is losing its redness.' He placed her hand back on her lap, noticing that she seemed to be reacting a little strangely. 'Jamie—are you all right, my dear?'

'Oh…yes. Yes, perfectly. It's just…' She giggled a little. 'I feel a little strange, that's all, as if everything were becoming hazy. I can't explain.'

'I can, I'm afraid,' he said flatly, remembering the champagne, which had been meant to relax her, not to make her sleepy. Obviously he had given her too much. 'May I suggest you retire now? You will feel better in the morning.' His voice betrayed the harshness of his self-criticism.

'Oh!' Jamie was conscious of the sudden withdrawal of all that enveloping warmth. 'Certainly, if that is what you wish, my lord.'

With surprising swiftness, considering her slight inebriation, she rose, bobbed a tiny curtsy and was gone, leaving him standing alone by the fire, cursing his own stupidity but quite unable to account for his wife's devastatingly sudden change of mood.

Tears were streaming down Jamie's cheeks as she ran up the stairs to her room and threw herself on to the bed. How could he change so much, so quickly, from gay and laughing to hard and withering? To send her to bed like an errant child! It was no better than Calderwood, to be sure! She continued to sob bitterly into her pillows, perversely grateful that she could indulge in her woes in private for once.

Jamie's sense of justice returned eventually. Hardinge House was nothing like Calderwood. Here she was cosseted, her every whim immediately gratified…except one. She wanted a true marriage, while her husband, however friendly he might be, seemed determined to keep her at arm's length. But he had wanted her before their wedding. Why not now?

Her inner devil whispered that he probably preferred the embraces of serving-girls to those of his lawful wife, maybe even unwilling serving-girls. No. No, that could not be, for he had not taken advantage of her when he had had the opportunity. She refused to believe him base.

And yet she could not account for his behaviour now. It was almost as if he were afraid of her. He never came into her chamber of his own free will— and he never stayed there a moment longer than necessary, even when he was forced to come. What if she were to go into his chamber instead?

She half-rose, wondering whether she had the courage to do such a thing. Why not? She was his wife! She tidied her hair before the glass, noting that the signs of her self-indulgent weeping had almost gone. Then she slipped her feet back into her evening shoes and crossed into their sitting-room.

There was no sound from Richard's chamber. He could be asleep. He might even be angry at being disturbed. She hesitated a moment. Then, squaring her shoulders and swallowing hard, she knocked softly and opened the door into Richard's room.

The fire blazed in the grate, the huge canopied bed was turned down and the brandy decanter stood ready on the table. But apart from those, the room was empty.

In the silence, the clock on the mantelshelf chimed twice. Two in the morning! How long had she lain in despair on her bed? And where was her husband?

Assailed by thoughts of where he might be—and with whom—Jamie ran from the room.

Chapter Eighteen

Next morning, Jamie forced herself out of bed at the usual hour, in spite of overwhelmingly low spirits and an aching head. How much champagne had she drunk last evening? She supposed that must be the chief cause of the terrible state she was in, although it could equally well be the shock of finding Richard absent in the middle of the night.

Annie took one look at her mistress's face and disappeared, returning five minutes later with a glass of murky liquid. 'Drink this, my lady,' she advised sternly. 'It will settle your stomach—and your head.'

Jamie bridled. 'What is it?'

'Sovereign remedy for the after-effects of overindulgence, m'lady,' said Annie smoothly, making little attempt to hide her disapproval. 'The valet's secret potion. If you swallow it quickly, you won't hardly taste it.'

Jamie flushed deeply at the thought that the whole household knew of her predicament. 'You asked Gregg for this for me?' She was outraged.

'No one else knows, m'lady. Gregg was making it

for his lordship in any case, so he just made a little more than usual. Do drink it.' Her disapproval had been replaced by concern now.

Jamie sniffed at the cloudy liquid. 'Ugh!' Then, gritting her teeth, she tossed it off. 'Good God!' she spluttered, after a moment of gasping for breath. 'What on earth is in it?'

Annie shrugged. 'Gregg will not say. He won't let anyone watch when he mixes it either, so your secret really is safe.'

After a few minutes of distinctly odd churnings in her stomach, Jamie found she was indeed beginning to feel better. Time to satisfy her curiosity. 'I am surprised my husband needs such a remedy this morning, Annie. I had not noticed that he drank much at dinner last night.'

The abigail commented airily, 'Oh, his lordship never overindulges at home, my lady. At his clubs, it's different of course, especially when they're playing deep. Last night, he...' She stopped, flushed, and began to brush Jamie's hair.

Gaming! No wonder his chamber had been empty. Dear God! If Richard were addicted to the tables, who knew how it might end? Jamie knew well enough that most of the Calderwood financial problems had resulted from her father's insatiable appetite for gaming. Richard certainly lived well, but surely no estate, however large, could withstand continued losses? Especially after that iniquitous loan to her father. What if...?

She forced herself to halt this totally unwarranted descent into pessimism. One night at the tables—and she knew of only this one—did not mark her husband out for a gamester, even if she dearly wished that he did not gamble at all. And at least it was better than what she had suspected last night.

She found herself wondering again if he kept a mistress, like so many men of his rank. A man who was past thirty could not be expected to live like a monk, even if he were now married. A cold lump settled in the pit of her stomach, like a lead weight, at the thought of Richard in the arms of another woman, any other woman.

Annie's bustling activity recalled her to the real world. She must join Richard at breakfast as if nothing had happened. She must try to use their time together to re-establish their rapport.

But there was no need, for her husband had already reached precisely the same conclusion and was a much more skilled practitioner of the art than she. He smiled a little apologetically as she took her seat at the breakfast table. 'Morning, m'dear.' Richard's greeting was quite breezy, considering the night he had had. 'Are you well this morning? I fancied I should make you an apology for plying you with a little too much champagne last night but, to be frank, you look to be blooming on it! Should I repeat the offence, do you think?'

'If I am blooming, it is thanks to Gregg's magic potion.'

'Works miracles, don't it? I was wondering why I seemed to have had short measure this morning. I shall have to speak to Gregg.'

'Oh, no, please,' gasped Jamie, blushing scarlet at the thought. 'If you—'

Richard grinned wickedly at her. 'I shall have to tell him that he must on no account provide his remedy to my wife when she is foxed. She should be left to endure the consequences of her own excesses. An appropriate penance, don't you agree?'

'Oh, by all means, my lord—on condition that you impose the same penance on yourself, of course,' Jamie retorted. 'For sin does not distinguish between the sexes, does it?' she added, with a sweet smile and a decidedly warlike glint in her eyes.

Richard raised both hands in token of surrender. 'I yield to your superior force, madam. Believe me, without Gregg's ministrations this morning, I should not be sitting here.'

'Indeed?'

He had the grace to look a little guilty and to admit that he had been rather too self-indulgent on the previous evening, both in terms of his gambling and his wine. 'But, thanks to the invaluable Gregg, we are both able to face the world again. And we shall have the whole day to ourselves. My agent will not send his report until this evening, and there's nothing more I can do until it arrives.' He smiled generously. 'So— I suggest we make that trip to Westminster Abbey. Can you be ready in half an hour?'

Jamie was just about to don the sables once more, when a maid brought up a message that some visitors were with his lordship in the blue saloon and her presence was requested. Intrigued, Jamie allowed Annie to hang up the sables again. It was very strange that Richard should be prepared to receive callers while the family was in deep mourning. 'I wonder who it may be?' she said almost to herself as she checked her appearance in the glass.

Richard came to take her hand as she entered the saloon. 'I have a delightful surprise for you, my dear. I want you to meet Sir Edward Fitzwilliam and his daughter Emma, two of my dearest friends.' He led her across to the visitors, continuing cheerfully, 'We have never stood on ceremony with one another, you must know. Why, Emma and I were thick as inkle-weavers when we were children.'

Jamie forced her leaden feet to move across the room to meet the visitors. If Richard noticed that she was pale, she hoped he would put it down to shyness.

The introductions were rapidly completed. Sir Edward was a large hearty gentleman, rather red-faced, which Jamie attributed to a love of good living. He took Jamie's hand in his own much larger one and expressed himself delighted to make her acquaintance. He had been intrigued to hear of Richard's sudden marriage, he admitted, but now that he had met the new Lady Hardinge, he could understand it perfectly.

Jamie was a little embarrassed by such fulsome compliments, especially from the father of the girl who had been Richard's intended bride, but she could detect no hint that Sir Edward's words were at all insincere. She smiled prettily, if a little shakily, and said all that was proper.

Miss Fitzwilliam seemed to be as open and friendly

as her father, both in her congratulations to the newly-weds and in her hopes that she and the new Countess might come to know each other better. Although Jamie agreed readily to the proposal, for to refuse would have been churlish, she shrank inwardly at the thought of friendship with the lovely Miss Fitzwilliam. On closer inspection, she proved to be everything that Jamie was not—tiny, blonde, blue-eyed, apparently possessed of every perfection of form and manner, and with the easy confidence which comes from long experience of the society world.

By contrast, Jamie felt large and clumsy, and ill-prepared for her new elevated station in life. No wonder Richard had planned to marry such a pattern card of feminine virtue! Jamie's small stock of confidence seemed to be ebbing away as she watched the easy intercourse between her husband and this lovely girl. It had been more comfortable to be a gardener's boy.

'I am so glad you have both come up to London, Richard, for otherwise we should not have seen you until the Season is over.' Miss Fitzwilliam had adroitly avoided asking directly why they had come, though the question was clearly uppermost in her mind.

'I had to come on business, Emma, so naturally my wife accompanied me. I am sorry I shall not have the pleasure of waltzing with you this Season, but no doubt there will be so many other gentlemen vying for your hand that you will not notice my absence.'

'Rogue!' exclaimed Miss Fitzwilliam. 'That is nonsense, and you know it! Not one of them waltzes half as well as you do.'

'Well, my dear,' interrupted her father, 'you will have to make the best of it, for Richard cannot possibly dance while he is in mourning. Perhaps that will encourage you to pay a little more attention to the eligible bachelors among your cavaliers instead of giving your hand to all comers. This will be your fourth Season, my girl. Beware! You are almost on the shelf!' It was clear from the indulgent smile which accompanied this warning that Sir Edward did not believe a word of it.

'I have paid attention to them, Papa,' protested the young lady, throwing him a look of reproach. 'You know that most of them covet my fortune rather than my person. I do so wish to marry a man I can both love and esteem, rather than one I must suspect of base motives,' she said a little wistfully. 'I suppose that means I shall have to marry someone with a fortune of his own, like Richard.'

'Well, we'll see, we'll see,' said Sir Edward placidly, smiling at his daughter. 'I have no wish to see you leave my roof, I'll readily admit.'

'Nor I,' echoed Richard. 'You must find a husband within ready striking distance of Harding, Emma, so that we may continue just as before.'

Suddenly, Miss Fitzwilliam laughed wickedly. 'I can tell you now, Richard, that Papa once had ambitions in your direction.'

'Emma!' Her father started to cough and turn very red.

She continued regardless. 'I had to tell him that we should not suit. A woman cannot marry a man who has been like a brother to her. We should have strangled each other before a month was up. Do you not agree, Richard?' Her eyes were dancing with suppressed mirth.

Richard laughed too, and nodded, moving to refill Sir Edward's glass. He threw a conspiratorial glance at Jamie and said, 'I doubt we should have lasted a week.'

Jamie was astonished. Richard did not look in the least embarrassed. Perhaps he was relieved to learn that Miss Fitzwilliam would have refused him?

Sir Edward had recovered his composure as he downed his sherry. 'Heaven preserve me from my wilful daughter,' he said, shaking his head. 'My only consolation is that she behaves with the utmost propriety when she is in company.'

'I am delighted to hear it, sir,' said Richard with an indulgent smile. 'And I know it to be true. I am only sorry that she and Jamie will not be able to go into society together—at least, not this Season. But perhaps they may become better acquainted in private. I am sure Jamie would welcome a chance to have a friend of her own age and station.' He looked enquiringly at his wife.

'"Jamie"?' repeated Miss Fitzwilliam, turning to Jamie with a friendly smile. 'Forgive my impertinence, ma'am, but may I ask about your unusual name? I have never heard of "Jamie" as a lady's name before.'

'My given name is Jessamyne,' admitted Jamie with a genuine, if rueful smile. Emma Fitzwilliam was no rival, that much was now clear. And she might even become a friend. '"Jamie" was a name given me by my mama. I much prefer it to Jessamyne.'

'No wonder,' added Richard with a grin. 'And I hope you will allow Emma to use it, my dear. I should hate to see you both standing on ceremony, such old friends as we are.' He raised his eyebrows expectantly.

'Of course,' conceded Jamie immediately.

'And you must call me "Emma", of course,' beamed that young lady. 'I do so hope we shall become friends.'

Jamie returned her smile with interest. 'I am sure we shall,' she said, with decision.

It was late afternoon by the time they returned from their delayed expedition to Westminster Abbey. Richard had insisted on taking Jamie all over the building, exploring every corner. And in the face of his determined good-humour, she had found herself enjoying every moment in his company and forgetting her lingering doubts.

When Jamie came upstairs to change for dinner, she saw that Annie had left the green gown in view, as a silent reminder. No such hint was necessary now. Jamie had already decided that she must take the initiative with her husband—somehow—and that it could no longer be delayed, if the distance between them were ever to be bridged. Waiting could only make matters worse for their marriage.

Not for the first time, she wished she had more experience of dealing with men, as she embarked on what would, she fervently hoped, be a seduction.

Heavens, she did not even know how to flirt, far less seduce! Still, if she let her love lead her... Love?

As she stood gazing fixedly at the green silk gown, she at last admitted to herself how she felt about her husband. She loved him! And now, she could see that it had been so for weeks, perhaps months. No wonder she had accepted his proposal, though all her finer instincts had prompted her to refuse him. He might have been better off with someone more like Emma Fitzwilliam, but he had chosen Jamie instead, and she could never give him up. She was able to recognise, finally, that her heart would be broken if she lost him now.

These moments of soul-searching served to strengthen her nerve for the encounter ahead. She would have to behave in a way she had never done before, never in all her life. And she must be prepared for her husband to reject her advances, as he had seemed ready to do every time the possibility of intimacy arose.

She had supposed that he still desired her, but what if he did not? Perhaps he was even thinking about someone else? She swallowed hard, trying to slow the thumping of her heart. She had to know the truth, she decided, whatever the cost to her self-esteem. If he did not want her as a true wife, she would be ready to settle for whatever lesser status might be on offer. Galling though it was to her pride, she knew there was no other choice for her. She could never leave him now.

Annie was allowed free rein over her mistress's appearance that evening and surpassed even her own high standards. The sea-green gown fitted Jamie to perfection, gliding over her slender figure, yet emphasising her feminine curves. With the matching ribbon threaded through her loose titian curls and Richard's emerald pendant clasped round her neck, she looked the complete antithesis of the pasty-faced dowd of Calderwood Hall.

Annie sighed as Jamie started to descend the stairs. 'Good luck,' she whispered softly.

Richard turned at the sound of the door opening and then stood transfixed as Jamie entered the room. He had not expected this. If she had been blooming before, she was now quite breathtaking. His heart lurched and began to beat very fast. Pushing aside all the questions which rose in his mind, he strode across the room to take both her hands and raise them, one by one, to his lips, drinking in the faint breath of her jasmine scent. This time she did not pull away. He felt a slight pressure of her fingers as she smiled up into his eyes.

'My dear, you look quite lovely tonight,' he began, a little uncertainly, searching for the proper words, 'and that green is exactly right, even more becoming than the black.'

She wondered for a moment if he were teasing her, but no, his eyes were warm and serious, perhaps too serious. 'I am glad you approve, my lord,' she answered rather primly, but smiling still.

'Madam, you tempt me with your words,' he said, with a mischievous twitch of the lips, trying to assume a stern tone of voice.

Jamie frowned a little, unsure of his mood, but did not pull away.

'Have you forgotten so soon, my dear, what I promised your punishment would be, if you continued to address me so formally?' He had forced his black brows together into a frown which was totally at variance with the sparkle in his eye.

'Oh,' gasped Jamie, 'but you would not!' She tried unsuccessfully to retreat. He was clasping her hands too tightly. 'Richard, you—'

'Better,' he pronounced solemnly, kissing her hands again and looking warmly into her eyes, 'but if I were you, I should not hazard too much on my husband's capacity for mercy. I pride myself on never making idle threats.'

'I had not thought that applied to your wife.' She allowed him to lead her to a seat and turned to look him full in the face. 'Does it?'

'Now, what am I supposed to say to that?' he teased. 'If I tell you that I shall never lay a finger on you, I shall be inviting you to become a disobedient, unmanageable wife. But if I promise to force your obedience with threats and violence, I risk losing your trust altogether.' He sought and held her gaze. 'Advise me, wife. What should I say?'

Jamie knew instinctively how she must reply. She did not hesitate. 'You should remind me of my marriage vows, husband, to love, honour and obey. You should ask me if I have so quickly forgotten all that I then promised.'

'And have you?' His voice had become suddenly husky.

She looked deep into his blue eyes, searching for some sign which would reveal what he wanted her to say. She could not be totally sure of what she saw there, but she quickly decided that she had no choice any more. The offer must be made—now—while her courage was high. In a low voice, which surprised her with its firmness, she said, 'I married you most willingly, my lord husband, and I shall keep my wedding vows—every single one—if I am permitted to do so.'

His sharp intake of breath proved that he had not misunderstood the import of her words. His cobalt eyes glowed with a new fierceness as he looked down into hers.

Richard could not tear his eyes from the green ones gazing unflinchingly into his. She was offering herself to him in the only way she could and waiting, totally vulnerable, like a cornered doe, to learn her fate—whether her husband would accept or reject her.

Richard's hand was gripping Jamie's so tightly that her fingers were starting to go numb, but she did not move a muscle to pull away.

Richard was quite oblivious of what he was doing. He was lost in those limpid eyes.

A discreet knock on the door broke the spell. 'Dinner is served, my lady,' intoned the butler and then quickly withdrew.

'Damn,' muttered Richard, releasing her hand. He rose from the sofa and turned to find that Jamie was still seated, apparently lost in thought. Had she even heard the butler's words?

'Jamie,' he said softly.

She looked up into his face and rose, a little unsteadily. Her eyes seemed to be brimming with tears.

Richard felt an answering tenderness welling up within him. Did she believe he was rejecting her? For a moment, he was at a loss for words as he gently cupped her face in his hands and gazed at her tempting lips. When he eventually spoke, his voice was very serious. 'Jamie, my dear, are you sure? Do you know what you are doing? I gave you my word, and you have it still. You do not need to do this.'

A single tear overflowed, running unheeded down her cheek and on to his hand. 'But I do, Richard,' she said simply. 'You gave me your word. Now I give it back to you, if you are willing to receive it.'

Richard found he had no words any more. Trying desperately to master the tide of passion which was threatening to drown him, he kissed her lips, gently at first, tasting her sweetness, but then, as she began to respond to him, with increasing fervour, pulling her tightly against his hardened body. For what seemed an eternity, both were lost in the whirling waters of that deepening kiss, until the realisation that Jamie's legs were no longer able to support her brought Richard back to a sense of where they were.

He tore his mouth away from hers, gasping for breath. Her eyes were huge and brilliant in her pale face. Her body was trembling. Without his arm around her, she would have fallen.

'I think we should go in to dinner, wife,' he began prosaically, trying to regain control of his treacherous body.

Jamie responded, not to his words, but to the tender

inflection in his voice and the warmth and desire in his eyes. He did want her—and he would make her his true wife, she was sure of it now. For the moment, it was enough. 'As you command, husband,' she said, bowing her head in mock obedience. 'Will you give me your arm?'

For Jamie, the meal passed in a dreamlike haze. She picked at the food served to her and drank a little—a very little—of the champagne which accompanied it. Although she was once again seated on her husband's immediate right, they did not touch once throughout the meal, for both were fully aware of the dangers which lay along that path. None the less, Jamie felt as if the warmth and tension in his body were radiating out to hers, making her nerves tingle and setting a whole flock of doves fluttering in her belly.

She could not know how much the play of these emotions enhanced her looks. Not daring to touch, Richard feasted his gaze on her instead—the brilliant eyes, the petal-soft complexion framed by silky curls, the wide mouth, ever so slightly bruised from his kisses, the elegant column of her neck tempting him down towards the beautiful breasts rising above her low-cut gown. The vision fired his flesh. He wanted nothing more than to slam his chair back from the table and carry her upstairs on the instant.

He tried instead to concentrate on the food on his plate and the wine in his glass. Presently, the second course was served. He watched as Jamie toyed with a little vanilla cream. Her wineglass, never more than half-full at the outset, was barely touched. 'Will you take a little more champagne, my dear?' he asked politely, ready to summon the butler from his post.

Jamie shook her head, murmuring something incoherent. The meal was clearly becoming something of an ordeal for her.

Richard threw down his damask napkin. 'I am afraid we are neither of us very hungry tonight, my dear,' he said, in his best conversational voice, starting to rise from the table. As he escorted Jamie into the hallway he said, in a voice loud enough to be heard by the servants, 'I fear the excesses of the last few days are taking their toll. Will you allow me to suggest we retire early? We shall have another long day tomorrow, I fancy.'

Jamie was just able to nod slightly but, luckily, not conscious enough to be embarrassed by the blatant invitation in his eyes. She allowed herself to be led up the stairs to their suite where, magically, neither abigail nor valet was to be seen.

Richard kicked the door shut and pulled her roughly into his arms, covering first her face and then her neck with urgent kisses. She arched into him, helpless, her hands gripping his strong body for support.

He made to pick her up and then stopped, placing his hands on her shoulders so that she was forced to face him. 'Jamie. Oh, Jamie, if you want to change your mind, you must do it now, else it will be too late.'

She shook her head, lifting her mouth for his kiss. There would be no going back now.

He lifted her in his arms then and carried her

through the connecting door to his chamber, to lay her on the huge canopied bed. She watched, in something of a daze, as he methodically snuffed all the candles in the room, leaving only the flickering firelight to cast ghostly shadows across his handsome face.

He came to her then, stretching out beside her on the bed as he had done once before, and drawing her into the encircling strength of his arms. He held her close, resting his lips on the top of her head to drink in the jasmine fragrance of her hair.

'Oh, Jamie,' he whispered, pulling the pins out of her hair one by one so that her curls fell free on to the pillow, 'how beautiful you are, my little wife.'

Then he began to kiss her, more gently than before, for he knew he must not allow his own desire to dictate the pace, lest he frighten her.

But he had reckoned without Jamie's own responses. She had loved and desired him for so long that, innocent though she was, the first touch of his hand on her breast set her whole body aflame. Her every sense was alive to his presence, eagerly responding to his lead as her clothes disappeared, one by one. She was no longer in the real world, but in a sensuous paradise where she felt as if she were floating towards oblivion.

Richard had stopped kissing her. Her eyes flew open to find he was simply gazing at her, with loving tenderness. Apart from the emeralds at her throat and in her ears, she was now naked, her body glowing rosily in the warm light. The glint of desire in his eyes was unmistakable. Jamie found she was blushing all over. Without thinking, she tried to cover herself.

He laughed throatily, pushing her hands gently back to the bed. 'Your blushes make you even more beautiful, love. Do not try to hide yourself from me, please. Just let me look at you.'

In spite of herself, she felt her blushes deepen, but she no longer tried to resist. 'But you...' she whispered, half-accusingly, her eyes wandering to his body which was still fully clothed, apart from coat and waistcoat.

Richard guided her hands to the buttons of his shirt. 'Will you help me then, love?' he asked softly.

A shiver ran through her body as she undid a button with clumsy fingers, touching the bare skin beneath. He looked at her in alarm, covering her hands with his so that she shivered again, more noticeably than before.

'Jamie, why are you still afraid of me? I swear to you there is no need.'

Jamie's heart turned over at the catch in his voice and the anxiety in his eyes. She smiled shyly up at him, dropping a tiny kiss on the back of his hand where it clasped hers. 'I am not afraid of you, Richard, nor have I ever been. It is just that, whenever I touch you, I...' She broke off, blushing fiercely again, and buried her face in his shirt front.

'Dear God, how could I have been so blind?' he moaned, as he began to kiss her deeply once more, pushing her on to her back so that he could tear off his own clothes without lifting his mouth from hers.

Then there were no more words, only the nerve-tingling excitement of touching and teasing, stroking and suckling. Her breasts seemed to swell to fill his ministering hands, the rosy peaks hardening beneath the expert touch of his fingers and his lips. The fluttering in her belly had become a churning, longing ache.

She moaned, pleadingly, as his fingers explored lower, discovering just how ready she was. That sound was almost his undoing as he parted her thighs and moved to enter her. She arched towards him, unconsciously raising her hips to meet him.

'Forgive me, my love,' he whispered hoarsely, covering her mouth with his as he thrust deeply into her soft warmth. He heard her gasp beneath him and saw her eyes fly open, wide with shock. He held himself totally still, wishing he could draw all her pain into himself, could see the return of desire to her eyes. 'Forgive me, darling,' he said again, achingly sad.

The pain quickly melted away as Jamie became more and more conscious of the beloved warmth within her and of her overpowering need to be closer to him. She tried to shake her head, to tell him there was nothing to forgive, but she was not given the chance to speak.

The moment he saw the love and passion returning to her eyes, he took her mouth again in fierce possession.

And then he began to move within her, in long slow strokes, stretching his control to breaking point as he strove to bring her to the fulfilment he longed to give her, ruthlessly suppressing his own needs as he concentrated on fuelling Jamie's rising passion.

She moaned again, writhing beneath him. 'Oh, Richard. Please,' she pleaded incoherently. The tension was mounting in her body, begging for release, driving her to undiscovered heights of awareness, until finally it exploded in spasms of kaleidoscopic ecstasy.

As the shudders of completion racked her, Richard's rigid control was shattered. He drove into her one last time to find his own release and collapsed on top of her. His selfless consideration for his virgin wife had brought him to a climax which fulfilled him in a way he had never known. He had not thought such paradise existed, this side of heaven.

After a moment, he rolled on to his side, bringing Jamie with him, waiting for the pounding of their hearts to slow. They lay together for a long time, intimately entwined, savouring the glowing aftermath of their lovemaking. Only the sound of their breathing broke the stillness. At last Richard stirred. He needed to hear her speak, to hear her words of love and reassurance, but still he could find no words of his own. So, softly, he kissed her bruised lips as if to ask forgiveness for her pain.

She looked at him in wide-eyed wonder. 'I never thought…' she began tremulously. 'Oh, Richard! Is it always like this?'

'Between us, it will always be so, I hope,' he vowed tenderly, stroking her cheek. 'Darling Jamie, my little love, forgive me for hurting you. That, at least, will never come again, I promise you.'

She was puzzled for a second. Then she smiled, radiantly, allowing her free hand to stray down the length of his back. 'It is already forgotten,' she said, daring to explore lower.

He rolled quickly on to his back to trap her wandering hand. 'Madam wife,' he grinned, 'I am sure that you will wish me to return you to your own bed before morning. But if you continue with such tantalising behaviour, you are like to be disappointed.'

She transferred her hand to his chest and began to walk her fingers down towards his flat stomach, an age-old smile on her face. 'Disappointed?' she repeated innocently. 'No. I don't think so.'

Chapter Nineteen

The house was already stirring when Richard carried Jamie back to her own bedchamber, tucking her lovingly beneath the covers. 'Sleep now, my love,' he insisted gently, smiling as he remembered just how much she needed it. 'I shall return later when you are rested.' He started to leave.

'Richard?' She sounded anxious. She should have no reason to be so.

'What is it, darling?' He turned quickly at her question and came to sit down on the edge of the bed, not touching her, though his gaze travelled lovingly over her face, seeking for the cause of her concern.

'What are you going to do?'

He looked suddenly grim. 'I am going to visit my agent again. He reports that he may have discovered who your father's London man is. I admit I am not very hopeful, but this is the only lead I have. Please understand, Jamie. I must do this alone. It might not be safe for you to come.'

'I do understand, Richard. But please take care.'

'I shall.' His gaze softened once more. She really

was an exceptional woman, in more ways than one. He grinned mischievously. 'Besides, I need my wife to be fully recovered before this evening, lest she...er...lack the energy for more enjoyable pursuits.' Ignoring her obvious confusion, he reached forward to pick up her hand for a gentle kiss, affectionate but with the promise of passion to come. Tonight, he would slip the Hardinge betrothal ring on to her hand. The diamond belonged there now, surely? 'Until this evening, then?'

'Yes,' she whispered. 'Until this evening.' She snuggled down contentedly and he left her to sleep the morning away.

It was early afternoon before she was wide awake, bathed and ready to face the world. But there was nothing pressing for her to do. Hardinge House ran perfectly smoothly without any intervention from her. Emma Fitzwilliam would not call again until the morrow, so there was no one but the servants for her to talk to. Richard's unpleasant errand would surely keep him occupied for hours.

Books and letter-writing held no attractions for her—this was no time for quiet pursuits. Jamie felt so vibrant, so full of life and love, that she wanted to sing and dance and shout from the rooftops. She longed for a good gallop, to feel the wind in her hair and the power of a horse beneath her. None of that was possible, not for a lady in mourning, so she decided to make do with fresh spring air and exercise— a good, brisk walk in the park. She would look for ideas for a spring garden at Harding.

* * *

An hour later, much invigorated and still bubbling
with happiness, she was just about to cross the square
to return to the house, when a closed carriage over-
took her and drew up beside the flagway a little
ahead. Her heart sank as she recognised it—
Calderwood! Her glorious day was suddenly clouded.

'My lady, perhaps we should go back to the
house?' urged Annie. But her warning words were too
late. A white head was poking out of the window and
calling to Jamie.

'Papa!' cried Jamie, shocked by the sudden encounter. Her mind was in a whirl.

'Come here, girl,' he commanded. 'You don't expect me to shout across the square, do you?'

Automatically obedient to her father's penetrating
voice, Jamie approached the carriage, trying to read
her father's stern expression. What was he doing
here?

'That's better,' he said curtly, 'but it's cold with
the glass down. Come, step inside for a moment, I
need to speak to you.'

Jamie hesitated and then backed away a little.

'It's about your sisters,' he added, swinging open
the door. Her father had drawn away from the door
as he spoke, so that she could no longer see his face
in the shadowy interior. 'Come, do as I bid you!'

His insistence made Jamie increasingly suspicious.
'Papa—'

As she turned round to look for Annie, she realised
that the two grooms had climbed down from the back
of the carriage and were almost upon her. She started
to run, but they seized her by the arms and bundled

her through the open door before she had gone more than a few steps. A sudden violent movement of the carriage threw her back on to the seat. Her father calmly leaned across her to pull the door closed while the coach gathered speed out of the square.

'What are you doing, Papa?' she cried.

'What I should have done long ago,' he growled fiercely. 'Making sure you do your duty by your family.'

'But I am married, Papa,' she pleaded desperately. 'You know that I am. My husband wrote to you.'

'Your marriage was illegal and will be annulled,' he stated flatly. 'I gave my word that you would marry Ralph Graves, and I intend to see my pledge redeemed. You may forget your precious Lord Hardinge. He is lost to you now.'

Jamie looked round anxiously for some means of escape from the swaying vehicle. Anything was preferable to letting her father carry her off to Ralph Graves! The only option would seem to be to throw herself out of the carriage. She might be injured in the process, but even that was preferable to what her father intended for her. She began to edge towards the door.

'You may be easy, my dear,' said her father sarcastically. 'There will be no more escaping. My servants will foil any attempt you might dare to make. There is no hope for you in that direction, you may be certain. Who would dare to help a wilful girl against the lawful claims of her father?'

There was no point in saying that the lawful claims of her husband should come first. Her father was obsessed with preventing her from thwarting his plans. Logic would never reach him, not from her.

Jamie forced herself to sit back in her seat, closed her eyes and tried to regain control of her thoughts. She must keep calm if she were to have any chance of escaping from this nightmare.

She took a deep breath, willing her pulse to slow. Annie had seen what happened, she told herself. Annie would tell Richard. Surely he would come to find her? She held tightly to that hope, a talisman and a shield against despair, as the Calderwood carriage sped out of London.

Annie stood petrified on the flagway, watching in disbelief as the Calderwood horses were whipped up and the carriage rattled off at top speed. She had recognised the white head, and now she knew the thin hand which reached out to pull the door shut. Sir John—and he was kidnapping Miss Jamie!

She tried to shout, but there was no one about to heed her cries. Besides, who would take the part of an abigail against a gentleman? Her only hope of finding help would be Hardinge House, so she picked up her skirts and ran as fast as she could round the square, banging urgently on the knocker of the front door.

The butler opened the door in the midst of her hammering. He looked more than a little taken aback to find only a servant standing there. It was a flagrant breach of etiquette. 'Whatever is the matter, Miss Smithers?' he asked, moving aside to let her enter. 'Where is her ladyship?'

'Is his lordship back yet?' gasped Annie, trying to master her distress.

'Why, no. He sent a message for her ladyship, just after you went out, to say he would be late. He was being taken to meet someone who had important information.'

'Oh, God!' moaned Annie. 'What are we to do?'

'I think you had better come and sit down, Miss Smithers,' said the butler kindly. 'Perhaps I can be of some assistance?'

It did not take her long to tell him what had happened. He was suitably concerned, but he had little practical help to offer for recovering Jamie, other than the obvious remedy of sending to ask for his lordship at his clubs.

No trace of Lord Hardinge was to be found. It was more than three interminable hours before he eventually returned.

'My lord,' began Annie, dropping a slight curtsy as she hurried across the hall, 'thank God you are come back!'

Richard recognised immediately that her words could mean nothing but trouble. 'Annie!' he cried, using his wife's mode of address for the first time, for it was his wife who was uppermost in his mind. 'What is the matter?'

'She is gone, my lord!' exclaimed Annie somewhat vaguely, preparing to launch into her tale of woe.

Richard raised a hand to stop her in mid-flow. 'Come into the library. Now, Annie,' he continued anxiously as he closed the door, 'tell me what has happened.'

As she explained, the colour drained from his face and his jaw clenched tight. His anguish was almost unbearable when he realised just how much time he had lost. The trail would be well-nigh cold by now. Pray God her father had taken her to Calderwood. If she were anywhere else, he might never find her.

'There is no chance that my wife went willingly, is there?'

'No, my lord, none,' answered Annie immediately. 'She was forced into the carriage, and her father drove off without even closing the carriage door. The coachman whipped up the horses as soon as her ladyship was inside. It was obviously pre-arranged.'

'But why on earth are they still pursuing her?' he cried angrily. 'There must be more to this than injured pride.'

Annie shook her head helplessly.

'No matter,' Richard continued, without giving Annie time to respond. 'We can resolve that later. There is no time to lose now. First we must find her, and get her out of her father's clutches. By God, if he...' He broke off abruptly, refusing to allow his emotions to rule him when there was so much to be done to rescue Jamie.

He then proceeded to issue precise and detailed instructions to his servants about his imminent departure. In barely twenty minutes, his carriage was on its way to Calderwood Hall.

Their progress was slow. The streets of London were thronged with traffic. It seemed to take hours to make their way out of the city, in spite of all the coachman's efforts. They would make only slow progress after darkness fell, especially if the sky did not clear.

Richard tried to make the time pass by imagining the worst possible punishments he could inflict on his father-in-law, but it did not serve. Jamie's pale face, with her eyes full of fear, could not be banished from his thoughts. He could not even pray.

It was almost three in the morning when they drew up at Calderwood. The journey had been accomplished remarkably quickly in the circumstances, thanks to the skill of the coachman and some welcome intervals of moonlight. The passengers inside had lapsed into silence long before. Anything they might say would simply intensify their fears.

Calderwood Hall stood dark and totally silent. Somewhere an owl hooted eerily. Inside the carriage, Annie shuddered.

Richard wasted no time. He leapt down from the carriage and ran up the steps to the main door. He lifted the heavy brass knocker and began to pound it, venting his frustration on the dark oak panelling. The sound echoed strangely in the darkness.

Eventually, a candle was seen at an upstairs window. Someone in the Hall was checking on the identity of the noisy arrivals. The candle disappeared again, but no one came to open the door.

Richard continued his pounding.

'Will you cease than infernal noise?' shouted a man's voice from an upstairs window. In the darkness, it was impossible to discern the owner of the voice.

'Not until this door is opened,' yelled Richard, attacking the knocker with increased ferocity.

'There is nothing for you here,' shouted the voice in reply. 'Go away.'

'I have come for my wife, and I shall not leave without her.'

The upstairs voice cackled nastily at that. 'Will you so? Will you indeed? You will be here a vastly long time, then, my impetuous young friend, for your wife, as you dare to call her, is not here. *My daughter* is safely tucked away where you will not find her and where she will remain until she has done her duty. You will never set eyes on her again. Now, begone! Before I set the dogs on you, you misbegotten abductor of children!'

Richard was suddenly very still. 'So you think to deprive me of my wife, do you, Sir John? I warned your crony of the risks of that. I now warn you. Unless you release her immediately, it will be the worse for you. You have my solemn word on that!'

Sir John's disembodied voice cackled again, louder this time. 'And now I warn *you*, my lord. She is *my daughter, not your wife*, not any more. You have no power and no rights.' His voice rose, almost to a scream. 'And in any case, it is too late!'

The window slammed shut, the sound echoing in the sudden silence.

Richard closed his eyes for a brief second, then turned sharply on his heel and covered the distance back to the coach in three strides. 'Drive to the nearest inn for fresh horses, William,' he commanded, flinging himself into the coach.

He opened a concealed flap in the carriage to withdraw a pair of wicked-looking pistols. He began methodically to check their priming, his lips set in a grim line. If he had to use them, he would make sure he did not miss—even if he were hanged for it.

'My lord?' Annie whispered apprehensively. 'What will you do?'

He looked quickly up at her, smiling mirthlessly. 'I am not about to murder my father-in-law, Annie, much though he may deserve it. No. In fact, I should thank him! He has been just a little too clever this time. He has told me where she is!'

He put the pistols back in their hiding place. 'Sir John can wait. I have a score to settle in another quarter now. Pray heaven we are in time!'

Chapter Twenty

Jamie awoke to total darkness. She had no idea where she was or how she had come there. All she knew was that she felt dreadful. Her head ached abominably, her mouth tasted foul, and her body was stiff and bruised.

She tried to move to ease the stiffness, but she could not. Her arms were bound beneath her. Even her ankles were tied. All she could do was to roll on to her side, to take the weight of her body off her hands and upper arms.

Memory began to return, haphazardly at first. She remembered the start of her journey quite clearly, from her total stupidity in going anywhere near that carriage in Hanover Square, until the point where they had reached the posting-inn for the first change. Her father—she could not think of him without being overcome with fury—her father had not permitted her to leave his carriage at the inn. He had merely condescended to order a cup of coffee for her, to keep out the cold, he had said. And she had drunk it, as the only shred of warmth being offered her.

After that, the memories were only fragments. She did not know how long they had travelled, nor the route they had taken. She had only a vague recollection of other changes of horses and of driving for many hours, sometimes on very poor roads. She had been asleep—drugged, she concluded bitterly, by her own father!

What a fool she had been. She should have run the moment she saw him. He did not care for her in the least—only for his own warped desires. But she refused to allow herself to dwell on what her father intended for her. More important to set about trying to escape! She forced her mind to sift methodically through the few facts she had about her perilous situation.

When the first light of dawn began to filter through the window of her prison, it revealed a small, unfamiliar room under the eaves of the house. From the look of the layers of cobwebs and dust, and the smell of damp, the room was not used. The bed on which she lay had no covering on the thin, lumpy mattress. Apart from the bed, there was a chair and a table. The stout door was bound to be locked.

Jamie swung her legs to the floor and pulled herself into a sitting position. Then, with an effort, she forced herself to stand, praying that her legs would not buckle under her. So far, so good! At least her legs were not totally numb.

She hopped across to the little window, trying to be as quiet as possible, and peered out through the grimy pane. Below her was a large park with fine trees, bordered on one side by dense woodland. In the distance, she could see cows grazing and smoke rising from cottage chimneys. It was an idyllic picture—which she had never seen before. She had not the least idea of where she was. So much for her hope that she was at Calderwood, where some of the servants might be persuaded to help her to escape. Here there would be no one. Her heart sank a little.

At the sound of heavy footsteps on the stairs, she hopped quickly back to the bed and flopped on to it, resuming her earlier position. The footsteps stopped outside the door. She held her breath, listening to the sound of the key turning in the lock. Then the door swung open to reveal a huge and menacing figure—Caleb!

In her shock at seeing him again, Jamie recoiled, her green eyes huge in her pale face.

'Well, so we're awake, are we, missy?' he sneered, advancing towards the bed to tower over her, clearly enjoying the sight of her panic. 'Never thought ter see me again, did yer, you an' yer precious lord?'

Jamie was not about to let this man believe he had the upper hand, no matter how hopeless her situation might be. But she was acutely conscious of his clenched fists and the veins standing out livid purple on his forehead. He was unpredictable—a very dangerous man. She must force herself to be calm.

'What is this place?' she asked quietly.

'Ye'll find out soon enough, missy,' he replied with a nasty laugh. 'Soon enough.'

'I need a drink, Caleb. Will you bring me one?'

He shook his head. 'Master'll see ter that. I ain't ter do anything fer ye, 'cept'n ter keep yer all right an' tight 'til he arrives. Nice little spot I've chosen fer yer, ain't it?' He looked round the miserable attic with a satisfied smirk. 'But this'll be like paradise ter yer *after*, once master's seen ter ye. Not long ter wait now.' His smirk had widened to a gloating grin.

He said no more. He was waiting for her to ask who the 'master' might be, but she knew he would merely continue to torment her if she did, so she said nothing. She gazed past him as though he were not there, refusing to betray her fear and loathing.

'Toffee-nosed little hussy!' he spat. 'But the master'll soon change all that, never you fear! Not long now!' he said again, with relish, and left the room, locking the door behind him.

Jamie heard him retreating down the wooden staircase. Silence descended once more.

She lay on her side, staring vacantly into the middle distance, trying to make sense of what was happening to her. Caleb again! Caleb, who had tried to kidnap her once already! But how could he be involved with her father? Unless…

She remembered again Richard's words on their wedding eve—a gentleman's servant had paid Caleb and his accomplice to kidnap her. Her father? She wished she could dismiss such wickedness in him, but, in truth, she could not. Her father seemed like a man obsessed, willing to go to any lengths to achieve his ends. He might even be mad. She shuddered involuntarily, before hauling her thoughts back to her immediate predicament.

Where on earth was she? She had never been to a house with a park like this one. Who might—?

The sound of returning footsteps on the stairs interrupted her fevered train of thought. The door was thrown open. Without a word, Caleb crossed to the bed. He reached his huge arms towards her and picked her up as though she weighed no more than a feather. 'Let's go,' he growled, tossing her so roughly over his shoulder that all the breath was forced out of her body.

Caleb carried her down the stairs, making light work of her attempts to struggle. The stairwell was dark and smelled of dust. Reaching the floor below, he flung open a door and carried Jamie into the room beyond, throwing her on to a large bed with a grunt of satisfaction. Then he took some cord from his pocket and tied her feet to the bedpost. 'Don't want yer ter go wanderin' about, do we?' he sneered. 'Master's decided my choice o' room ain't fitting, but he'd be mortal offended if yer was ter leave his.' As the door closed, his laugh echoed in the hallway.

Jamie lay helpless, desperately trying to control the fear which flooded through her at this new turn of events. 'Richard,' she whispered, over and over again, 'Richard, I love you. I know you will come.' The constant repetition slowed her racing pulse and her over-rapid breathing. She refused to believe he would not come. And she had to be ready to help him.

She found that this second room, though neglected, was a great improvement on her earlier prison. It was quite large and furnished with heavy old-fashioned pieces, dulled through lack of care. The bed on which she lay was soft and made up with linens. The bed hangings above and behind her were silk, sadly faded and torn, as were the curtains at the tall windows. It must once have been a fine chamber.

'How very pleasant to see you again, my dear,' said a voice from the door. 'I do apologise for the mistake about your earlier accommodation.'

Jamie gasped and then steeled herself as she turned towards the sound. The door had opened so quietly that she had not heard it. The voice, however, was the unmistakable high-pitched whine of Ralph Graves!

'I am sorry I was not present to do the honours myself when you arrived but, nevertheless, welcome to Bathinghurst, Jessamyne. I promised you a visit, did I not?'

'This is not quite what I had in mind,' retorted Jamie hotly, giving her anger full rein to prevent him from seeing how frightened she was.

'Ah, no, nor I, but it has its compensations, as you will soon find out. We shall enjoy getting to know one another better, my dear, I promise you.'

His lascivious smile made her skin crawl. 'My husband will kill you for this,' she hissed venomously through clenched teeth. 'But, if you let me go, you would have time to escape—'

Ralph Graves' cruel laugh echoed round the chamber. 'You have no husband, Jessamyne, not yet. Your so-called marriage was illegal and is to be annulled. Your father will already have set the wheels in motion, you may be sure.'

Jamie gripped her lower lip between her teeth to hide its trembling.

'Our wedding will take place in due course, my

dear, just as your father intended. In the meantime, you will remain here at Bathinghurst, learning the duties of a wife. You take my meaning?' he leered.

She lifted her chin proudly. 'I shall never submit to you,' she vowed. 'Never.'

'Never is a long time, Jessamyne. And there are ways of making you change your mind. You might like to think about that. Unfortunately, I have business to attend to today, so I cannot stay to...further our acquaintance. For the moment, I shall leave you to consider your position.' Then he was gone.

After the briefest moment of reflection, Jamie cursed her foolish pride. Antagonising him would not help her. He would keep her trussed up like a fowl for plucking. He would enjoy humbling her, depriving her of every last vestige of her will to resist. She must gull him into believing she had given up all hope of rescue—humour him a little. A shudder ran through her, at the thought that she might have to suffer his hands on her. But she refused to be ruled by her demons. She set about planning her tactics for their next encounter.

No one came near her for several hours but when, eventually, the door opened once more, she was ready for him.

'Cousin Ralph,' she pleaded through parched lips, 'may I have something to drink?' She had schooled her features to hide every trace of rebellion.

He gazed down at her, clearly gratified to see that his tactics were working. 'Very well, my dear, since you ask so prettily.' From somewhere behind one of the huge cupboards she heard the sound of liquid being poured. He approached the bed, carrying a half-full tumbler.

In spite of the numbness in her limbs, Jamie struggled into a sitting position before he could get near enough to touch her. 'Will you not free my hands, sir?' she pleaded, trying to make her submission appear complete. 'They are so very painful, tied as they are.'

He assessed her thoughtfully for several moments. 'You cannot escape from here in any case,' he concluded with evident satisfaction, 'since the door will be locked and there is no other way out of this room. I advise you not to try the window, by the bye. It is locked, naturally—and it is quite a long drop,' he added nastily, savouring the shock on her face. He placed the tumbler on the bedside table and then, taking a vicious-looking knife from his pocket, he cut her hands free.

She gasped as the blood rushed back into her fingers. The pain in her shoulders was excruciating as she moved her hands from behind her back. Automatically, she began to rub the red weals on her wrists, ignoring the gleeful smile on his face.

'A timely reminder, I suggest, my dear, that willing compliance with my wishes is advisable. For this is a mere token of what I *might* do.' He handed her the tumbler of water which she drank greedily, refusing to look at him.

'You will remain here for the present. This chamber is perfectly adequate for your needs. Caleb will be on guard outside the door, so do not attempt anything foolish or I might find a need to chastise you further. Caleb would welcome such an opportunity, I am sure. He abhors half-wits. And he hates you!'

Jamie continued to concentrate on rubbing her wrists.

'Caleb will bring your meals to you and anything else you need,' continued Graves. 'I shall join you here for dinner this evening, I think, and afterwards we can get to know each other a little better, hmm?'

Jamie would not allow herself to dwell on what lay behind his ominous words. She forced herself to smile up at him. 'I did not know Caleb was in your service. It was you, then, I suppose, who tried to carry me off from Harding?'

'A sadly botched business but, luckily, the man who was caught knew nothing of my part in it. And as for Caleb—well, he was the best I could find nearby at such short notice. It helped, of course, that he was so keen to take revenge on you, young lady. I should beware of giving him any opportunity, if I were you.'

She ignored his threat. 'But why go to such lengths?' she exclaimed. 'Is it simply because I slighted you? Let me go! Please! After all, I can bring you nothing.'

Graves went off into peals of laughter which almost doubled him up. 'How little you know, my dear, you and your precious Earl. What a pity I shall never be able to tell him, face to face!' He crossed to the door, still chortling at his private joke. 'I shall leave you to untie the rest of the knots yourself. It will help to bring the feeling back into your fingers!'

The door closed behind him with a thud, and the key was turned in the lock.

First things first! Jamie struggled to undo the cords which bound her. It took several minutes, for her fingers seemed to have lost all feeling and the knots were more than thorough. But at last she was free.

She put her feet to the floor to try her legs. It was very painful, but she could just about walk. She moved with difficulty at first, but soon she was pacing up and down the room, trying to get the strength back into her limbs again, while she reviewed her situation.

Most decidedly, it was not good. There was nothing in the room that she could use as a weapon. The water jug was not stout enough. Apart from that, the room and all the cupboards were empty. There was not even a set of fire irons by the grate.

An idea came to her, a mad, perilous notion. At first she pushed it aside because of the enormous risk. She continued to pace, seeking for some alternative solution. She found none.

If she were to have any chance of avoiding the attentions of Cousin Ralph, she must make do with what she had, whatever the risk. She had no choice. She went to the door, before she lost her nerve.

'Caleb,' she called through the thick wood, 'are you there?'

'Aye. What is it?'

'Your master said you would look to my needs. I am freezing in here. I need you to light a fire.' She heard a low grunt and then nothing more. She spoke his name again, but there was no answer. There was no way of knowing whether he would comply with her request.

Amazingly, he did. Some fifteen minutes later, he opened the door to bring in logs and kindling. Jamie retreated prudently to the furthest corner of the room, putting as much distance as possible between them. He seemed so unpredictable—and she doubted whether Graves would restrain his violence. Still, he seemed marginally less terrifying with his back to her, kneeling at the grate.

'I never suspected you worked for Mr Graves, Caleb,' she ventured, trying to keep her voice even.

'Lots o' things you don't know, ain't there, eh?' he replied nastily, without bothering to turn round.

Jamie allowed herself a tragic sigh. 'Yes, I have been a fool. But how was I to guess that a mere gardener could plan a kidnapping?' She noted with satisfaction how the muscles in his massive shoulders tensed at her biting sarcasm.

He turned his head for a moment to glare at her. 'This "mere gardener" can plan a deal more'n that, I'll have yer know, Miss High an' Mighty. Who do yer think made sure we got yer in London, eh? Yer father's plan wouldn't never have worked. I told him yer wouldn't get in his coach unless we forced yer.'

'I'll admit you have been very clever, Caleb. But why did you throw your lot in with Graves in the first place? If you're caught—'

'Won't be,' Caleb grunted, laying the final logs in the grate. 'His way, I gets my revenge and I gets paid as well.' He laughed. 'Followed ye all over London, I did, and yer never once suspected. Never once. A feeble pair y'are, ye and yer lordling. And now he's lost ye fer good. Or p'rhaps it's fer bad, eh? Eh?'

Jamie did not speak. She knew she would not be able to keep her voice steady.

Caleb turned back to the grate to light the fire, which was soon crackling merrily. 'Won't be leaving yer no extra logs, though,' he said, rising from the hearth. 'The master may think ye're tamed, but I knows better. Think ter hit me o'er the head wi' one o' these, did ye, dearie? Well—think again!' Gathering up all the unburnt logs, he left.

'No, Caleb,' she whispered softly as the key turned once more in the lock. 'I might have tried it, if you had given me a chance. But there are other options you have overlooked. I have a better plan than yours.'

It took the best part of an hour to make all her preparations. Everything she did had to be quiet and careful, lest she arouse Caleb's suspicions. Once, as a curtain tore suddenly under her desperate tugging, she thought he must hear and come in. But he did not.

She continued her painstaking work. She dared not rush, for her very life might depend on the care she took now.

When at last all was ready, she crossed to kneel by the grate, pulling a long brand from the flames. She could feel the searing heat from it on her face. She moved swiftly to the door and set the flame to the pile of torn hangings she had heaped there. Dry as dust, they caught immediately. Within seconds, there was a huge blaze licking at the door and the panelling around it.

Jamie did not stop to admire her handiwork, or the speed with which the flames were taking hold. She picked up the water jug and hurled it through the locked window with all her strength. Glass flew everywhere. If only the fire could hold Caleb for a few minutes!

She grabbed hold of the rope of twisted bedclothes which she had tied to the four-poster. It was nowhere near long enough to reach the ground. No matter! Anything was better than the fate which awaited her with Ralph Graves!

Hitching up her skirts, she climbed nimbly over the sill. She began to descend the rope, hand over hand. Halfway down, she thought she heard distant shouts from above. She needed to climb faster.

At last, she came to the end of the rope and looked down. It seemed a very long way to the ground—but perhaps the flower-bed would break her fall.

She had no choice now. She let go of the rope.

Chapter Twenty-One

Richard was on the box for the final stretch of the journey, allowing William a last, well-earned rest. As the carriage rounded the bend to enter the long driveway leading to Bathinghurst, Richard saw part of the house in the distance, half-hidden by the rise—and there were flames shooting out of the roof at one end!

Dear God, the house was on fire. Jamie… He whipped up his lathered team in a desperate attempt to gain a little more speed. If only he were in time…

Nobody seemed to be fighting the fire. A small knot of servants stood huddled together on the front lawn, shoulders slumped, watching helplessly. Of Jamie—and of Graves—there was absolutely no sign. Richard groaned aloud. The house seemed to be an inferno, apart from the few rooms on the ground floor by the entrance. If she were anywhere but there…

The horses were already snorting in fright at the smell of the fire, as he pulled them to a screeching halt, twenty yards short of the house. Leaping from the box, he sprinted to the partly-open main door and pushed his way inside. The hall was surprisingly smoke free.

For a moment he heard nothing, except the voracious sound of the fire, inexorably consuming the house. Then, a cracked voice spoke to him from somewhere above, its source indistinguishable. 'You have come then, Hardinge? Ah, but you are too late. Too late. Your precious *wife* set the fire herself, and now she has perished in it, damn her. I am glad you are here to see it. I may not have her, but neither will you. Neither will you!' A shout of hysterical laughter was followed by silence, and then the sound of something heavy being dragged across bare floorboards.

Richard refused to believe the evidence of his eyes and ears. Most of all, he refused to believe Graves. All through the journey from Calderwood, he had seemed to hear her voice, repeating his name, over and over, with the words 'I love you'. He thought he could hear them still. She could not be dead. Somehow he would have known if she were. He refused to believe it.

Heart pounding fit to burst, he raced out of the house. He must find something to shield him against the smoke and flames. Precious minutes ticked away as he and his companions searched for water. The few house servants were useless—they seemed to have been frozen into immobility.

At last a bucket of water was found by the stables. Pulling a dripping rug over his head, Richard ran back to the house. The eerie sound of scraping could still be heard, seemingly farther away now. The smoke was thicker than ever. Only by the doorway could he see his way at all.

He began to feel his way up the stairs, step by step. The acrid smoke was soon choking him. In his head he could still hear her voice calling 'Richard! Richard!' He must find her! He must save her!

Her voice seemed to be getting louder. He prayed that he was not imagining it. No. She must be here. She must be closer to the top of the stairs than he had dared to hope. He made his way along the landing, wondering desperately where to begin.

The first doorway was engulfed in flames. The door itself was long gone. The room beyond was a blazing furnace. He called her name, once, twice, in rising desperation. There was no response. He forced himself to go on to the next chamber.

There the fire had less of a hold, though the room was full of smoke. Dropping to his hands and knees, he crawled inside. Was there a corner where Jamie might have taken refuge? Again he called her name. Again there was silence.

Dear God, if he could not hear her any more, did that mean she was dead? It came to him then, like a bolt of lightning, that if she were lost to him, his life would be hollow and empty. Without her, life would be nothing. He must, *must* find her—even if he perished in the attempt.

He began to make his way farther along the landing. He was starting to lose his sense of direction in the dense smoke. It was beginning to affect his breathing. The dripping rug had almost dried. Parts of his clothes were beginning to singe as he crawled across the hot floorboards.

'Richard!' came that voice again. 'Richard! Please come back! Oh God, please don't let him die!'

The change in the now familiar litany brought him suddenly to his senses. It *was* her voice. Surely it was coming from down below, nearer the door? He began to feel light-headed. Was he dreaming? Was he already dead? Perhaps her voice was calling to him from beyond the grave? He shook himself out of his wandering thoughts. The smoke must be getting to his mind. It was certainly choking his lungs. He pushed himself even closer to the floor and began to edge painfully back towards the staircase.

The voice came again, more distinctly this time. 'Richard! Oh, Richard, where are you?'

Jamie! She *was* there! She was alive! 'I'm coming, my darling!' he croaked, through raw lips. It was barely audible. He reached the top of the stairs, gasping for air. He was exhausted. He had not the strength to move another inch. But if he remained where he was, he would surely die. With a silent prayer, he allowed himself to go limp and roll down the stairs.

The body which reached the bottom was senseless.

'Help me, William!' shrieked Jamie. 'He is here!' Together Jamie and the coachman dragged the inert body across the hall and into the blissfully fresh air outside. As they laid him on the cool grass, an enormous sheet of flame burst through the roof and the main timbers collapsed inwards on the floors below. What little had been left of the house was now completely engulfed by the fire. Bathinghurst was doomed.

Ignoring the tears streaking down her smoke-grimed cheeks, Jamie set about trying to revive her husband. 'Bring me some more water! Quickly, Annie! And you, William, the rugs from the carriage!'

She was cradling his poor blackened head in her arm while she bathed his face with cool water. 'Richard! Oh, Richard, I love you so. Don't leave me!' she cried in desperation, willing him to come back to her. Then pure, mutinous anger took possession of her. Nothing would be allowed to take him from her, not now. 'I won't let you die! I won't!' She repeated those stubborn words over and over as she gently tended her husband's hurts and tried to cool his over-heated body.

She was rewarded, at last, with a croaking attempt at a laugh as he came to himself again. 'It will take more than a little smoke to carry me off,' he whispered hoarsely. 'Especially now that I know I love you.'

Joy flooded through every fibre of Jamie's being. She was so overcome with emotion that she could not say a single word. She simply flung herself on to his chest, sobbing in relief.

His hand came up to touch her hair. 'Hush, my dear love. It's all over now. We are together. No one shall part us now.'

Jamie allowed herself the indulgence of tears for only a few moments before her practical side reasserted itself. Richard was hurt and exhausted. He must be taken at once to somewhere safe where his injuries might be tended.

'William! Help me bring his lordship into the carriage!' she commanded incisively.

Richard was now struggling to rise and would have collapsed again without the help of his wife and his coachman. Even as it was, Jamie was buckling under his weight, for he was too weak to support himself.

'You there!' cried William to one of the Bathinghurst servants watching open-mouthed. 'Get over here and make yourself useful!' The man hastened to obey, relieving Jamie just in time. His lordship's tall, athletic body was quite a burden, even for two men.

Jamie rushed to ready the carriage, but Annie was before her. She had spread the rugs and made a makeshift pillow with the clothes from his lordship's valise. It was no easy task to get Richard inside—he had lost consciousness once more—but eventually he was safely bestowed along the seat. Jamie took the seat opposite, anxiously chafing his hand and holding a damp cloth to his forehead to cool him.

William stood by the open door. 'Where to, milady?'

Jamie looked down at the faithful retainer, seeing his fatigue for the first time. How many hours had he been driving in search of her? 'There must be an inn hereabouts, William. Try if you can find it.' She forced herself to smile at him reassuringly. 'His lordship must be tended. And you must have some rest.'

William coloured slightly. 'Oh, no, milady. I'm

good for hours yet. But we'll need a change, if your ladyship wants to go any further. This team is spent.'

'The nearest inn will do very well for us all, William,' she repeated, with a calm she did not feel. 'Where is Annie? We must go!'

'She is travelling with me on the box, milady, all right and tight,' he replied with a grin and closed the door.

Although it seemed like an age to Jamie, anxiously watching over her husband's motionless body inside the carriage, it took William barely twenty minutes to make his way to the nearest inn. As the carriage turned into the yard, Richard stirred and opened his eyes.

Jamie breathed a sigh of relief. 'Thank God, you are come to yourself again. William has brought us to the nearest inn. You can be tended here.' She removed the damp cloth from his brow and made to pull back the rugs.

'Is that my neckcloth you have there?' croaked Richard.

'Oh!' For the first time, Jamie registered what she was holding. She looked hard at her husband. In spite of his pitiful state, he seemed to be amused. 'I fear it is,' she replied sternly, 'since there was nothing else to hand. And what is more, your head has been pillowed on the rest of your linen, so—'

Richard groaned theatrically and choked out a single word. 'Gregg!'

Jamie allowed herself the luxury of a giggle. If Richard could indulge in such levity, his hurts were not as serious as she had thought. 'Don't worry,' she added blithely. 'It was Annie's doing. I shall let them fight it out.' She paused. 'And my money will be on Annie!'

Richard grinned, rather weakly, which brought Jamie back to earth.

With help from William and the landlord, Richard was conveyed into the inn and taken upstairs to the best bedchamber. The landlord and his wife fussed about, bringing hot water, soap and towels for the high-born but dishevelled guests. And the gossip ran through the inn like wildfire.

Jamie's attention was fixed solely on her husband. She removed his ruined clothes and bathed his smoke-blackened body. He needed a shave too, but there was nothing she could do about that. 'You look a positive fright,' she said brightly, when he reached out to take her hand with his bandaged one.

Richard tried to speak but could not, even when he had sipped the water she handed to him. He pressed her hand.

'I'm sure you will be better soon,' she said encouragingly. 'There's no need to talk now. What matters is that you are safe.'

His eyes spoke for him. *And you*, they said.

'Shall I send for some brandy?'

He nodded.

'And some food too, I think,' she added, ringing the bell and ordering bowls of broth to be served to them. The look on Richard's face spoke volumes, but she pretended not to notice. As the little maid turned to leave, Jamie remembered her other responsibilities.

'My servants are to be given a hot meal and good beds, if you please.'

'Yes, milady. I'll tell the landlord, at once. Will there be anything else, milady?'

'Yes. I pray you ask the landlord if he can find a coat for my husband. His own was ruined in the fire and it will be some time before his valet arrives with another.'

'Oh, yes, milady, I'm sure he can.'

In no time she was back with the brandy and a black coat, no doubt the landlord's best. Since he was a burly man, the coat was broad enough for Richard's shoulders, though it fitted nowhere else.

Richard swallowed a gulp of brandy and turned to grin wickedly at Jamie. He could just about speak again now, thank goodness. 'You shall get your just deserts for this sacrilege, wife.' He rose unsteadily and made his way to the fireplace. One glance in the mirror there confirmed the worst. He shuddered. 'What a sight!'

Jamie joined him. 'Then we are a matched pair, my lord, are we not?' And indeed they were, for Jamie was still clad in the gown in which she had been kidnapped. It was now filthy, torn and crumpled, fit for nothing but the fire.

Richard smiled sweetly down at her. 'Perhaps the landlord's wife has a gown for you?'

Since the landlady's girth was at least twice Jamie's, that was more than a little unlikely, and he must know it. '*Touché*, my lord,' responded Jamie with a grin. 'I shall see if I can surpass you in...er...elegance!' She put a finger across his lips as he made to reply. 'Hush! Don't try to talk now. Wait till you have recovered a little more. We have plenty of time now.'

He nodded, gazing down at her with glowing eyes, and opened his arms to fold her against his broad chest. It was an embrace of comfort and of reassurance, of tender love but not of passion. He rested his cheek on her disordered curls and drew her ever more closely to him.

If Jamie had had any lingering doubts about whether he truly loved her, that embrace removed them all. With her arms wrapped around his waist, she leaned into his protective strength. Now was not the time for words. Later, when he had recovered a little and they could talk about the ordeal they had shared, then she would tell him how much she loved him. She smiled blissfully into his borrowed coat.

Richard and Jamie were sitting in companionable silence in front of the fire in the inn's private parlour. Both were still too exhausted to speak much, and Richard's throat was too raw. It was enough that they were together, and that the danger was over.

The little maid returned to report that her ladyship's instructions had been fulfilled—their servants had been well fed and had been provided with beds. Jamie nodded contentedly. For the present, she needed nothing more.

'Beg pardon, milady, but there is a visitor to see his lordship.'

Who would have the impudence to intrude on them

at such a time? Jamie raised an eyebrow, for all the world the great lady, in spite of her appearance.

The little maid continued bravely, 'It is Mr Peacock. The magistrate,' she added shyly. 'About the fire.'

Richard nodded wearily. The law must take its course.

Thomas Peacock, Esquire, seemed more than a little taken aback when he entered the private parlour to meet the Earl and his young Countess.

Richard hauled himself stiffly to his feet and extended his bandaged hand, pulling his ill-fitting coat together as best he could. 'Mr Peacock,' he said. 'I am afraid you find us in rather a sad way, for which I must ask you to accept my apologies. Will you not sit down?'

'Forgive me for disturbing you, my lord,' began the magistrate formally. 'You will understand that I have my duty to do.' He sat stiffly on the edge of the chair Richard had indicated. 'I understand you were involved in the fire at Bathinghurst, my lord?'

Richard nodded mutely and resumed his seat.

'Will you be so good as to tell me what happened?'

Jamie intervened quickly, before Richard could overtax himself. 'My husband was caught inside among the smoke and flames, sir, and can barely speak, but I was there when the fire started.'

The magistrate turned to her in surprise.

'Ralph Graves, the owner of Bathinghurst, is a distant relation of my family,' Jamie began crisply, keeping strictly to matters of fact, while watching out of the corner of her eye for any signal from Richard that she should not tell everything that had happened. None came. He was smiling slightly at her, which she took for encouragement. 'He…he had me abducted from London and was holding me against my will in that house.' Jamie had decided, almost without thinking about it, to omit any direct reference to her father.

'But this is unbelievable!' exclaimed the magistrate. 'What on earth could a man like Graves hope to gain from such a wicked act? Criminal, I should say, rather!'

Jamie looked towards Richard who nodded imperceptibly, still smiling warmly. 'Ralph Graves believed that my marriage to Lord Hardinge was not legal and could be set aside. He wished to marry me himself. He told me I would become his wife whether I willed it or no. That was the reason for my abduction.'

'Dear God,' breathed Mr Peacock, turning pale. He frowned, puzzled now. 'But what about the fire? I am afraid I fail to understand what that has to do with your abduction, my lady.'

'I started that deliberately,' she admitted immediately, with disarming candour. 'It was intended as a diversion, so that I could escape from the house without being seen by Graves and his people.'

Richard laughed throatily. 'Some diversion! I was wondering how you had managed to get away. I am still all agog to learn the way of it,' he added, reaching for the tumbler of water at his elbow.

'It was nothing so mysterious. As with the fire, there was really no other choice. I twisted a rope out of the bedcovers so that I could climb down from the window. Since it was locked fast—as you would expect—I had to break it first.'

'I don't dare ask how you did that!' smiled Richard.

Jamie shrugged. 'I flung the water jug through it. There was nothing else to hand.'

'Of course! I should have known!' nodded Richard, leaning back in his chair to admire his modest, courageous wife.

Mr Peacock coughed discreetly. He looked to be a little embarrassed by the loving byplay in that exchange. 'Forgive my plain speaking, my lord, but you must understand this is a formal investigation,' he said reprovingly. 'Pray continue, my lady.'

'I managed to reach the ground without being hurt—the flower-beds under the window were quite soft, considering how little they had been tended— and I escaped into the woods which border the park. Nobody saw me. At least, nobody followed me. I suppose they were too busy with the fire.'

'They thought you were still inside, my love,' interposed Richard seriously. 'They did not know you had escaped. Graves himself told me that you had set the fire—and had died in it. He gloated over the fact that he had taken you from me.' He reached out his hand to cover hers.

The magistrate pricked up his ears at that. 'Graves spoke to you, my lord? Where was he?'

'Upstairs somewhere. I thought at the time that he was on the first floor, though when I reached there, he still seemed to be some distance away. The mind plays very strange tricks in the dark, I'm afraid, amid all that smoke. I thought I heard my wife's voice too.' He threw her a strange sidelong look, half-mocking, half-serious.

'But you did!' exclaimed Jamie instantly.

Richard looked round sharply at her. 'What?'

'When I saw the carriage arriving, I shouted and shouted, but apparently no one could hear me. I suppose I was too far away. So I started to run back to the house. I tried to get to you before you went into the fire, but it was such a long way from the woods to the house that I was too late. You must have been somewhere on the first floor by the time I reached the main hall with William. You must have heard me calling from there.'

'Yes,' he agreed slowly, fixing his eyes on her face, 'but not only from there. In my mind, I heard you all the time, almost from the moment I knew you had been taken.' The look which passed between them then was filled with wonder, as they tried to come to grips with what he seemed to have experienced. Was it possible...?

Mr Peacock coughed again, more deliberately. 'Could Graves have been on the second floor, my lord, on the landing above you?'

'Possibly. Why? Does it matter? Did he escape from there?'

'He did not escape at all, my lord. That is to say, we found two bodies after the fire. One was a great bear of a man, scarcely recognisable. The other was much smaller, and almost untouched. The servants identified that as the body of Ralph Graves.'

Richard nodded. 'Yes, that makes sense. And the

other would have been his henchman, Caleb, who was acting as my wife's gaoler, I believe. What happened to him?'

'Trapped by a falling beam, my lord, and burned to death.'

Jamie shuddered and put her hand to her lips, picturing the scene. What a terrifying end, even for Caleb. And she was responsible! She had started the fire!

'And Graves?' asked Richard sharply, apparently unmoved by the deaths his wife had caused.

'We think he was on the second floor, trying to move a huge strongbox down the staircase. It must have meant more to him than the house or anything in it, even her ladyship. When the roof fell in, it took all the internal floors with it. Graves and his strongbox came down together and ended in the cellars, with Graves under his precious box. I'm afraid it killed him.'

'Justice,' said Richard harshly, without a moment's pause.

'I beg your pardon, my lord?' asked the magistrate, rather shocked.

'I said "justice", Mr Peacock,' repeated Richard deliberately. 'I learned yesterday that Ralph Graves was a blackmailer and a miser, who made his money by preying on the weak. He loaned money at exorbitant rates to people at their wits' end and, when the debtors could not repay, he sucked their lifeblood like a very leech. Many were totally ruined. I believe my wife's father was one of his victims. The man was an out-and-out villain. At least his death will give his

victims back their peace of mind, if all his papers
have been destroyed. I assume they have?'

Jamie had barely registered the end of Richard's
recital. She was staring at her husband, wide-eyed
with shock. Her father?

'I am most grateful for that information, m'lord,'
said the magistrate. 'It explains a great deal. There
can be no question of any action against Lady
Hardinge, given the circumstances. The man Caleb
was certainly an accomplice in Graves' criminal activity. And Graves was as culpable in the matter of
his servant's death as in his own. The irony is that
Graves risked his life to pull his strongbox out of the
fire, but the box survived intact anyway. I may tell
you—in confidence, of course—that it contains a
great deal of money. It also contains documents, almost all of them undamaged.'

He cleared his throat. 'You might be interested in
one of them,' he said, with a slight smile, the first he
had ventured during the whole interview. 'It records
a loan from your father to Sir John Calderwood,
which was subsequently taken over by Graves. You
should be able to recover the capital from the dead
man's estate—once the formalities are completed,
naturally.'

Richard nodded soberly, trying to conceal his surprise.

'One other thing, if I may,' said the magistrate,
rising from his seat and turning to Jamie. 'You said
Graves was related to your family, my lady. Would
that be the Calderwoods?' Jamie nodded, bemused.

'And would you be Jessamyne Calderwood?' Jamie nodded again.

The magistrate smiled more broadly now, reaching into his pocket. 'Then, I see no need to retain these papers. They did not belong to Graves. I think these are your property, my lady,' he said, offering her a sheaf of legal documents.

Jamie was too astonished to move. Richard had to take them from the magistrate's hand.

'Your dowry, I believe, my lady,' continued the magistrate. 'You *are* married, I take it?'

Jamie began to protest at his question, but she was overtaken by a shout of hoarse laughter from her husband. 'Oh, yes, sir, I promise you, we are truly man and wife, though there was never any thought of a dowry when I proposed, I can assure you.' He laughed again, ignoring the strange looks from Mr Peacock, who probably thought the smoke had affected his lordship's mind.

'Come here, wife,' commanded Richard when they were alone once more. Jamie came to stand in front of him, still looking puzzled. With one swift move, he pulled her on to his lap and into his arms.

'Cease your frowning, my love. Those papers are the deeds to lands which were left you by your mother, to be under your control when you came of age, or on your earlier marriage. Although he had no right to do so, your father seems to have pledged them as security for his debts to Graves. I imagine he could not redeem them, so you were to be the means by which Graves would take possession of the forfeited land. There was no other legal way. It explains his illogical desire to marry you. It also explains the rush to tie the knot before you came of age and learned of your inheritance.'

Jamie stiffened in his arms. 'Illogical, is it, my lord, to wish to marry me? Why, you—'

'For him, since he already had you in his power. Not for me, you little vixen,' he admitted, silencing any further protests with a long, thorough kiss.

'And now, my love, my lady wife, I think it is time for bed, do not you?' She blushed delicately, but did not protest.

Much later, as they lay together in the intimacy of sated passion, Jamie voiced the question which had been on her mind since their arrival at the inn. 'You have told me you love me, Richard, but you have never asked me if I love you, or even given me a chance to say so. Why is that?'

'Because I already know, my love,' he announced, in tones of maddening certainty, beginning to stroke the lock of hair which lay across his shoulder.

Jamie dug a fingernail into his chest to regain his undivided attention. 'You are very sure of yourself,' she accused, 'considering I have said nothing.'

He picked up the offending finger and carried it to his lips, where he nibbled it gently. 'Wrong, my love. You told me over and over again, all through my journey from Calderwood to Bathinghurst. I could hear your voice calling my name and saying "I love you". Was it not so?'

'Yes...' she breathed in an awed whisper. 'It

helped me to keep my sanity. But I never really thought that I could reach you.'

'You have not enough faith in the power of love, my darling—which is strange, considering how much under my mother's influence you have come. And that reminds me...'

He reached across to the bedside table for the box that rested there. Then he took the Hardinge betrothal ring out of its velvet cushion and slid it on to her finger. 'Where this diamond is given and received in love, it brings blessings on both giver and receiver,' he said solemnly, his eyes locked with hers. 'I believe we have those blessings already. I love you, Jamie Hardinge.'

* * * * *

Don't miss the conclusion of Joanna Maitland's Regency duet in Volume 14 of
The Regency Lords & Ladies Collection,
available in August 2006

The *Regency*

LORDS & LADIES

COLLECTION

*Two glittering Regency
love affairs in every book*

6th January 2006	Rosalyn & the Scoundrel *by Anne Herries &* Lady Knightley's Secret *by Anne Ashley*
3rd February 2006	The Veiled Bride *by Elizabeth Bailey &* Lady Jane's Physician *by Anne Ashley*
3rd March 2006	Perdita *by Sylvia Andrew &* Raven's Honour *by Claire Thornton*
7th April 2006	Miranda's Masquerade *by Meg Alexander &* Gifford's Lady *by Claire Thornton*
5th May 2006	Mistress of Madderlea *by Mary Nichols &* The Wolfe's Mate *by Paula Marshall*
2nd June 2006	An Honourable Thief *by Anne Gracie &* Miss Jesmond's Heir *by Paula Marshall*

*Available at WH Smith, Tesco, ASDA, Borders, Eason,
Sainsbury's and all good paperback bookshops*
www.millsandboon.co.uk

MILLS & BOON®
Live the emotion

0706/04b

*H*istorical
romance™

ASHBLANE'S LADY
by *Sophia James*

Lady Madeleine Randwick was his hostage, and a way to
get under her brother's skin. As a willing player in
the murky game of borderland politics, Alexander Ullyot,
Laird of Ashblane, should have had no compunction
about using her for his own ends. He should ruin her as
surely as he wanted to ruin her brother. And instead,
he found he was complimenting her... Was Alex in
danger of falling for the woman who was his means
of revenge...?

THE MISTAKEN WIDOW
by *Cheryl St.John*

Sarah Thornton could only bring disaster on herself and
her infant son by revealing her identity. Yet looking into
Nicholas Halliday's dark eyes, it was hard to remember
why she mustn't confess. Nicholas sensed that his newly
widowed sister-in-law was hiding something. Sooner or
later he would have to choose: family loyalty, or his love
for a woman he just couldn't trust...

On sale 4th August 2006

Wicked

– A novel steeped in darkness, danger and desire

The Earl of Carlyle was known as a beast.

Camille Montgomery is aware of the Earl's reputation. But as an expert in antiquities, she also knows his family's Egyptian artifacts are the finest in England. Unfortunately Camille's wayward stepfather knows this too. When he's caught in the act of robbing the 'Beast of Carlyle', Camille must swallow her fear and confront the man whose mask is said to hide a face too loathsome to behold.

On sale 21st July 2006

Look out for the spellbinding sequel,
Reckless *– coming in August 2006*

www.millsandboon.co.uk

M&B